Beverley Harper w the age of twent intending to stay Instead she stayed various times in S Coast and Malawi. Beverley is married with three sons and now lives in the New England Tablelands of New South Wales. *Echo of an Angry God* is her third novel.

Also by Beverley Harper

ECHO
of an
ANGRY
GOD

BEVERLEY HARPER

PAN
Pan Macmillan Australia

First published 1998 in Macmillan by Pan Macmillan Australia Pty Limited
This edition published 1999 in Pan by Pan Macmillan Pty Limited
St Martins Tower, 31 Market Street, Sydney

Reprinted 2001 (twice), 2003, 2004 (twice), 2006

National Library of Australia
cataloguing-in-publication data:

Harper, Beverley.
Echo of an angry god.

ISBN 0 330 36127 9.

I. Title.

A823.3

Typeset in 11.5/13pt Bembo by Post Pre-press Group, Brisbane
Printed in Australia by McPherson's Printing Group

*This book is for my family
and especially
Mona and Fairy.*

*This book is also dedicated
to the memory
of Debbie Gange-Harris.*

I wish to thank Associate Professor Peter Flood,
Head, School of Physical Sciences and Engineering
at the University of New England for his assistance
in matters dealing with oil exploration.

And a thousand thanks to my friends
Margie and Terry O'Callaghan
in Malawi
for their hospitality.

No book is ever as good as it might be without
considerable input from editors.
Cate Paterson and Alexandra Mohan – two of the best.
Thank you.

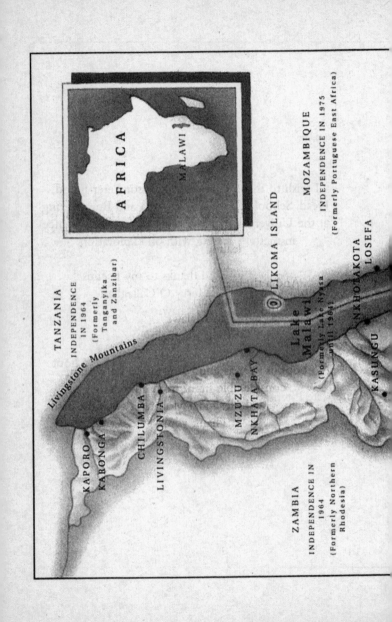

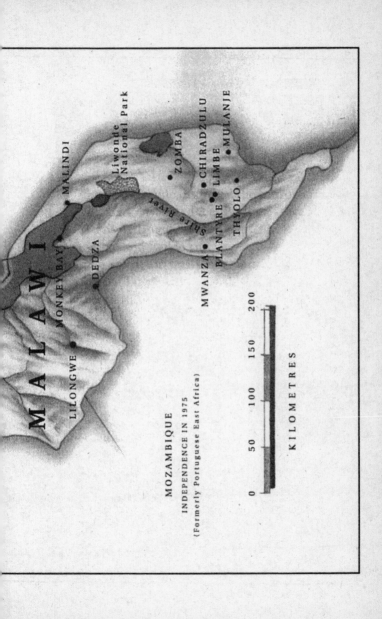

MALAWI

LILONGWE

MONKEY BAY

MALINDI

DEDZA

Liwonde
National Park

ZOMBA

CHIRADZULU

MULANJE

LIMBE

Shire River

THYOLO

MWANZA

BLANTYRE

MOZAMBIQUE

INDEPENDENCE IN 1975

(Formerly Portuguese East Africa)

| 0 | 50 | 100 | 150 | 200 |

KILOMETRES

ONE

LIKOMA ISLAND – 1694

The barest ripple disturbed the mirror surface of dark water. Reeds along the shore swayed, languid and serene. A fish eagle called, high and wild, and was answered by its mate. The sultry air was heavy and redolent with anticipation. Tiny wavelets ran silently onto the sandy beach and slid, with no energy, back again, leaving a watermark no more than the length of a man's little finger on the absolute whiteness of the unblemished sand.

Rocks separated the beach from the small cove – smooth, round boulders of a sandstone colour, their external features revealing evidence that once, when the lake was higher, they had been submerged. In the gathering gloom of approaching night, the deep water of the cove appeared silky black, cut by ribbons of silver as unseen currents flowed below the surface.

Diogo Pegado was not a coward. At thirty-eight, he had fought many battles. He regularly travelled the largely unexplored African hinterland where most men feared to tread. He navigated Africa's wild and unpredictable coastline. He had seen men die of disease, of snake bite and of their injuries in battle. Aware that his own fate was as insubstantial, as unpredictable as that of others, he nonetheless perceived life to be a set of challenges, there to be conquered, with no place for regret and recrimination. Such was life. Diogo Pegado had no time for cowards and milksops. He believed men brought their own sufferings onto themselves. He was immune to suffering.

But what Diogo Pegado was about to witness in the deepening velvet night brought him out in a sweat of dread that prickled in his armpits and threatened his legs with collapse.

King Lundu was an immense man of indeterminate age. He bore his status with a precise, almost pedantic dignity which his subjects knew tolerated no disobedience. Rolls of fat under his chin, along arms and legs and around his waist gave his almost hairless body authority and presence. His subjects took his size to mean enormous strength of limbs and heart. He ruled his small kingdom in the manner of all kings of the day – with fear, obedience and blind worship being prerequisites for staying alive.

At a signal from the King, torches were lit, throwing their flickering light onto the inky water of the cove and made shadows of the gathered people of King Lundu dancing on the rocks like disembodied stick figures. The big bonfire at the burning place up on the hill was also set alight, flaring immediately, sending flames into the air which could be seen from the mainland. Diogo Pegado shivered in spite of the warmth of the evening. Death could surely not be more horrible than what was about to take place.

Ng'ona saw the flames. At three metres beneath the surface, he flicked his tail and glided in a circle. His small reptilian brain made the connection – food. He waited. At the first splash he would propel himself upwards, taking the body around the waist as a bird would grasp a fish in its beak and, rolling backwards in a spiral, spin down to the bottom, where he would hold the victim until it stopped its ineffectual attempts to escape, until the last bubble of oxygen floated in an effervescent string upwards and death stilled the flailing limbs. Then, and only then, would he glide effortlessly to the place he took all his food and stash the body for several days, until the flesh began to rot and the putrid smell of it would tell *Ng'ona* that the food was ready to tear and grind.

Diogo Pegado glanced across at the intended sacrifice. A proud young man in the prime of life. Muscles bulged under very black skin and, in the bonfire's red glow, the sheen of nerves glistened, accentuating the man's strong body. He stood erect, head held high. His fate was sealed and there was nothing he could do but die with dignity. Diogo saw the slight tremor in his limbs and wondered what was going through the man's head right at this minute. Would he jump? Or would he need to be thrown? To die a coward in these people's eyes meant he would remain an unhappy spirit for eternity. What kind of courage was required to throw oneself from the high boulder where he stood, into those dark and dangerous waters? Despite his dispassionate regard for other men's lives, Diogo could not help but reflect that this man's death would be a waste of a good, strong warrior.

Sweat ran down the Portuguese man's face but he dared not wipe it away. Any sign of weakness on his part would be noticed. The natives placed great importance on a man's courage. Diogo was being tested as surely as the unfortunate wretch on the boulder. He needed the King's help more than the King needed his, and so he willed himself to ignore the sweat stinging his eyes and the biting discomfort of mosquitoes as they rose in their hordes and enjoyed their nightly feasting on human blood.

To keep his mind busy, Diogo wondered why the King had chosen this particular young man to die. His decision had seemed casual, a response to Diogo's question, 'Will it be safe?' The King had clicked his fingers and the warrior had stepped forward with no hesitation. No expression of fear crossed the young man's face as the King ordered him to die.

Drums began an awful death roll.

Three metres down, *Ng'ona* felt, rather than heard, the throb of the drums. Still he glided in lazy circles. The food thrown to him from time to time was easy prey, no match for his speed and strength. At just over five-and-a-half metres long, he was powerful enough to bring down a rhinoceros and fast enough to catch a full-grown impala if the need arose. He was 164 years old and, unless some misfortune befell him, would live another fifty to seventy years. Longevity seemed assured. No-one dared to even think of harming him. He was, it was whispered, the spirit of King Lundu's ancestral great-grandfather, returned to this earth in the form of a crocodile, to protect the King and those favoured by the King. He lived in a cave under the water and patrolled the small cove and the waters beyond, secure in his size and strength, protected, revered and feared.

Diogo looked back at the boulder. The warrior stood alone, unguarded. He supposed the man could run, but where would he go? The island of Likoma was eight kilometres long and no more than four kilometres wide. The closest land was thirteen kilometres away. Like most of King Lundu's subjects, Diogo suspected the man could not swim more than a few strokes.

It was fully dark now, the silky black water tinged pink by the fires. King Lundu rose slowly from his Stool of Life, his beaded crown glinting, the special serpent design seeming to come alive in the flickering light. Beside him, musicians blew loud mournful notes on their *siwas* – intricately carved ivory horns of varying tones – and, added to the beating drums, the night air throbbed with a message of death. The King raised his arms and the sudden silence was almost painful.

Diogo Pegado saw the man on the boulder gather himself to jump. With no hesitation, no final words, no last-minute look at his family, he leapt high in the air, as if to postpone the final, horrible moment of terror, and plunged, feet first, into the jet black embrace of unimaginable horror. He disappeared under the glassy water and bobbed to the surface immediately. Almost in slow motion, he struck out for the shore, swimming with the awkwardness of one who can barely stay afloat. *Ng'ona* hit him midriff with such force that man and beast rose from the water by nearly two metres, foam coursing back over the long snout and slit yellow eyes. Diogo saw the black man's eyes go wide as terror, disbelief, pain and the inevitability of his own death hammered into his brain. He was held in the crocodile's mouth, fastened by teeth already crushing flesh and bone from the sheer strength of those terrible jaws. The warrior's arms and legs flailed uselessly, still in a swimming motion, as if he had not yet realised he was out of the water. *Ng'ona* slapped back on the surface with a spray of water that was already redder than the light from the fires. Diogo caught one more glimpse of the young man as the crocodile rolled and vanished with an almost casual flip of his powerful tail. Flickering torches played over the water in the cove. Within minutes, the mirror surface returned and the dead man and the reptile might never have been there.

Without a word, King Lundu sat down on his Stool of Life and bearers raised the palanquin in one fluid movement, so as not to anger him. Six young men, hand-picked for the job for their

6

strength, sureness of foot and the ability to work as a team. The King had to be carried up a narrow and steep stairway, fifty-eight steps carved into a gigantic rock face, which led from the beach directly to the largest of his five courts atop a hill. To do this without rocking or unsettling their ruler required their utmost concentration. Priests and elders followed the palanquin. Diogo Pegado, as guest of honour, climbed the steps behind the priests. The rest of the village kept a respectful distance behind him. The last allowed up the steps were the family of the dead warrior.

Lamp niches, hundreds of them, glowed and lit the way. The courts of King Lundu stretched away towards Macholo, the highest point on the island, an astonishing feat of architectural and stone masonry excellence. Having reached the top of the hill the bearers, with no discernible shift in their rhythm, carried the King across the audience court and along an arcade which ran down the far side. At the entrance to one of his reception rooms he was gently lowered. Courtiers stepped forward to remove the Stool of Life, the swords and umbrellas which always accompanied King Lundu and hastily bore them away for safe-keeping. Diogo waited in the arcade. A movement at his side told him his interpreter had found him.

The King beckoned and entered the reception room. There, seated at one end on stone steps and flanked by priests, elders and soldiers, he waited until Diogo and his interpreter were settled in front of him. 'Are you satisfied?'

'Yes, Holy One. The treasure will be safe.'

'Tell us how you came by such treasure.'

The King had been greatly impressed with the volume of necklaces, carvings, bowls, masks, ceremonial staffs and stools of all sizes and designs. Some were solid gold. Others were constructed of wood and then covered in sheets of beaten gold. Diogo had filled the hold of his ship with them. A second vessel had been loaded with grain and cloth, beads and ivory, live animals and barrels of rum – gifts for the King.

Diogo had done business with King Lundu before. Until last year, his ships contained the results of legal trading – coiled wire of iron, copper, bronze and gold; sheets and beads of gold; necklaces, bracelets and masks of gold, bronze and copper; ingots of copper; copper jewellery; metal gongs; idols and carvings; soapstone dishes; even tools made from gold filled his ships. He traded from Sofala on the east coast, inland to the Zambezi. Then he headed south to the trading fairs along the Limpopo and Sabi rivers, before returning north to Great Zimbabwe and finally, northeast to cross the great lake to Likoma island where the King, in return for other goods, would store his products until slavers heading east could be hired to transport the goods to Kilwa and Zanzibar.

Last year, however, the Great Zimbabwe ruler, the Mambo, had banished all Portuguese traders from his kingdom. In a clean sweep, he also routed the Munhu Mutapa and his Shona followers from the plateau, setting up his own Shona state of the

Rozvi people. While the Portuguese were still welcomed to the trading fairs of the Munhu Mutapa in the north, the gold-rich plateau of Great Zimbabwe was suddenly off-limits. For a time the Portuguese – Diogo included – employed specialised African traders, the Vashambadzi, as their agents. This became impractical since the Vashambadzi did not consider themselves to be full-time traders and, for most of the year, they farmed and herded cattle.

Diogo Pegado knew that the King was aware that he could not have come by such treasure through normal trading procedures. The talking drums of Africa – those hollowed out tree trunks, some as long as two metres and measuring a metre-and-a-half thick, which could send their message up to thirty kilometres – would have informed him of the Mambo's decree within hours of it being made, despite having to travel more than 900 kilometres to reach the King's ear. Diogo was, by nature, a prudent man. In the volatile lands of Africa, an incautious remark had cost more than one foreigner his life. He wondered how much to tell the King. Lundu had dealt fairly in the past but how would he react to an admission of theft? Realising the King was waiting for an answer, that lying was probably a waste of time anyway, and aware of how fond the King and his subjects were of a good story, Diogo told him the truth.

'The Mambo of the Rozvi people is no friend to the Portuguese,' he began. 'Last year he forbade us to trade with him.' Diogo spat. 'He fears we will take his kingdom.'

King Lundu nodded. 'I have heard this. He is gaining power for himself.'

'He makes many enemies in the process. Beware, Holy One, for he sees himself as ruler of all the lands.'

The King scowled.

'We Portuguese have traded here for centuries,' Diogo said. 'Have we tried to take your lands?'

The King's face was impassive as he said, 'The Munhu Mutapa is little more than a puppet of the Portuguese.'

Diogo's respect for King Lundu grew. He was very well informed. 'It is true, we helped the Munhu Mutapa as we wished to help the Mambo.'

King Lundu's belly fat wobbled as he found a more comfortable position to sit. 'Then the Mambo is a fool who does little to help his people,' he said lightly.

Diogo was encouraged. The King obviously couldn't care less that the treasure was stolen. 'You are wise in the extreme, Holy One. The Mambo has learned a lesson he will not forget. Great Zimbabwe has been stripped of its treasure. It was not a difficult task.'

King Lundu shrugged, unimpressed. 'Why would it not be so? They build their towns with no thought of defence. A child could take their treasures.'

'Careful,' Diogo thought. 'Do not make him despise you.' 'You are right, Holy One. Even a child could steal their treasures.' He hesitated, then added craftily, 'But a child could not escape the wrath of the Rozvi. Many men were lost in the battle. Fortunately most were the Rozvi.'

'Tell us,' the King commanded.

Diogo paused for effect, then went on. 'It was a dark night, Holy One. The moon was young and not yet risen. We hid in the trees outside the Great Enclosure and waited for all sound to cease.'

'How many of you?'

'My men numbered twenty-five. We brought nearly two hundred Nguni with us as well,' he added, naming the tribe to which the King himself belonged.

The King sneered. 'Then you had as many as lived there.'

'Only to carry the treasure, Holy One. The Nguni did not enter Great Zimbabwe with us.'

Finally, the King looked impressed.

'The treasure was stored in the Mambo's tower. We killed the four guards and took everything. My men and I made many trips between Great Zimbabwe and the trees. We were not seen or heard.' Diogo permitted himself a small smile of self-congratulation. 'By the time the moon had risen we were on our way.'

'And the battle?'

'Ah, Holy One, what a battle it was. The Rozvi caught up with us four days later as we approached the Zambezi River. By the end of the day, not one Rozvi remained alive. The river ran red with their blood. I lost seven of my men. Of the Nguni, only two dozen were killed.' Diogo refrained from mentioning that 300 of the Munhu Mutapa's warriors

11

joined his side of the battle. He was gambling on the fact that news of such an insignificant scrap would not have reached the King's ears. King Lundu's words confirmed that it had not.

'That is good. And now you sail for Malindi?'

'In the morning,' Diogo confirmed. 'The treasure will remain here until arrangements can be made to transport it to Kilwa. I will let you know when.'

Their business conducted, the tale told, the two men had little left to discuss. King Lundu left the reception chamber and Diogo went to a guest sleeping room where he would spend the night.

Three days later, in a ferocious storm which whipped up waterspouts reaching high into the air, Diogo Pegado's ship sank, drowning all hands, off the rugged Makanjira Point. King Lundu, waiting to hear from him, soon forgot about the treasure (which was meaningless to him in terms of value) as a virulent strain of malaria took hold of his small kingdom, eventually claiming the life of the King and eighty per cent of his people. Those who survived left the small island of Likoma and headed for the mainland, leaving the large fortified building, which had been their home, to the invasion of surrounding bush, ants, the passage of time and erosion. By 1886, nearly 200 years later, when the Anglican Church decided, in their wisdom, to build a cathedral on Likoma, all trace of King Lundu and his people had disappeared. Ironically,

St Peter's Cathedral was erected at Chipyela – the burning place – above the beach where Diogo Pegado witnessed the young warrior's execution. The aim of the Anglican Church being to bury the evil history of the place with good intentions.

Ng'ona lived for sixty-three more years. Although the food so obligingly thrown to him on occasion by King Lundu ceased, the great lake abounded in fish. Coinciding with *Ng'ona*'s death, Likoma Island was once again settled, this time by Nguni fishermen. They nonetheless avoided the cove where the great crocodile had once lived. In 1871, though nowhere near as large, another *Ng'ona* took up residence. The sheltered cove with reeds covering the bottom, the large, dry cave containing strange golden objects, were very much to his liking.

TWO

NORTHERN LAKE NYASA – 1887

The woman knew she was about to die. She knew too, that long before she was dead, she would have lost her sanity in unspeakable agony.

The hard, rasping cough of a male leopard as he called for a mate was close. The growling, sawing snarl sliced through the soft velvet warmth of the African night with savage malevolence. However, it was not the big cat that kept the woman, and the man standing next to her, frozen with fear.

Tightly woven fibrous walls, reinforced with hard-packed river mud, surrounding the Nganga's enclosure danced in sinister waves in the flickering firelight. Behind the walls, the long, pestle-shaped *mapondela* pounded its morbid death knell, mocking the woman as it pulverised the poisonous bark from a mwavi tree.

Fear was a palpable blanket over the bowed heads of Chief Mbeya's people. Fear of the unknown, of the magic spells of the Nganga, fear that one day they too might stand accused like the man and woman in the centre of the burning place. Fear ruled the Nkonde people and kept them obedient.

Those who broke the rules, those whose usefulness had ended, had good reason for fear.

The villagers sat or stood in a tight circle around the accused, leaving a path for the Nganga once he emerged from his hut. The woman tried to still the tremors in her hands. The prospect of death was less terrifying than her superstitious dread of the Nganga. His power was said to be supernatural, his displeasure brought instant and awful reprisal, his appearance, daubed and painted to look fierce, struck terror into every heart, and adornments of teeth and bones, gruesome reminders of past enemies or wrongdoers, rattled on his chest and ankles.

The pounding behind the wall ceased abruptly. Agonising silence followed. Then the drums began their chilling death message, spreading the woman's shame from village to village until the whole of central Africa knew that another witch was about to be tested. Although her eyes were lowered, the woman knew the instant the medicine man stepped from his enclosure. The warm night air turned icy cold and goose bumps rose on her flesh and itched at the base of her skull.

'You may look upon my magnificence.' The Nganga's voice was reedy with extreme age.

The woman raised her eyes. A hideous grinning hyena mask covering the medicine man's face appeared alive in the light of dancing flames. She could see the steely glint of cold appraisal through slits cut for the Nganga's eyes. The drums reached a crescendo then stopped abruptly, and the only sound left was that of the leopard as he passed in the night. The Nganga squatted on the ground in front of the accused. Monkey tails hanging from copper wire around his waist fanned out around him in a perfect circle, protecting him from evil.

Opening a bag made from baboon skin, he emptied the powdered mwavi bark onto a banana leaf. Onto this he spat sap from the same tree. While the bark was poisonous, the sap was not, but only the Nganga knew this. Taking the hollowed end of a nyala horn, which was strung around his neck on finely woven fibre, he added a generous proportion of mixed owl and hyena excrement. Using his fingers, the witchdoctor mixed the ingredients into a sticky paste. Then, scooping up the poisonous brew he scraped it into two roughly sculptured containers of mud. His concentration was total as he thinned the paste with water.

Satisfied that the poison was ready, the medicine man rose and gravely observed the two terrified people in front of him. Then he took the first steps of his 'smelling out' dance which would continue until he was foaming at the mouth in an eyes-glazed, body-convulsed trance, at which point he would stretch an accusing finger at one or both of the trembling suspects.

The dance took an agonising twenty-five min-utes. It seemed the Nganga must surely collapse from exhaustion. Finally, with a chilling scream, he pointed a bony finger at the man and then the woman. Both had been 'smelled out' and now had to prove their innocence.

No-one noticed that one of the cups contained a much larger dose of poison than the other. Cunning, as his calling required him to be, the witchdoctor did not want the man to die for, although he had strayed too close to the Nganga's enclosure yesterday, he was a fine and strong young man with many years of usefulness left. The woman, however, was of no consequence. She had no man to take care of her, her parents were dead and she had no brothers or sisters. Her five small children needed feeding and she and her offspring were a drain on the village. If she had been more agreeable perhaps she could have found a husband but her sharp tongue made her unpopular. Someone had to die; a death kept the villagers obedient. Accusing both victims of witchcraft gave the Nganga a perfect excuse to get rid of the woman and reinforce his authority.

The Nganga's power was awesome. No-one questioned it. Omens and dreams, rigid rules of behaviour, the witchdoctor reigned supreme. Two river stones in the corner of the woman's hut were proclaimed proof that she was a witch. That was all it took.

The poison, if given in large enough quantities, brought about violent vomiting, which was considered a sign of innocence. A smaller amount, however, induced agonising convulsions which inevitably led to death.

The Nganga handed the woman the smaller amount.

With trembling hands she put the cup to her

lips and swallowed the foul-smelling paste. The drums started up again. No-one moved or spoke. Then the man began to vomit and the woman knew her fate. Someone always had to die. As she was gripped by the first painful cramp and her limbs began to twitch, the villagers pressed closer, raining insults and blows down on her. Her last sight on this earth, just before the agony of her death blotted out all other considerations, was of half-a-dozen warriors running to her hut to kill her children.

The Nganga's powers and medicines had been handed down from father to eldest son for countless generations. But while he used tricks and stage-managed most ceremonies, he also possessed the gift of second sight and this, coupled with his special effects and gimmicks, had earned him the fearful respect of everyone in his own and surrounding villages.

Three days after the 'smelling out' ceremony, the awful prediction he had made that night came true.

Ferig sat in the shade of an enormous sycamore tree with a dozen other young, married women, and kept glancing up from the blanket she was weaving to look with awe, fear and revulsion at the strange looking man who had stormed into the village and demanded to speak with the Chief. She wondered how the witchdoctor could possibly have known.

'I have had a terrible vision,' he had said, removing his mask and gazing sternly at the villagers clustered around the convulsing woman on the ground.

Ferig had shuddered. The last time he warned of danger he predicted death by water. Four nights later the river flooded with no warning and twelve people had drowned.

'You have heard of the man with skin so white it burns in the sunlight?' The Nganga had rattled three sticks in his hand to protect himself and the others from the evils attributed to the white man. 'One such man is coming here very soon. He will warn of bad things affecting Nkondeland.'

Chief Mbeya, who stood in as much awe of the witchdoctor as the rest of them, stepped forward. He never made an important decision on behalf of the village without first consulting the Nganga. 'What will this white man want from us?'

'He will tell us to move to the big village where he lives. He will say he can protect us.'

There was shuffling and unease among the men. They needed no white man's protection.

'What am I to tell him?'

'You are Chief. You will tell him that which you know in your heart is right.' Neatly shedding responsibility, the Nganga knew that if Chief Mbeya made the right decision it would be whispered that the Nganga had known he would. If the wrong decision was taken, the blame would belong to the Chief entirely. Either way, the Nganga's reputation remained intact. Before the Chief could question this decision, the witchdoctor had dismissed the villagers.

And now, as the Nganga had said, a white man had come to the village.

Monteith Fotheringham presented an astonishing spectre to the unsophisticated inhabitants of the isolated Nkonde village. His face, surrounded as it was by a bristling and wild red beard, seemed to have adopted the same colour. His eyes looked like those of a fish which, Ferig had been told, was considered a great delicacy by the Wahenga people who lived on the shores of the great water. The only skin she could see, other than that on his strangely red face, was on his hands. They were the colour and shape of cattle udders and she wondered whether, if squeezed, milk would squirt from them. His body was encased in the skins of an animal unknown to Ferig. That is, she assumed it to be an animal, never having encountered cloth. And what a strange animal it must be, for she had never seen one the colour of fire and milk.

Ferig herself wore only a tiny apron of bark cloth, as did all the women. The men wore nothing more than copper wire around their waists. She wondered what the white man was hiding to wrap himself from head to toe.

The Wankonde, those who belonged to the Nkonde tribe, lived in small villages scattered across fertile plains from the top of the great water and extending north, east and west along the soft contours of the southern end of the Rift Valley. Some lived on the shores of Lake Nyasa. Others, like Ferig, lived two days' walk from the great water.

Only a handful from Chief Mbeya's village had ever glimpsed a white man before. The villagers were filled with curiosity but good manners required that he not be approached, stared at, harmed or ridiculed.

He had brought with him, however, three Nkonde tribesmen from the town of Karonga. Ferig and her friends lured one of them away with the promise of food and bombarded him with questions. He told them that, behind his back, the white man was called 'thunder and lightning', an apt name since his voice alternated between a crackle and a rumble. To his face he was called 'Montisi' which was as close as they could get to 'Monteith'.

He had come to Karonga to build a big house which kept many items of value which could be traded for other items. Men brought him tusks from the elephants they hunted. Ferig could not imagine what they would want in return. She was content. The Wankonde lived almost exclusively on bananas and cattle. The banana fruit was pounded into porridge; the leaves were used for a variety of purposes including thatch, plates, towels or were burned in their cooking fires; the sap was used as soap; and strong fibre was used to weave baskets and blankets.

The man also told Ferig and the other women

that Montisi owned a thunder stick which made such a terrible noise that those who had the stick pointed at them fell down dead, the noise being so loud that it made holes in their bodies. Montisi, however, must have swallowed some medicine to protect him from such a noise for, although others fell, he always remained standing.

To Ferig, the white man was so utterly and incomprehensibly unlike any human she had seen that she wondered if he was a real person or some strange god from across the great water. Her life was spent in a radius not exceeding one day's walk and she had never spoken to anyone other than a fellow Nkonde tribesman or woman. This one was so strange that she was both fascinated and repulsed. His appearance, and the rude manner in which he had entered the village, were enough to frighten everyone. His utterings were garbled noises that no-one else could possibly understand. He showed no deference to the Chief and had walked straight past the Nganga shaking his head. In a society where pleasantries were always eagerly exchanged and haste taken as a sign of either fear or guilt, this white man appeared to be in a suspicious rush.

She peeped up at him again. The isolated villages thrived on the gossip of travelling storytellers, men whose life work was to spread stories of tribal history, news of distant relatives and interesting tidbits collected in their wanderings. The last one to visit her village had told of the coming of a white race. Ferig hadn't believed him. He had told of how they were supposed to be so clever and have many miracles. Hau! If this man was so clever why then did he have to crane his neck to look up at the Chief. Clever people were leaders and leaders could not lead unless others had to look up to them.

Only the Nganga was allowed to be small. But even the Nganga would ask, 'From how far did you see me?' The only prudent response was, 'I saw you from very far away.'

The white man turned abruptly and stomped away from the Chief in the same brusque manner as he arrived, with rapid aggressive steps. She watched him from under her lashes, her fingers busy weaving. As he drew level with the spot where Ferig and the other women sat he slowed and stared at Ferig. She raised her head and looked at him and he appeared to be lost in thought as he looked back. Then, shaking his head, he set off again, saying something in his own language.

Ferig, like all the Wankonde, had a high proportion of Egyptian blood in her. Unlike other tribes in Central Africa with their very black skin and short stature, the Wankonde were generally tall, with bronze skin, finely chiselled features and proud bearing. Although she had not understood his words, they frightened Ferig. She'd have been more frightened had she understood.

Monteith Fotheringham, struck by the beauty of the Wankonde, and especially by the young woman who stared back at him in a manner which was innocent, calm, aloof and apprehensive all at once, had been moved to say, 'Aye, lassie, you'll be gracing the court of the Sultan afore this year's oot, you mark my word.' Then, as he turned to go he added savagely, 'If you live.'

The women had to wait until the men returned from hunting to hear why the white man had come, for the Chief spoke to the women only through their husbands, fathers and brothers. Pambuka, Ferig's husband of five moons, related the Chief's words.

'The chief at the village of Mpata has allowed a stranger to build a small city there.'

Ferig glanced at him. In the flickering light of her cooking fire, his handsome face was serious. 'Mpata is very far from here.'

Pambuka nodded slowly. 'Indeed.' He adjusted a stick in the fire and grinned cheekily when Ferig readjusted it to her liking. He often teased her because her gentle reprimands delighted him. 'This man has the name Mlozi. He is a very evil man. He is a friend of the ruga-ruga.'

Ferig shivered at the mention of the ruga-ruga although she had never seen them herself. Once they had ruled and raided the whole of central Africa. Savage and cruel, without a shred of compassion, they were rumoured to run with the evil spirits and eat the flesh off live captives. Although tales of their deeds circulated, Ferig, like most Wankonde, half believed the ruga-ruga to be myth. 'This man Mlozi must be a devil who walks the earth.'

Pambuka hunched forward. 'Listen carefully, wife. Mlozi and the ruga-ruga are taking the Wankonde for slaves. The white man warns of lines of captives so long that they would stretch from one end of our village to the other. Mlozi wants to take our lands for the Wahenga. Those he does not take for slaves are killed. The white man is a good man. He tells of terrible deeds, of slaves so hungry their bones poke out, of women being used by the ruga-ruga against their wishes, of flesh split by the *kurbash*.' Pambuka took a deep breath. 'They are travelling great distances to take our people. The white man wants us to move to Karonga where we will be safe.'

Ferig said nothing. This was men's business. Her role was to obey whatever decision they reached.

'Our Chief has refused.' Pambuka could not keep the pride from his voice. The Wankonde were peaceful and gentle people but they were not cowards. The Nganga had told Chief Mbeya that he would find the answer to the white man's request in his own heart. If this was the right decision, and Pambuka would not dream of questioning it, then the Nganga had put it there.

Convinced as he was, however, Pambuka was a man who loved his wife and wanted to protect her. 'If this terrible thing comes to our village and I am killed, you must promise to kill yourself.' He reached over and stroked the velvet bronze of her cheek. 'Believe me, wife, it is better you die from your own hand.'

Ferig stared at him wide-eyed, her heart fluttering at the enormity of what he was asking. To take

25

your own life meant your spirit wandered restlessly forever.

'Promise me,' Pambuka said softly, his dark eyes penetrating and commanding.

Ferig nodded slowly. 'I promise, husband.' She had no option. If he told her to jump in the fire she was obliged to obey.

Pambuka smiled, relieved. He knew what he was asking of her. But he had to make sure she understood. 'I know your blood has stopped running, wife. For two moons you have not journeyed to the women's hut.'

Ferig hung her head, embarrassed. A women's bleeding was not a fitting subject, even between husband and wife. When the bleeding was upon a woman she had to sleep in a special hut, for fear of contaminating her own home.

'Look at me, wife.' Pambuka knew he had overstepped the boundary of good manners. But he had more to say. He was prepared to die at the hands of the ruga-ruga but he feared for Ferig. She was the most beautiful woman in the village and the white man had been specific. The women's fate was worse than death itself. 'If the ruga-ruga come after our child has been born, they will kill him.'

Ferig placed her hands over her stomach, as if to protect the small being which had only begun to grow a short while ago.

Pambuka went on remorselessly. 'They will kill our child and take you away. You will go far away, wife, to distant lands. There you will be the wife of a stranger. But before then, the ruga-ruga will treat you as their own. They are cruel men, wife. They do terrible things to women. Animal things. Do you understand?'

Ferig's heart beat wildly at the horror of what Pambuka was saying. She had never heard anything like it in her life. 'I will do as you say, husband. No-one will touch me as you do. I would rather be a restless spirit.'

Pambuka nodded, satisfied. 'What are you doing with our food, wife?' he teased, to take the terror from her heart. 'Are we to eat it in the morning?'

The women of the village clustered together next morning, each one aghast at the terrible warnings of the night before. The events of recent days, ever since the Nganga told them of his vision, had them buzzing with a multitude of mixed emotions. The white man's visit alone was enough food for speculation to last them many months. Each one had made some small observation, unnoticed by the others. Ferig's fantasy about the white man's fingers spouting milk had them all rocking with laughter.

In the normal course of events, the stories about their strange visitor would circulate and grow until reality was replaced by make-believe and the truth lost in legend.

Added to the excitement now were the unbelievable things the white man had told the Chief, things which had then been related back to them by their menfolk. The advice the women had received varied. Some had been told to run, others to fight, a few had been advised to submit in order to save their lives. Only Ferig had been ordered to kill herself.

Pambuka's instructions frightened them nearly as much as the threat of the ruga-ruga. 'What is your man thinking?' one of them asked angrily of Ferig. 'Does he know what he is saying?'

'He knows,' Ferig replied, ready to defend her beloved husband. 'He knows it is wicked. But he is a wise man as you all know. He would not ask it of me if he did not think it best.'

The others nodded, each one wondering why their own husbands did not love them the way Pambuka loved Ferig.

As the days passed the dire warnings of the white man slipped into their subconscious lives. There was work to be done, cattle byres to be cleaned, huts to be swept, blankets to be woven, food to be cooked. The villagers returned to their daily lives and the prospect of the slave-trader Mlozi and his terrible ruga-ruga faded to a vague possibility, not to be dwelt upon in case they willed it to come true.

Ferig was dreaming. In her dream she was walking through banana groves, and the lovely sycamore and cotton trees which grew between them. Her as yet unborn son, in the strange way of dreams, rode high on Pambuka's shoulders. They were all laughing. Dimly, through the soft corners of her dream, she heard Pambuka stir and mumble something in his sleep. Her dreaming eyes saw her son's hand reach out in slow motion and take a banana. He handed it to Ferig and she took it, happy and content, for the banana symbolised food in plentiful supply. Feeling secure, she rolled on her sleeping mat and curled her body into Pambuka's. The strength and warmth of that familiar back sent her into a deeper sleep where no dreams can reach.

It was an hour before dawn and three weeks after the visit of the white man. The slumbering inhabitants of the isolated Nkonde village, like Ferig and Pambuka, slipped into that delightful predawn slumber which would ensure vitality and enthusiasm for the daily chores which lay ahead. One or two cooking fires smouldered still, their smoke rising far above the banana groves and the tidy clay brick and bamboo huts to dissipate in the cool mountain breath which sped down from the Livingstone Mountains and flattened out over the northern tip of Lake Nyasa, fanning little waves.

Ferig and Pambuka lay curled together like children.

Outside, in the byres, a wave of unease ran through the cattle, corralled for the night to protect them from predators. A scent, alien and unpleasant, was suddenly all around them. Ghostly figures flitted past. The cattle, usually content to doze through the night, began to move restlessly, sensing danger. But the figures ran on and were soon out of sight and the smell of them, which had so disturbed the cattle, went with them. One by one the cows settled down.

Five minutes later a scream split the silence. It was the war cry of the ruga-ruga. Loud and hideous, bloodcurdling in its savage ferocity, it sped its chilling message into the huts and jerked even the deeply asleep into a dry-mouthed, nameless terror. Blinking away his dreams, Pambuka sat up. His heart was beating wildly. *Was it a dream? A wild animal in pain?*

In the next instant he knew. Gunfire was intermingled with loud shouts. Pambuka had never heard the sound of guns but the aggressive brutality of it was a violent penetration of the harmonious and peaceful village and Pambuka knew with absolute certainty that he was about to die.

Ferig clung to him, crying with fear. 'Remember your promise, wife,' he whispered fiercely. 'My spear is my love for you. Go where the spirits take you. I will find you.'

Ferig could only cry harder.

He heard his neighbour and friend call his name from the hut next to his. He hugged Ferig roughly and stumbled up, ready to defend the village. 'Do it quickly,' he bellowed, bursting from his hut, ancient warrior traditions flooding his body in one last desperate act of unremitting bravery.

The ruga-ruga were waiting for him. One on either side of the door. Pambuka was clubbed to death. The two ruga-ruga men rained blows down on his head until it became a bloody pulp. Ferig sat rooted to the spot with fear, listening to the sickening sound of Pambuka's head being crushed. She delayed obeying Pambuka because her paralysed

mind could think of nothing. Violence was everywhere, where a minute earlier there had been
nothing but the gentle sound of his breathing and
the warm security of his body next to hers. A rustle at the door broke through the panic which had
arrested her body. She lunged for Pambuka's spear.
But she had delayed too long. The ruga-ruga
grabbed her and hauled her outside.

Dawn was rapidly lighting the eastern sky. Ferig
could just make out a group of villagers, huddled
together in terrorised stupor. Women were wailing.
Not in full-throated harmony as they did at the death
of a loved one in order to encourage a happy passage
to the spirit world. Fear constricted their throats so
that their wails were like those of an ailing baby.

Children clung in sleepy confusion to their
mothers. A few men, their heads hung in shame
that they had not died in defence of their village,
stood among the women. The Nganga stood with
them and Ferig, in a blinding realisation, saw him
for what he really was: a short, skinny old man who
trembled with the rest of them as he faced the
prospect of his own death. 'Why did he not warn
us?' she thought angrily. She had no way of knowing that the Nganga's second sight came and went
at will and that he had no control over his visions.
Of the Chief there was no sign. Ferig was pushed
roughly into the crowd.

Shaking from head to toe, with silent tears running down her face, she confronted her fate. The
truth of it was so horrible she began to wail out
loud in fear.

31

'Be silent, you foolish girl,' an older woman next to her hissed. 'Do you want them to kill you?'

'Yes. Oh yes.' Ferig wanted that more than anything. She had failed in her promise to Pambuka. He had died defending her and she had failed him. The knowledge gave her the courage to act. She broke from the huddle of her friends and ran straight at the ruga-ruga.

She was seized by half-a-dozen eager hands and flung to the ground. She lay there, anticipating the blows from their clubs, or the searing, stinging pain of their spears. A voice shouted, loud and menacing. From the corner of her eye she watched the filthy bare feet of the ruga-ruga shuffle away. Another foot, one clad in sandals, hooked under her side and flipped her on her back. Ferig stared upwards into the coldest eyes she had ever seen. They flicked over her body, assessing, contemptuous, unfeeling eyes, and she knew he was not seeing her as anything other than an animal. He eyed her as dispassionately as she would pick through a bunch of bananas, in search of the most succulent.

His white robe flowed down to his feet, a red sash thrown over one shoulder. A small white cap sat on his shaven head. She felt a horror which ran through her body and sat in her bowel like a hard, red-hot object.

Mlozi! The one who walks with devils. His half-caste Arab/African face – with a tidy beard and two protruding front teeth which pushed out his top lip and sat, like white pebbles, over his bottom lip – was almost benign. But his eyes were dead and deadly all at once. Ferig felt deeply afraid.

He snapped out an order in an unfamiliar tongue and the ruga-ruga stepped forward and pulled her to her feet. Mlozi gestured impatiently and they broke the twine holding her modesty apron so she was naked before him.

Mlozi moved around her slowly. Ferig had no idea how beautiful she was but there was no way she could misinterpret the appreciation on this man's face. She tried to place her hands over her *mons veneris* but the ruga-ruga snatched them away. She was trembling so badly she believed she would fall down. She was certain that Mlozi was planning to eat her.

But Mlozi had things commercial rather than culinary on his mind. This one was a treasure. She would fetch far more than the average slave. The sultan in Zanzibar would pay handsomely for one so proudly beautiful, yet so fearful. He hoped she would survive the trip – not a foregone conclusion; the ruga-ruga were not oblivious of her charms and there was nothing he could do to protect her. Although he controlled the savage band of ragged and inhumane warriors with food, wages and use of the slaves, he, like everyone else, was also afraid of them.

He nodded and Ferig was pushed back into the huddle of mute and fearful villagers. Then he nodded again and ran his finger under his throat in an obscenely murderous gesture and the ruga-ruga, grinning and laughing, pulled each of the captives forward and, depending on a nod or shake of Mlozi's head, either led the wretched villager away to stand in a bewildered huddle with others, or killed them on the spot with clubs or spears.

Ferig quickly realised that a dispassionate selection process was taking place, where only the fittest were left alive. The elderly, pregnant, ill, deformed or very young were killed. The all-powerful Nganga was killed with one blow to the head and in death his once indestructible body became a pathetic jumble of arms and legs, a sight so shocking to those who had regarded him with awe that they dumbly submitted to their own death. 'Please let me die,' Ferig begged silently, wishing the baby which had only just begun to grow inside her was more obvious. But she was led away to join the chosen few where she was yoked by the neck with a forked stick, a *goree*, the long end of which stuck out behind her. The front was locked into place with an iron staple and the fork narrowed so rapidly it rubbed the skin on either side of her neck. The stick at the back was bound to another *goree* which in turn was placed around another's neck, this time with the fork rubbing cruelly at the front of the captive's throat once it was secured by a staple at the back. Ropes, tied around the waist, linked a line of some forty people and then children were tethered by a neck-iron with the other end of their chain attached to the length of *goree* which stretched between two people yoked together.

Those yoked by the *gorees* quickly realised that

34

any movement by them, or the child linked to them, caused instant pain as the sticks rubbed their necks and threatened to cut off their breathing. Trembling and fearful, the captives stood in mute lines, their minds unable to take in the carnage around them.

Ferig's village was burning. The ruga-ruga ran through it setting it alight, amid shouts of encouragement from each other. Mlozi seemed content to let them take their time. It crossed Ferig's mind that he could not have stopped them even if he wanted to. The ruga-ruga's eyes were glazed in the aftermath of human slaughter and the joy of looting and burning. She did not see her own home set alight since she was facing the other way and to move was too painful. So she was spared the sight of Pambuka's once strong and loving body, mutilated beyond recognition and set alight. Ferig was, in any case, staring at the mountains, devouring the familiar sight which she vowed she would not forget until the chance came for her to fulfil her promise to Pambuka.

Finally the ruga-ruga, smeared with fresh blood and displaying large yellow teeth in a dreadful parody of a grin, appeared to have satisfied their blood lust. Mlozi realised they were under his control once more and barked an order. Reluctant to move away from the only home they had ever known, and despite having understood they were supposed to move, the bewildered captives stared dully at him. Ferig heard a hissing sound, followed by a tremendous crack and a cry of pain from someone.

The Arab *kurbash*, in the hands of Mlozi, danced and hissed and split tender flesh with its needle-thin end until the slaves realised the only thing to do was obey the command to move immediately. Shuffling, reluctant, with terror pounding in their hearts, they moved away from the burning village, leaving the bodies of loved ones and friends to the scavenging village dogs and the already circling vultures.

They walked all day. The ruga-ruga marched beside them, beating tom-toms, lashing them with the *kurbash*, taunting and poking them, particularly the women. Very few adult men had been spared.

The first part of the journey was a nightmare. Coming down from the foothills of the mountains meant the slave in the front yoke was always below the level of the one yoked behind. The chafing on Ferig's neck was bleeding. She could feel the warm blood running down either side and trickling over her shoulders. But she bore the discomfort quietly. As bad as it was for her, it was worse for Pambuka's sister, Makeba, who was behind her. Several times she heard her friend and sister-in-law choking for air as they laboured down a particularly steep slope.

The ruga-ruga made no effort to take them around thorny stands of acacia trees. Ferig's arms and legs were torn in several places. Flies, attracted to the blood, followed the pathetic caravan like a sinister cloud, inflicting stinging bites onto the torn flesh. They were given no food or water.

By the end of the day Ferig was so tired she could barely put one foot in front of the other. Mlozi called a halt just as the sun disappeared behind the mountains. The ruga-ruga went among the captives, removing their yokes. These were immediately replaced by neck-irons. Sharp, rusty edges cut into the soft skin rubbed raw from the sapling yokes but, so glad were they to be able to turn their heads, no-one made a sound. Once the ruga-ruga had moved away Ferig asked softly, 'Are you well, sister?'

'I am as well as you,' Makeba replied.

Freed from the restraining *goree,* the two women moved together and clutched each other in terror.

'I am going to kill myself,' Ferig said. 'I promised Pambuka.'

'I will kill myself also,' Makeba agreed. 'But how?'

'We will find a way, sister.'

Up and down the line of bone-weary captives, speculation was whispered back and forth.

'What will happen, what will happen? They're going to eat us. Will we be sacrificed to their devils? Roasted alive? Turned into monsters?'

The speculation fell silent as the ruga-ruga dispensed small quantities of food. Corn kernels, raw and hard, poured into the sand at the feet of each slave. They were so hungry that, despite misgivings that the little yellow beads would poison them, they ate ravenously.

For the first time since her capture, Ferig forced

herself to look fully at the ruga-ruga. They were very black. The whites of their eyes were tinged with the yellow trademark of those who lived by the great water and fell ill with the mysterious water-sickness. Tribal scars disfigured their faces and bodies. They stank as bad as a rotting carcass. Their faces and bodies were streaked with paint and blood. Long, greasy ringlets of hair had battered and dirty feathers tied into them. Necklaces of human teeth hung around their necks and rattled and clacked together each time they moved.

She remembered Pambuka's words: 'They will use you against your wishes,' and her own reply: 'No-one will touch me as you do.' But how could she stop them? She glanced towards Makeba, wondering if she feared the same as herself.

Makeba read her thoughts. 'Get some rest, sister. It will be worse when the night is full on us.'

But the ruga-ruga were not prepared to wait until dark. They moved among the captives and fell on them like starving hyenas at a freshly killed zebra. The young girls and boys were first. Their distraught mothers could only sit helpless, crying tears of frustrated rage as their precious and dearly loved children were defiled by these monsters from hell.

Ferig knew her turn would be soon. She prayed for night to fall so she did not have to see those who took her. But the good spirits did not heed her prayers. Their hideous features grimacing in carnal pleasure above her, Ferig was raped three times before nightfall obliterated the sight of them

38

and left her to deal only with the stench of their foul bodies, the invading outrage of their male parts, the animal grunting of them and the pitiful cries of the children in their pain and fear.

In the cold light of dawn, the carnage was terrible. Several children were dead. Others would clearly be unable to walk. Mlozi, who had not taken part in the savagery, examined the fallen. Those too damaged to keep up were casually speared where they lay. As he withdrew his spear from a little boy who still twitched in his death tremors, he turned to the shattered mother, spread his hand, palm up, towards the child, shrugged and smiled. It was almost as though he were saying, 'See . . . I have lightened your burden. Am I not a good friend?'

Yesterday Ferig had used disbelief, anger and grief to keep up her strength. As she had stumbled along in her cruel yoke a tiny flame of hope had burned in her breast. Pambuka was not really dead, he would rescue her. The white stranger would save them all. Wankonde from other villages would fall upon the ruga-ruga and destroy them and set the captives free.

Today, after the horrors of the night, she, like all the others, felt that hope die, to be replaced with dumb, aching despair. There was not one spark of anything positive left in the entire tragic caravan of captives. Ferig had even forgotten her promise to Pambuka.

On the third day they reached Mlozi's stockade

at Mpata, a holding place where the slaves were kept until enough of them had been caught to make the trip across the lake in dhows. The sixty or so from Chief Mbeya's village who survived that dreadful march had, up until then, been able to take some small comfort in being in the company of each other. At the stockade, in the same frightful condition as Ferig and her companions, other Nkonde people huddled together in village groups. But, Mlozi decided that with the arrival of the latest slave caravan, he had enough captives to fill several dhows and so the miserable Wankonde, numbering nearly 600 in total, were assembled and subjected to a grading process which separated Ferig from her friends. She did not know it but, with her youth and beauty, she had been picked, along with five others, for the sultan's harem in Zanzibar.

Others would work on Portuguese estates, toiling in the fields or homes of the landowners, some of whom were nearly as cruel and indifferent to their suffering as the ruga-ruga. Some were destined for such faraway places as Turkish harems, Brazilian plantations, Indian courts or the pavilions of Chinese emperors. Each group was kept separate. All the males, irrespective of their age or final destination, were castrated without the benefit of any pain-killing herbs. Eunuchs fetched more money. Many died from loss of blood that night.

Ferig and the other five women considered comely enough to please the Sultan of Zanzibar were placed in a filthy cell which carried the stench of fear, death and human faeces. The walls of the stockade consisted of some 260 cells – formed by the construction of a parallel wall two metres from the outer wall. Most of these were for Mlozi's fighting force. Occasionally slaves selected for special reasons would be placed in one. Ferig and her companions huddled together in abject misery. Screams and moans from the men and boys kept them awake. Because they were the cream of the crop, the ruga-ruga demanded access to them and Mlozi was too afraid to refuse. However, he warned that this would be the last night. 'From tomorrow,' he told his ghastly soldiers, 'they are to be saved for the Sultan.'

The ruga-ruga paid special attention to them that night. In the morning two were dead and not one of the remaining four could move without excruciating pain. At some stage during that terrible night, the seed planted in Ferig's womb by Pambuka as she had lain in the security of his strong arms and whispered her love for him, died. For Ferig, the last link with everything she had ever known had gone. For the first time in her life, she was truly alone. In the morning, listening to the soft weeping of the other women, she knew they felt alone too. But they were all too sick with fear and pain to make any attempt to seek solace in each other.

Around midmorning, the four women were removed from their cell and taken to a special building within the stockade where they were ordered to bathe. The feeling of water around her

41

was like a soft protective cocoon and Ferig's desperately cowed spirits lifted sufficiently for her to again think of her unfulfilled promise to Pambuka. As she washed away her own excreta, dried blood, dust and the horrible spent sullage of the ruga-ruga, she looked around for something, anything, she could use. The room contained nothing more than rough towels, too small and thick to make any kind of rope. She knew it was no use but, under the watchful gaze of the two Wahenga soldiers guarding her, she submerged herself completely in the bath. The Wahenga had seen it before. They allowed her thirty seconds before moving in and pulling her out of the water.

Crying tears of frustration, Ferig barely felt the open-handed slaps of punishment. She was dried by angry hands and then bundled into another room where the other three stood, each one guarded by two men.

Each of these women was of astounding beauty, their Egyptian ancestry giving them an aristocratic haughtiness which could not be hidden. Tunics of soft white material were lowered over their heads. None of them had worn anything but modesty aprons. They were women and they were beautiful and they were powerless to stop their lifted spirits as they cast admiring looks at each other and enjoyed the feeling of caressing silk against their skin.

Healing ointment was rubbed onto the raw flesh on their necks, on the whip and thorn cuts and on the scratches made by the filthy fingernails of the ruga-ruga. A greasy red substance was applied to their lips and Ferig was astonished at how it changed the appearance of the others. She licked her lips. It had a pleasant enough taste. She was told not to lick it off.

They were led into another room where Mlozi waited to inspect them, like a proud father, before providing a highly spiced meal of meats with maize meal. The food was so strange that Ferig wondered if she was being poisoned but she was too hungry to care.

The women ate with their hands. Mlozi had lost several girls to sharp utensils in the past and these four had not yet lost their will. The bath, the clothes and the food had revived them to a point where, he could see, they would try anything to escape their fate, even death. That was good. The Sultan liked spirited women. But they still had some lessons to learn.

After the meal, Mlozi clicked his fingers and the Wahenga bodyguards moved in, ripped the tunics off the women and half-pushed, half-dragged them back to their cell where, as a gruesome reminder, the bodies of their two dead companions still lay, rigid and real.

That night, well after the visiting time of the ruga-ruga had passed with no incident, one of the women called timidly, 'I am Chikanga.'

'I am Ferig.'

One by one they introduced themselves.

One by one they voiced their fears.

One by one they told of life in their villages, of

43

their experiences on the way to Mlozi's stockade, of husbands and children, mothers and fathers, brothers and sisters, friends and relatives murdered or captured.

One by one they slipped into fearful sleep, expecting the ruga-ruga at any time, each woman's dreams filled with wild-man images and eyes which belonged in the land of evil spirits.

They were woken at daybreak and herded into the open area of the stockade. Ferig was prevented from joining her friends but she could see the dreadful condition some of them were in. Those men and boys who had survived their savage and crude surgery were in a weakened and cowed state. Pambuka's sister had a *kurbash* lash on her shoulder which had gone septic. She called softly to Ferig and told how her skin was red-hot and the flesh had swollen up to resemble a melon. She was sweating and complaining of feeling cold. 'I do not wish to leave you, sister, but I am growing weaker.'

'Leave me and go with your husband's spirit, Makeba,' Ferig called back. 'I will join you all as soon as I can.'

Screams from other parts of the enclosure warned her of a new terror. It soon became clear what it was. Each of the slaves had to be branded with the mark by which they had been graded. Women trembled and wailed in fear as the stench of burnt flesh filled the stockade. As the wailing spread through the groups it took on a rhythm of its own. The slaves took comfort in familiar words and harmony. They sang of their homeland, plundered and

44

burning, of mountains and skies they would never see again, of loved ones gone to the spirit world. The shame of central Africa pulsated from hundreds of fear-stricken throats and rose in abject misery to speak of despair and suffering and cruelty. But their spirits had been broken and they could not bring themselves to sing for long and soon the stockade was filled with heartbroken sobs.

Ferig was branded on the breast. Other women endured the searing pain on the shoulder or buttock. While they were still moaning with pain from this new horror, Mlozi examined each woman methodically. He scrutinised their faces and, with the help of the ruga-ruga, forced each woman to stand erect so he could examine their posture. Next, he wrenched open their mouths in order to examine their teeth. Their arms and legs were pulled and pushed and, finally, they had to lie on the ground with their legs apart while he examined their genitals for any sign of venereal disease. Those found wanting in any way were quickly eliminated by the ruga-ruga.

Now that they had been branded Mlozi allowed them to mingle with each other. They were placed in neck-irons and linked in chains of forty. All of them – men, women and children – carried enormous elephant tusks on their heads. Although slaves fetched Mlozi as much as five English pounds each, the trade in ivory was nearly as lucrative. Not one to waste an opportunity, Mlozi saw this final march to the lake as an ideal occasion to use free transport for the tusks, some of which weighed as much as one hundred pounds. Already weakened by hunger, fear, unspeakable acts of cruelty by the ruga-ruga and deeply in mourning for the loss of loved ones, and with the ruga-ruga again beating time on their tom-toms, the slaves made the half-day journey to the lake. There, they were herded into stockades like cattle and left, still fettered, to await loading into dhows for a three-day journey down the lake to Losefa, where they would be joined by other slaves coming up from Makanjira and Mponda. After that, an 800-kilometre march to the coastal port of Kilwa.

In the morning, with the weather looking favourable, Mlozi was anxious to load the dhows. First, the slaves were used to load the heavy ivory. There were so many tusks they filled one entire dhow.

Mlozi watched the loading process carefully and made a mark in his ledger for each tusk as it was carried through the shallow water and passed to a crew member on board. He consulted constantly with the Arab captain who stood with him on the beach. Once the ivory was loaded the captain gave him a receipt on which he had written the number of tusks, their estimated collective weight, the date, Mlozi's name as the owner and his own name as the carrier. He would have the slaves carry the tusks to the coast, sell them to traders and bring the payment, less his commission, to Mlozi. The two men regularly did business together and had developed an unlikely but necessary trust in each other.

The slaves were loaded next, packed in like sardines. Those first on board had to lie on the deck, alternately head to foot. They were jammed so tightly together they could not move their arms or legs. Then, amazingly, their captors managed to squeeze a child between each adult. Once the deck had been carpeted with human bodies, a bamboo platform was placed over them, leaving less than two centimetres of headroom, and this new level was loaded with more slaves. The tiers rose high off the main deck until the captain considered the dhow could take no more. Mlozi watched this process as carefully as he had watched the ivory being loaded. Four dhows were filled with slaves. He and the captain compared tallies. 'There is no room for food or water,' the captain warned. 'There will be deaths.'

Mlozi shrugged. There were always deaths. They were of no consequence. There were plenty more slaves where they came from.

Ferig lay under three tiers of others. She could barely breathe but she wondered how those below her must feel. A man above her defecated. 'I am sorry, sister,' he said quietly.

'Do not apologise,' she replied as softly. 'There is no need.'

Someone above her panicked and thrashed about. 'I can't move, I can't move,' the woman cried. The Arab crew simply moved in and nailed one of her feet into the platform. Her shrieks, and subsequent sobs drowned out the swishing of the water as the dhow found wind and sped south-east towards the centre of the lake.

All five dhows made good time during the first day and night. The captain of the fleet, who preferred to sail with the dhow carrying the ivory, blessed his good fortune. Once the slaves were loaded they were stuck until offloading at Losefa. Despite sailing up to fifty metres apart, the stench of excrement, death and illness always accompanied the dhows. A good wind carried the smell away but on one previous occasion he had been becalmed for two days. On the third day, with no sign of wind, he had been unable to stand the smell any longer and had set the slave-carrying dhows alight. The odour of burning flesh was infinitely preferable.

Late in the afternoon of the second day, after another day of excellent weather, he noticed a fringe of light coloured cloud just below a mass of storm clouds off to the north. The sight of it filled him with unease. The mountains far to the west and east formed natural funnels and he knew that winds could whip up to storm ferocity in very little time. Top-heavy as the dhows were, the sight of thunderclouds could mean trouble.

There was nothing much he could do. When thunderstorms collapsed in the cooler air above the lake, it happened so quickly that evasive action was a waste of time.

The rolling motion of the dhows, as the wind picked up, added to the misery of the slaves. Many were seasick and, being unable to move, some even drowned in their own vomit.

Ferig prayed to the good spirits to take her away

with them. 'I want to die,' she told them. 'I want to be with my Pambuka.' The dhow lurched heavily to one side. The wind was whipping up the waves and water was sloshing over those on the lower tiers. Terrified screams, choking and coughing came from below her. 'Please take me away,' she prayed.

The thunderstorm broke directly overhead just after nightfall. In a flash of lightning the Arab captain saw one of the dhows capsize. He spared a moment's irritation as he mentally calculated the worth of the slaves who went rapidly to a watery grave. But then he forgot about his financial loss. With incredible speed, and faster than the crew could lower the sails, the full force of the wind pushed the waves to three-metre rollers. Ferig's dhow, with only two sails down, went broadside to the oncoming wall of water. The heavily over-loaded vessel stood no chance at all.

Ferig's prayers were answered. She felt no fear, just an overwhelming sense of peace. As the cool waters of the lake closed over her head she was smiling.

THREE

LONDON – FEBRUARY 1983

John Devereaux resisted the urge to look at his watch. He was irritated beyond belief. *Bloody London cabbies! If the man had taken my advice and gone down Gloucester Place we'd never be stuck in this snarl. Traffic is hell in London at this hour but it's worse in Oxford Circus than most places. Surely he knew that.* He looked moodily through the window. *It's pissing down with freezing rain and we're seven blocks from York Gate.* The urge to check the time was almost overwhelming. John steeled himself not to. *Damn the man! I'm going to be late.*

Through the steamy window he stared out at a sea of black taxis. All around him were square black shapes with meters running. John Devereaux tried to mentally calculate the worth of the collective hire charges but his normally analytical mind was diverted by one bright red car with a young man behind the wheel, the sole occupant. The traffic jam did not worry him. He was singing lustily to something on his radio, oblivious of the stares from bored commuters and the scowls from down-to-earth taxi drivers.

'Bloody 'ell,' his driver muttered, more to

himself than his passenger. 'I'm off duty in ten minutes.'

'Hard luck,' John thought callously, blaming the man. But he said, 'It should clear once we're into Regent Street.' No point in getting the driver's back up and reminding him this was his own fault. He looked back to the young man in the red car. Whatever he was singing, it was giving him a great deal of enjoyment. His left hand was curled around an imaginary microphone while his right tapped out the rhythm on the steering wheel.

The traffic moved half a car length. An oncoming taxi and his own driver vied for the same space, neither man prepared to give in until the last moment. By the time they stopped, the two vehicles were a cat's whisker apart. The drivers turned their heads slowly to stare at each other. Both men had the same craggy Cockney face, full of character and hard-bitten humour, with tough and uncompromising eyes, unless you knew where to look. John had seen those eyes dissolve into compassion, laughter, love and kindness on more than one occasion. Not this time though. Two sets of brown orbs were fairly crackling with indignation. His driver had dark blond hair, the other's hair was black but the styles were identical. Unkempt, badly cut and over-long, with strands straying inside the collars of imitation leather jackets. Two peas in a pod. The drivers didn't think so.

The cabs sat, facing opposite directions, blocking everyone behind them. 'This'll be interesting,' John thought. London cabbies took great pride in their driving skills and could, on nearly every occasion, come up with colourful and varied reasons as to why they couldn't possibly be at fault. Now here were two clearly in the wrong and just as clearly making the congested traffic even worse. His driver was breathing heavily.

They pushed their windows down in unison. John was reminded of the slow, tense walk down dusty, empty streets as gunslingers squared up to each other in old western movies. 'The driver's hand flashed down for his window,' he thought in amusement.

The air in the small space between the two vehicles was electric. 'Haven't you got a horn then, mate?' the other cabbie asked finally, his voice heavy with sarcasm.

His driver mulled this over for a full two seconds. Then, with no trace of a smile, responded lazily. 'What? Sitting here looking at your ugly face?'

Devereaux laughed. Good stuff. He must remember to tell Karen tonight.

The other driver took it in his stride. 'What's it like up yonder?'

'It's jammed all the way to Marble Arch,' John's driver told him with a degree of satisfaction. He knew he had come out of the encounter in front.

John's mind drifted while the two cabbies discussed the traffic. Born and educated in England he may have been, but the language of Cockneys and East Enders was a mystery he could not unravel. He loved their dry humour, when he could understand it, but was more at home with French, the language of his childhood spoken by his French-born father and English mother.

'Black,' he was thinking. 'Black is the colour of London. Black taxis, black umbrellas, black coats and scarves, all going God knows where, all intent on getting there, all irritated and frustrated, cold and wet and miserable. What a way to live.'

He looked down at his own black shoes, dark grey trousers, black umbrella dripping sullenly on the floor of the taxi. Then he thought of Karen, his wife. She was South African. The drabness of London was something to which she refused to conform. Karen's coats were either cherry red, midnight blue, moss green or caramel yellow. Her umbrellas were always white. She stood out in a crowd with confident ease which was why he noticed her in the first place and probably why he married her – something he had never regretted.

The traffic inched forward again. The would-be rocker in the red car was now belting out an old Beatles number. John could read his lips. 'Song-writers,' he mused, his mind drifting sideways again, 'didn't exactly need talent in the sixties.' Alana loved that song. Having found it on one of John's old records she sang it incessantly.

Alana (she preferred Lana, and obstinately refused to answer to anything else), his twelve-year-old daughter, was a source of constant delight to him. John had inherited his father's Gallic dark good looks and had passed the best on to his daughter. While John was considered handsome,

Lana was undoubtedly breathtaking. '*Mon Dieu*, hearts will be sore over this one,' John's father had said on introduction to his grand-daughter when she was five days old. Twelve years later he hadn't changed his mind. Tall for her age, slim and supple, already possessed of a penetrating and questioning intelligence, unruly dark curls framing the alabaster skin of her perfectly oval face. Dark, winged brows over sparkling deep blue eyes – an unusual combination, made more so since John and Karen both had brown eyes. Her nose would go aquiline once it lost its baby button look, an inheritance from French ancestors. Her mouth was pure Karen – wide, with a smile which curled at the ends and put mischief into her eyes. At twelve, Lana knew exactly what she wanted to be when she grew up – a geologist like her father. She certainly had a mind of her own.

John found himself smiling and adjusted his face back to neutral. 'A pity we couldn't have had more children,' he thought. 'There should be more Lanas in this world.' He was besotted by her and didn't give a damn who knew it. Discipline was normally left to Karen. Lana had him around her elegantly long little finger.

'Gotcha.' His driver found a gap and went for it. Travelling down Regent Street at thirty-five kilometres an hour felt like they were speeding after the snarl left behind. John allowed a glance at his watch. Four twenty-two. The meeting started in eight minutes. He'd be okay if there were no more traffic jams.

Portland Place was flowing freely. Park Crescent appeared congested but the driver, with consummate skill, slid into a space not even an insane cyclist would try and caught the lights in time to cross Marylebone Road. From there the traffic eased considerably. They turned left into Regents Park Outer Circle and left again into York Gate. 'What number, guv?'

'All the way to the end.'

The driver clearly felt an explanation was required as to why he got them tangled up in the congestion at Oxford Circus. 'Want to know why I didn't go down Gloucester Place?'

'Why?' John didn't want to know but good manners prevailed.

'That way takes you past Madam Tussaud's. Bleedin' place gives me the creeps, know wot I mean?'

John didn't. 'I know what you mean.'

'All them wax dummies. Mate of mine told me they use the real eyes.'

John didn't think so. A lot of the wax effigies were of living people. He rather thought they still required use of their eyes.

The driver was on a roll. 'Seems kind of pagan. Know wot I mean?'

'Quite so,' John murmured. 'This'll do, driver.'

The taxi swerved into the curb. 'Sorry, guv. All that waitin's going to cost you. That's twelve quid neat.'

John tipped him a pound and the driver looked at it sourly. 'Ta,' he said finally.

The freezing rain had turned to snow. Flakes drifted down and settled on Devereaux's black hair and the collar and shoulders of his coat. He shook open his umbrella and hurried through the gate and up the path towards an imposing granite building which sat squat and solid within its own grounds, its cream paint somehow sunny and out of place in the surrounding drabness.

'Evenin', Mr Devereaux, sir.'

John believed doormen to be an endangered species and was always relieved to find Duncan still at his post. 'Evening, Duncan.' Ever cheerful, ever helpful and usually courteous, Duncan was a relic of Britain's more formal past. Nothing escaped him. He was a walking encyclopaedia of snippets of gossip, knew everybody's name and, more often than not, the name of their spouse and children, had his favourites and treated those who did not meet his approval with profound but scrupulously polite disdain. John, he liked.

'Go through reception today, Mr Devereaux. She's in one of her moods.' Duncan was referring to the receptionist, Cecilia Bagshaw, for whom he harboured a secret admiration. Years ago he had been incautious enough to inform her of his feelings and, as far as John could see, Duncan was still licking his wounds.

John went through the heavy, double glazed glass doors on which 'Petroleum and Gas Exploration Technology' (PAGET) was gold leafed in discreet lettering, and into the large and formal reception area. Miss Cecilia Bagshaw presided over this space like a jealously possessive Great Dane. He could have taken the lift and bypassed the receptionist, he often did that. But when she was in a bad mood, as she obviously was today, it was more than anyone's life was worth to get on her wrong side.

Cecilia Bagshaw had her own methods of dealing with recalcitrants. Messages that were not delivered. Phone calls cut off (she was especially gifted in this regard when one was making a call from some far flung and under-developed place where a telephone call to London could take several days to get through). Another favourite of hers was to pass on blatantly incorrect information. She was blandly indifferent to the truth . . . 'Mr Devereaux is out of the country and cannot be contacted', when Mr Devereaux had just passed her desk on his way to the boardroom.

On her own, Miss Bagshaw had probably lost PAGET more business than the rest of the staff put together. However she was devoted to Bernard Pickstone, the Managing Director. No-one, but no-one got to see Bernard without an appointment. No-one, but no-one's work took precedence over Bernard's. And absolutely no-one could ever say a bad word to her about Bernard without receiving a tongue-lashing so impressive that they rarely recovered. And she was always ready to drop everything, including visits to her ailing mother, if Bernard asked her to. She had been with the company for over a decade, since its humble beginnings. On principle, she personally disapproved of each new staff member until they could show that her own authority would not be threatened. For his part, and for reasons of his own, Bernard rewarded her aberrations with a blind eye.

Pre-warned by the doorman, John knew the moves. 'Evening, Miss Bagshaw. You've done something different with your hair. It suits you.'

Miss Bagshaw's downfall was her vanity. At thirty-eight, her often sour disposition had left a legacy of permanent disapproval imprinted on her face. Even smiling, something she didn't do very often, she managed to look critical and picky. 'Are you sure? I didn't do much, just, sort of, you know.' She patted her hair nervously then, using her little finger, wiped an imaginary lipstick smear away from the corner of her mouth.

'Absolutely,' John said sincerely. He felt sorry for Miss Bagshaw. True, she owed her solitary existence to her own personality but the poor woman knew no better. 'It makes your eyes larger.'

Her eyes went wide. 'Mr Pickstone is waiting for you, Mr Devereaux.'

As he ran up the wide main staircase to the first floor, Miss Bagshaw stared after him with eyes forced as wide as they would go. So wide in fact that fifteen minutes later she would develop a blinding headache.

At this hour, people were leaving their offices to do battle with London's peak-hour traffic. John knew most of them. Although he was not a full-time employee of PAGET, he had been consulting for them for nearly eleven years, since the days when they operated out of a dingy suite of six rooms opposite Euston Station. A spare office was kept in the York Gate building for his exclusive use. Bernard Pickstone, geophysicist, founder and Managing Director of PAGET, was a close personal friend and a man for whom John held profound respect.

The two men shook hands warmly. 'Like your tie,' John said, eyeing the gold, brown and purple monster which shrieked against the blue of Bernard's shirt. Bernard Pickstone was happiest in the field wearing old khaki shorts, shabby boots of indeterminate age and bottle green T-shirts. Now he resided permanently in London and rebelled by means of his ties, the variety of which ran the gauntlet from psychedelic, through pornographic to wildly imaginative. At present he was emerging from an Aztec phase and was entering an Australian Aboriginal one. This tie straddled the two cultures.

'Designed it myself,' Bernard said, pleased and quite unnecessarily. 'How are you, John, how's the lovely Karen?'

'Lovely as ever. How's Maggie?'

Bernard's wife, Margaret, had been the victim of a hit-run accident two years previously. She lay in a coma on a life support system just across the road in the Princess Grace Hospital. Bernard spent every lunchtime with her. She was the reason he refused all field work for, as dearly as he loved being in the field, he loved Maggie more. 'No change.'

'Damn! Wouldn't you think –'

'The doctors want to switch her off,' Bernard cut in. 'I keep telling her to get her act together and wake up but you know Maggie. She'll do it when she's good and ready.'

John knew she wouldn't. Maggie had been declared officially brain dead two months after the accident, a fact Bernard simply refused to acknowledge.

'What are you reading to her now?'

Every day, between twelve o'clock and one-thirty, Bernard read to Maggie who had loved books passionately before the accident. 'Rudyard Kipling.'

'Now this is the Law of the Jungle – as old and as true as the sky,' John quoted from a boyhood memory.

'And the Wolf that shall keep it may prosper, but the Wolf that shall break it must die,' Bernard finished. 'Stirring stuff, John. Maggie loves it.'

'A lady of extreme good taste,' John said gently. Talking about Maggie was a joy to Bernard most of the time but John always trod warily since, once or twice, a memory too painful to recall, or an incautious remark on someone's behalf, would upset this grieving man to the point where he would have to leave the room. Miss Bagshaw, for all her sins, tenaciously shielded Bernard from confronting the truth.

'Did you drive up?' Bernard changed the subject abruptly.

John and Karen lived in Sevenoaks, some thirty-five kilometres away. 'Karen dropped me in

Greenwich. She's picking me up here later. We're going on to a show.'

'What have you done with my goddaughter?'

'Staying over with a friend. She sends her love.'

Bernard gave a lopsided grin. He doted on Lana. He and Maggie had no children. 'Like a scotch?'

John shook his head. If he had a drink he'd want a cigarette and Bernard loathed the smell of cigarette smoke. Woe betide the unfortunate wretch who incautiously lit up in his office. John watched the golden liquid splash lazily into Bernard's crystal glass. Whisky was something Bernard took seriously. Where wine buffs were common enough, whisky buffs were somewhat rarer. Most whisky drinkers tended to like one brand and stick to it. Bernard liked to experiment. He saw John watching him. 'Glenallachie,' he said. 'Fairly new distillery up near Aberlour. Used for blending mainly but this is a single Glenallachie malt, eight years old. Not a bad drop, slightly tarry but pleasant enough all the same. Sure you won't have one?' Without waiting for a reply he poured a second glass.

John held out his hand for the glass, cursing inwardly the cigarette craving he knew would follow. 'Thanks,' he said.

Bernard crossed to his desk and sat behind it. John waited in silence. Bernard would tell him in his own time the reason he had requested this meeting. Finally. 'We've lost a man.'

John's heart skipped a couple of beats. Oil and gas exploration had its dangers. Forefront of these were the unpredictable politics in some of the countries geologists were sent. 'Who?' He steeled himself for bad news. Over the years of consulting for them, he had worked with most of the permanent staff of PAGET and had a number of good friends among them.

'Cunningham.'

Robin Cunningham. Solitary nature, shy to the point of unfriendly, a brilliant geochemist and an alcoholic. No-one knew much about him. His alcoholism was on record only because he insisted on mentioning it at any time he discussed anything other than work. Perhaps it was part of his therapy but he was not generally liked. 'What happened to him?'

Bernard sipped his scotch. 'He seems to have done a runner.'

'Robin! No way. He lived for his job.'

'His marriage was in trouble.'

'He told you that?' The information was no surprise, the man must have been hellishly difficult to live with.

'She did.'

John had never met Robin's wife. 'What's she like?'

Bernard rose and went to the side cabinet to replenish his glass. John shook his head at the proffered decanter. 'I've only spoken to her on the phone. Seems nice enough.' Bernard returned to his desk. 'We called her. He's been away two weeks. We haven't heard from him and neither has she.'

'Where is he?'

'Malawi.'

'Malawi! What for? There's no oil in Malawi.'

Bernard inclined his head. 'I agree.' He raised his hand to stop John's next words. 'At least, if there is, it will be thousands, if not millions of years before it's worth looking at.'

'So what else did Robin's wife say?'

Bernard hesitated. 'I'm only telling you this because I want you out there. It could be relevant. I'm breaking a confidence here.'

John nodded. Bernard knew he could trust him.

'She ummed and erred a bit but finally told me that just before Robin left for Malawi she had told him she wouldn't be there when he got back. Seems his drinking is out of control. He's dropped out of the AA program. Apparently, in his current frame of mind, his wife thinks he's capable of just about anything. In fact, she's a bit concerned for her own safety.'

'So she thinks he's just legged it?'

'She believes he's gone on a binge somewhere and decided to hell with it. If that's the case, he's taken his Malawian assistant with him. They've both gone missing.'

John sipped at his scotch, aching for a cigarette. 'What is it you're not telling me?'

'I'm not entirely convinced.'

'Why not?'

'Like you said. Despite his drinking, Robin lived for his work. And there's something else.'

'What?'

'The Malawian Minister who commissioned our survey took great pains to emphasise that it was to be conducted in absolute secrecy. Apparently the President regards the lake as his own personal property. Even changes of land ownership on the shores of Lake Malawi have to go across his desk. Several South African consortiums have wanted to build casinos there and have been refused. He wants nothing to spoil the pristine beauty of his lake. He was not informed of the survey.'

'How the hell did they expect to keep it from him? From the little I know he keeps an iron grip on everything.'

'Maybe that's the key to it. President Banda has become something of an autocrat. Perhaps there is dissension in the ranks. Who knows how many of his ministers are prepared to go against him? Robin may have got himself caught up in some kind of internal strife.'

'A coup of some kind? The papers haven't said anything about it.' John had been in Nigeria in 1970 when Biafra was overthrown. It had not been a pleasant experience.

'God knows. All I'm saying is that something smells.'

John shook his head. 'Robin wasn't interested in politics. He certainly wouldn't get involved. If anything, he might just have been in the wrong place at the wrong time. At worst he would have been kicked out.'

'He hasn't left the country, that much I do know. The whole thing is rather odd. The British

High Commission is looking into it for us.' Bernard looked unhappy. 'I don't like it much, John, I've got a bad feeling about it.'

'Robin is probably pissed as a newt in some bar.' John didn't like it either but he could see it was worrying Bernard that he was asking him to go to Malawi.

'Something's brewing in Malawi,' Bernard ignored John's words. 'Do you read the *New York Times*?'

'Sometimes. Not often. Why?'

'They've been running a story about the leader of the opposition out there, Orton Chirwa. He and his wife Vera were tried for treason last year. No sentence has been passed yet but they're expected to get death.'

'Come on, Bernard, these things happen in Africa. You know that.'

'Not like this. The Chirwas were tried before a Traditional Court which was presided over by a Malawian chief. That means they were not allowed to engage counsel for their defence. The International Commission of Jurists has requested that President Kaunda of Zambia intervene on their behalf, and the United Nations Subcommission on Human Rights has asked the Malawian Government for some answers. The Chirwas' son was arrested at the same time. He appears to have dropped off the face of the earth. Apparently Orton and Vera Chirwa are lawyers. The African Bar Association has sent an appeal on their behalf directly to President Banda.'

'Why is this worrying you? It's just internal politics. Robin's disappearance couldn't possibly have any connection.'

'I spoke with a Martin Flower at the British High Commission in Blantyre. He's as puzzled as we are about Robin.' Bernard sipped his drink. 'The High Commission has taken the unusual step recently of appointing wardens for each district. Every British subject in the country is accounted for.'

'That *is* serious. Sounds like they're expecting a full-scale war out there.'

Bernard grimaced. 'Heaven forbid, no! Martin Flower tried to tell me it was perfectly normal for the High Commission to instigate such a plan. Nothing to worry about. All part of a day's work, that sort of thing.' He spun his chair and stared through his window to the rapidly darkening day and the fat snowflakes falling. 'The point is, John, where the hell is Robin?' he asked finally. 'We know he hasn't flown out. We're reasonably certain if he were in Malawi the British High Commission would have him on their lists. He's either slipped over a border somewhere or he's dead.' Bernard looked back at John. 'I don't like sending you there.'

'I've been to worse places.'

By way of a response Bernard flipped a thin file across the desk. 'Not much in there. Copies of correspondence mainly. Read them and memorise them. You can't take them with you.'

John didn't open the file. 'I'll do it at the weekend.'

Bernard nodded. 'This is a rum do, John. Nothing

text-book. I've never handled a job like it.' He stared glumly at his whisky. 'We'll worry about finding Robin. I don't want you to get involved. Just get out there and do the survey. Shouldn't take more than a couple of months. Keep your head down and stay out of trouble and, if it gets dicey, get back here fast. Don't take risks.'

'I never take risks, you know that.' He grinned across at Bernard remembering how he had been airlifted out of Biafra. 'You'd better fill me in.'

Bernard leaned back in his chair and said in a resigned voice, 'You're dying for a cigarette aren't you?'

'You know it.'

'If you have another scotch I'll pretend it's not happening.'

John handed the empty glass to Bernard and hastily produced a flat thirty-pack of Rothmans.

'Those things will kill you,' Bernard said, giving him back his glass which had been half filled.

John eyed his glass. 'Nah,' he said, grinning. 'The bloody scotch will get me first.'

Bernard laughed. 'How does Karen put up with you?'

'She loves me.'

'I love you too but not enough to put up with that stench.'

'Get on with your story.' John drew on his cigarette. 'Open the window if it bothers you.'

'It's below freezing out there.'

'Okay, okay.' He stubbed out his barely lit cigarette. 'Better?'

'No,' Bernard said morosely. 'The smell will last for days.'

John looked regretfully at his bent cigarette in the ashtray.

'Okay.' Bernard leaned back in his chair. 'I'll start at the beginning.' He picked up a pencil and tapped it on an executive notepad on his desk. 'Last summer we received a letter from the Minister without Portfolio who, incidentally, is also the administrative secretary and secretary-general of the ruling Malawi Congress Party. The letter was handwritten and postmarked Zambia. He invited us to tender for a reconnaissance survey of the Lake Malawi area for signs of natural oil and gas reservoirs. Apparently he got excited by the discovery of fossil fuels at the bottom of Lake Tanganyika and figured that if Tanganyika had oil, then Malawi might too.'

'But Tanganyika is the oldest of the Great Rift lakes,' John cut in. 'I think I'm right in saying that Lake Malawi is the youngest, despite their proximity.'

'Perfectly correct,' Bernard acknowledged, appreciating the fact that even though John had never worked in central Africa, he was at least familiar with its geographic features. 'The find at Tanganyika has got Zambia, Zaire, Tanzania and Burundi claiming a share. They all expect instant profits if a major reservoir is found. Each is boasting that this will make them as rich as Nigeria. The Minister no doubt is prepared to fund a reconnaissance survey in the hope . . .' Bernard smiled. 'The very vain hope, that Malawi has oil too.'

John made a steeple with his hands and looked

at Bernard over the top. 'This is not like you. I've never known PAGET to accept a job where they know before they even start that it's hopeless.'

Bernard shrugged. 'We told them there was less than a five per cent chance that we'd find anything. The Minister remains unconvinced. Seems he started a geology degree which he never finished. A number of things, in his opinion, add up to oil.' Bernard ticked them off on his fingers. 'One. It's been recently discovered that where the lake drops down to depths of around 700 metres, natural terracing is evident. Two. The deepest part of the lake is assumed to have a mud floor. However, sandstone and sand cover the bottom to depths up to 300 metres. Three. Oil-stained sand has been reported in the north of the lake.'

John interrupted his flow. 'What colour?'

'Greenish.'

John raised his eyebrows.

'Four.' Bernard went on. 'He thinks he's found source rocks. He's done some form of field evaluation himself, God knows what, and believes he's discovered kerogen and bitumen organic matter.'

John's eyebrows went higher.

'Five. These source rocks have been found near where the North Rukuru River runs into the lake north of Karonga. Six. Seems like some fellow decided to put a match to gas escaping from a spring in the area.'

'Ouch.'

'Quite,' Bernard said crisply. 'There wasn't a whole lot of him left. Or the village for that matter.'

'Did Robin leave any reports or notes here?'

'Only what's in that file.'

'Okay,' John said slowly. 'You want me to find out what progress Robin made and take it from there?'

'We don't think he even started. You'll find a second handwritten letter in the file from the Minister asking what the hell is happening with the survey.' John slid the notepad from under Bernard's fingers and held out his hand for the pencil. Bernard passed it over. 'Get out there and speak to the Minister. His name is Dick Matenje. Next to Banda, he wields more power than anyone else in the country. He knows you're coming. And for God's sake remember it's hush-hush. Get up north and see if this bloody Matenje really did find source rocks and do some field testing yourself. If you find anything we'll commission a proper basin analysis.'

'I suppose it's too much to ask if there has been any seismic survey?' John was scribbling furiously on the notepad as he talked.

Bernard laughed.

'I thought so. Virgin territory.'

'We'd like to determine the type and distribution of rock types, John, and the burial history of that area.'

'Mapping?' John asked.

'A structural map will do for a start. If it's looking good we can undertake more geological analyses. But you should include a report on accessibility options.'

'How about aerial surveys?'

'Not at this stage. This is strictly reconnaissance. I personally doubt we'll ever get as far as a detailed survey.'

'How about an assistant?'

'The Minister has arranged that. You'll be met at the airport.'

'That's it?'

'Yes.'

John threw down the pencil.

'What's your gut feel?' Bernard asked him.

John thought for a moment. '*If* this man . . .' he consulted his notepad '. . . Dick Matenje has found kerogen in source rocks then I'll lay odds to even it's Type-III which makes it gas, not oil prone. *If* terracing has been discovered under the lake I very much doubt it's of a folded structure. The Rift is still developing. Most of the lakes in the western chain are relatively new *and* most of the rocks are igneous. That much I *do* know.'

'Your gut feel, John,' Bernard pressed him.

'The lake bed has not been sampled, however one presumes there is a good deal of marine organic matter,' John mused to himself. 'Could be some fractured shales down there. To the best of my knowledge there are no volcanic necks or plugs under the lake.'

'So. What do you think?'

John smiled over at Bernard. 'Anything's possible, my friend. But my gut feel is that Malawi is wasting money which could probably be put to better use.'

'That's what our initial report told them.'

'Okay. It's their money. When do I leave?'

'Yesterday would be fine.'

John shook his head. 'Karen's birthday next week. The big four zero. Can't miss that.'

'Heavens!' Bernard sipped his scotch. 'I'd forgotten. What can Maggie and I get her?'

FOUR

MALAWI – MARCH 1983

The slimly elegant Air Malawi BAC 1-11 belly-flopped in some clear air turbulence, hitting nothing more than thin air with the force of a body falling on water from a great height. John cursed silently as his coffee slopped over the side of the inadequate cup. He looked through the window to the land below. Heavily timbered hills and valleys with ribbons of rivers and tiny pockets of water glinting through. It looked uninhabited although he knew it wasn't. He had done some reading on Malawi in the ten days since Bernard had briefed him.

When Life President Dr Hastings Kamuzu Banda took control of what used to be the British Protectorate of Nyasaland, he had encouraged his people to stay on the land rather than head for the towns and cities. Malawi, as it was now called, could feed itself. 'Not bad going,' John thought, staring down at the land beneath him. 'Considering that sixteen years ago the country was bankrupt, dependent on aid from Britain for even the most basic of services, people were starving, had no commerce or industry to speak of and most of the inhabitants were illiterate.'

At thirteen, Banda had apparently walked 1500 kilometres to Johannesburg in search of an education. On the way, he worked as a hospital orderly in Salisbury, the capital of Rhodesia. This experience gave him the determination to one day qualify as a medical doctor. He never wavered from that ambition. In South Africa he worked in the goldmines and then as a clerk and an interpreter until he could afford to travel to the United States. Once in America, with incredible fortitude, Banda completed his secondary education, then studied philosophy, political science and economics before entering medical college and graduating as a doctor. Not satisfied, he had then moved to Edinburgh University in Scotland to obtain further medical qualifications. 'What would motivate a thirteen-year-old semi-illiterate boy to such an extent?' John wondered.

It was with the same tenacity which, when he returned to his own country, he fought Britain's proposed Federation of Rhodesia and Nyasaland. His cry as he travelled around the country: 'To hell with the Federation! Independence now, now, now!', was heard across the land and taken up by the people. The British, with predictable indifference to the wishes of the majority, promptly threw Banda into prison in Rhodesia where he stayed for just over a year.

John, along with his father's looks, had inherited a Frenchman's distaste for Britain's convenient about-face in dealings with her African colonies. He had not been surprised to learn that as soon as difficulties arose in the form of open rebellion by the people at Banda's imprisonment, Britain had conveniently developed a conscience whereby they effectively dumped Nyasaland, released Banda from prison and, after three years of haggling and with as much dignity as they could muster, finally agreed that the Federation might just be a bad idea.

On 6 July 1964, as the national flag – a red rising sun symbolising the dawn of freedom, superimposed on a horizontal tricolour (black representing the people of Africa, red for the blood of the martyrs of African freedom, and green for the lush colours of Malawi) – was raised for the first time, Dr Banda might well have been contemplating his next challenge. Instead, he rolled up his sleeves and got down to the business of being a hands-on president, determined to turn Malawi into a model for all independent African countries.

'And he's done it,' John thought. Exports had gone from 27 million Kwacha in 1964 to 230 million now. Tobacco, tea, sugar, groundnuts, seed cotton, maize, pulses and paddy rice. The country fed, clothed and educated itself. The people were reputed to be the friendliest, healthiest and most determined in Africa. Malawi promoted itself as 'The Warm Heart of Africa' and was a Mecca for South Africans whose nationality precluded them from visiting many parts of the world. In holiday mood, South Africans flocked to the huge body of fresh water which occupied one-fifth of the entire country.

'A pity if success has gone to Banda's head,' John

thought. He admired the man's achievements. Against all the odds, he had proved that a dream really could be followed.

John felt the throttling back of the twin Rolls-Royce turbofan engines. They were starting their descent to the new Kamuzu International Airport. A Malawian stewardess moved along the aisle checking seat belts. John stopped her. 'When does the next flight for Blantyre leave?' His travel agent in London had been unable to establish flight times between the new capital of Lilongwe, and Blantyre which was still the main business centre of the country but 300 kilometres south. He had a ticket but the best London could do was advise him to sort it out when he got there. John was about to discover why.

The stewardess smiled, shrugged her shoulders and said, 'I think there are no more flights today. The timetable has just been changed so I am not sure.' She moved on before he could ask if the pilot would radio ahead and check.

'Great!' he thought. 'A night in Lilongwe is the last thing I need.' Minister Matenje wanted to brief him personally but had insisted on doing it far away from any prying eyes in the capital. They had arranged to meet at the Minister's small holding near Chiradzulu Mountain, just beyond the small village of Njuli, some twenty minutes' drive north of Blantyre. The meeting was scheduled for the following day.

Ten minutes later the BAC 1-11 landed gracefully and sped down the runway. The brand new airport had an almost unused look about it . . . as if it was a really good idea but someone forgot to mention it was finished. One KLM jumbo was loading meals, a boxy looking Britten Norman Islander was taxiing away from the terminal and several smaller planes were parked on the apron. The two-storey terminal building, long and modern, sat behind emerald green grass and newly established gardens. John, watching the departing Norman Islander, had a gut feel that the last flight to Blantyre that day was about to take off.

Stepping from the aircraft, the March heat hit him like a blast from an oven. His slacks and long-sleeved cotton shirt soon felt like a heavy, winter-weight suit. Inside the building, however, was mercifully cool.

Getting through Health, Immigration, the baggage counter, Customs, Foreign Exchange and Security was tedious but John had seen worse. The officials were courteous and friendly, even at Security where a *Punch* magazine was confiscated because it contained an advertisement showing two women wearing jeans. He was given a brief lecture about dress codes – no skirts above the knee, no trousers and no shorts for women; no long hair or bell-bottomed trousers for men – then offered the option of having the magazine taken away or have someone blot out the offending legs with a felt-tip pen. John told them he didn't need the magazine and was left in no doubt that it would enjoy a long, though undercover, life.

He had invented a story that he was an author,

researching a book, as his reason for requesting three months in the country. The need to do so made him uneasy. In every other country he had worked, the respective governments had been so anxious that oil be found that they rolled out the red carpet and treated him to every courtesy. The undercover nature of this assignment was worrying.

The man at Immigration gave him four months, asked what other books he had written and told John, who hastily invented a couple, that they were very good books. The Customs official wanted to know why he had four dozen small glass bottles and several glass funnels in his suitcase. 'I collect sand,' appeared to satisfy him.

Bernard had said he'd be met. A tall African, holding a white card with John's name written on it and yelling, 'Mr Deborie, Mr Deborie,' was the likely candidate.

'I am John Devereaux.' He put out his hand.

'Mr Deborie, sir, I am Mr Kadamanja, your assistant.' The man seemed flustered by John's out-stretched hand but finally offered his own and they shook in a thumb, palm, thumb African clasp.

'I take it I've just missed the Blantyre flight?'

'Not a problem, Mr Deborie. We will drive. There are no more flights until tomorrow.'

John groaned inwardly. A four hour drive after travelling from London via Johannesburg, when all he wanted to do was shower and get into fresh clothes, was a very large pain in the arse. He questioned the sanity of whoever had scheduled a shuttle between the capital and the business centre to miss an incoming flight, and speculated briefly on the intellect of one who considered ten-thirty in the morning to be the perfect time for the last flight. But all he said was, 'You drive, Mr Kadamanja, I'm a bit tired.'

On the way he tried to talk Mr Kadamanja into calling him John but was told, 'I could not, Mr Deborie, it would be too very rude.' So John spent some time trying to get the man to say his name properly. He did not believe he could spend the next couple of months with someone who insisted on calling him something which sounded suspiciously like 'debris'. No luck there. Kadamanja simply could not get his tongue around 'Devereaux'. Finally, at the African's suggestion, it was agreed he would be called 'sir'. 'When we know each other better perhaps I can call you sir John,' Kadamanja said helpfully, blissfully ignorant of British titles.

John let it go.

Kadamanja talked in fits and starts and John was content to let him. In the first place, the man was a terrible driver and John preferred to think his attention was entirely on the road. Besides, Malawi interested and impressed him and he was happy to watch the scenery, rather than the near misses with oncoming traffic. He noticed how clear of litter the roadsides were. Neat villages, with thatched-roof mudbrick huts nestling under shady branches, appeared every few kilometres and each showed the industrious and self-sufficient nature of rural Malawi. Banana groves, maize and ridged rows of cassava grew all around the villages but space had been left for children to play, meetings to take place and for chickens to scratch and peck to their hearts' content. Goats and hump-backed zebra cattle grazed under the watchful eyes of their owners. Colourfully dressed women worked in the fields, gossiped to each other as they queued at wells for water, or tended young children. Everywhere had a busy, contented and well-ordered appearance.

The few small towns through which they passed had none of the urban slums found throughout Africa. Shops showed the influence of Indian traders, with brightly coloured facades advertising everything from headache powder to shoes. Bustling markets displayed their wares and bartering was conducted in smiling, friendly banter.

'This looks like a very happy country,' John observed.

'Yes, sir,' Kadamanja agreed proudly. 'Malawians have no need for sadness.'

'I wonder,' John thought. But he said, 'You are very lucky then. In other parts of Africa the people are not so well off.'

Mr Kadamanja shook his head. 'So sorry,' he said, making it sound as though he were personally responsible.

Just south of a place called Dedza, where the land on their left was Malawi but, on the other side of the road, Mozambique – although no border fence separated the two countries – Kadamanja stopped the car and pointed eastwards. 'There is the lake, sir.'

John got out of the car. The crisp air surprised him. He knew they had climbed since leaving Lilongwe but had not realised how high. Stretching away to the east the highland country seemed endless but, right on the horizon, he could make out a smudge of pale blue which followed the land as far as he could see. The view was magnificent. He felt as if he were standing on the very top of the world. The lake must have been forty to fifty kilometres away. 'It's beautiful,' he said, getting back into the car. 'I've never seen a view like it.'

Mr Kadamanja nodded and smiled. 'Thank you, sir.'

An hour later they might have been on a different planet. Dropping down from the mountains, the land became typically African savanna and, winding down his window, John felt the stickiness of sultry valley air. They crossed the Shiré River along a long low bridge and he watched a dozen or more hippopotamus playing in the water. 'That is Liwonde National Park,' Kadamanja told him, waving his hand to the left of the road. 'They have many angry elephants in there.'

From Liwonde, the land became undulating and wooded. Despite his earlier irritation at having to make the trip by car, John watched the passing country with increasing interest. Malawi seemed to have everything. The variety was incredible considering the size of the place.

Blantyre, named after the birthplace of Scottish missionary David Livingstone, was another pleasant surprise. Modern shopping facilities and office blocks sat side by side with imposing church architecture of the last century, street vendor markets and squat Indian trading houses. The city was a multicultured integration of the best of all worlds. The scrupulously clean streets were wide enough to turn a full span of oxen and the pavements could accommodate at least eight pedestrians abreast.

John had been booked into the Mount Soche Hotel. It was just before three in the afternoon when they pulled up outside the five-storied neat white building set in luxurious gardens right on the edge of the central business district. Inside, John was relieved to find the air-conditioning working perfectly. Mr Kadamanja, having handed him over to the Assistant Manager, departed saying, 'I am seeing you at nine-thirty tomorrow, sir.'

Left to his own devices John checked in. A shower and change of clothes eased the tiredness of almost twenty-four hours of non-stop travel. The banks, he learned from the receptionist, shut at one o'clock but the hotel offered a limited banking service. He changed some traveller's cheques to the local currency, Kwacha and tambala, observing with some surprise that they had a fifty tambala note which equated to about twenty pence.

At four-thirty he made his presence in the country known at the British High Commission, a precaution he always took when working in the Third World. 'Is Martin Flower available?' he asked the girl at reception. Bernard had told him not to concern himself with Robin Cunningham's disappearance but he figured he might as well see if there had been any new developments.

'Do you have an appointment?'

'Fraid not.' John gave her his best boyish grin, the one which melted even Miss Bagshaw's impenetrable armour.

The receptionist was made of sterner stuff. 'I'm sorry. He's very busy. Perhaps tomorrow . . .'

'Won't be here tomorrow,' John said breezily. He raised his voice an octave. Several doors opened onto a passage behind the reception area. If Martin Flower occupied one of the inner offices, he might overhear. 'Actually, I'm making enquiries about a friend of mine who seems to have disappeared.'

Bingo! A man appeared. 'It's okay, Miss Anderson. I have a few minutes to spare.' He looked towards John. 'Please come in, Mr . . .'

John went through an opening in the counter. 'Devereaux. John Devereaux.'

'Ah yes, Mr Devereaux. London mentioned your name. Please, do come in.' John followed the man. 'I'm Martin Flower. Sit down please.' Flower shut his door. 'Now,' he said, crossing to his desk. 'How can I help you?'

John looked at him carefully. Dark curly hair, penetrating eyes, and the build of a man who liked to keep in shape. His suit could not hide powerful shoulders, or well-developed muscles on the man's upper legs. He had about him a kind of controlled alertness with which his manner, bland and polite, did not seem to match. John was willing to bet he was British Intelligence. 'Just checking in really.

Thought I'd ask about Robin Cunningham while I'm here. I'm his replacement.'

Martin Flower sat opposite him and leaned back in his chair. 'No sign of him unfortunately.'

John frowned. 'How could he just disappear?'

Flower seemed lost in thought. Then, 'Tell me, Mr Devereaux, exactly what is it you and your friend Cunningham are doing in Malawi.'

So. Bernard hasn't confided in the High Commission. 'Geological survey of the lake bed.'

'Why?' It was lightly asked but the man's eyes were attentive.

'It's never been done. About time it was, wouldn't you say?'

'Who commissioned it?' Flower's earlier blandness had been replaced by professional interest and he was making no attempt to hide it.

John thought rapidly. *If* this man was what he thought he was, it would be best to keep him on side. He probably knew the truth anyway, or most of it. 'Minister Matenje.'

Flower's eyebrows rose. 'Dick Matenje? Are you sure?'

John nodded. 'It's all a bit hush-hush but I have a meeting with him tomorrow. Why?'

Flower ignored the question. 'What's he up to?' he mused quietly. He appeared to reach a decision and leaned towards John. 'Be careful. I don't like the way Cunningham disappeared. Dick Matenje is big league in this country right now but . . .' he hesitated. 'All I can say is there are some alarming undercurrents. You're likely to hear all sorts of stories.

Mainly untrue I might add.' He allowed a small smile to escape. 'We can't be sure about Cunningham but we're assuming he's in trouble. The best advice I can give you is don't stick your nose into anything but the job you've come to do. Get it done and get out.' He rose and held out his hand. 'And don't be seen with Matenje,' he added. 'Shit sticks. Good luck.'

John shook his hand. 'Thank you.' Then he added, 'give my regards to Jean-Claude Bourquin.' Jean-Claude was a cousin who worked for French Intelligence and John knew he had been involved with the British on several occasions.

Flower looked him over carefully. 'Never heard of him,' he replied mildly. As he moved towards the door he said softly, 'Besides, dear boy, the Foreign Office would *never* employ a Frenchman, no matter how good his credentials.'

With no car and no contacts, John made his way back to the Mount Soche and spent what was left of the afternoon by the pool reading the local newspaper, *The Daily Times*. There was virtually no international news but much comment on local events and praise for the President. In the entertainment section his eye was caught by a small article:

DRUNKEN HYENA KILLED
On Friday morning, a man killed a hyena with an axe in Nthache Village.

Some people in the village say that the hyena had drunk some beer which was brewed outside a certain woman's house on the previous night.

'The hyena looked so drunk that it could not harm anyone,' the people said.

He was still chuckling over this when a shadow fell across the newspaper. Looking up he could make out nothing more than a large shape blocking the setting sun. 'Mind if I join you?'

The accent was South African, with the rasp of a forty-a-day man.

'Please do.'

The man lowered himself into a canvas chair. 'Karl Henning,' he said, sticking out his hand. The flimsy chair creaked and lurched in protest.

'John Devereaux.' The hand was huge and calloused. His grip almost painful.

'Found something funny in our newspaper I see.'

'This.' John showed him the article.

Karl Henning laughed with his belly. 'Bloody typical. Last week we had a front page story about a rat in a tie.'

'Slow news day?'

'No such thing in Malawi. Bad news is forbidden so most of the time they're scratching around to find something to put in the paper. This is the land of cotton wool.'

John wasn't sure if he was joking or not. He looked the man over. He must have weighed around 130 kilograms but, because of his height, the weight sat comfortably on his frame although there were the definite beginnings of a beer belly. He appeared to be about forty but had one of those faces which could belong to a much younger man, or one who was as much as ten years older. Square jaw, broken nose, faded blue eyes, reddish-brown face and thick straight blond hair. His nicotine-stained moustache was in urgent need of clipping. His etched granite face said, 'I'm a nice guy but don't cross me.'

A waiter appeared. John asked for a gin and tonic. Henning ordered an 'MGT'.

'Do you live here?' John asked.

'Not in Blantyre. Up north. Kasungu.' He saw John's puzzlement and added, 'Just over a hundred clicks north of Lilongwe.'

'What do you do up there?'

'Tobacco. I farm flue-cured.'

'Must be a bit lonely?'

Again the belly laugh. 'Lonely? No way, man. Some of the biggest flue-cured tobacco estates in the world are up there. And now we have the bloody academy, all expat staff. Mind you, they're a waste of a good white skin most of them. Bloody academics. They're a fair way out of town, which is just as well. They keep to themselves mainly. Stuck-up bunch as ever you saw.'

John wondered what the teachers had done to deserve such a scathing attack. 'What academy would that be?' In his research John had not found any mention of an academy.

Henning laughed derisively. 'What else would they call it? Kamuzu Academy. It opened last year. They *say* that H.E. funded it personally. Free education for the nation's brightest. Run along the same lines as one of your public schools.'

'Sounds like a good idea.'

Henning frowned. 'Good idea sure, but I hate to think what it's costing the government.'

'Maybe His Excellency *is* funding it himself.'

Faded blue eyes observed him. There was something in them, something behind their smile which made John cautious.

'You're not an *academic* are you?' He made the word sound like a four-letter one.

John smiled and shook his head.

'So what brings you to the Warm Heart of Africa?'

John considered his author story but discounted it. It was one thing to use it as a cover with the immigration authorities but quite another to try and deceive this man, Karl Henning. 'If you're going to tell a lie, keep it as close to the truth as possible.' He remembered a housemaster at school telling him that after falling foul of an outrageously audacious lie as to why he had liquor on his breath.

'I'm a geologist,' he told Henning. 'I work for myself and accept freelance work from a number of different companies in London.' That much was true. 'I'm doing a seismic survey.'

The waiter reappeared with their drinks. The MGT ordered by Henning looked exactly the same as John's drink and he commented on it.

'It is the same. That's how it's ordered. There's a distillery here making the stuff. Not a bad drop, better than most of the big brands.'

'Will mine be Malawi gin?'

'Nope. You have to specify, otherwise you get an expensive imported brand.'

John laughed. 'Thanks for the tip.'

The faded blue eyes penetrated John over the rim of his glass. Then Henning swallowed half the MGT in one go, not seeming to mind that the liquid had to be strained through his moustache. 'Not many earthquakes in this area,' he said finally, returning to the previous subject. 'Why would anybody want that information?'

'The lake bed has never been properly mapped. Scientists want to know what's under there.'

Henning laughed derisively. 'Bugger-all I'd say.'

John shrugged. 'You never know until you look,' he said mildly. 'Malawi could do with some resources.'

'Malawi has plenty of resources,' Henning said, sounding belligerent. 'Trouble is, the silly sods don't know what to do with them.'

John was starting to dislike him. 'I disagree. You've got to start somewhere and this is as good a start as anywhere. The company commissioned to undertake this work –'

'Would do better to stay at home and mind their own business,' Henning interjected rudely. 'What do you hope to find anyway?'

'Whatever's there,' John said evenly, refusing to be drawn into further explanation.

Karl Henning looked reflective. 'I see,' he said slowly. 'I wonder if H.E. knows about it.' He drained the rest of his drink and heaved himself out of the chair. 'Well, nice talking to you. See you around.'

'What was all that about?' John wondered,

89

watching the tall man stride away. Henning appeared to have deliberately struck up a conversation, then gone out of his way to be disparaging. John had the uncomfortable feeling that the man had been probing for information. Why? The survey was supposed to be a secret. And that remark about whether President Banda knew about the survey. Was it a threat? He shook his head, troubled. He'd had a bad feeling about the secrecy from the start. The sooner the job was over the better as far as he was concerned.

John dined alone in the hotel's Michiru restaurant, experimenting with smoked kampango, a local catfish served on lettuce leaves, liberally sprinkled with ground black peppercorns and fresh lemon juice which, the waiter told him proudly, was as good as any smoked salmon. 'It might be,' John thought, putting down his knife and fork, 'if it weren't still frozen.' Rather reluctantly he tried the grilled fillets of chambo. It was the finest fish he had ever eaten, except perhaps for the sea trout he occasionally fished in Scotland. Still in experimental mode, he washed his meal down with a bottle of two-year-old South African Chenin Blanc from the Cape Province, dry but refreshingly free of astringency.

Pleasantly tired, John left the dining room and headed for the lifts. On his way through the foyer he found Karl Henning in earnest conversation with a tall, meticulously dressed Malawian. So deeply engrossed were they that although John nodded and said, 'Good night,' Henning did not even acknowledge him.

In the morning after breakfast John checked out of the hotel. But when he went to pay the bill he was told the account had already been taken care of.

Mr Kadamanja collected him at nine-thirty precisely. The road they took out of Blantyre was the same one they had travelled yesterday. John was impressed again by the lack of slums. It was so unusual he commented on it.

'The Ngwazi takes care of all his people,' Mr Kadamanja told him proudly.

'The Ngwazi?'

'Our President.'

'What does Ngwazi mean?' It seemed to John that Life President Hastings Kamuzu Banda had more names than he needed.

'It means . . .' Mr Kadamanja sought the right words. 'There is no-one else like him in the world.'

'Unique,' John suggested.

Mr Kadamanja shook his head. 'No, sir, not unique.'

'Like a King?'

'Exactly so. That is how he is known to us. A King of Kings.'

'How old is the Ngwazi?'

The car swerved to the side of the road and stopped. Kadamanja turned off the engine. 'Mr Deborie,' he said seriously, not looking at John but at the road ahead. 'You are new to this country so I will try to explain. It is not good to speak of the Ngwazi, especially if you are white. Some people might hear and misunderstand your words. It could get you into great trouble.'

'But I only asked his age.'

Mr Kadamanja shook his head. 'Even so,' he said, still staring ahead. 'You should be careful. There are many spies.'

This was nothing new to John. Most African countries thrived on intrigue and it was usual for Europeans to check over their shoulder before saying most things. He remembered hearing of a dinner party somewhere where the cook kept shutting the door between the kitchen and dining room, much to the irritation of the master of the house because the cook was then unable to hear the bell summoning him to wait on the table. Finally the exasperated man asked his cook why the hell he kept shutting the door. 'We are supposed to report your conversations,' said the loyal cook. 'If I cannot hear what you say, how then am I to repeat it?'

'Are you telling me to be careful of you, Mr Kadamanja?' John asked softly. Might as well ask, although he didn't expect a straight answer.

'Yes, sir,' came the sober reply. 'You must be careful of everyone.'

Mr Kadamanja looked so distressed, John realised that if the man was reporting his every move it was something he did not enjoy. 'The machinations of the Third World,' he mused to himself. Then he decided to probe further. 'Have you any experience in the work we're going to do?'

'No, sir.'

That settled it. Kadamanja was spying on him. But for whom?

Chiradzulu was an impressive oblong-shaped mountain, with the large village of Njuli spread out along the foothills. John's suspicions of his assistant were further enhanced by the man's refusal to accompany him beyond a small trading store in the village. 'I will stay here and talk with my brother. You take the car. Just follow the road through the village. The man you are meeting will be waiting on the other side.'

As he drove along the rutted track, John speculated on who Kadamanja really worked for. It didn't bother him. He'd been on assignment in too many political 'hot spots' to be surprised that he was being monitored. But, coupled with the secrecy of this meeting, he wondered what exactly was going on. Everything he had read about Malawi pointed to a happy, well-adjusted people who clearly adored their President. Was The Warm Heart of Africa cooling off perhaps? Why was Kadamanja reluctant to go with him to the meeting? Why was the meeting being conducted in secret? Did the Minister have his own agenda and could any of this have a bearing on the disappearance of Robin Cunningham?

He wrenched the steering wheel violently to avoid a sorry-looking dog whose teats were swollen with milk and whose ribs stuck out painfully. Several children watched, laughed and waved to him, their teeth startlingly white in very black faces. John smiled and waved back. He loved the unaffected, unsophisticated innocence of African children who took delight in the simplest of things and showed only kindness to each other. It crossed his mind that some of London's street kids could benefit from a year in a rural African village. If they were given the opportunity to experience the consistent loving and approval accorded to African children, then their view of the world must surely change and that, in turn, must penetrate the tough protective armour they erected around themselves. 'Or would the reverse happen?' he wondered as he drove. 'Would the harmony here suffer?' He shook himself mentally. His heart went out to those children back home with their hard, suspicious eyes or lack-lustre, drug-filled stares. 'No child in Africa would ever be abandoned that way.'

The track wound randomly through the village. It was not a road as such, simply a route taken by most people, animals and vehicles. It obligingly curved around trees, houses, stock enclosures and a couple of wells. Children, dogs, goats and chickens were everywhere. A school lesson was taking place in the shade of a huge tree, the teacher using a small blackboard, the children listening avidly and writing on slates. John slowed and watched. He always felt strongly that life in an African village had a lot to teach the outside world, if only the outside world would listen. These children were learning because it was what they desired. He could tell by their faces. They were actually *enjoying* the process of learning. They regarded it not as a chore, as Lana tended to do, but as a privilege.

Women gossiped contentedly, babies strapped to their backs, baskets of washing or loads of firewood on their heads, their hands busy knitting or weaving. Men greeted him as he passed, raising their right hands politely, showing their palms. Karen had told him that in the old tribal war days, Africans meeting each other would transfer any weapons to their left hand and raise their right, showing it was empty with no harm intended. John had always believed this to be a custom further south but clearly it extended to central Africa too.

He looked at his watch. He had no idea how much further he had to travel.

Fifteen minutes later, just as he was thinking he must be on the wrong road, he saw a vehicle up ahead which was so brand spanking new that it had to belong to the Minister. As he drew closer the driver's door opened and a man stepped out. John looked at him in disbelief. He was wearing a pale cream suit with a maroon polo-neck sweater. He must have been hellishly hot. The clothes looked new and, by the way he tugged at the jacket and patted it into place, John could tell the man thought he looked absolutely terrific.

He pulled up behind the car, an imported German Ford Granada Ghia complete with tinted one-way windows and sun roof. 'Mr Devereaux?' the man called to him.

'Minister Matenje?' John climbed out of his vehicle and they shook hands. 'I was beginning to think I was on the wrong road.'

'There is only one road, Mr Devereaux. All the tracks lead back to it sooner or later. Please follow me. We will go to my house.' He turned to go but spun back theatrically, like a model on a catwalk. 'Where is your driver?'

'He stayed in the village. His brother lives there.'

'His name?'

'Kadamanja.'

John was watching the man's eyes. Deep, deep brown, the whites tinged with yellow, he saw a kind of panic pass through them. But all he said was, 'Come, we will go to my house.'

It was off the main track, tucked behind a small hill. John was surprised by its simplicity. After the clothes and the car he had expected something grander. Made of wood-fired bricks with a corrugated iron roof and a verandah at the front. The bricks were newly whitewashed and dark green paint sparkled on the metal door and window surrounds. John had to duck his head as he went inside.

The interior was clean and cluttered with cheap modern furniture, a notable exception being an old-fashioned sideboard painted green with red doors and yellow drawers. 'Please sit down.' The Minister shrugged off his jacket and then removed the polo-necked sweater. Naked from the waist up, he sat opposite John. 'Your colleague, Mr Cunningham, is dead,' he said, with no preamble.

'What happened to him?' John felt sorry for Robin Cunningham. His constant battle with the bottle, devotion to his work and a crumbling marriage was not much of a legacy to leave.

Matenje shook his head. 'We do not know. His body was washed up near Karonga. He appears to have drowned.'

'Have you notified PAGET?'

'Yesterday. As soon as the report came in.'

'Did they have any messages for me?'

'Mr Pickstone just said you should complete your work.'

John nodded. He studied the man opposite him. Short and thickset, he had the blackest skin John had ever seen. His body was soft, a man not used to hard physical work. He had an unusual face. Broad forehead, large eyes and, for an African, a small nose. The top half of his face was round but then it ended with a small pointed chin. There was something boyish about his looks. 'I believe Bernard Pickstone has expressed an opinion that the likelihood of us finding oil is about five per cent in the affirmative.'

'Is that your opinion too?'

'Yes, Minister. Lake Malawi is too young for oil to have formed, even if source rocks look promising.'

'But, Mr Devereaux, if oil has entered a migration stage, its source could be many tens of kilometres from the lake shore.'

'That's true. However, terrestrial higher plants, as you well know, will only produce gas-prone Type-III kerogen. At best you could expect gas, not oil.'

'The entire western Rift is constantly changing. We know that Lake Victoria, as it is now, once covered an area one hundred kilometres to the east of its present position. It is my contention that Lake Malawi could once have covered territory to its north and west. Oil has been discovered in Lake Tanganyika. It's possible the two lakes were once joined. If that's the case there would be marine organic matter in abundance. I believe there is a case for a survey.'

John looked at him. 'But your President does not,' he stated bluntly.

Matenje blinked. 'Our President has no knowledge of such things. He is only concerned with keeping the lake in its current unexplored state. He is worried about the environmental impact should oil be discovered.'

'Then he has nothing to worry about,' John said firmly. 'Lake Malawi is too young for oil to have accumulated in commercial quantities.'

'I have found oil-stained sand.' The Minister was not about to be put off.

'Vegetable stain most likely.'

'Also I've found source rocks.'

'Doesn't mean there's oil. Even if there were, what I'm trying to tell you is that it probably needs a couple of million years to mature at the shallow depths below the lake floor. OPEC are not even remotely interested in Lake Malawi.'

The Minister was unimpressed. 'The Organisation of Petroleum Exporting Countries thumbed their nose at Tanganyika too but they found oil there. What's the matter, Mr Devereaux, doesn't PAGET want the work?'

'It's not the work, Minister, it's the waste of this country's money that concerns us.'

Matenje smiled and John braced himself for the 'don't you worry your pretty little head about that' speech. He was not disappointed.

'Very well,' John said curtly when the Minister was finished, angry that so much money would be thrown away when the country had only just got its financial nose out of the water. 'I'll do a reconnaissance. You'll have my report within two months.' He went to rise.

'Mr Devereaux, please do not be in such a hurry to leave. Would you like a beer?'

John looked at his watch. Ten minutes to eleven in the morning was a bit early for him. But then, he reasoned, it would be ten minutes to one in England. 'Thank you.'

'Green or brown?' Matenje saw puzzlement on John's face. 'That's how we order beer in this country. By the colour of its label. A "green" is a lager, a "brown" is more like your English beer. We also have a "gold" which is our export beer, but I'm afraid I have none.'

'A green will be fine.'

The Minister leaned sideways and flipped a wet towel off a dozen or so bottles standing on the floor. 'I have no refrigerator,' he explained.

99

'I notice that in spite of your position in Malawi you live very simply.' John hoped Matenje would not take offence.

The Minister handed him a bottle and laughed. 'Glass?'

John shook his head. 'Bottle will do fine.'

Matenje stretched his legs out in front of him, leaning backwards into the cracked leather of his sofa. 'I have a house in Lilongwe which is as good as any you'll find. It's convenient, it's modern and it impresses the people I need to entertain. When I come back here, back to where I was born, I like to shed the European influence.' He smiled. 'No offence, Mr Devereaux, but, like most Malawians, I believe simplicity is best. Besides,' he laughed again, 'if I had a house here filled with expensive items how long do you think they would last? I am away three-quarters of the year. As soon as I turned my back my possessions would grow legs.'

'They'd steal from you?'

'Steal?' The Minister thought a minute. 'I think the word should be "borrow".' He hunched forward. 'You see, Mr Devereaux, there is no English word to explain a Malawian's regard for another's property. It is not stealing to help yourself. It is borrowing without permission. If the item comes back there is no justification for anger against the borrower. If, on the other hand, it does not come back, to make enquiries as to its whereabouts is to accuse and then the borrower feels justified in keeping the item since he will reason that the accuser might have been wrong. The fact that the accuser was not

100

wrong does not enter into the equation. Therefore, it is better not to put temptation in the way of one who might borrow, not so?'

'What about your possessions in Lilongwe? Surely that's putting temptation in the way of would-be borrowers?'

Dick Matenje chuckled. 'Ah, Mr Devereaux, but in Lilongwe I live behind a security fence. I have guards and burglar bars and security lights and three very large dogs. For one to come to borrow my belongings under these circumstances it could be assumed that he means to steal. Besides, a man in my position could also assume that an intruder meant harm, not so?'

John smiled at the man's logic. 'You aren't so different to us, Minister. We have holiday cottages to fill the same purpose as you use this place.'

Matenje slapped his knee. 'You see then, already we have found common ground.' Once again, some kind of panic passed through the man's eyes and over his face. 'Tell me about Kadamanja,' he demanded abruptly.

In the past, when caught in intrigue, John had always found it best to tell the truth straight and let those embroiled in whatever games they were playing sort it out as best they could. 'I don't know much about him. He met me at the airport, told me he was my assistant, knew about our meeting and then, on the way here, warned me to be careful about what I said, even to him.' He thought for a moment. 'Oh yes, someone paid my hotel bill, I assume it was him.'

'I took care of your hotel account but I did not organise this assistant,' Matenje said slowly. 'The man I arranged for you was known to me.' He seemed to reach a decision. 'Beware of him,' he said curtly. 'I'll make a few enquiries. Perhaps one of my colleagues . . .' He rose, looking unhappy. 'There could be something funny going on.'

'You're telling me.' John also rose and spoke crisply. 'A reconnaissance survey which is kept secret from the man running the country. This meeting. What exactly *is* going on?'

The Minister was pulling on his polo-neck. As his head appeared through the rolled opening he said, 'Our President was a very fine man, Mr Devereaux. He has done wonders for this country in the short time since Independence. But when he was made President for Life . . . well, it's affecting his judgment. He's started believing all the legends and stories circulating about him. He's become . . . well, let's be kind . . . senile. If we can find oil under our lake, this country will prosper. Without something major we're destined to plod along as we are. We have to try. Can you understand that?'

John nodded. 'I understand your concerns but I feel I have to warn you yet again. There is no oil under the lake. Trust me on this.'

Minister Matenje nodded slowly. 'I hear you.' He was shrugging into his jacket. 'Some of the biggest oil fields have been found exactly where they were least expected – you know that. Preserving our lake is a noble idea, I admit, but it doesn't put food into bellies. We have to look.'

John could sympathise with the man's hopes. 'You'd do better to develop the tourist industry,' he warned. 'That's my advice.'

The Minister smiled. 'Have it your way, Mr Devereaux.' He laughed out loud. 'And then do it my way.'

John laughed too and put out his hand. 'Where do I send my reports?'

'Send them to London. They have ways to contact me.'

Driving back through the village, John thought, 'I hope Bernard has been paid in advance.' There was something about Minister Matenje . . . he could not put his finger on it, something almost intransigent. It was as though he was detached, both from the survey and from his position as Minister without Portfolio. He shook off the idea as ridiculous.

Kadamanja was waiting for him on the side of the road outside the small trading store. 'I'll drive for a while,' John said. They had a long way to go. Robin Cunningham had been working near Karonga and that was where John intended to start. Karonga was over 600 kilometres to the north.

FIVE

LAKE MALAWI – MAY 1983

M r Kadamanja's face resembled an oil slick. Sweat-greasy, an unhealthy sludge grey, with fever blisters dotted like suds above his top lip. The malaria burned him until he shook uncontrollably. 'So sorry, sir,' he managed through chattering teeth.

John pushed two Chloroquine tablets through the trembling lips and held a glass of water against Kadamanja's mouth so he could wash them down. The man's skin was fever-hot through sweat-soaked clothing but he complained of being freezing. John had piled every available blanket over him but to little avail. 'Get some rest,' he said gently. 'I'll be back later.'

Kadamanja nodded and sank gratefully back under the covering layers.

John left the tent and stood shading his eyes from the shimmering glare off the lake. The Livingstone Mountains on the eastern shore rose straight up, over 2000 metres sheer out of the water. They looked deceptively close but, in fact, were nearly fifty kilometres away. With the sun setting behind him, the mountains had lost their clarity and were bathed in soft shades of misty sepia, pink and red.

The lake, too, appeared stained by the sun's last probing rays. Local fishermen were returning, effortlessly guiding their bwatos across the glass-like water. John had earlier watched two men on the beach as they worked on a new boat, patiently chipping away at the hardwood heart of a single trunk with nothing more than a crude adze, mallet and chisel. It crossed his mind that if he had visited this spot 300 years earlier the scene would be no different.

The wind, which had ruffled whitecaps through the day, had dropped. Voices of the fishermen, as they called to each other, carried clearly over the water. It was a beautiful and peaceful sight. Dark wakes followed the bwatos but, very quickly, the pink tinged lake reclaimed its mirror surface. In anticipation of a good catch, smoke rose all along the bay as women stoked their cooking fires.

'Good evening, Mr Devereaux.'

John turned, momentarily startled. Sarah Fotheringham had walked to within two metres of where he stood without his being aware of her presence. 'Good evening, Miss Fotheringham.'

'How's our patient?'

'On the mend I think. It's the worst case of malaria I've ever seen.'

Miss Fotheringham smiled. 'Not up here, Mr Devereaux. Thousands die of it every year but they will not take prophylactics.' She stepped towards him holding up a flask. 'I've brought him some more broth.'

'I doubt he'll have any.'

Her head went up. Chin out, with a steely glint in her clear grey eyes which John had already learned meant 'you'll do it my way or else', she said, 'He'll take it, Mr Devereaux. Excuse me,' and went into Kadamanja's tent.

John turned back to the lake but his thoughts were of Sarah Fotheringham. She was a woman who would not take 'no' for an answer. After Kadamanja was struck down with malaria – and how she got to hear about that remained a mystery – she had insisted they both accompany her to Karonga so he could be looked after. She had simply appeared at the place where John and his assistant had been working, some twenty kilometres out of Karonga, and taken charge of Kadamanja. There, with brisk efficiency, Mr Kadamanja's recovery became her number one priority.

John knew his assistant was in good hands. There was no doubt that Miss Fotheringham knew what she was doing. He did not know much about her, but the little he did know intrigued him. She must have been in her late sixties yet her walk had the spring of a much younger woman. Her calm eyes twinkled with some kind of secret amusement, unless she had decided someone needed bullying for their own good. Her bearing was proud and erect, untouchable and barren. So why did she inevitably have half-a-dozen small children vying for the clasp of her hand? She spoke with an enchanting Scottish accent which left no doubt that she was a good, God-fearing woman. So why did she leave John with the impression she was unshockable, and ready to discuss anything from politics to prams, moral standards to motherhood?

She was tiny, no more than 150 centimetres tall, with a thin frame more like that of a boy than a woman of her years. Snowy white hair was pinned back in an enormous bun but strands strayed around her face, giving a youthful look. She wore rimless glasses which kept slipping down a bird's beak of a nose. Her skin reminded John of delicate parchment. A faint scent of Lily of the Valley always surrounded her.

It was the way she dressed which gave the biggest clue as to her true personality. She favoured brightly floral, badly homemade skirts to her ankles. Her blouse was invariably white, of a loose design and never tucked in. On her feet she wore white canvas tennis shoes with neat socks always meticulously turned at the top. She was intelligent, kind-hearted, had a will of iron and no time for fools. Above all, she was harmlessly eccentric and loved the people of Karonga with a passion that went far beyond any simple desire to help them.

She came to Karonga in the fifties she had told John. She was the great-niece of Monteith Fotheringham, who had run the trading store in Karonga until 1895 when a bout of malaria ended his life. 'I wanted to see where he lived,' she had explained to John proudly. 'He was much revered at home you know for his part in ending the slave trade.'

From others John gathered that after her arrival she had seemed to lose interest in the history of her ancestor, becoming totally engrossed with the present. Appalled by the sickness and poverty, and despite protest from the few whites in Karonga who viewed her as a threat to their supremacy, she set up a clinic at her own expense. Missionaries in the area complained to the authorities that she was unqualified to administer medication. Angrily, Sarah Fotheringham had taken her nursing diploma to the District Commissioner. Two local chiefs went with her to support the contention that she had as much right to run a clinic as anyone. Along the way, this determined trio were joined by hundreds of lake-shore dwellers, all of whom had come to regard this tiny but obstinate woman with deep affection and respect. Faced with a possible uprising, the District Commissioner told her she was free to carry on, providing she did not obstruct the real work being done by the missionaries.

He should have known better. Infuriated at his condescending remark, the indomitable Miss Fotheringham had gone on to open a school, a clearing house for woven artifacts and a fish market of sorts. She also ran classes for women to try and educate them in the ways of hygiene, nutrition and contraception.

Her interference in matters of birth control alarmed the missionaries. While they had sought to confine the villagers' marital activities to one partner – rhetoric regarded with open amusement by all but the most fervent converts – Miss Fotheringham had gone to the women behind their backs and advised them to 'spurn God's gifts'. A delegation was sent to her.

The small group, made up of three indignant missionary wives and a young man of strong religious fibre but questionable sexuality, returned to the mission station with the words 'bugger off' ringing in their ears.

In truth, Sarah Fotheringham made little headway with her birth-control program. It did not stop her trying, however, and the villagers listened to her politely because they liked her, then went on with the business of giving birth every two years, making sure they apologised with great sincerity over each pregnancy.

During the turbulent years of independence, she had quietly and efficiently carried on with her work. Dr Banda was so impressed when he learned of her achievements that he offered Malawian citizenship. She accepted immediately and became one of the very few white people ever recognised in this way. As far as Malawi's society matrons were concerned, she was an eccentric spinster who was much too friendly with the natives. The men speculated that she would benefit from just one night in their virile company. To all of this, Sarah Fotheringham reacted with dignified indifference.

To John Devereaux she was an angel. He had not been unduly worried when Kadamanja fell ill. However, two days later, the man's condition had deteriorated, showing no response to anti-malaria treatment. When Miss Fotheringham appeared and demanded that they return immediately to Karonga, he gratefully handed Kadamanja into her competent care. John doubted that Kadamanja would still be alive if it weren't for her.

'He's a little better.'

Damn! She's done it again. How does she move so silently over sand? 'Thanks to you,' John said, turning from the lake to look at her.

She smiled. 'Poppycock! Jonah has the constitution of a hippo.'

'Jonah?'

She cocked her head and looked at him. 'Surely you didn't doubt he had a first name.'

'He never told me.'

'Did you ever ask?'

'He's a very formal individual,' John said defensively. Kadamanja persisted in calling him 'sir' and had resisted any attempt John made to put their relationship on a more friendly basis.

Clear grey eyes regarded him seriously. 'One of the things to impress me most when I first arrived in Nyasaland was the gently polite manner with which these people conduct themselves. They're not formal, Mr Devereaux. At least, not in the stiff British way. They are very shy people and, unless you do something which upsets them, extremely respectful to their own kind and to us as well. I am constantly delighted that independence has not altered them unduly.' She smiled a wicked little smile. 'I am also continually relieved that, despite their best efforts, the missionaries have failed to

110

interfere with the Malawians' own high moral standards.'

John laughed. 'I hope Dr Livingstone can't hear that.'

Sarah Fotheringham laughed too. 'I think the good doctor was more realistic than some. He at least accepted that moral codes, even if they differed from ours, were better than none at all.' She squinted across the lake to the mountains which bore the Scottish missionary's name. 'How long have you known Jonah?' she asked abruptly.

'Six weeks.'

She smiled at him. 'That's all right then. He'll tell you his name fairly soon.'

'What makes you so sure?'

'My dear man, I'm one of them.' She peered at John over her spectacles, her eyes bright with amusement. 'Besides, I had to ask his name. It's difficult to wash a man's undercarriage while you're calling him mister.'

John chuckled. He liked her. Her personality was that of a modern woman but her precise manner of speaking was straight from the previous century, except of course when she was telling someone to 'bugger off'. 'Would you mind if I leave Mr Kadamanja with you tomorrow?' he asked. 'I'd like to finish off up at the camp and bring our equipment back to Karonga.'

'After more of my broth, Mr Devereaux, I assure you Jonah will be up and about by the time you get back.' Again, the wicked grin. 'It's laced with sherry you see.'

John pretended to be scandalised. 'Miss Fother-ingham, how could you! Mr Kadamanja doesn't drink.'

'Well he does now,' she said gleefully. 'And he appears to be thriving on it.'

John left Karonga before dawn to return to the site where he and Kadamanja had been working: on the border between Malawi and Tanzania about twenty kilometres to the north near where the rivers Kaparo and Songwe run into the lake. With a geologist's knowledge of what lay under the earth's surface, John had located a possible basin which looked as though it might once have been part of Lake Malawi. They had collected sand samples and were about to start testing them when Kadamanja fell ill. John could easily finish the work on his own.

Oil geologists, John included, believed that all the easy oil in the world had already been located. Back in the fifties, oil fields of less than a billion barrels were discounted as economically unviable. But with dwindling resources of natural gas, oil and petroleum, the smaller fields were being reinvestigated. Some of the world's most inhospitable places were now traversed in the quest for petroleum.

John knew that Malawi had no large reserves of oil. All his training, years of experience in the field, all his instincts told him it was impossible. *But what if . . .* It was the 'what ifs' that made this business an exciting challenge, attracting mavericks from all over the world. John was no different to the rest of them. 'What if' was the reason he left his assistant in Karonga. He was too impatient to wait for him to get better.

As he drove along the sandy road John was not actually thinking about oil. He was wondering why the big South African tobacco farmer, Karl Henning, had paid them a call the previous week. John did not believe the visit was coincidental. There was something about Henning that disturbed him. It was entirely possible that the man was spying on John. The question was, who for? Should John inform Minister Matenje? 'Damn them and their bloody intrigue,' he thought, changing down a gear to negotiate a steep and rutted water causeway. 'There's no way Henning just happened along.'

John had been working on a structural map of the area and glanced up from the portable table to catch sight of a ketch-rigged motorsailer as she rounded the headland. Straightening, he watched the vessel with admiration as she sliced smoothly through the water. It was unusual to see such a large craft up here. The lake shelved away from the land very slowly. Indeed, John had seen cattle several hundred metres out from shore with the water lapping just above their hooves. Obviously the skipper of the ketch knew the area well and kept the craft in the deep channel where the Kaporo River ran into the lake. John estimated the boat to be about a forty-five footer and, in the light southerly breeze, she appeared to be making about

113

five knots. An aft cockpit accentuated her sleek lines. A bit of an armchair expert, he nonetheless preferred the racy appearance of a cockpit to stern rather than the more solid looking centre-well favoured by leisure sailors. Light blue sails and a gleaming white hull gave the ketch a clean, eager appearance.

As he watched, the sails had come down and she dropped anchor some fifty metres from shore. From where he stood, John could see only one person moving about on the deck. The ketch was close enough for him to read her name, *Silver Bird*.

Ten minutes later a small runabout had been lowered on davits extended back over the transom. Since he and Kadamanja were the only two people in the vicinity John assumed the visit to be delib-erate and wondered, with some disquiet, if perhaps there was bad news for one of them. As the dinghy drew closer he recognised its sole occupant as the large South African he had met briefly in Blantyre at the Mount Soche Hotel. He walked down the beach to greet the man. 'Bit out of your way,' he commented.

Karl Henning stepped easily from the dinghy, turned and heaved it further up the beach. 'Doing a bit of fishing. Saw the tents. Assumed it was you,' he said. 'Thought I'd drop in to see how you're doing.'

The two men walked up to the camp. Henning glanced at the table John had been working at. 'Looks complicated,' he commented.

John had wanted to draw his unexpected visitor's

attention away from the map. Clearly it was not of Lake Malawi and, since he had told Henning he would be mapping the bottom of the lake, he did not wish to arouse suspicions. 'I've been a bit diverted. Looks like this used to be under water. I wanted to take some measurements but we're nearly finished. Heading south later in the week. Somewhere near Likoma Island.'

'How's the survey going?' Henning was glancing around as he spoke, his eyes missing nothing.

'Could be finished in a couple of weeks. It's all going very well.'

'Found anything interesting?'

There was something wrong. Henning was trying too hard to appear casual. John's earlier suspicions – that the man was prying for something specific – returned. 'Rock formations, rise and fall of the substratum, composition of rocks, that sort of thing.'

That was usually enough to turn the conversation elsewhere. But Henning hadn't finished. 'How about wrecks?'

John laughed. 'I'm not in the salvage business, Mr Henning. Wrecks don't interest me.'

'Yes, but have you found any?' the man persisted.

'No,' John said bluntly. If Henning was after an easy line on sunken treasure he was wasting his time.

The South African did not believe him and it showed. 'As you wish.' He smiled coldly. 'You've got yourselves nicely set up here,' he remarked, changing the subject. 'What's it like being cooped up with a kaffir for weeks on end?'

Mr Kadamanja had been carefully mixing sand samples about ten metres away. Henning made no attempt to lower his voice and, although the Malawian did not appear to have heard, John saw the black man's back stiffen. 'Mr Kadamanja and I work well together,' he replied, not allowing his anger to show.

Karl Henning knew his words were offensive, John could tell. But all the man said was, 'So you're off to Likoma next week.'

'Yes, that's the plan.' John, in order to divert Henning's attention, had said the first thing to come into his head and had no intention of going anywhere near Likoma. It was 200 kilometres south, inside Mozambique waters and of no interest whatsoever. In reality, he and Kadamanja had nearly finished their work. They had one more area to investigate and then he'd be returning to London, writing a final report and that would be an end to it. And, he hoped, an end to whatever game Karl Henning was playing.

After one final penetrating look at the map John was drawing, Henning turned to go. 'I'll be off then. May catch up with you later.'

John walked with him to the dinghy, they shook hands and he watched as Henning pulled away from the beach, hoping another encounter could be avoided. There was something almost predatory about the way the man just happened to appear, ask questions and then abruptly leave. John watched until Henning reached his ketch, then returned to where Kadamanja was working. 'That comment was inexcusable. I apologise on his behalf.'

Mr Kadamanja had smiled, shaking his head. 'It was not your fault, sir. Please do not worry. We are used to it.' The following day Kadamanja had come down with malaria and, two days after that, he and John had gone to Karonga at the insistence of Miss Fotheringham.

It was fully light when he reached their camp site. They had left behind one large tent with most of the survey equipment. Miss Fotheringham, impatient to get Kadamanja back to Karonga, had said, 'For God's sake, my good man, who is going to steal bags of sand?' Reluctantly, John had packed everything into the tent and left it there. It was a relief to find it unscathed.

Checking the soft ground, John saw no new footprints other than the spoor of animals, including a family of hippopotamus who spent their days in a large, sandy-bottomed pool a few hundred metres inland from the river mouth, and their nights grazing the sweet grass along the shore. He had half expected to see signs of Henning having returned but there was nothing even remotely suspicious.

Bags of sand, each weighing around two kilograms, had been stacked and labelled ready for testing. John got to work.

The sand had been thoroughly dried by Kadamanja but John emptied each bag into individual mixing bowls using his fingers to check for moisture. Satisfied that the sand was completely dry, he mixed each separate sample thoroughly, working the grains in the same manner his mother had used when she was rubbing butter into flour to make biscuit dough.

Taking the sample bottles from a cardboard box, he lined them up on the mapping table and then placed a tablespoon of sand from the first bowl into a bottle. Over this he poured carbon tetrachloride until it saturated and covered the sand. Then he corked the bottle, shook it vigorously and attached the label from its sample bag around the neck of the bottle. He did this with each different sample until he had sixteen bottles corked and labelled, their numbers corresponding with exact locations in the basin he was mapping. If John found evidence of oil, exploratory drillers would come in to do some down-hole logging, an expensive process and one which required the most accurate data possible.

Each sample needed at least twenty minutes in the liquid so John filled the time by packing equipment into the vehicle. Half an hour later, with his heart beating wildly, he was ready for the next stage. This was crunch time. If the sand contained any evidence of oil, now was the time it would be revealed. Taking a glass funnel, he folded a disc of white filter paper inside and held it over a white enamel dish. Then, picking up the first sample, he deftly flicked the cork from the bottle with his thumbnail and upturned it over the funnel. He held his breath. A brown or black ring on the filter paper would do nicely.

An explosion of pain at the back of John's head came from nowhere. His legs buckled and he groped frantically to stop himself falling. His fingers closed around something cold and hard but it slipped from his grasp. His knees hit the ground and he toppled sideways. There was a roaring sound in his head and, even though his eyes were open, he could see nothing. Dimly, just before he slid into deep unconsciousness, John thought that what he had grabbed had felt like the barrel of a pistol.

SIX

Terence Parker-Brown eyed with distaste the shrilly ringing telephone on his desk. He was halfway through pulling on his jacket and had been about to leave the office. It had been a long day, he was tired, cranky, and had the beginnings of a tension headache. The Africa desk, his responsibility, had obligingly served up a revolution in Ethiopia, another bid for independence in Namibia, more problems in Somalia, anarchy in Uganda and post-independence violence in Zimbabwe, to name but a few. Just another day at the office.

Now, at six in the evening, he needed time to think. The soft May air outside beckoned. It held the promise of a good summer. He wanted to get out there and breathe it in. He wanted to let it flow over his tired mind until the problems of Africa were encased in a balmy English spring evening. 'I'm too old for this,' he thought, hating the telephone.

He was tempted to leave it ringing. What he wanted more than anything was a leisurely stroll along Victoria Embankment before catching the tube at Charing Cross Station. 'A day at the Foreign and Commonwealth Office,' he mused, 'is a bit like fighting the War of the Worlds every day of your life.'

Parker-Brown stared balefully at the telephone. 'If there was ever any justice in this world, Alexander Graham Bell would never have been born,' he thought sourly. He finished shrugging into his jacket and crossed the office to his desk, muttering aloud. 'What is it this time? War in Angola? A coup in Tanzania? You people out there think all you have to do is press a few buttons, dump your troubles on me and then bugger off to the club for a drink. *I'm* the one with the ulcers. *I'm* the one with the sleepless nights. Oh for heaven's sake, do stop that infernal racket.' He snatched up the receiver.

'Parker-Brown,' he snapped irritably. He heard his own voice bounce back. International. Well, at least it wasn't Susan asking him to pick up some fish for dinner.

'Oh good, you haven't left.' The tinny, disconnected voice of Martin Flower came over the line. 'We've had some interesting developments.'

Parker-Brown had protested the need for one of his men in Malawi. The country had no wealth, it was on the road to nowhere, internal political strife might affect a handful of British citizens, but it was nothing the High Commission staff couldn't handle. The war raging in Mozambique was of interest, certainly, but he had several operatives in South Africa who could gather intelligence just as

121

easily as Flower. As far as he was concerned Britain was holding Dr Banda's hand a little too long. 'I was on my way out,' he informed Flower peevishly.

Martin Flower ignored the obvious pique of his boss. 'Banda dissolved Cabinet and Parliament yesterday.'

'We knew that,' Parker-Brown said impatiently. 'What's the problem?'

'He's postponed the elections.'

Despite his irritation, Terence was a thorough professional with a comprehensive understanding of African politics and a nose for trouble. What was the old man up to? 'Reason?'

'Take your pick,' Flower said cheerfully. 'Officially, it's to give candidates time to sit their English proficiency test. Unofficially, Banda has decided to take a year out. John Tembo has been named as his replacement, although he's strenuously denying it. Forty ministers were not even nominated for re-election. Their names got as far as Banda's desk and went straight into the circular file at his feet. There's a lemming-like rush for the border and Lusaka is overflowing with out-of-work Malawian top brass. Rumours are flying everywhere. It's my guess that Banda is delaying the elections until the stories stop circulating. There's a kind of low-key hysteria over here but it's rapidly getting out of control.'

'African games,' Parker-Brown growled. He'd seen this sort of thing many times before.

'Not really,' Martin Flower said, suddenly serious. 'Dick Matenje and three others are dead.'

Parker-Brown's interest quickened. 'Tell me.'

'Dick Matenje, Aaron Gadama . . .'

'Who's he?' Terence interrupted.

'Minister for the Central Region.'

'Who else?' Parker-Brown was scribbling furiously on a notepad as Flower spoke.

'John Sangala.'

'Health Minister. Met him once. Not a bad chap.'

'David Chiwanga, the former legislator,' Flower concluded.

Parker-Brown frowned at the names on his notepad. 'What happened to them?'

'Their bodies were discovered in a burnt-out car. It's being reported as an accident.' Flower paused for effect. 'It's the funniest damned accident I've ever seen.'

Parker-Brown steeled himself. Flower had a habit of leaving the worst news till last. It was the man's one fault. 'What's funny about it?'

'They all had bullet holes in them,' Flower told him soberly.

Dick Matenje's name jumped off the page of the notepad. The other three had probably been in the wrong place at the wrong time, but Matenje? If Banda was planning a year's sabbatical then Matenje should have been a strong contender for his replacement. Terence didn't know much about John Tembo except that he was the Governor of the Reserve Bank *and* uncle of Mama Cecilia Kadzamira, President Banda's companion and official hostess.

123

'Some kind of power struggle between Matenje and Tembo?' he asked.

'Matenje's been a bit of a loose cannon lately. Not toeing Banda's line. We've had our eye on him for a while.'

'No need for that now,' Parker-Brown commented sourly. 'What else?'

'Mama Kadzamira has her King Air tanked up and the pilot's on twenty-four-hour standby.'

'Prudent lady,' Parker-Brown said. 'Any word from SAMACO?' The Save Malawi Committee recently formed in neighbouring Zambia had proved an invaluable source of intelligence.

'According to them, nearly sixty army officers and at least ten politicians are dead. Banda is apparently implicated. The nickname "crocodile feeder" has been bandied about.' Flower paused, then added darkly, 'I suppose that's one way of getting rid of the evidence. Matenje and the other three were found near Mwanza. SAMACO say they were trying to get into Mozambique and from there up to Zambia. The route they chose is not the usual one into Zambia. Looks like they saw this coming and fled.'

Parker-Brown agreed. 'Anything else?' he asked.

'There's been some kind of attempted coup. We heard shots coming from the palace earlier today. We're all standing by. The whole country is holding its breath.'

'Can Banda hang on?'

'Looks like it.'

Parker-Brown's mind raced over the implications.

Banda was the devil they knew. Dick Matenje and his followers were a wild card. Right and wrong didn't enter the equation at the moment. Order, if it was possible, had to be restored. 'What's the word from Sanjika palace?'

'Deafening silence. A statement was released a while ago about the car accident. The mood is rather thundery. Questions about the shots we heard are probably not a good idea.'

'How about British subjects?'

'No immediate danger. All the whites have their heads well and truly down but word is they're safe enough for the time being. The next twenty-four hours are critical. If Banda stays in control this will pass. If half of what we're hearing is true, he'll be ruling by fear for a good few years.'

'Fine, Martin. Keep me posted.'

'There's just one more thing.'

Parker-Brown moved the receiver away from his ear and scowled at it, as if it were solely responsible for delaying his departure from the stuffy confines of his office. 'What?' he snapped.

'Can someone get in touch with Bernard Pickstone at PAGET. They've lost another man.'

'Was he caught up in this?'

'Not directly, no,' Flower said. 'Although he was doing a survey commissioned by Dick Matenje. He appears to have fallen foul of something quite different. Not that it matters. It stinks just as bad.'

'Body?'

'Not yet.'

'Are we involved?'

'No. It's a criminal offence, nothing political.'
Flower had regret in his voice.

Parker-Brown sympathised. In the course of their work, field operators often stumbled over criminal matters. The very nature of their work, however, required them to keep a low profile. Flower was waiting for him to say something. Parker-Brown spread balm on his conscience. 'Then keep out of it, Martin. That's an order.'

SEVEN

LONDON – THE PRESENT

At the age of fifty-four, Martin Flower felt like a teenager. It was many years since he had been the youngest man in the room. He looked around. They had come from all parts of Britain, from all forms of retirement – once-powerful men who had influenced the nation's leaders. Men who, some would say, had been the true rulers of Britain. They had come at his bidding, intrigued by the brief message, 'A matter of supreme national importance . . . a matter of utmost secrecy'. Bound, as they all were, by the Official Secrets Act, asking them here was a gamble. Crumbling old bodies, crusty old personalities, still fiercely patriotic even in their declining years, these men held in their heads so many unforgotten but unspoken secrets of the past. But would they talk to him?

His former boss, Terence Parker-Brown, long since retired, sat enveloped in an overstuffed armchair, his frail body and age-reedy voice deceptively screening a mind that was still razor sharp. At seventy-three, and fighting cancer of the bowel, Terence Parker-Brown MBE spent most days tending roses in his rambling two-acre garden in Hertfordshire, doting on an overweight and hyperactive King Charles spaniel called Muffy and, with ill-concealed bad humour, replenishing glasses at his wife's soirees which she insisted on holding at least twice a month.

Godfrey Winterbottom, nearly blind, well into his eighties, had once controlled the Foreign and Commonwealth Office with an iron fist. 'And he still does in a way,' Martin thought. No-one discounted his wisdom when he cared to share it. Not that he did very often these days. A confirmed bachelor, Godfrey had fallen in love four years ago with a charming and delicate woman of similar age to himself. They spent six months each year travelling extensively. Godfrey liked to say, 'There is so much to see and do that we're going to have to live forever.'

Admiral Fairy Stanley used to stalk his six foot four inch frame through the halls of Admiralty House, casting a shadow with which no-one quibbled. His real name, Anthony, was not known to many. He had been nicknamed 'Fairy Feet' more than half a century earlier by some quartermaster joking that navy issue shoes did not usually come in size fourteen. Confined to a wheelchair now, feet hidden under a blanket, his once massive frame bowed and thin, disguising the fact that, in his youth, he had played rugby for Scotland. To get to this meeting, Fairy Stanley had to be driven down from Edinburgh, something which caused him to exclaim to Martin when he telephoned, 'My dear

chap, do you actually *know* where Edinburgh is?'
But he came anyway.

Sir Thomas Tomlinson, deaf when he wanted to
be, had been a major player at the Home Office
during Margaret Thatcher's reign. A minor scandal
involving a secretary ended his public career but,
for many years after that, the Iron Lady consulted
him in secret. His bellicose features had softened as
age padded his face but he still resembled a belligerent bulldog with jowls which actually quivered when he spoke. His wife of fifty-six years
called him 'Pug'. No-one else dared.

Lord Rawson, 'Banger' to his friends for some
long-forgotten bedroom indiscretion, had advised
the Queen on matters of national and international
importance. An extremely religious man, he had
vigorously opposed the divorce of Prince Charles
and Princess Diana and, making his objections
loud and clear, had fallen foul of Royal favour. Not
that it bothered him. He carried in his blood
enough blue to make the Royals envious and was
one of the richest men in England. More at home
wearing plus-fours and stomping around the
grouse moors of Yorkshire, Lord Rawson nonetheless had been sufficiently intrigued by Martin's
message to cut short a spot of duck shooting and
make the trip to London.

Now eighty-one, he was inclined to break wind
involuntarily, something he tried to cover up by
coughing repeatedly, although the timing was seldom properly synchronised and he often sounded
like an ailing Model-T Ford.

And finally, the enigmatic David Chisholm, ex-war correspondent for *The Times* who retired back in the seventies. Since then he had written several books which were considered to be definitive works on African aspects of the Second World War. Socially, he lived a high-profile life. Seen at every opening night in London, his cynical observations were devoured avidly by readers of the society columns. He was so often the first to break scandalous news that the newspapers competed fiercely to buy his pieces – as Chisholm himself once commented to an indignant society matron, 'Your indiscretions, darling, are my champagne and caviar. Sod the bread and butter.' Openly homosexual, he had attempted suicide twice, been thrown out of more bars than most people enter in their lives and then astounded his critics by getting a thirty-four-year-old editor pregnant and marrying her. The marriage lasted two weeks but he was now the bemused and somewhat reluctant seventy-six-year-old father of a four-year-old son.

The minds of these six men were bank vaults for government cover-ups and political connivings from the thirties through to the eighties. What lurked there was best left alone. Martin Flower knew this but had asked them to the meeting because he was desperately worried.

Observing crystal whisky glasses charged with Scotland's finest, cigars glowing, and each man comfortably settled, Martin thanked them for coming.

'Why here?' Parker-Brown asked querulously. 'Why all this secrecy, Martin?'

They were assembled in the lounge of a large penthouse apartment on the Prince of Wales Drive in London's south-west. The apartment was owned by the Foreign and Commonwealth Office and occasionally used as a safe-house. The lift stopped at the floor below the penthouse which could only be accessed by a steep flight of stairs. If other occupants of the building wondered about occasional comings and goings to and from the top floor, they were too discreet to mention it.

Admiral Stanley sniffed his whisky appreciatively. 'Damned inconvenient,' he growled. His driver and personal valet – he refused to call the large ex-navy engineer a chauffeur – when faced with the stairs had simply carried him to the penthouse, returning for the chair and depositing one protesting Admiral back into the only mode of transport he really trusted.

'I'm sorry, sir.' Martin smiled sympathetically. He liked Fairy Stanley and recognised the frustration caused by dependency on others.

'C'mon, man,' Lord Rawson snapped impatiently. 'What's this all about?'

'What?' Sir Thomas cupped his ear. 'Speak up, damn it.'

David Chisholm leaned towards him. 'He said twist and shout.'

Sir Thomas's jowls quivered and runny eyes observed Chisholm with distaste. 'No he didn't.'

Martin Flower cleared his throat. 'Gentlemen, if I may have your attention.'

Six pairs of veteran-wise eyes observed him,

silence suddenly loud in the room. In their time, these men had wielded enough power to bring down a government. They knew when to speak and when to listen.

Martin spoke loudly for the benefit of Sir Thomas. 'The FCO has been approached by one Frederick Hamilton who has made an extraordinary claim. So extraordinary in fact . . .' Martin leaned forward in his chair, '. . . that I have spent the past two weeks trying to verify whether it can possibly be true.'

Lord Rawson coughed suddenly and broke wind loudly. He did not apologise.

'At first . . .' Martin went on as if Lord Rawson had not farted, '. . . I was inclined to think he was making it up. His motives for contacting us were less than honourable. Not to put too fine a point on it, gentlemen, Mr Hamilton is after money in return for his silence.'

Godfrey Winterbottom humphed. 'Been tried, been tried, dear boy. Happens every year or so. Some damned bucko thinks he can –'

'Do shut-up, Godfrey. Let the boy speak.' Lord Rawson nodded to Martin. 'Carry on.'

Martin might have grinned if the issue had not been so serious. 'The first thing I did was run a check on Hamilton. I came up with surprisingly little. He is British, grew up in Tonwell and was educated at Haleybury College near Hertford. Obtained a driving licence in 1968 and hasn't picked up so much as a parking ticket since. First applied for a passport in '75, one extension and then had it reissued in 1990. He's clear with Tax Department, saw a dentist regularly and rarely went to the doctor. His appendix burst in '72. That's it. No library fines, no convictions, no marriages, no mortgage, no credit cards.'

'What a boring little man,' Lord Rawson said in total disapproval. 'But what does he do?'

'Everything he told us about himself tallied,' Martin went on. 'In 1978 he joined the Universities Mission to Central Africa and was sent to Malawi.'

'Serves him right,' David Chisholm muttered.

Martin did grin this time. Chisholm was a well-known atheist. 'Last month he was fired,' he told the listening men.

'Are we still sending missionaries out to convert the heathens?' Admiral Stanley said to nobody in particular.

'They concentrate on more practical matters these days,' Chisholm responded drily. 'Leper colonies, hospitals, schools and the odd church service. After all, dear boy, they're a business just like anything else.'

Godfrey humphed again but otherwise kept silent.

'Why was he fired?' Parker-Brown asked.

'Apparently he was posted to Likoma Island,' Martin told the men. 'In its day, it was a thriving missionary station but there's not much left of it now, a sodding great cathedral that's seen better days and a small fishing community. It would appear that our friend, Hamilton, discovered a sealed crypt of some kind under the cathedral. That's why the man was fired. He opened the crypt.'

'Perfectly natural thing for a chap to do,' Chisholm observed. 'Why fire him for that?'

'Someone gave him express instructions not to,' Martin said. 'I'm still trying to get to the bottom of that one. All I've discovered so far is that the crypt is older than the cathedral by several hundred years. It was never used and they sealed it in 1939. The Bishop who ordered it sealed died two years later, vegetation grew back as the building deteriorated and, over the years, the crypt was forgotten. Just who ordered Hamilton to leave it alone is unclear. He was apparently doing some gardening, found the crypt and was still contemplating whether to open it or not when he received an anonymous letter, postmarked London, saying that under no circumstances was the crypt to be disturbed. Hasn't a clue how whoever sent the letter even found out about his discovery.'

'Bit rum,' Winterbottom grumbled. 'Bit high-handed too if you ask me.'

'Hamilton thought so too. He went ahead and opened the crypt.'

'And got fired,' Parker-Brown said. 'By whom?'

'By the Mission's head office here in London.'

Parker-Brown opened his mouth.

'I know, I know, Terence,' Martin said quickly. 'The assumption could be made. I asked them straight if the order not to disturb the crypt had come from them. They denied it. All they're saying is that Hamilton should have known better. A sealed crypt is not for the rank and file to open.'

'I assume that he found something inside the crypt which caused you to ask us here?' Chisholm's sarcasm was barely hidden. He was getting impatient.

'Yes,' Martin said soberly. 'If he's telling the truth and goes public it will not only cost us the next election, gentlemen, it could be the end of the Conservative Party.'

David Chisholm laughed. 'That old chestnut,' he scoffed. 'Come on, Martin, you know better than that.'

'Shut-up, Chisholm,' Parker-Brown snapped irritably. He looked at Martin. 'Still can't see how we come into this. What do you expect from us?'

'Your memories,' Martin said seriously.

'Why?' Godfrey Winterbottom asked.

'Because I need to know if Hamilton is telling the truth. Because I have top priority clearance yet can find no documented evidence of his claims, just a few annoying coincidences that might, or might not, mean he's telling the truth. Because if what Hamilton is saying is true I have to get somebody into Malawi as a matter of urgency. Because there are supposedly three documents on Likoma Island, the contents of which will not only bring an end to the Tories, they will have devastating international ramifications for Britain too.'

Lord Rawson looked down his profoundly aristocratic nose. 'What's this damned Hamilton fellow saying?'

'Mind if I top up my glass?' David Chisholm rose and looked around. 'Anyone else?'

Martin waited until the decanter had done the rounds and Chisholm was back in his seat. 'In the spring of 1939, intelligence confirmed that Germany intended to invade France. We expected Italy to join in and it appeared likely that Japan would favour Germany. We, for our part, could rely on France. If Hitler invaded Russia we could also count on them as allies. As regards any commitment of armed forces, America simply didn't want to know.'

Heads were nodding, several of them impatiently. They hadn't come here for a history lesson. 'Hell,' Martin thought, 'these men wrote the book.'

'There were several countries we were certain wouldn't join us,' he went on. 'What Britain had to do was make sure they didn't join Hitler.'

Fairy Stanley nodded. 'There was a bit of pushing and shoving in India as I recall.'

Martin nodded back.

'We were worried about Spain,' Godfrey Winterbottom said. 'Civil War just ended and Franco a military man. If he'd taken a side it wouldn't be ours.'

'Are you saying we made deals?' Lord Rawson spluttered. 'I say, Martin, do watch what you're saying.'

'Wouldn't be the first time,' Chisholm commented.

Rawson favoured him with a filthy look. 'What could Britain offer Spain to encourage her neutrality?' he asked. Then he stared at Martin. 'Good grief, surely not.'

Martin nodded again. 'Gibraltar,' he said softly.

'Speak up,' Sir Thomas bellowed.

'He said Gibraltar,' Chisholm told him, exasperated.

'You can't possibly mean . . .' Godfrey Winterbottom rubbed at his failing eyes as if by seeing better he could take in what Martin was saying.

David Chisholm laughed cynically. 'I don't know why you're so surprised. Spain and Britain have been using that rock as leverage since the Treaty of Utrecht. It's been offered in exchange for territory or favours more times than I've had baked dinners.'

Terence Parker-Brown was staring at Martin. 'There's more isn't there?' he said, his voice a thin rasp.

Martin nodded. 'Portugal was to get Likoma Island.'

'That makes sense,' Parker-Brown said. 'Portuguese East-Africa demanded a portion of the lake when Britain and Germany were drawing lines on Africa's map. Likoma is smack in the middle of, what is now, Mozambique water. The only reason Likoma remained as part of Nyasaland was because the missionaries raised hell at the time.'

'Correct,' Winterbottom agreed. 'Mind you, it was a bit more than just drawing lines, dear boy,' he reprimanded gently. 'There were strategic considerations.'

'Don't get me started, Godfrey. You know how I feel about that. Lines were drawn through villages, for God's sake.' He turned to Martin. 'Let's have it. We're not here over Gibraltar and Likoma.'

Martin delivered the punchline. 'Argentina got the Falklands.'

'Jesus Christ!' David Chisholm rose and headed back to the bar. 'Jesus Christ!' he said again, turning to face the room. 'We lost 250 people down there.'

Lord Rawson's usually reddish face had drained of colour. 'We wouldn't . . .' he whispered.

'Speak up,' Sir Thomas shouted in frustration.

'I'd have known of it,' Godfrey boomed, staring at Sir Thomas. 'It would have gone over my desk.'

'They all stayed neutral,' Parker-Brown said slowly. 'So if it's true . . .'

'We've reneged before,' Chisholm cut in. 'The British people won't give a shit that we've done it again. Gibraltar and Likoma don't count. It's the Falklands that matter.'

'Where's the proof?' demanded Winterbottom.

'He's not telling. It's my guess they're still on Likoma. Maybe even in the crypt.'

'How the hell did they get there in the first place?' Parker-Brown wanted to know. 'And why did the idiotic man leave them there?'

'He's probably hidden them.' Martin looked around the room. 'What would you do?' he asked. 'Hamilton plans to hold the British Government to ransom, he's hardly likely to leave his proof lying around. The documents could be anywhere but he'd want to be able to get his hands on them if needed. I don't think he'd travel with them. Too risky. They're not in his flat in London – we've checked.'

The room fell silent. Each man was busy with his memories. Martin waited tensely. These six men were the only ones left in Britain who might, just might, be able to confirm or disprove Hamilton's extraordinary claim. If they could remember it.

'Anyone here remember Burleigh Marks?' Admiral Stanley asked suddenly.

'Marks,' Winterbottom mused. 'Wasn't he that chappie who went missing somewhere in Africa? On some kind of mission. Let me think.'

'By Jove, I remember him,' Lord Rawson said loudly. 'Damned scoundrel. Got that serving girl up the duff and –'

'That was his brother, you old fool,' Sir Thomas said.

Lord Rawson took no offence.

David Chisholm drained his glass and stood.

'Haven't you had enough of that stuff?' Parker-Brown snapped.

'My dear boy, you can never get enough of this stuff,' Chisholm said languidly, moving to the bar. He spoke with his back to the group. 'I did try to get up a story. Something about secret meetings. We were all very suspicious. Burleigh Marks, if I recall, was a name that kept popping up. Never met him personally. The War Office had him under wraps.' He turned suddenly. 'Good God, I do remember something.'

'What?' Sir Thomas asked, his jowls shaking.

'They sent me into Russia to cover . . .' he looked crafty. 'Well, never mind what I covered. The point is, I was away for six weeks. When I got back the War Office, Foreign Affairs, the whole damned lot of them were acting normal. Well . . .' he laughed cynically, '. . . as normal as a bunch of cut-throat, conniving –'

'Yes, yes,' Parker-Brown cut in. 'Get on with it, man.'

'It rather looks now as though I was sent to Russia to get me out of the way,' Chisholm said, aggrieved. 'It looks as though I got too close to the truth.'

Parker-Brown glanced at Martin. 'Why hasn't anyone staked their claim?'

'There would have been a mere handful of people involved in negotiations on that level,' Martin said.

Parker-Brown nodded agreement.

'I've checked though, Terence. There appears to have been a plague of unexplained deaths. They all took place within six weeks of Germany surrendering.'

'Circumstances?' Parker-Brown asked.

'Extreme prejudice,' Martin told him.

'Charming!' Chisholm muttered.

'Burleigh Marks,' Admiral Stanley said stonily, upset by the interruptions, 'went to Spain, Portugal *and* Argentina in the spring of '39. I know he did. Never returned.'

'How can you be so emphatic?' Lord Rawson asked.

'He owed me money.'

'What? What did he say?' Sir Thomas cupped his ear.

'He said he owed him money,' Chisholm yelled at him.

'Oh.' Sir Thomas subsided into his chair, crossed his hands over his formidable stomach and dropped his chin to his chest. He appeared deep in thought.

Godfrey Winterbottom yawned. Chisholm went back to the bar. Parker-Brown's disapproving gaze followed him.

'Marks was a bit of a lad,' Admiral Stanley continued. 'Never said what he was up to but couldn't help bragging a little. Something about a mission which would change the world map. You know how he was. I didn't take too much notice at the time. It's possible though, isn't it?'

Martin nodded. 'Entirely possible, sir. We have to assume that a meeting of some kind took place between Portugal, Spain, Argentina and Britain, and, if we assume that, we might take it a step further and presume that the meeting took place on Likoma Island. It makes sense. Likoma was one of the carrots we held out; the Germans were watching our every move; we would have needed to find somewhere remote that was still on British soil to hold such a meeting *and* Africa back then was such an intricate mishmash of colonies that it would have been easy to reach Likoma without raising too many suspicions. The island was perfect. And what better place to hide documents of that nature? An ancient crypt on some practically unknown island in the middle of a forgotten lake. Far safer than have Marks bring them back to London. Quite fortuitous as it happens, especially

141

if, as you say, Burleigh Marks went missing shortly after that in Africa.'

'It should have gone across my desk,' Winterbottom said peevishly.

Chisholm didn't bother to move away from the bar this time. He leaned on it and said, 'Actually, 255 British subjects died during the Falklands War. If what this man Hamilton says is true, how the hell do we explain *that* to the British people. The Tories will have lawsuits coming out of the woodwork. If I were you, Martin, I'd get a man into Malawi pretty damned fast.'

Martin looked at Admiral Stanley. 'Burleigh Marks could have negotiated it,' the Admiral said crossly. He hated to be interrupted. 'It was right up his street. He was certainly in Spain, Portugal and Argentina that spring. Don't know about Africa though. It's your responsibility, Martin, but I think David's right.'

'Godfrey?' Martin asked.

Godfrey Winterbottom was also peeved. 'Pig in a poke,' he said huffily. 'My guess is you'd be wasting your time. Everything went across my desk.'

'I'm not so sure,' Parker-Brown said. 'They were trying times. In your place, Martin, I'd want to make certain.'

Martin looked over to Lord Rawson who shrugged. 'Never heard a whisper of it. Knew all the chaps. *Someone* would have said *something* surely. I'd boot this Hamilton out, damned man is just a scoundrel.' He coughed and broke wind. 'Mind you, if it were true . . .'

'Sir Thomas?' Martin said loudly.

But Sir Thomas Tomlinson had fallen asleep.

'Well?' demanded Parker-Brown.

Martin sighed. 'Do I have a choice? There's too much at stake. All hell will break loose if Hamilton goes public.'

'He could meet with a tragic accident,' Chisholm suggested with a degree of sarcasm. 'After all, you chaps do that sort of thing rather well.'

Martin looked uncomfortable. 'Who warned him against opening the crypt? How much does that person know? Who else knows? No, gentlemen, our only safe option is to locate and destroy the documents – if they exist!'

'Doesn't sound to me as if Hamilton has the kind of imagination to make it up,' Chisholm observed.

There was general agreement to Chisholm's comment.

'Then, my boy . . .' Chisholm said, reaching for the decanter yet again, '. . . You can take it from me. The documents exist.'

EIGHT

Lana Devereaux stared through the window of the South African Airways 737 Stretch Boeing, impatient for the aeroplane to take off. The passengers had been on board for almost a quarter of an hour but the stewardess was still waiting by the open door, glancing at her watch every few minutes. A couple of ground crew were standing aimlessly on the tarmac, bored. One of them was studiously picking his nose. In the distance, across the aprons and runways, a row of sheds glinted in midmorning sunlight, a low line of buildings huddled together as if for protection in an otherwise flat landscape.

No stranger to this city – Lana had visited South Africa nearly every year with her parents, and then, after her father's disappearance, with her mother – she nonetheless wondered again what on earth it was that attracted South Africans to live in such a sprawling, unattractive concrete jungle. Surrounded by ugly, barren mine dumps, their dull yellow nudity a testament to man's indifference in his quest for the gold hidden under the ground, the dumps distributed fine yellow dust when the wind blew, thick yellow mud when the rain fell and were the closest thing to a mountain Johannesburg could muster. The only redeeming feature of Johannesburg, as far as she could see, was the high-veld crystal clarity weather. Cape Town, far to the south, was cosmopolitan, quaint and beautiful with its mountains and seas. Durban, on the east coast, hot, tropical and flavoured by its large Indian pop-ulation. Johannesburg, despite the opulence of its buildings and lushness of gardens, irrespective of being the commercial capital of South Africa, appeared to lack a heartbeat, a rhythm, any form of personality.

She shifted in her seat, trying to relieve the best efforts of her right leg which seemed hell-bent on cramping. Twelve hours in the air from Heathrow, three hours on the ground waiting for a connect-ing flight and now this. 'If you've got time to spare, fly there.' The expression was certainly true more often than not. Lana had lost count of the delays she'd experienced around the world, cooling her heels in various airports, while the mechanics or paperwork of flying took their time.

There was a sudden flurry of activity at the front of the aircraft and a large windswept man appeared, rumbling an apology. The stewardess took his coat, nodded and smiled that it didn't matter, although the fixed quality of her smile said otherwise. Lana, diverted from her thoughts, watched the man make his way down the aisle and realised, just as he reached her, that he was looking for the empty seat beside her. He sat down with a grunt, strapped himself in, then glanced at her. 'Sorry. The delay is my fault. The London flight was late.'

Lana, who had herself landed in Johannesburg on the only London flight that morning, nodded briefly and turned away. She'd had plenty of time to make the connecting flight to Malawi. The pilot of the 737, either under instructions from the control tower to hurry up, or irritated by the delay, taxied across the endless aprons and onto the runway well over the legal speed limit. He turned at the end and, with no further ado, slammed the throttles forward surprising most of the passengers, who were expecting the usual few seconds slowdown, thrusting everybody back into their seats as the big plane leapt forward like a thoroughbred and raced eagerly down the runway.

This was the part of flying Lana didn't like. She remembered watching Spike Milligan on television once saying that people who were scared of flying had got it wrong. Flying wasn't dangerous. It was *crashing* that was dangerous. Lana didn't mind flying, she just wasn't overly fond of taking off. Her analytical mind accepted airflow and lift. However, the self-preservation gene within questioned how something so obviously earthbound could leap into the air and stay there. That first minute was, to her, critical. She shut her eyes and tried to think of something else. When she opened them they were several thousand feet into the air. Relaxing, she busied herself counting the number of Johannesburg homes with swimming pools. Finally she concluded that about two in ten did *not* have one.

'All that water,' she reflected. 'I wonder if South Africa can spare it?'

She let her mind drift. She was going to Malawi; a strange-sounding land, about which most of her friends had never even heard. 'And why would they?' she asked herself. A country 900 kilometres long, on average less than 100 kilometres wide with one-fifth of its surface area covered by water, and surrounded as it was by Mozambique, Zambia and Tanzania, Malawi would need to turn itself inside-out before it made world headlines.

'The bottom of the Rift,' Bernard had told her. The way he said it made it sound like the arse end of the world. As a geologist Lana knew about Africa's Rift Valley. A 9600 kilometre fissure in the earth's crust in which, for the past twenty-five million years, volcanoes and earthquakes had seethed and pushed, creating huge valleys – some as wide as fifty kilometres – between parallel fault lines and forming high mountain plateaux on either side. At university, she had studied the immense series of cracks which ran from the Red Sea all the way south to Mozambique. She had learned that thirty still-active volcanoes continued the rifting process and that many scientists believed the north-east corner of Africa, the Somali plate, would ultimately drift away as a new ocean sliced through the continent. She knew too that Lake Malawi was considered to be the youngest of the Great Rift lakes and yet Lake Tanganyika, the south end of which was a scant 250 kilometres west of the northern tip of Lake Malawi, was supposed to be the oldest in Africa's chain of deep, freshwater inland lakes.

Lana shifted in her seat and sighed. Interesting as the Rift Valley may be, it was not its geological features that drew her to central Africa. When her father disappeared in Malawi fifteen years earlier, all she could think about was that, one day, she would go there and try to find out for herself what had happened to him. She swallowed, and the bitter bile of grief rose in her throat. It had never gone away, not in all these years, and sometimes, like now, it would engulf her with such intensity that she found herself defenceless against the feeling of despair that followed. A sudden, heart-thudding sense of hopelessness which, even at the age of twenty-seven, would bring back the fear, disbelief, pain and anger of that day, nearly fifteen years ago, when her world was shattered into tiny fragments of memories leaving only a yearning for the picture to be whole again.

She remembered the day clearly. A still and beautiful day, late in May. Britain was enjoying an early start to summer that year, the air had a soft clarity that her mother called 'champagne'. It was a champagne kind of a day and Lana had been upstairs doing her homework, wishing she could go outside and play with the dog. Staring through the window of her bedroom she gazed wistfully at the sweep of gravel drive with bright green lawns on either side. Encouraged by the warm weather, the flowerbeds were already a riot of pinks, reds, yellows, blues and white. The oaks framing the garden, and the birch lining the drive had lost their spring green and had turned darker, providing deep shade.

Portia, Lana's wet-nosed, soulful-eyed Labrador, was sitting in the middle of the front lawn looking hopefully up at Lana's bedroom window, a tennis ball at her feet. Lana smiled and waved and the dog bounded in a circle before sitting down again. Lana giggled, remembering her father's comment, 'I swear, poppet, that damned dog believes she should be sitting cross-legged on the sofa watching television, with a gin 'n' tonic clasped firmly in one paw.'

The dog was spoiled, pampered, thoroughly loved by the family and she could practically speak. She obeyed commands – when the mood took her – in English and French, even responding to Lana's mother's occasional outburst of '*voetsak*', which Karen solemnly promised was Afrikaans for 'get out of the way, darling' but which caused Lana's father to grin in such a way that Lana knew it meant something a little more basic.

On special occasions, like when Lana had been sick with flu, her mother allowed Portia to sleep in her bedroom. It was such a treat that Lana never once mentioned that the dog kept her awake with loud snores, yelps as she dreamed of chasing rabbits and regular dispensations of gas which had Lana wondering what on earth her mother fed her.

Lana had just decided that the day was simply too good to waste on homework and had rebelliously snapped her English exercise book shut when she heard the crunch of tyres on the gravel and looked up to see a long black car ease to a stop outside. She watched, intrigued, as a driver emerged briskly and snapped open a rear door, executing a brief salute to a small, dapper man in a charcoal grey suit who emerged from the back, tugged down his jacket and brushed at something on his lapel before turning to look sombrely at the Devereaux house. Portia, as intrigued as Lana, trotted over and sniffed the man's legs before losing interest and finding shade under some rhododendrons. Lana had never seen the man before. Her mother was, she knew, in the back garden. The housekeeper would not be back until later. So Lana ran lightly down the stairs and had the front door open before the man could ring the doorbell.

'Hello.'

He seemed surprised to see her. This annoyed Lana since she believed, and occasionally voiced the opinion to her friends, that children lived in houses and had as many rights to be there as their parents, whether adults liked it or not. 'Well hello, young lady.'

Lana immediately didn't take to him. He was the hearty type, that curious breed of adult who could hold the floor at parties, speak in public, and yet found themselves completely tongue-tied in the company of children. Good manners, and an innate politeness, prevailed. 'Do you want to see Mummy?'

'Yes please, if it's no bother.'

She led him into the lounge. *Never let a strange*

man into the house. Lana knew the rules but reasoned that someone with evil intent would hardly arrive with a chauffeur. She could see he was impatient and ill at ease. Inside Lana resided what her father called the mischief monkey. This often stubborn, contrary, questioning and perverse little creature offered the stranger tea, made certain he was comfortably seated and brought an ashtray before letting him off the hook and going in search of her mother. She found her in the greenhouse, thinning seedlings ready for planting into the vegetable garden. 'Hi, poppet. Finished your homework?'

Lana shook her head. 'There's a man inside who wants to see you.'

'Who?' Karen Devereaux looked surprised. Lana knew most of their friends and would have named the man if he had been one of them.

'I don't know. He didn't say.' Lana took a deep breath. 'Mummy, if I promise to finish my homework later can I please, please go outside and play with Portia?'

Karen smiled at her daughter fondly. Headstrong and independent she might have been but she had a highly developed sense of fair play and could always be trusted to honour a deal with no complaints. 'No television if you do.'

'I promise.'

'Okay then, off you go.' Karen wiped her hands on a cloth and made her way towards the kitchen door.

Lana ran around the side of the house calling to Portia. Five minutes later, as the dog trotted back

151

over the lawn, tennis ball in her mouth, something made Lana turn and stare at the house. It was nothing tangible, no noise, nothing she could identify that suddenly drew her gaze. In fact, it was almost an absence of sound, rather like the house and garden had become frozen at a moment in time when nothing moved or breathed. Something creepy ran up her spine and settled on the back of her neck. Portia nudged her leg with a wet nose. Lana took the ball absently and threw it but whatever was bothering Lana appeared to have suddenly affected the dog as well because Portia sat down and, like her mistress, stared at the house.

An inner force compelled Lana to walk towards the front door. She went reluctantly, her heart hammering. Her twelve-year-old mind was trying to tell her not to be foolish but her heart knew. Something was badly amiss. As she opened the front door and heard her mother's soft sobbing, Lana went cold. The sympathetic murmurings of the stranger screamed a warning. Moving slowly, as if in a dream, Lana willed herself to walk towards the lounge. She did not want to know why her mother was crying but she was helplessly in the grip of fatalistic curiosity. A terrible trembling started suddenly and she shook uncontrollably.

The man saw her standing by the door of the lounge. 'Oh, my dear. You run along.'

'No!' It was wrung from Karen. She held out her arms to Lana. 'Come here, darling.'

On leaden feet, Lana moved to where her mother sat. 'What's wrong, Mummy? What is it?'

But she knew before her mother told her. She knew it was dreadful, she knew it had to do with her father and she knew, as her heart broke, that things would never be the same again.

Terence Parker-Brown waited with embarrassed impatience as Karen and Lana Devereaux faced the first few awful minutes of despair. He had never broken this kind of news to anyone in his life and was ill-prepared and unqualified for the task. A telephone call from the Home Office at eight the previous evening had sent him reluctantly to the Devereaux residence near Sevenoaks. Terence had answered the persistent ringing, hating whoever it was for interrupting an extremely good wildlife program.

'Taylor here.'

Terence had groaned inwardly. Taylor – Terence probably knew his first name but could never be bothered to think of it – was too fond of getting mixed up with international politics. Privately, Terence referred to him as 006½. The man only ever phoned him at home, always spoke as though he were fearful of being overheard, usually sent Terence, or one of his overworked operatives, on a wild goose chase, inevitably avoided responsibility when something went wrong but, on those few occasions where congratulations were called for, was there with his hand out. He had absolutely no business interfering in African affairs, a fact he studiously ignored. Unfortunately, he was also the nephew of Terence's boss.

'Oh yes, good evening,' Terence said without enthusiasm.

'Not interrupting you am I?'

'It's our bridge night,' Terence lied.

No apology. The man never apologised. 'Bit worrying this Malawi thing.'

'Only for Malawians,' Terence answered sourly.

'My dear chap! What about the missing Englishman?'

'He was half French,' Terence growled. He had spent some time after Martin Flower's call finding out what he could about John Devereaux. It hadn't been much. Terence waited. Taylor didn't disappoint him.

'Er . . . yes, quite, dear boy, but the FCO will need to know . . . I mean, after all, you don't want a scandal. Could prove very embarrassing for someone, don't you think?'

'Typical!' Terence thought, irritated. Taylor never mentioned his uncle. He just made sure that you knew he had personal reasons for interfering.

Taylor was still whittering on. '. . . can't be too careful, old man. Who knows what these chappies get up to once they're out of England.'

Terence had had enough. Taylor was a blithering halfwit but he was like a terrier with a grip on a bull's nose. He had to be shaken off. 'What are you suggesting?'

The man huffed happily. 'Well, dear boy, far be it for me to tell you how to run your office.'

But you will, you half-arsed, moronic buffoon! With that uncharacteristic but thoroughly satisfying thought behind him, Terence's voice went silky. He knew from experience that the only way to get Taylor off his back was to pretend to be interested in what he had to say. 'Not at all, old man, two heads and all that.'

Taylor did what Terence expected. With his voice lowered to nearly a whisper, he rattled off a series of suggestions which sounded to Terence as if he were reading from a list. 'The family don't know yet. Get someone out to Sevenoaks to tell them.' A pause.

'Lost your place?' Terence thought nastily.

But the man was only pausing for breath. 'No, better still, go yourself. Have a snoop – the man must have a study – check it out, his wife won't mind, she'll be too upset to stop you. Grab that opportunity, Terence, grab that opportunity.'

Terence Parker-Brown gritted his teeth.

'Phone bills, locked drawers, invoices, go through the lot. You know the drill, I'm sure.'

Terence let that go.

'Devereaux was working for a company called PAGET. You'll have to let them know of course.'

'Of course,' Terence said faintly.

'Yes, yes, quite. I'm sure you were planning to.'

'In the morning?' Terence asked timidly.

The sarcasm was lost on Taylor. 'Stall that. We don't want his wife surrounded by well-meaning friends; they'll get in the way. I want his study turned over. A man like Devereaux would be meticulous. Bring out anything that looks even remotely contentious. We're up a blind alley here.'

'The family should be told immediately.'

'Tell them yourself. Half a day won't hurt. You can always say you were trying to verify it.'

It crossed Terence's mind that Taylor was being unusually forceful. Taylor usually distanced himself from personal involvement. Terence wanted to know why. 'Who told you about Devereaux?'

'My dear chap, do you mind?'

Parker-Brown grinned. The way to Taylor's mouth was to first ask a question you knew he wouldn't answer, then hit him with the one you wanted. The man's mind was usually so busy wondering if he'd done the right thing refusing to answer the first question that he invariably blabbed more than you needed with the second. 'Well then, what's your interest?'

Taylor obliged him immediately. 'We don't want the press on it. Banda's visiting Britain next month and is scheduled to meet Her Majesty *and* the PM. The visit will be difficult enough as it is. Britain has billions tied up in joint ventures in Malawi and Banda's well behind with royalty and dividend payments. He knows he'll be under pressure. If he gets bad press he'll use it as an excuse, you know what these people are like.'

'Money,' Terence thought. 'It's always down to money.' He knew he could simply ignore Taylor's phone call and go ahead as planned – inform PAGET in the morning and leave them to deal with the family, forget Devereaux, who had clearly fallen foul of something other than politics, and leave the entire Malawi issue in Martin Flower's capable hands. He sighed. Taylor, he knew, would not let it go, especially since the Home Office had, on this occasion, a vested interest in containing any possible media circus.

'Are you still there, old boy?'

'Sorry.' Terence wasn't. 'Just wool gathering. I'll get onto it, leave it with me.'

He had meetings he couldn't put off in the morning and early afternoon. In truth, he knew he was stalling. Impartial as his profession required him to be, he did not relish the task of shattering the lives of Devereaux's family. Now, as he stared down at the two distraught people on the sofa, he was wondering how long it would be before he could decently request a look in the missing geologist's study.

Karen raised her tear-stained face. 'Thank you, Mr Parker-Brown,' she said quietly, earning his respect with her dignity. 'I'm sure you're a busy man. We'll be fine on our own.'

Terence cleared his throat. 'I'm sorry to ask this now but do you mind if I have a look in your husband's study?'

'Why?' She was surprised and it showed. 'Why are you here at all?'

Parker-Brown wondered how much to tell her. 'We don't normally get involved,' he said gently. 'To tell the truth, we'd rather not.' He glanced at the child who was observing him with wide and solemn eyes. A pretty child, about twelve he guessed, a girl who would one day grow into a beautiful young woman. Her scrutiny disturbed him. He took a deep breath and sought refuge in professional misinformation. 'There's been an attempted coup in Malawi. Under the circumstances, anyone unaccounted for must be investigated by us.'

'Surely you don't think that John . . .' Karen's voice broke.

'Daddy was working out there,' the child said stonily, surprising Terence with her grasp of the situation. 'You won't find anything in his study.'

She appeared set to challenge him and Parker-Brown was disconcerted. 'I'm sure I won't, my dear, but I'm afraid I still have to look.'

The girl opened her mouth to argue but Karen Devereaux stood suddenly and said coldly, 'Very well, follow me.'

As he shut himself in the study he heard the child's voice outside. 'I don't care. I'm waiting here,' and her mother's reply, 'Very well, darling, I'll phone Uncle Bernard.'

Uncomfortably aware that on the other side of the solid oak door waited a mutinous but grieving little girl, Terence searched John's study thoroughly, finding nothing more noteworthy than a collection of old ceramic toothpaste jars in a glass cabinet and a letter, written in French, from someone who was obviously a relative inviting the Devereaux to a family reunion next month in Paris. In a locked drawer in the desk – which Parker-Brown expertly picked – he found a folder and scanned the contents. A letter written to PAGET from Minister Matenje, introducing himself and authorising a preliminary

survey seeking to establish the presence of oil in
Malawi; a response from PAGET to the effect that,
in their opinion, such a survey would be a waste of
money; and a second letter from Matenje asking
what progress had been made. The correspondence
was interesting only because Matenje had insisted
the survey be conducted without Banda's knowledge. Parker-Brown photographed all three letters
to give Taylor something to do.

Searching other people's belongings was nothing new to Terence. Putting everything meticulously back in its place was. The need to do so
irritated him but he knew he could never face
those large serious eyes if he didn't.

She was waiting for him, sitting on the floor
and leaning back against an antique grandfather
clock. Her eyes told him she did not like him poking around her father's belongings. 'What were you
looking for?' she demanded.

The absence of Devereaux's body annoyed Terence. He did not like messy mysteries. He realised,
however, that it could work to his advantage in this
situation. 'Anything that can help us find your
father . . .' He left it unspoken: dead or alive.

'He's not dead,' she stated flatly. 'I would be able
to feel it if he were.'

Something akin to sympathy finally squeezed at
Parker-Brown's hardened heart. Death is especially
hard on the young, particularly so when there is no
proof. He was no policeman, had no experience of
mysterious disappearances, no knowledge of the
criminal mind. John Devereaux was, he believed,

an honest, upright and thoroughly nice man. He was also, in Terence Parker-Brown's opinion, as dead as a dodo. 'Could you call your mummy please?' he said lamely. 'God,' he thought, 'what a shitty job this is.'

'Haven't we met before?'

Lana came back to the present with a jolt. The man beside her had said something. 'I beg your pardon?'

He smiled and she noticed how it changed his hard, craggy features – softened them somehow. 'I asked if we'd met before.' He shrugged apologetically for having disturbed her. 'You look very familiar somehow.'

His accent was South African through a throat made gravelly by smoking. He looked to be in his mid-fifties, thickset, iron grey hair and faded blue eyes. He had one of those moustaches which reminded Lana of a scrubbing brush. His face was a contradiction, craggy, weather-beaten and hard, but there was an element of open boyishness too. His eyes showed humour and intelligence but ruthlessness – or was it competence – lurked at the back. They watched her now, waiting for a response to his question. 'I don't think so,' she replied.

The man gave a wry smile and Lana turned back to the window. She knew the effect she had on men. Her grandfather's prediction, that she would break hearts, had not been far out. Tall and slim, intelligent and practical, she bore her beauty with an unassuming acceptance that was in itself endearing. She made no effort to enhance the bounty with which she had been born. Not because none was needed, which it wasn't, but because she couldn't be bothered. Her dark curly hair was cropped very short, but tendrils still crept enchantingly around her face. Pale alabaster skin which had never experienced the trauma of teenage acne stretched taut over high cheekbones and an aquiline nose. Winged dark brows over eyes the colour of lapis lazuli and framed by thick black lashes. A mouth ready to smile and, when it did, the smile reached her eyes and glowed there long after it had left her mouth. Jawline sculptured by a maestro and a slender neck added elegance to a face already rich in beauty.

Dismissing the man beside her from her thoughts, her mind drifted again.

Events over the weeks after that dreadful day came to her in fragments. There were whole chunks of memory wiped clean. She supposed there was nothing much to remember. Grief and rage overtook her and life was a blur of trying not to cry or lose hope, forcing herself to eat and sleep, spending hour after hour high in her favourite tree staring up the lane, willing her father's car to turn into view, even though she knew it was in the garage at the side of the house. She and her mother each put on a brave face for the sake of the other, as well as for all the well-meaning friends who visited them.

Every morning she would sigh and think, 'What an awful dream,' only to be confronted by an inescapable reality, and the grief would come back as strongly as before.

She had returned to school, at her own request, after three days. It was preferable to the mental isolation of staying at home. Her friends offered sympathy and macabre interest. Her teacher pussy-footed around her, determined to make allowances, until Lana snappily told her she needn't bother, her father wasn't dead, and could she please have extra homework so she could catch up. Shocked, the teacher complied.

The house was full of horribly formal flower arrangements and horribly formal people, both of which Lana banned from her bedroom. Her grand-parents came and went, one grief-stricken pair from France – her French grand-pere flamboyantly expressing *cri de coeur* for all to see, while her English grandmother tried to keep a stiff upper lip and failed. Her mother's parents came from South Africa, but, shocked as they were, they were more concerned for their daughter's grief than anything else. Uncle Bernard was there often, the only one willing to mention her father by name for which Lana was profoundly grateful since everyone else avoided mentioning him at all – almost as though he'd never existed. Aside from Uncle Bernard, Lana wished all the other visitors would go to hell. The thought both pleased and shocked her.

Sometimes she felt she was the adult and all the rest were children.

162

Finally they all left and Lana and her mother began the long climb back. Bernard Pickstone came to see them again in June, three weeks after Parker-Brown's visit, a sober expression on his usually cheerful face. 'Come over here, Lala,' he was the only person Lana permitted to call her anything but Lana, 'I have something to tell you and your mother.' He patted the sofa beside him.

Lana adored her Uncle Bernard – although he was not her real uncle – because he spoke to her as her parents did: like an adult. She sat next to him and leaned against the comforting bulk of his side as he put his arm around her.

'You remember I told you that I'd sent someone out to Malawi to see if they could find your father?'

Lana nodded. Karen Devereaux leaned towards him. 'You've heard from him?'

Bernard pulled a wry face. 'He's back in London. I'm sorry, Karen, he's not much wiser than when he left.' Bernard handed Karen three sheets of paper. 'Here's his report, my dear.'

Lana waited impatiently for her mother to go through the pages, searching for any sign of hope in her mother's face. It seemed to take an age for her to read and Lana was fidgeting with anxiety by the time her mother lifted her eyes. 'You can read this if you like, darling. It doesn't tell us much. No-one seems to know anything.'

Bernard tightened his arm around Lana. 'You see, little one, since the attempted coup, the local people have been frightened. Even if they knew anything about your father the chances are they would be scared to say so. No-one wants President Banda to think they're not loyal. Frankly,' Bernard looked over to Karen, 'I believe the government is telling the truth. Anyone who knew anything about the survey is dead.' He looked horrified by his own words. 'I mean of course, Minister Matenje and his followers.'

Karen rose and paced the room. 'I know what you meant, Bernard.' She spun to face him. 'What about the British High Commission out there? What do they think?'

Bernard looked disgusted. 'Misadventure,' he spat out.

Karen's mouth went tight. 'Misadventure!' She could not believe she heard him correctly. 'This report . . .' she slapped her hand against the three sheets of paper, '. . . says Robin Cunningham was washed up near Karonga. His assistant was pulled from the water by local fishermen near Nkhata Bay. That's 160 kilometres south, Bernard.' She stared at him, too angry to be cautious with words for her daughter's sake. 'Both men's wrists showed signs that, at some stage prior to drowning, they had been bound with rope. For God's sake, Bernard, what went on out there?'

Bernard went to say something but Karen gave him no time to respond.

'John's assistant . . .' she consulted the report, 'Kadamanja. He was found dead on a deserted beach on the Tanzanian side of the lake, fifty kilo- metres east of Karonga. He had clearly been hit by

something or somebody; his skull was fractured.'
Karen paced again, rattling the report in her right
hand. 'The coroner blames rocks. Rocks, Bernard!'
She was back in front of him again. 'I can just
accept that rocks might fracture a skull if the boat
ran aground in rough weather. I can't accept the
rope burns were caused by rocks. What does this
coroner think we are – idiots?'

Bernard knew her anger was not directed at
him. He held out his free arm and Karen came to
him and curled against his other side. 'They were
all alive when they went into the water,' she said in
a small voice. 'Oh God, Bernard, why?'

'I'm sorry to be so persistent but I'm convinced
we've met somewhere before.'

Lana turned to her fellow passenger, ready to be
curt. She had no interest in being chatted up by
him.

'My apologies. I tend to get talkative on aero-
planes. Relieves the boredom.' He smiled disarm-
ingly. 'You're English aren't you?'

He was regarding her with nothing more than
friendly interest. She relented. 'Yes I'm English. My
mother is South African though.'

'Ah!' He nodded. 'Perhaps it's your mother I
have met.'

'Perhaps.' Lana didn't think so. Her looks were
her father's.

'Have you been to Malawi before?'

She shook her head. 'First time.'

'What brings you to The Warm Heart of Africa?' He wore a quizzical look, as though he were still trying to place her.

'Just a holiday,' Lana said evasively.

'Do you have friends there?' He laughed suddenly. 'Don't mind me, I'm just naturally nosy.'

Lana relaxed slightly. He seemed harmless enough. 'No, I don't have friends there. I've always wanted to visit Malawi. My mother told me about it years ago. I believe it's very beautiful.'

'Beautiful?' He frowned, as though this were a new thought. 'I suppose it is. Hard to say really. I've lived there thirty years. I find Europe beautiful.' He picked up his newspaper, smiled at her and began to read it.

Seven years after John Devereaux's disappearance – Lana could never accept that he had gone – he was declared officially dead. It seemed such a final act. Legally alive one minute, legally dead the next. Up until then she had held on to the hope that one wonderful day he would come swinging into the house as if he'd never left. She always referred to him as though he were still alive – 'When Daddy gets back; Daddy will; Daddy is', peppered her conversations. Grief counsellors had explained to a worried Karen that it was a normal denial for a child who had no body, no coffin, no burial to assist in the acceptance process.

Seven years later, all that abruptly changed. A piece of paper, an official declaration, a rubber stamp, and John Devereaux was no more. Lana was shocked by the impersonal nature of it all but in truth, she had to admit it helped. She was finally able to say 'Daddy was', without the dreadful thought that she was, in some way, being disloyal. It was like the final piece in a seven-year-old jigsaw had finally been found, slotted into place and the puzzle was no longer a challenge, it had become a complete picture.

She was nineteen years old, in her first year of university and, despite finally acknowledging that her father was dead, she was still consumed by a burning need to know what happened to him and inwardly vowed, 'One day I will know the truth.' The determination to know what happened in Malawi never went away. No-one, not even her mother, guessed at the strength of this tenacious, single-minded pledge to herself.

Life, so it seemed, picked Lana up and took her with it. She lost her virginity one freezing winter's evening to a fellow student with brooding eyes and warm, gentle hands. They had been to the pub and, halfway through the evening she had looked over at his sensitive face and seen the longing in his eyes. She was ready, her body told her that, waiting for the right time and man. 'Yes,' she thought, hugging the knowledge to herself, scared by the power of yes or no in her mind over the need in those dark eyes. On the way to his college, huddled together for warmth, her decision translated to him – she had no idea how – and what had been an arm offering warmth became a possessive arm secure in what was to come. They made love in his room, on a bed which squeaked its protest and informed anyone passing in the corridor what was happening behind the closed door. The student wanted her to move in with him. Lana declined and the relationship went sour. All she felt was a profound sense of relief which she could not explain. She put it down to youth.

In the back of her mind though, she knew she would never be ready for commitment to a relationship until she had lost the excess baggage she always carried with her of her father's disappearance.

To keep fit more than anything else, she worked her way up to a black belt in defensive karate. The instructor spent the first six weeks trying to get into her pants. When he finally realised that he would never get inside her flat, let alone her pants, he went out of his way to make training as difficult as he could for her. Challenged, Lana gritted her teeth, worked harder than anyone and rose through the ranks, earning grudging respect from the other students. When the day finally came that she was able to fling the instructor flat on the mat, she stood over him and, without any undue breathlessness, said calmly, and with no trace of sarcasm, 'Thank you. Without your help I could never have done that.' She walked from the gym with her head held high and never went back. She wondered occasionally why, after putting herself through all that training, she simply dropped it. She put it down to experience.

She also knew that a woman travelling on her

own in Africa was likely to be a lot safer if she possessed a black belt in karate than if she didn't!

She learned – much to the discomfort of anyone who lived within a one mile radius – to play the bagpipes. When pressed by her mother as to why, she would grin and answer, 'To bother people.' The truth was that the sound of the bagpipes always stirred something ancient within her, although with a South African mother and a half-French father, she had absolutely no idea from where it came. She put it down to one of nature's aberrations.

And one of nature's aberrations it had stayed. Whichever way she looked at it, she could not think of a single benefit – in Malawi terms – other than developing healthy lungs which she thought might come in handy at some stage.

She developed a passion for Indian food and nearly drove her mother mad whenever she came home for weekends by insisting on cooking up something spicy. Karen, a quiche and salad disciple from way back, had no taste for her daughter's heavy hand with the olive oil bottle and fresh chillis. Leftovers were given to Portia once Lana had returned to London, until that unfortunate animal developed an ulcer and spent her remaining days on a diet of porridge and milk. Lana put that down to Portia's age since her mother lacked the courage to confess.

In short, Lana Devereaux was perfectly well-adjusted, happy, ambitious, intelligent, slightly quirky and beautiful. She was also consumed by a need to know what went wrong in Malawi and was perfectly well aware that qualifications and skills acquired were all very well but really, all she was doing was filling in her time until she was ready to go there.

She was not delaying. Lana knew that maturity was a prerequisite for her proposed journey. She had no idea what the trip might achieve, if, in fact, it achieved anything at all. She had to be prepared for disappointment as well as grief. So, in her own patient and determined way, she waited for the moment to arrive when she would know it was time to go.

She graduated with a Bachelor of Science (Honours) degree, majoring in Applied Geology. Bernard offered her a job at PAGET which she readily accepted. One day, nearly six months later, Lana fell in love with a Fat Boy. It was the most beautiful thing she had ever seen. Black and gleaming chrome, its winged Harley Davidson shield proclaiming its pedigree, as soon as she saw it Lana knew she had to have it. The practicalities never entered into the equation. Britain's weather or how to ride a motorbike wearing a tight skirt were not even considered. Lana grimly ignored the former and took to wearing skirts split up the front. Weaving through London's traffic, shapely legs exposed, she caused more than one near miss as drivers craned their necks to see better. Lana didn't care. She was in love. And like any woman in love, she was blind to the negatives.

Her mother, having raised her eyebrows slightly,

steadfastly ignored the machine. Portia, who was going deaf, on her first introduction to the Fat Boy, fled under a rhododendron bush and refused to come out. That was okay. Lana was, by now, living away from home and the disapproval of her family was something she could live with.

She had been working for PAGET for almost a year when her mother telephoned and invited her down to Sevenoaks for the weekend. Mystified, Lana said she'd come. She spent many weekends at home but always at her own suggestion. Her mother never nagged her to come home for which she was grateful. Arriving on Friday evening, Lana was not surprised to find Bernard Pickstone there. Always a close friend of the family, for the past few years he had been spending more and more time at the house.

Bernard had finally let his beloved wife, Maggie, go ten years earlier. With her life support system turned off, he had sat with her while her body shut down. It had only taken a couple of hours. Bernard had been devastated by the swiftness of it all. 'Her body has been ready to go for a long time,' the doctor had told him gently.

When John Devereaux disappeared, Bernard had been a rock in the lives of Karen and Lana, there whenever they needed a shoulder, a strong arm or just a sympathetic ear. In turn, they freely gave him their compassion, support and understanding. Over the past couple of years it seemed to Lana that her mother and Bernard had developed an even deeper friendship than before, one that had strengthened with shared grief.

Karen had said little during dinner, completely unlike her usual breezy self. Bernard too had been quieter than usual. With dinner over, the three of them took coffee and liqueurs into the lounge where Karen, giving a clear sign of nervous energy, paced the room incessantly.

'For God's sake, Mummy, do sit down.'

Karen shot a glance at Bernard. Lana turned her head slowly and stared at him. He had a strangely apprehensive, yet pleased look. A smile of understanding suddenly spread across her face. 'You two are an item!' she said happily. 'How marvellous.'

The relief on her mother's face was almost comical.

Bernard lumbered to his feet and stood in front of Lana. 'You don't mind?'

Lana looked up at him fondly. Next to her mother and father, she had loved Bernard best all her life. When Maggie died she had cried, not for Maggie, but for the grief she knew Bernard was feeling. 'I think . . .' she said slowly, '. . . that this is the best news I've heard in a long time.'

'Oh, darling, are you sure?' Her mother was still anxious. 'We were worried that you . . . well, you and your father were very close.'

Lana rose, went to her mother and put her arms around her. 'Daddy has been gone a long time. You deserve some happiness, both of you. I'm very pleased, honestly.'

Later that night, lying in her old bedroom, Lana wondered if she was pleased. Her mother was . . . well, her mother. Uncle Bernard was Uncle

Bernard. They fitted into different slots in her life. Now she had to rearrange things in her head and fit them into the same slot as each other. How did she feel about it? Strange? Resentful? Happy? She tossed in bed and tried to look at it as honestly as possible. Her mother and Bernard had been friends for years. They had both known loss. They got along with each other very well. Neither of them, as far as she knew, had so much as looked at another person since they lost their respective partners. Were they in love? Or was this a marriage of companionship? She couldn't ask them. In the end she concluded that she had mixed feelings about it. It did feel strange, there was probably the teeniest bit of resentfulness inside her but she was happy for them. It was the best she could do.

Over the next two years she could see how right the marriage was for both of them. They loved each other in a quiet sort of way. The gaiety and passion which had been there between her father and mother was missing, instead there was contentment and companionship. Seeing them together, especially when they went upstairs to go to bed, still gave her a strange feeling. Most of the time though, she accepted their togetherness as being the most natural thing in the world.

Lana received steady promotion at PAGET, earned on merit and hard work with no hint of favouritism over her colleagues. She did field work in some of the most inhospitable places on earth, living rough with no complaints. Her on-again, off-again relationship with London life meant there was no time for long-standing commitments with the opposite sex. She had only once allowed a relationship to develop into something deeper. The experience left a bad taste and a reluctance to repeat it. In any event, Lana felt deep inside that she was simply cooling her heels for the main event. She never lost the belief that, when the moment was right, when she was ready, she would go to Malawi. She was twenty-seven years old before that time came.

'Good morning, Miss Bagshaw, wonderful day.' Lana strode into the foyer of PAGET and paused in front of the reception desk, as she always did, to pass a few pleasantries with the indomitable Cecilia Bagshaw. Years of disapproval, suspicion and professional misery were etched on Miss Bagshaw's face and she tended to over-compensate by applying too much make-up. No-one at PAGET possessed the courage to tell her it wasn't working except Lana, and even she trod warily and chose her words carefully. Miss Bagshaw's disposition had not improved, in fact, it had grown worse. However, she had a very soft spot in her heart for John Devereaux's daughter, mainly because she mistook Lana's directness for friendship whereas all Lana was trying to do was tone down the first impression visitors received on entering the building.

'Welcome back, Lana. How was New Guinea?'

By way of an answer, Lana slapped a magazine down on the reception counter. 'Page twelve,' she said briefly. 'Soon as I saw it I thought it would suit you.'

Miss Bagshaw found the page quickly. 'I don't know.' She eyed the article about ageing gracefully with some doubt. 'I've never worn pink lipstick.'

Anyone else would have backed off at that, if indeed they had the courage to show Miss Bagshaw the article in the first place. Not Lana. 'Rubbish!' She produced a lipstick. 'Knew you'd say that so I bought you one to try.'

'Oh, Lana, how kind, I couldn't possibly accept . . .' Miss Bagshaw's hand crept out and closed around the gift. 'Well maybe I'll just try it.'

'Good,' Lana said. She intended to coerce the staff of PAGET into commenting on how much the new colour suited the woman. Anything was better than the slash of bright red Cecilia Bagshaw had favoured for years. 'And as for New Guinea, I've known worse.'

Lana had just returned from three months in the highlands of Papua New Guinea. She had lived in a temporary bush camp near the Mubi River, where the canopy of rainforest dripped water constantly, the terrain was vertical and the temperature fluctuated from suicidally humid to homicidally hot and where best friends hated each other within days of arrival. She hadn't known worse. The continuous cloud cover made aerial photography impossible. The densely foliaged mountain region made access roads out of the question. The contractors and geologists arrived and left in helicopters. By the end of the first week Lana was wishing she had a couple of mountain goats for ancestors.

Sitting in her prefabricated hut, watching the drops of water falling monotonously, bored by constant inactivity due mainly to the interminable rain, unmotivated to join the others playing cards, Lana concentrated on a single droplet of water as it slid down a fat leaf, flared dramatically as it hung, trembling, on the edge then dropped onto the next leaf. 'What the hell am I doing here?' she asked herself.

A burst of masculine laughter came from the open mess tent. 'False,' she thought. 'They're as bored as I am.' Her mind flicked to her father. 'Dad never mentioned boredom. He must have experienced it, just never talked about it.' Then it hit her. It was time. She was ready. She didn't question it; she always knew it would happen this way. Now all she had to do was tell her mother and Bernard.

'An hour to go. That's Zimbabwe down there.'

Lana looked politely. Brown African bush, a couple of rivers, a mountain range and one small town. From 35,000 feet, it had no soul. 'Really,' she murmured, feeling he was waiting for her response.

'Ever been there?'

Her fellow passenger had tucked his newspaper into the pocket in front of him and lowered the folding tray. A stewardess was wheeling a refreshments trolley towards them. 'No, thank you,' Lana looked up and smiled at the woman before turning to the man at her side. 'No, I've never been there,' she replied.

He opened a plastic snack-pack and rummaged disinterestedly for something to take his fancy. 'Great country. Cecil Rhodes knew a good thing when he saw it.' He buttered a rock-hard scone and smeared it with jam. 'Malawi's different; more tropical.' He glanced over at her. 'In some parts anyway.'

'I'm looking forward to seeing it.'

'Are you going to the lake?'

'Doesn't everyone?'

He smiled. 'It's what attracts most of our visitors. How long have you got?'

'Two weeks.'

'Two weeks!' He shook his head in mock disapproval. 'Not enough time, my dear.'

'It's all I could get off work.'

'What do you do?'

'I'm a geologist.'

A shadow passed his eyes, fleeting and deep. 'How interesting,' he murmured. He put the scone in his mouth and took a bite.

Seeing he was occupied, Lana turned back to the window.

Lana had expected opposition to her plan. Her mother and, to a lesser extent, Bernard, had not disappointed her.

'Of all the harebrained schemes I've heard, this takes the cake.' Karen Devereaux-Pickstone literally strode around the room. 'Tell her, Bernard. Tell her to forget this foolishness.'

'I could send an investigator,' Bernard offered.

'You tried that, remember?' Lana smiled to take the sting out. 'This is something *I* have to do.'

'In God's name, why you?' Karen sat down, crossing her legs and throwing an imploring look towards Bernard.

'It was so long ago,' Bernard said. 'Have you really thought this through?'

'It's ridiculous,' Karen snapped. 'Thoughtless and selfish. Ridiculous.'

'Thank you, Mummy.'

'Tell her, Bernard.'

There were times when Bernard believed he knew Lana better than her own mother did. This was one of those times. 'I might be able to get a name for you. Someone at the High Commission out there.'

Karen fixed her husband with a stare hard enough to stop a charging buffalo. Bernard shrugged helplessly, started to smile, thought better of it and stared mournfully back.

'I'm going and that's that.' Lana set her jaw.

'Your father's assistant was called Kadamanja,' Bernard offered. He knew that look.

Silence was loud in the room. Bernard was frantically trying to think up an excuse to go and do something, anything, as long as it was away from here. Karen saw the determination on Lana's face and, although her mind was telling her she understood her daughter's need, her heart was scared for

Lana's safety. Something had been badly amiss in Malawi fifteen years earlier. Too many had died or simply disappeared. But she knew it was no use. Defeated, she looked at the practicalities. 'How long do you plan to be away?'

'Two weeks. That's all I can spare her,' Bernard said, startling himself with his note of authority. He had studiously avoided exercising any discipline over Lana, except in a work environment, because he was aware she would resent it. He knew her of old. Telling her not to do something always seemed to be taken up as a challenge. As a frustrated school-teacher once said to Karen and John, 'The only way to be certain your daughter will do something seems to be to expressly forbid her to do it.'

Bernard knew this was not true. It was senseless rules, rigid disciplines or unfair decisions which Lana immediately dissected, digested and spat out again in the form of an honest request for things to make sense. Even as a child, she appeared well aware of the consequences in going head to head with authority but this did not prevent her from doing so. Bernard respected this and loved her all the more for it and he could see why she wanted to go to Malawi. Bernard also loved her mother. Under these circumstances Bernard knew that he was somewhere between a rock and a hard place. Having contributed but one time-related directive, Bernard thought he should quit while he was ahead. He went outside to examine the roses even though Karen and Lana both told him in even tones that it was raining.

'Poor man,' Lana said, smiling fondly at the door which Bernard had quietly closed behind him.

'He hates confrontation,' Karen agreed. She turned to her daughter. 'Do you *really* have to do this, darling?'

'Don't you want to know what happened?'

Karen looked troubled. 'I always believed I did. Lately . . .' she shrugged and spread her hands. 'Oh I don't know, Lana. Lately I think it's best if we let sleeping dogs lie.'

'I can understand that, Mummy, really I can.' Lana crossed to her mother and hugged her. 'Your life has moved on and I'm pleased for you.' She looked intensely into her mother's face. 'I made a vow fifteen years ago. I made it to Daddy. I won't rest until I find the truth. Please try and understand.'

Karen reached up and brushed Lana's cheek. 'I do understand, darling,' she said softly. 'But I won't sleep a wink until you're safely back in England.'

Lana stirred in her seat and sighed. What lay ahead? Heartache? Frustration? Was this an emotional wild goose chase? Thanks to Bernard she had two names. Tim Gilbey at the British High Commission in Lilongwe and Moffat Kadamanja in Karonga, son of her father's assistant. She wondered about his Christian name. As far as she knew, Moffat was a Scottish surname. David Livingstone's wife had been a Mary Moffat. 'Strange kind of name for an African,' she mused. She shrugged mentally. Strange name or not, would Moffat Kadamanja or Tim Gilbey be able to help?

'Just starting our descent,' the man in the next seat said unnecessarily. She had felt the engines throttling back. 'Gets a little bumpy sometimes.'

Lana smiled at him. 'Clear air turbulence I guess.' The sky was endlessly blue but the aircraft began to judder as though they were flying through storm clouds. Next to taking off, she wasn't particularly fond of landing either. To take her mind off the bumps, she asked, 'What do you do in Malawi?'

'I farm tobacco about a hundred kilometres north of Lilongwe.'

'Tobacco?' She raised her eyebrows. 'Is there *any* market left for tobacco?'

'You'd be surprised,' he said. 'It might be a dirty word in some places but cigarettes are very much the go throughout the Third World, all over Asia and the Middle East and in most of the Eastern Bloc countries.' He paused, then asked, 'Do you smoke?'

Lana shook her head. 'Never had the urge.'

'Bright lady,' he commented. 'I can't kick the habit.' The aeroplane hit an air pocket and dropped alarmingly. When they were flying straight and level again he gave her a lopsided grin. 'Besides, I'm more likely to die flying than smoking.'

Lana laughed. His humour was wry and she enjoyed it. He was a man with hard edges, she could see that. It didn't bother her. Very often, in her experience, the harder the edge the softer the centre. Then she remembered he had lied about delaying the flight. She liked mavericks but she liked them honest. Caution was the word in her head.

'Perhaps I should introduce myself,' he said suddenly. 'After all, I'd hate to die next to a stranger.' He put out his hand sideways. 'Karl, with a K not a C, Henning at your service.'

Lana took it. 'Lana Devereaux,' she said, shaking his hand.

His smile froze, and so did his eyes. 'Devereaux,' he said softly. 'Did you say Devereaux?'

'My father was French.'

He closed his eyes a fraction longer than a blink. When he opened them there was nothing but friendly interest in them. 'I think it's a charming name.'

'Thank you.' She wondered if she'd imagined it. He seemed to be having trouble collecting his thoughts.

'I met a Devereaux once,' he said quietly, looking at her intently. 'In Blantyre actually. He was a geologist too.'

Lana's heartbeat quickened. 'John Devereaux?'

He nodded. 'I believe that was his name, yes.'

She could not believe her luck. 'He was my father,' she said quickly.

'I see,' he said slowly, still nodding. 'That's perhaps why I thought you were familiar. I can see the family resemblance.'

'Did you know him well?'

He pulled at his earlobe. 'Not really. Only spoke

to him briefly at the hotel. He was heading north as I recall; something about a seismic survey of the lake.'

Lana felt something like panic well in her. Her father's death had taken so long to accept. Now, talking to this man Henning, it seemed to bring him back, make him real again. It was an oddly disturbing feeling. She wondered why Karl Henning would remember her father if he only met him once. 'He must have made quite an impression on you,' she commented.

His expression didn't change. 'I never forget a face or a name.'

She let that go but decided to probe further. 'He disappeared in Malawi,' she said quietly. 'No-one ever found out what happened to him.'

He was regarding her with unreadable eyes. 'I'm sorry, I heard he'd gone missing. Is that why you're here? To try and find out?'

He sounded sincere but instinct warned her not to say too much. 'Not really. It was so long ago. I just wanted to be where he had been.' She smiled suddenly, brushing away her melancholy. 'I expect that sounds morbid.'

'No.' He looked at her seriously. 'I might be able to help you though. I keep a yacht moored up north. I was planning to do some sailing next week. Perhaps you'd like to join me.' He produced a slightly dog-eared business card. 'If you come with me you might meet someone who knew him. Give me a call if you can make it,' he said lightly.

Lana took the card, looked at it briefly before putting it into her shirt pocket. 'Thank you,' she said, not intending to take him up on it. 'That's very kind of you.'

He pointed past her. 'There's Lilongwe.'

She looked. From the air the city appeared fresh and bright, spacious yet orderly. They were a few thousand feet above the ground and she had a good look at ultra-modern buildings, green lawns, wide, tarred roads and sprawling houses. 'I didn't expect this.'

He smiled, amused. 'Most people don't. Lilongwe is a model city. There are very few like it throughout this continent. Our previous government was determined to make Lilongwe different, a showpiece for post colonial Africa.'

'Dr Banda you mean?'

'It was his dream,' Karl Henning told her, 'to build a symbol of independence.' He smiled. 'It may surprise you that much of the initial architectural work and funding for our new capital actually came from South Africa.'

'When?' She was fascinated. For a good thirty years, under that country's white regime, South Africa had been the big bad wolf of Africa. Generosity towards northern neighbours was seldom reported, giving rise to international belief that it never happened. Lana knew this to be untrue. A magazine she remembered seeing in her father's study told how South Africa flew petrol to Malawi during a critical shortage in 1980 – eleven plane loads a day for two weeks – until the rail line connecting Malawi to the Mozambique port of Beira could be considered safe from RENAMO terrorists who consistently blew it up to prevent FRELIMO troops from using it. The cost? Regular wholesale prices for the fuel, nothing for the cartage. She mentioned it to Karl, concluding, 'Malawi and South Africa seem to enjoy closer than usual relations.'

Karl nodded. 'When Banda came to power he took pains to stress that his struggle to free this country from colonial rule had nothing to do with racism. He created a bridge between South Africa and her black neighbours, giving them all a common meeting ground. He received a great deal of international flak but stuck to his guns. He always claimed that quiet and reasoned consultation was better than confrontation.' Karl smiled. 'Pretoria loved him.'

'So they helped him?' Lana found she was enjoying listening to Karl Henning. He spoke in a measured way, giving no indication how he felt personally, imparting information in such a way that she could make up her own mind.

'Lilongwe was a way of developing the north of Malawi. South Africa saw the sense of that. Banda always said Malawi wasn't poor, just the victim of neglect. Having a brand new capital city, encouraging foreign investment, bringing in expatriates, it was all part of a larger picture to kick-start the economy. Lilongwe was on the drawing-board right from the start.'

'1964?' Lana shook her head. 'As far back as that? He must have been quite a president.'

Karl looked serious. 'He was in the beginning.' He shrugged. 'Things change, people change.' He had a strangely sad look on his face. 'I don't know how or why it happens, it just does. One moment you're young and full of ideals, the next . . .' He stopped abruptly, as if he'd said too much. 'The money for Lilongwe was given in 1965.' He changed the subject smoothly. ' The master plan was designed by a Johannesburg consultancy. South Africa came up with nine million Kwacha.'

Lana wondered what it was he'd been about to say but she let it go. 'That's not really much is it? Even in 1965, nine million wasn't that much.'

'It was enough. Think big and solve pragmatically was the phrase.' He leaned forward and looked at the land beneath them. In the distance they could see the airport's control tower. 'It's worked too. We're all very proud of Lilongwe.' He leaned back again. 'Are you staying here?'

'In Lilongwe? Not tonight. I'm catching a connection to Blantyre.'

He appeared to think. 'I'm having a luncheon on Saturday at the farm. Would you like to come as my guest? It will give you a chance to meet people who have lived here all their lives.'

She considered it. 'I'm not certain of my movements.' She patted her shirt pocket. 'I've got your card, I'll call you.' She was hedging. She did not want to waste her precious fourteen days on socialising. She would go to Blantyre and see where that led.

They said goodbye inside the terminal building.

As he strode away, Lana frowned thoughtfully after him. There was something about him – she couldn't put her finger on it – something that made her wary. Once or twice she had seen something in his eyes, hardness or cunning, she wasn't sure which. The fact that he'd met her father was exciting. She had wanted to ask him more about it. What had stopped her? Lana always trusted her gut feel for people but this time her guts were in two minds.

Should she accept his invitation to lunch? Or the one to go sailing? It would give her a chance to ask about her father. Something had held her back. Had she dreamed of finding the truth about her father for so long now that, when the opportunity to do so presented itself, she withdrew from it in the fear that the truth might be too hard to take? As soon as she had that thought, Lana discarded it. She had never run from the truth. 'So what am I scared of?' The answer evaded her but she had the uncomfortable feeling that, whatever it was, Karl Henning made her uneasy and it just might have something to do with him.

NINE

The connecting flight to Blantyre was scheduled to leave a mere forty-five minutes after her arrival in Lilongwe. Lana barely had time to complete immigration, customs and security formalities before checking in at domestic departures and an announcement called passengers to board the aircraft. She hefted her shoulder bag and joined yet another queue. 'I hope it's a white pilot,' a woman said loudly to her husband, seemingly oblivious of uniformed airline staff at the gate who were black and well within earshot.

'How rude,' Lana thought. The ground crew acted as though they hadn't heard and were equally polite to the woman as to everyone else. 'How do they do that?' she wondered. She had seen it on visits to South Africa, bland politeness in the face of cruel or thoughtless remarks. Years ago, Lana had decided that the jibes went in and stayed in, one day to emerge in a rage too intense to control. She had always, even as a young child, experienced deep anger at thoughtless racism, not so much for the hurt it caused at the time but for the cancer it fed, a cancer of hatred which would ultimately extract vengeance on the innocent as well as the guilty. She was grimly amused to see that the pilot *was* black, as was his first officer, and that the woman, silenced by some furtive words delivered in an undertone by her husband, stayed on board.

The flight to Blantyre took an hour. Lana watched the passing scenery below, impressed – as her father had been on the ground fifteen years ago – by the ever changing land. 'Did Dad fly to Blantyre?' she wondered. PAGET had received very little information as to his activities once he arrived in Malawi. He had landed in Lilongwe but there was no evidence that he had then flown on to Blantyre. They only knew he had checked into the Mount Soche hotel and registered with the British High Commission office there. In that his assistant's body had been washed ashore in Tanzania, that Robin Cunningham and *his* assistant were known to have been working right up at the far north end of Lake Malawi, it was assumed that John Devereaux had based himself somewhere near Karonga and it was from there that he had disappeared. It was all they had.

Lana intended to follow in his footsteps as best she could. The British High Commission no longer had an office in Blantyre but she could at least spend a night in the same hotel as her father and then she intended to drive back to Lilongwe. There, she would make contact with Tim Gilbey, though she didn't expect he could help her, before heading north to Karonga. Her plans were vague and she was beginning to think that her mother had been right when she'd said, 'You'll gain nothing from this trip but heartache, darling. Why put yourself through all that?'

'Why indeed?' Lana asked herself. For the past fifteen years her determination to do it had made sense. Now she was here what did she hope to achieve? Sitting next to Karl Henning on the flight from South Africa had been a stroke of luck. Maybe she should accept his invitation, at least to lunch. What harm could that do?

Lana reached into her bag and brought out a map of Malawi. Spreading it open she retrieved Karl's card from her pocket. He said he farmed about a hundred kilometres north of Lilongwe. His card gave his address as Kasungu. She located it on the map. It was on the way to Karonga, she had to pass right through. 'That settles it,' she thought. 'I'll give him a call from Blantyre.'

The woman who had not wanted to fly with a black pilot was complaining loudly to one of the cabin crew that they were too low over the hills surrounding Blantyre. 'It's dangerous,' she whined. 'And the turbulence is making me ill.'

Lana marvelled at the Malawian stewardess's ability to remain polite, although the look on the young woman's face, as she turned away from the troublesome passenger, gave Lana the impression that if the woman were to be sick, the stewardess would happily rub her face in it.

Chileka Airport, some twenty kilometres north of Blantyre, had obviously been downgraded in terms of financial priority to make way for the new international terminal in Lilongwe. The two structures were like chalk and cheese. Chileka had the look of an ageing beauty queen, fading and cracked, a sad relic of former glory. A paint job inside did little to hide the indifference it had suffered in favour of its glamorous sister to the north. Lana went to the Avis counter and, after some discussion as to the validity of her International Driver's Licence, was handed the keys to a pre-booked hire car. As she walked out to the car park, smilingly refusing insistent young boys' offers to carry her suitcase, she wondered why most so-called Third World countries were bound up in such a stifling degree of red tape. It was the same all over the world. 'We're to blame,' her father had once said, having told her about some difficulties he'd encountered in Nigeria. 'The colonial powers introduced red tape and enforced it rigidly. All today's lot are doing is carrying on with it.' He had grinned at her in that way she loved so much, just before he said something contentious, scandalous or even a little bit naughty. 'I don't know who I'd like to kick up the bum most, the colonials or their bloody successors.'

Lana smiled at the memory. She felt very close to her father in this strange land. Had he walked where she walked now? Had he sat in the airport at Lilongwe as she had? Could her room at the Mount Soche be his room? And what about Karl Henning? He had met her father. It was a link, an exciting and totally unexpected link, and she wondered, as she occasionally did, if John Devereaux was watching over her now.

She got the hang of the car pretty quickly – a Subaru four-wheel drive sedan – and found her way into Blantyre with ease. The Mount Soche was at the end of the main street. Lana booked in, changed a traveller's cheque into local Kwacha and went straight up to her room on the third floor. Tired, she intended to shower, change, have a quick meal and then treat herself to the luxury of being able to stretch out in the queen-sized bed. It was four in the afternoon, local time, only two hours behind London, but her body said it had been awake too long. She had just opened her suitcase when the telephone rang.

'Hello.'

'Miss Devereaux?'

'Yes.'

'Ah, thank you. This is the reception desk. A Mr Gilbey is here to see you.'

Lana was surprised. Tim Gilbey was supposed to be in Lilongwe. 'Ask him to come up please.' She hung up amused. Bernard had obviously contacted the man and requested that he look out for her, bless him. She quickly splashed water over her face and hands and ran a comb through her hair. At the discreet knock on the door she went to open it. 'Mr Gilbey, this is most unexpected, please come in.'

He made no comment. Pale blue eyes regarded her carefully, the interest in them purely professional. Otherwise, his long face was expressionless. He appeared to be summing her up.

Lana stepped back and indicated he should come in. After a moment's hesitation, he moved past her, giving a brief nod. She realised he had made no attempt to introduce himself. He went to the window and peered out through the curtains. 'Long way down,' he said lazily. Then he turned to face her. 'Why are you here?' he asked bluntly.

Lana had been watching him with increasing wariness. He was tall and elegantly slim. Greying hair combed back and impeccably cut. His light brown suit fitted perfectly. Face lightly tanned, a long nose adding character over thinnish lips. He had a mole on the right corner of his mouth. Good-looking, about forty, and, she decided, for some reason best known to himself he didn't like her one little bit. 'Didn't Bernard tell you?'

'Bernard?' He was off balance and it showed.

'Bernard Pickstone. Didn't he explain?'

His face cleared. 'Ah yes, Bernard.' Hands in the pockets of his jacket he rocked back on his heels. He appeared to be waiting for her to say more.

Lana didn't oblige. She folded her arms and observed him impassively. He had never heard of Bernard, of that she was certain. Silence stretched between them.

It was Gilbey who broke the silence. 'Just refresh my memory,' he said.

Lana was in two minds. On one hand, he was with the British High Commission and, whether he liked her or not, he was here, presumably prepared to help and, as such, had to be considered an ally. But instinct warned her against him. What was he doing here if not at Bernard's request? Fatigue made her blunt. 'Mr Gilbey,' she said crisply, 'if you have anything to say I would appreciate it if you would do just that and leave. I've had a long flight and I'm tired.'

Anger flitted over his face. He was being dismissed and didn't like it. 'You're here to find out what happened to your father.' It was a statement, not a question.

Lana inclined her head. 'If I can.'

'Why?'

Annoyance surfaced from within her. 'Why do you think? He disappeared without a trace. We were not given a satisfactory explanation. I want some answers.'

He took three steps towards her, measured steps, his eyes on hers. Lana felt he was trying to intimidate her. She held his gaze, her face expressionless. He stopped just in front of her. 'I'd hate to see such a pretty girl get hurt.'

A prickle of fear ran through her. Then reason prevailed. 'He's a diplomat, for God's sake!' she thought. His manner angered her.

'Say what you've come to say and get the hell out of my room,' she snapped. 'If you're not prepared to help, why on earth did you bother to come up here?'

He smirked, his gaze hard. 'Enquiries about your father will only lead to trouble. No-one wants to know what happened to him and no-one cares. Have a nice holiday and go home, there's a good girl. You'd do well to take my advice.'

Lana felt he was deliberately trying to provoke her. But why? 'What is the High Commission trying to hide, Mr Gilbey? Some kind of bureaucratic bungle perhaps? I must say, your attitude surprises me. You can't stop me asking about my father – how dare you even try.' She glared at him. 'I don't like your advice. I've a good mind to report this conversation when I get back to London.'

He shrugged elaborately. 'Go ahead, it won't get you anywhere. All I'm trying to do is warn you –'

'Warn me, Mr Gilbey?' Lana smiled grimly. 'You did say *warn* me didn't you, Mr Gilbey?' When he made no response she went on. 'British diplomats don't *warn* people, Mr Gilbey, they *advise* them. What section are you in anyway?'

He was losing his temper, she could see a flush spreading from his neck to his face. 'Warn, advise, what's the damned difference? Okay, I'm advising you, does that make it more palatable?'

Lana took a deep breath. 'You can shove your advice, Mr Gilbey, preferably somewhere the sun don't shine,' she said in a hard voice. 'Now, if you've finished . . .' She walked to the door and opened it.

He followed and slammed it shut, leaning towards her, his breath smelling of strong peppermints. 'I came here today to give you some friendly advice.' He was struggling to control his temper and failing. 'Fine. You don't want my advice so I'll tell you straight. Keep your nose out of the past. I'm warning you, don't stir up trouble or you'll be the only one in it.'

'Are you actually threatening me, Mr Gilbey?'

Lana asked coldly. Without thinking about it, she was flexed and ready to take him if he came closer. She might be out of practice but she knew she could have him flat on the floor in a fraction of a second. The consequences of decking a diplomat could be dealt with later. Lana was on automatic pilot, her instincts telling her that Tim Gilbey was not above physical methods of persuasion when he was angry. His height gave him an advantage but she had already worked out where to grab him, which way to lean to get him off balance and where to throw him.

Something must have warned him. He stepped back out of her space. 'I'm telling you.' He tried to smile but his face wasn't in the mood. 'For your own good, go home where you belong and forget it. You'd do well to listen to me before it's too late.'

Lana had had enough. 'You'd do well to get your arse out of my room. I don't like being threatened, Gilbey, and I don't like being patronised either. Either give me your reasons or take a hike – your choice.'

He was watching her uncertainly. Lana realised he had more to say but wasn't about to give him an opener. He reached into his pocket, producing a packet of cigarettes and lighter. 'Don't even think of it,' she said tersely. 'I detest cigarette smoke.' She had given him ammunition to use against her.

He put a cigarette to his lips and lit it lazily. 'Hard luck,' he said around the cigarette, blowing smoke towards her. 'There are no rules as yet to say that I may not smoke in this room.'

Lana willed herself not to step back from the smoke. She stared at him, saying nothing. She knew the effect her angry eyes had, when they went from deep friendly blue to the colour of oxide on polished steel, hard and every bit as cold.

'Miss Devereaux,' he said finally, heavily sarcastic and unmoved by her stare. 'I could have you deported if I choose. One word in the right ear and you'd be on the next flight out.' He drew on his cigarette, inhaled, and blew smoke towards her again, his earlier loss of temper back under control. 'So listen carefully, Miss Devereaux. Your father disappeared during turbulent times in Malawi. Neither the Malawi Government nor the British wish to stir up old memories, do you understand what I'm saying?' He opened the door. 'You may not like my advice but I'm officially warning you off. I'll be observing you closely, Miss Devereaux.' He watched to see the effect of his words. When she still made no comment he shrugged. 'Don't say you weren't warned. If you end up in trouble, don't come crying to me.' Then he was gone.

Lana paced her room, furious and frustrated. She was also shaken. The man was a toad but there was something else about him which disturbed her. In her experience, people who worked in the diplomatic services never voiced personal opinions to anyone other than their closest friends. They never indicated that any one individual was responsible for any one thing, always taking cover behind a collective 'we', 'us' or 'they'. Gilbey had made frequent references to himself. Thinking about it, he was the most atypical diplomat Lana had ever met, not to mention the most unpleasant.

She had dealt with British Foreign Office diplomats on a number of occasions. Without exception, they turned the word diplomacy into an art form. One man in Oman stood out in her mind and she often wondered how he managed to remain polite in the face of what she now regarded as excessive stubbornness and a fair sprinkling of stupidity on her part.

PAGET had been invited to conduct a detailed survey of natural gas potential. PDO – Petroleum Development Oman – worried that their reservoirs of oil were running out, were looking at diversification possibilities. Lana wanted to be on the survey team. Bernard had advised her against going on the grounds that the Omani men would never deal with a woman. Against his better judgment, he allowed her to talk herself onto the team.

Two weeks into her job there, after a threatened walkout by Omani jug hustlers – men who work with the seismic crew and handle the geophones – who refused to take orders from a woman even if they were distilled through a front man, Lana, with a little advice from a charming British diplomat, could see going to Oman had been a mistake. The diplomat had been kind, sensitive and sympathetic, despite having to drive 500 kilometres into the desert to talk her into leaving and then escort her back to Muscat. As she was leaving the country, irritated by his blandness, she asked him if part of his training was to practise smiling while people were slapping his face. He had smilingly replied that it wasn't, wished her a pleasant journey and turned to leave. It was at that moment she caught sight of controlled hysteria in his eyes, a look which shamed her every time she thought about it. She acknowledged that, if ever she had needed a boot up the bum, it was then.

This man in Malawi, this Tim Gilbey character, had been threatening, rude *and*, more to the point, appeared to possess none of the professional detachment required for his position. The more she thought about it, the more angry she became. 'Bugger him,' she said to herself. 'I'll go to his office in Lilongwe, register my arrival and demand to see someone else.' The idea had merit. Lana was not in the habit of getting people into trouble but she expected, and demanded if the occasion warranted it, simple common courtesy.

Putting Tim Gilbey out of her mind she explored the room, discovered a mini-bar refrigerator concealed behind the wardrobe door, examined the contents, selected a bottle of Carlsberg Green Label and used the wall-mounted opener. She drank from the bottle. 'Not bad,' she thought. 'Could have done with a bit more maturation though.'

The telephone shrilled. 'If that's bloody Gilbey again I'm about ready for him,' she thought crossly, striding across the room. She snatched up the receiver. 'Lana Devereaux.'

'Karl Henning.' There was no hesitation; he just barrelled in and announced his name, knowing she'd remember him.

She was surprised. 'How on earth did you . . .'

His deep laugh rumbled down the line. 'Lana, Blantyre only has two reputable hotels. You had to be in one of them.'

Lana was disturbed by his persistence. *Damn it! I don't need this.* 'Look, I'm really quite tired . . .' She was deliberately cool, not wanting the further complication of his attentions.

'That's a fine hello, Miss Devereaux.' His voice was light and teasing. 'You're a visitor to this country and don't know anyone. I just wanted to make sure everything is okay.'

She regretted her curtness. The man was only being friendly. 'I'm fine. It's good of you to call.'

'My pleasure,' he said warmly. 'I must confess to an ulterior motive though. I wanted to restate my invitation to join me on the yacht. I was thinking about what you said and it made me realise that some local assistance might actually be appreciated. In any event, it's not really safe for a woman on her own to go . . .'

Lana cut in. 'I can take care of myself.'

His deep chuckle sounded friendly and reassuring. 'I have no doubt you can.' He hesitated briefly. 'Now don't get mad at me but . . . well . . . if I had a daughter your age I'd feel a lot better knowing she was in good company. I know how independent –'

'Karl, you're very kind.' Lana relented. He was only trying to help. The knowledge made her voice warm. 'I'll think about your invitation, I promise.'

'You're about to say "but", I can hear it coming.'

She laughed. 'Not really, but . . .'

'There,' he said, delighted. 'I knew it. Listen,' he went on, 'your father told me he was doing some kind of survey of the lake bed. What better way to follow than by water?'

Lana was tempted. Karl Henning had at least met her father. 'I don't know,' she hedged. 'I don't really want to tie myself down.'

'No commitments,' he promised. 'Just say the word and I'll let you off anywhere you like.'

'Why are you doing this?'

Again the deep laugh. 'I'm not doing much. I planned this trip a while ago. I just thought you might like to join me. Besides,' he added, 'I would enjoy the company.' He laughed again. 'To be honest, I would enjoy *your* company and I don't say that to many people. How about it?'

As a rule, Lana had no difficulty in turning down invitations. Under any other circumstances she would have politely told Karl Henning 'no' and that would have been that. The fact that he had met her father was tempting but her wariness of the man made her cautious. 'Where is your yacht?' She was stalling and knew it was beginning to sound obvious.

'Normally I keep it at Nkhotakota. Know where that is?'

'Not off the top of my head,' she replied, loving the strange word.

'It's about a hundred kilometres from the farm. It has an airstrip so it's quite convenient to reach.'

'You have a plane?'

'Of course.'

The way he said it implied 'doesn't everybody'. 'You said normally you keep it there. Isn't it there now?'

'That's the reason for the trip and it's also why I thought you might like to join me. The yacht is currently up at Chilumba. I have to sail it back to Nkhotakota.'

Still she hesitated.

'Chilumba is about seventy kilometres south of Karonga,' Karl pushed.

Karonga! Her father had been in Karonga. She needed to go there anyway to speak with Moffat Kadamanja, this could be the perfect opportunity. She was on the verge of accepting but she heard herself say, 'Can I let you know? I'll call you in a couple of days.'

There was a slight hesitation at the other end. 'Fine,' he said at last, a little too heartily she thought.

As she hung up the receiver, Lana frowned at the far wall. The man was making it impossible for her to refuse without appearing rude. Resolved not to be pushed into something which could prove a waste of time, and deeply reluctant to closet herself on a yacht for several days with a man she hardly knew, but who was making it abundantly clear that he found her attractive, she nonetheless wondered why she had not accepted his invitation. At the same time, however, she found it hard to fathom why Karl Henning was being so persistent. It was his persistence which made her wary. She could not shake off the feeling that it was due to more than just finding her attractive.

202

Sipping her beer, Lana crossed to the window and looked out. Had her father seen the same view? She felt very close to him again, somehow treading only a little way behind a time span of fifteen years. Was that his Old Spice aftershave she could smell? 'Where did you go from here, Dad?' Bernard had said he'd met with a Cabinet Minister who, several weeks later, was one of four found in a burnt-out car. All had bullet holes in them. Had her father been caught up in some deadly political power struggle?

Irritated at the sudden onset of melancholy, Lana turned from the window, unpacked her suitcase and took a long, hot shower. Feeling somewhat refreshed, she dressed in slacks and T-shirt. 'Thank God they've changed the dress rules,' she thought. In Banda's day, trousers on women had been banned. Lana virtually lived in jeans, slacks or shorts. The dining room, she noted from the hotel information brochure, opened at six-thirty. Her watch was reading three forty-five. 'Can't be. It's getting dark.' Then she remembered that Malawi was two hours ahead of London time. She reset her watch and then, feeling the need of exercise and fresh air, decided to go for a walk.

Crossing the lobby, she intended to leave her key at reception but a noisy crowd of Japanese tourists milling there changed her mind and she pocketed the key and went into the street.

The May temperature was mild. Lana strolled down the main street of Blantyre, enjoying the balmy evening and the feeling of having nothing pressing which required her immediate attention. She did not notice Tim Gilbey following some one hundred metres behind.

There was very little traffic and only a few pedestrians. At a quarter to six, night was coming in fast as it tended to do in Africa. Street lamps had yet to be switched on. In the gentle twilight, descending like a mantle of sea mist, the air was redolent with scented flowers, unfamiliar spices and a soft dampness which coaxed an earthy fragrance from the soil. Lana walked slowly, the sensation of being far from the traffic fumes of London caressing her senses like that of a caring lover.

Most of the shops were shut for the day. They were a strange mixture of designs. Many showed a strong Portuguese or Indian influence, others were modern, still others had an old English look about them. Lana, who always looked for local arts and crafts wherever she went, was delighted to find a homecraft boutique displaying a comprehensive selection of carved wooden objects. She spent several minutes looking in the windows before stepping into an arcade which led to another craft shop. The arcade went back some ten metres to the lifts which serviced the eight-storeyed building. It was dark in the arcade, lit only by display lights in the shop windows. Absorbed, she barely registered hearing the long, drawn-out whistle at first. Then it sank in. The whistle hadn't been one of appreciation or one to get attention. It had sounded more like a signal.

Realising that the shadowy and deserted passageway was not a particularly safe place to be on her own, and sensing danger, Lana spun round. Something, an inner sense, warned that she was in trouble. As she pivoted on the ball of her left foot, a shadowy figure stepped in close and behind her. Lana had not seen anybody coming and only just had time to register his presence when an arm, scratchy in a woollen jacket, whipped around her throat, cutting air. She was pulled roughly backwards, a hand over her mouth and she lost balance, falling back against her attacker as he dragged her deeper into the shadows. The man's hand smelled strongly of carbolic soap.

A second assailant, outlined in silhouette against the fading light, stepped against her and she was sandwiched between them, their burliness hiding her completely. Acting instinctively, she forced herself to relax, sagging into the man behind, trying to get a precious few centimetres of space to bring a knee up into the groin in front of her. The men were too professional to fall for it, the one behind tightening his arm around her neck, the one in front sagging with her so that she was pinioned and helpless. Hands roamed her body but she quickly realised they were intent on picking pockets rather than thrill seeking. She mentally blessed a decision to leave all but a few Kwacha back at the hotel, along with her traveller's cheques and passport.

Lana's mind quickly assessed the immediate predicament. She ruled out rape – these men were too cool for carnal intentions. Mugging was the obvious motive and yet she could not shake off the feeling that she had been a deliberate target, rather than a random victim. Murder would, she reasoned, be unlikely in the middle of Blantyre, although she would be helpless to prevent the quick thrust of a knife if that were their intent. She was being mugged, rather expertly, by two large men. She had been taught that when the odds were against her to lie back and think of England. Typically, and without stopping to consider the consequences, Lana exploded into anger and action.

The arm around her neck slackened a fraction. The man in front of her, in an effort to search the hip pocket of her trousers, had his face two centimetres from hers and was the immediate recipient. Butting her head forward, she connected with the bridge of his nose. Ignoring the warm spurting blood and making the most of his shocked second of inactivity, she sank her teeth into his shoulder. The man shouted in pain and pulled away but Lana hung onto his flesh grimly. His attempts to get rid of the searing pain gave her the space she needed to deliver a punishing knee jerk which found the satisfying softness of testicles just before making hard contact with pelvic bone. The testicles had nowhere to go, crushed in an explosion of excruciating agony. At the same second she unlocked her jaw, falling limp and bending both legs.

Caught unawares, the man behind nearly lost his grip around her throat but quickly recovered and his arm tightened painfully. Instead of fighting for air, Lana used the added impetus to push up and back, her head making contact with teeth and lips. Cursing her sneakers as being useless weapons, she kicked backwards as hard as she could, a heel slamming into his shin. She nearly got away but he jerked hard, arching Lana back and off the ground.

Another shape loomed in the arcade and her heart sank. She hadn't expected a third attacker. 'What the hell is going on here?' He was halfway into the entrance before she registered that he had spoken in perfect English. He stepped over the man on the ground without even looking at him, making no attempt to stop him. The African staggered up and ran, bent double, down the steps and away across the street. 'You there, let go of her at once.'

The suffocating arm dropped away and Lana was pushed forward towards her rescuer as the remaining assailant dodged sideways and ran from the arcade. She slid down the shop window and sat on her haunches, head hanging, one hand on the ground for balance as she tried to lose the sudden dizziness and blurred vision.

'Are you hurt?' He squatted next to her.

She shook her head, fighting to gain control of her breathing.

The light of a torch shone on her. 'You're bleeding!'

'His,' she managed.

He grunted, half amused. 'They won't try that again in a hurry. You can certainly dish it out.' He put a hand on her arm. 'Can you stand?'

She raised her head to look at him but saw only

a dark shape. 'Give me a minute.' The warm pressure of his hand was reassuring. 'Turn the torch off will you.'

He played the light on her face, carefully avoiding her eyes. Lana stayed where she was. The rush of adrenalin and anger she had used to such good effect was waning. In its place, shock, nausea and dizziness had begun to kick in. She was trembling, and the urge to burst into tears was very strong. Breathing deeply, Lana concentrated all her willpower, her last reserves of strength, towards suppressing an overwhelming desire to give way to hysteria. 'That's incredible,' she heard her rescuer murmur, almost to himself, as he snapped off the torch. 'You're controlling it,' he added, admiration clear in his voice.

'What did you expect?' she asked, still looking up, glad her voice was steady. 'Tears?'

'As a matter of fact, yes.' He hesitated, then asked, 'Want to try standing up?'

Lana took his arm and he stood, bringing her up with him. They moved out of the dark arcade. 'Thank you,' she said, looking at him. He was tall, without a spare ounce of excess weight. Broad shoulders accommodated a blue Lacross shirt with elegant ease. Thick, dark, straight hair fell forward over his forehead. His eyes were dark too, she could not tell their colour, but his gaze was direct and warm. He was strikingly attractive.

He smiled, a lopsided grin exposing very white teeth. 'You look a little the worse for wear.' His accent held the faintest Scottish burr.

She glanced down at her clothes. The T-shirt

was blotched with blood. Her head ached and her jaw was sore. She touched the back of her head gingerly and looked at her hand. No blood. She looked back at her rescuer. 'It was preplanned, I'm sure of it. They were waiting for me.' She remembered the whistle.

'Where did you learn to defend yourself like that?' The admiration was still there.

'Black belt karate,' she said briefly.

He nodded. 'Then you'd know that what you just did was incredibly stupid.' There was no censure in his words, he was simply stating a fact.

She grinned. 'Non-practising.' She laughed out loud, the tension and fear slowly dissipating. 'I'm a little rusty. I forgot the rules. Besides, there were only two of them.'

He laughed with her. Then, 'Where do you live?'

'I'm staying at the Mount Soche.'

'Business or pleasure?' He had taken her arm, moved to the road side of the pavement and was leading her back towards the hotel.

'Holiday.' Lana noticed the old-fashioned courtesy. It was oddly reassuring.

'Try to stay out of dark places,' he commented lightly.

She didn't take offence. He was making conversation to divert her thoughts. 'Um . . . I don't want to walk through the lobby like this.'

'I know a back entrance.'

She wondered how he knew. 'Shouldn't I report this to the police?'

'You can,' he said calmly. 'It won't do you any

good though. The muggers won't be found and you'll be tied up for days in bureaucracy. Do yourself a favour and write it off to experience.' His dark eyes rested on her. 'Are you sure they were waiting for you?'

She nodded. 'Just before the attack I heard a whistle. It was a signal, I'm sure of it.'

He raised one quizzical eyebrow. 'Any reason why you would be singled out?'

She was grateful that he didn't disbelieve her, but said nothing about the warning she'd received from Tim Gilbey. Nor did she explain about her father. 'Not that I can think of,' she lied. 'Perhaps they mistook me for someone else.'

'Perhaps.' He didn't sound convinced but let it go. 'Here we are. How about your key?'

'I've got it with me. I'll be fine.' Her head was aching badly now. The rush of adrenalin had left her weak, in need of a stiff whisky and a chance to think. 'Thank you again.'

'My pleasure.' He grinned at the stupid inadequacy of his formal response. 'Well . . .' he said, cocking his head to the same side as his grin, '. . . you know what I mean.' He turned and left.

As he walked away Lana couldn't help noticing how perfectly his grey slacks fitted over a very attractive posterior. She tried to imagine him in swimming trunks. The vision was profoundly pleasing. As she made her way into the hotel she realised that she didn't even know his name.

*

In the morning, refreshed by a good night's sleep and after a very large breakfast to make up for her lack of dinner the night before, Lana was walking towards the lifts when she saw a noticeboard in the foyer of the hotel which displayed the various functions being held that day. The Tobacco Growers' Association were holding a lunch, the Malawi Congress Party were conducting an executive meeting in one of the boardrooms and a British High Commission representative was available for consultation in another. Lana looked at her watch. Nine-fifteen. She hesitated. It was more than likely to be Tim Gilbey. Then she decided, 'To hell with it!' She was a British citizen and she had been attacked in the street.

Pushing open the door to the boardroom, she strode into the room in no mood for any of Gilbey's nonsense. A woman sat behind a desk buffing her nails. She looked up and smiled. 'Can I help you?' The room had been divided into two by a screen.

'My name is Lana Devereaux. Is the representative here?'

'He's just stepped out for a minute. Would you like to wait?'

Lana said she would.

'In here, please. He won't be a moment.'

Behind the screen had been set up as a sparsely furnished office. 'Please take a seat.' The woman left, and Lana heard the outer boardroom door quietly closing. She was alone.

She sat beside the apparently unused desk and

looked around. 'Good God! I don't believe it!' Queen Elizabeth smiled knowingly at her from one wall. 'Have Queen, will travel.' Lana had wondered often why it was that diplomats of all nationalities needed to reassure themselves with photographs of their rulers. She speculated sometimes that it must be because they needed to remind themselves of their loyalties. To live constantly with photographs of their monarchs must have been a bit like having an overzealous school-teacher hovering over the shoulder during an examination. She blew the Queen a kiss. Five minutes later Lana and the British Monarch were still alone and Lana was beginning to feel annoyed. 'These people seem to think they can treat me any way they like,' she thought, rising. 'Well they can't.' She was just moving towards the door when it opened and a man came in.

'Miss Devereaux. Sorry to keep you.'

'You!' It was her saviour of the previous evening. His casual attire had been replaced by a pin stripe business suit which, despite its best efforts to stereotype the man, did nothing to hide the fact that he was very fit and, in the cold light of day, drop-dead gorgeous.

'Well!' he said, amused. 'We meet again.'

She would not be diverted. 'I was just about to leave.'

'Sorry,' he repeated. 'I was just saying goodbye to someone.' He crossed to the desk and sat down, indicating that she should do the same. She noticed that his eyes were as deeply blue as her own. 'You don't seem any the worse for yesterday.'

'I'm resilient.'

'And impatient.' He grinned. 'Calm down. No-one kept you waiting on purpose.'

Lana was still annoyed but it was waning. 'I'm calm enough. I just don't like people telling me what to do.'

He cocked his head to one side in that manner which had invaded her dreams last night. 'Have *I* told you what to do?'

'No. But if you're anything like that odious man, Mr Gilbey, I'm sure you're about to.'

He looked startled. 'Tim Gilbey?'

Lana nodded.

'When did you speak to him?'

'Yesterday, just after I arrived. He came to the hotel. He was extremely rude. That's one of the reasons I'm here now.'

He nodded, produced a folder from a desk drawer and a gold Cross pen from his pocket. Tapping the pen against the folder he asked, 'Who knows you are in Malawi?'

'No-one.'

'Your Mr Gilbey obviously knew.'

'I suspect my stepfather informed your office in Lilongwe.' She thought about that. 'Strangely, I got the impression that Mr Gilbey had never heard of my stepfather.'

He digested this. 'Who have you spoken to since you arrived?'

'No-one.' Then she thought about it. 'I did meet someone on the plane.'

He leaned forward. 'Who?' he asked intently.

'Karl Henning.'

'The tobacco farmer?' He frowned. 'How did you meet him?'

'He sat next to me on the flight to Lilongwe. Why do you ask?'

The man opposite her shook his head briefly. 'No reason. I'm just trying to make sense of a few things.'

'Be sure to let me know if you do.' Lana could not keep the sarcasm out of her voice.

Something passed across his eyes, a dark shadow, a secret of some kind. It was gone in an instant. He spun his chair and stared at the door. 'Miss Devereaux,' he said quietly, 'your assumption is correct. The man who came to see you at your hotel had not heard of Bernard Pickstone.'

'How do you know that?'

He turned his head and dark blue eyes looked deeply into hers. 'Because, Miss Devereaux, your stepfather spoke to me. I am Tim Gilbey.'

TEN

'What did you say?' Lana stared at him in disbelief.

'I am Tim Gilbey.' He stared back. 'Believe me, there is only one of me.'

'But . . .' Lana took stock. 'He said *he* was Tim Gilbey and implied that he was with the British High Commission. He threatened to have me thrown out of Malawi.'

The man sitting opposite her raised his eyebrows. 'That should have told you *something* surely. The British High Commission, irrespective of their true feelings, wouldn't make threats like that. We're not called the diplomatic service for nothing.' He picked up his pen. 'Can you describe him?'

Lana nodded. 'Somewhere between forty and death; ill-mannered; a bully *and* decidedly unpleasant,' she said succinctly.

Tim Gilbey dropped his pen back on the notepad. 'I mean, his physical appearance,' he said, trying not to grin.

Lana described the man and Gilbey wrote it down. She noticed his handwriting was bold and masculine. 'What exactly did he say about throwing you out of Malawi?' he asked, still writing.

'He told me I should not try to find out what happened to my father, that no-one would help me and some things were best left alone.' She stopped, thinking. 'He said he could have me deported if he felt like it.'

Gilbey observed her with compassion. 'You weren't to know but no-one in the High Commission can have a British subject deported without going through a hell of a lot of red tape. But what he said about your father, he's right about that.'

'Can't any of you understand?' Lana burst out angrily. 'Have you any idea what it's like? Not knowing, no proof, not even a reasonable explanation? Nothing but silence for fifteen years.'

Tim Gilbey clasped his hands on the desk and leaned forward. 'I do appreciate that. It's not what I mean. Of course you want to know. The trouble seems to be, from what little I have been able to learn since Bernard Pickstone got in touch with me, that your father's contact was one of four Malawian Ministers who were killed in somewhat suspicious circumstances. The police did investigate,' he shrugged dismissively. 'Their resources were meagre to say the least back then. Also, at that time they were more concerned with matters of national security. That makes our information a bit sketchy. However, there is no indication of involvement by your father or his assistant.' He leaned back and tapped his fingers on his desk. 'What was your father like?' he asked suddenly.

Without being aware of it happening, Lana's face softened. 'Very professional, decent, honest, funny, caring, intelligent . . .' she stopped. 'Why?' she demanded.

'The man in Malawi doing this job at the time your father disappeared is now my boss. He's all those things you've just said about your father. Please believe me when I say that your father's disappearance was not treated lightly. Martin Flower went out of his way to find out what happened. He got nowhere. Martin was as mystified then as you are now.' Tim Gilbey hesitated. 'I shouldn't tell you this but I will. Martin did some investigating of his own. It was strictly off record and must stay that way.' He waited until she nodded agreement. 'He came up with nothing,' Gilbey went on. 'Whatever happened to your father had nothing to do with local politics. We're fairly certain of that.'

'Fairly certain?' Lana repeated sarcastically. ' "Misadventure" was the word I think you used.'

He had the good grace to look embarrassed. 'A word for all reasons? Yes, it must have been very frustrating for you. Thing is,' he said, leaning forward again, 'the High Commission cannot throw its weight around too much. If your father had *committed* a crime while he was here . . . well . . . that would be different. The powers that be would have gone out of their way to involve us.' He smiled slightly. 'That's the way it works.'

'My father –'

Tim Gilbey held up his hands. 'I know. Your father committed no crime. It seems unfair and the

system makes no allowances for anyone's feelings.'
He watched her, waiting for a reaction but she just
looked at him so he went on. 'Look, our position
is clear cut and whether you or I like it, here's how
it goes. In that a crime appeared to have been committed *against* your father, all this office could do
was request a full investigation. They did that
immediately. The Malawi police were certainly
cooperative but with no body or known motive
the assumption was given as misadventure. We had
to accept it. Sure,' he smiled at her sympathetically,
'the High Commissioner rattled his sabre and
asked for more information but, at the end of the
day, he still had to accept their findings. You must
realise that, at that time, the country was going
through some very unstable times.'

'That's convenient,' Lana said sarcastically. 'The
other Tim Gilbey used unrest too.'

'It's true enough.'

'I know that,' Lana snapped. 'It's pathetic. My
father was probably murdered and all anyone can
talk about is politics.'

He was watching her sympathetically.

'I imagine the police will tell me the same thing.'

He nodded. 'I'm afraid so.'

She knew a brick wall when she saw one. She
didn't like it. 'If it's all so bloody cut and dried then
why am I being warned off? Somebody doesn't
want me around and that tells me that something
is most definitely being hidden.'

'Miss Devereaux,' he said patiently, 'I understand
your frustration, believe me. There's very little the

High Commission can do for you.' He pulled absently at his ear. 'We're as in the dark about this as you.'

Lana was not convinced. 'There must have been a file. Where is it?'

'London,' he said briefly.

'Why?' She didn't believe him. If all the files from all the British diplomatic missions around the world found their way back to London they'd need a warehouse the size of Buckingham Palace to store them.

If Tim Gilbey knew she doubted his word, he gave no sign. 'Things like this are always fully investigated. The file was sent to London so they could make their own enquiries.'

'MI6?'

He shrugged. 'I have no idea.'

She stared at him. 'Yes you do.'

'Miss Devereaux,' he said firmly, 'at the time of your father's disappearance I was a third-former at Glenalmond College.'

She smiled mirthlessly. 'Scottish boarding school or not, Mr Gilbey, as soon as my stepfather contacted you, you'd have made enquiries.' She looked for guilt, deception or discomfort in his eyes. All she saw was the deepest compassion. 'Fine,' she snapped. 'When I get home I assume I'll be given access to the file?'

Tim Gilbey looked embarrassed again. 'Probably not,' he said apologetically.

'And why would that be?' She was going round in circles and this man wasn't helping.

He shrugged helplessly. 'Because,' he said quietly and with great sincerity, 'the British Government doesn't operate that way.'

Lana knew she would get no more out of him. He was hiding something, she was sure of it, but he was too professional to say more. The knowledge irritated her but there was no point in persisting. 'Thank you,' she said, about to rise. 'I can't say you've been helpful but at least you've given me some answers. It's more than I thought I'd get.'

He gave his lopsided grin. 'Are we that secretive do you think?'

'Secretive?' She thought about it. 'It's not the word I'd choose. "Evasive" would do the trick.' She stood and looked down at him, irritation rising further. 'Let's not tell the general public what we know because we have decided, in our incredible wisdom, that the poor unintelligent, uninformed and misguided general public – who incidentally would be much more palatable to us if they dropped out of sight and let us get on with the real issues – can't handle the truth.' She blinked back tears of frustration. 'There's more to this than anyone is letting on and I certainly don't intend to let the matter drop.'

'Sit down please.' He waved his hand at the chair. When she remained standing he said, 'I didn't expect you to let it drop.' He looked up at her. 'Oh for God's sake sit down, you're making my neck ache.'

'A teacher said that to me once.' She sat down again.

'That you're a pain in the neck?' He grinned.

She smiled back. 'Exactly her words.'

'Were you?'

'Probably.' She looked serious again. 'I don't want to be. All I want is to understand what happened to my father. That's reasonable isn't it?'

He changed the subject abruptly. 'How do you feel this morning?'

'Fine,' she said shortly. 'My head is sore, that's all.'

'Your head?'

'I hit it against . . .' she stopped. 'What's my head got to do with things?' she snapped.

'I was merely asking how you felt,' he replied mildly. 'You gave a pretty good account of yourself last night but I wondered if –'

'If being female didn't leave me with a fit of the vapours?'

He leaned back and folded his arms. 'Miss Devereaux, you can sometimes be pretty hard to like.'

Lana stared at him coolly. 'I'm not here for a popularity contest, Mr Gilbey. Can we get back to the subject?'

His arms were still folded. 'Let's talk about Karl Henning.'

'What about him? I met him on the flight up from Johannesburg.'

'Does he know why you're here?'

'No.' She thought about it. 'He knows who I am, who my father was, and that he disappeared. He actually met my father in Blantyre before Dad went up north. I told him I just wanted to visit the

221

places Dad had been.' She watched him watching her. 'Why?'

'Do you plan to see him again while you're here?'

'Do you answer every question with a question?'

'No more than you. Well? *Do* you plan to see him?'

'Maybe. He's invited me to go sailing. I might.'

Tim Gilbey raised his eyebrows. 'He's a bit old for you isn't he?'

Lana lost patience. 'My private life has nothing to do with you, Mr Gilbey,' she said stiffly. 'Can you help me or can't you?'

'I'm trying to if you'd give me a chance.' His dark blue eyes twinkled briefly, then went serious. 'Last night could have been a warning. Think about it. A total stranger, who says he's me, warns you off asking questions about your father. Why? Then you're attacked in the street and think it was deliberate, that you weren't simply the victim of random violence. Why?'

'Someone is determined to let sleeping dogs lie. My turn. Why?'

'Who else in Malawi knows what you're doing here except Karl Henning and me?'

Lana narrowed her eyes. 'There's something you're not telling me.'

He spread his hands. 'Not really. I don't know much about our farming friend but it is rather odd, don't you think?' He hunched forward on his elbows. 'Be careful, Lana Devereaux,' he said softly. 'Somebody obviously knows why, if not how, your father disappeared and that knowledge could prove to be seriously dangerous.'

'And you think Karl Henning is involved?'

He shrugged. 'I don't know. All I'm saying is be careful.'

'I have another name,' she said. 'Moffat Kadamanja.'

Tim Gilbey nodded. 'The son of your father's assistant.'

Lana inclined her head, acknowledging that he'd done his homework. 'I'm going to try and find him.'

'What good will that do?'

'He might know something.' She pulled a wry face. 'If he does he'll be less likely to keep it from me than you.'

'What are you doing tonight?' he asked abruptly, ignoring the criticism.

'Nothing. Getting an early night. I'm driving to Lilongwe tomorrow. I only came to Blantyre to see where my father started his time in Malawi.'

'Can't have you dining alone. I feel it's my duty to take you to dinner.'

'Duty?' she asked in a steely voice.

He grinned at her. 'Pleasure?'

'How do you know it will be a pleasure?'

'I'm having grave misgivings.' Again the twinkle.

Lana grinned suddenly. 'I'm not that bad, Mr Gilbey. Socially I come up quite well and the only thing I bite is my food.'

'Tim.'

'Lana.'

'What time?'

She rose. 'How about six-thirty?'

He rose with her and put out his hand. 'Fine. Do you like Chinese?'

'Love it.' She took his offered handshake. It was firm but not excessive. 'I warn you, I know you're hiding something.' She studied him carefully. 'I keep asking myself what the Commercial Attache is doing in Blantyre when the business capital is Lilongwe.'

'Six of one, half-a-dozen of the other. Effectively, I should divide my time between the two. The chap who usually comes to Blantyre couldn't make it this month. It suited me to come here. I'm new in Malawi and it gives me a chance to meet people.' He spoke lightly.

Lana was still scrutinising his face. 'I also keep asking why the Commercial Attache was given to me as a contact? Rather odd wouldn't you say?'

He grinned wryly. All he said was, 'Nope.'

She nodded. 'Have it your way.' She left it, knowing he would say no more.

He walked her to the door. 'Tonight's informal.'

'So am I.'

'Yes,' he said quietly. 'I rather thought you would be.'

It was a compliment but she was still annoyed that he obviously knew more than he was saying. 'I'm not letting this thing drop. Take it or leave it.'

He scratched his head. 'I'll take it.' He laughed suddenly. 'Could be quite an evening.'

'Why?' She looked at him quizzically.

'I'm an old-fashioned kind of guy.'

'What kind of guy is that?'

'Oh, you know.' He shrugged. 'Wine, roses, good listener, just your average lovable, huggable kind of guy.'

Lana laughed. Despite herself, she was beginning to like Tim Gilbey.

As soon as he was alone, Tim went to his briefcase and dialled the combination lock. He pulled out the false bottom and extracted a slim manila file marked 'Devereaux'. At his desk he paged through the scribbled notes Martin Flower had written some fifteen years earlier. He knew what they said, almost by heart.

Four days earlier Tim had been contacted by Bernard Pickstone who had spoken at some length in brusque tones, leaving Tim in no doubt that the safety of Lana Devereaux was, in Bernard's opinion, the sole responsibility of the British High Commission. Dismayed, because the last thing Tim needed was some hysterical female on a sentimental journey, as soon as he finished speaking to Bernard Pickstone he had telephoned London and spoken to his boss.

'Sorry, Tim, I had to give him a name. I didn't expect him to ring you though.'

'His stepdaughter is coming here. Her father . . .'

'I know. He told me as well. I do remember her father actually. John Devereaux went missing in my time.'

'Anything you can tell me?' Tim asked.

'There's a file, should still be there. Have a look for it. I wrote some notes at the time and bunged the police report in it too.'

'What should I tell the daughter?'

Martin Flower went silent, thinking. 'Nothing,' he said finally.

'That's a bit unfair,' Tim protested.

'You're not there for that. Devereaux was a civilian thing. I had my suspicions at the time but nothing was ever proved. Steer her off, Tim.'

'I could suggest she try the police?'

Martin laughed mirthlessly. 'She can try, no harm in that.'

Tim felt sympathy for the family. 'Pickstone said that Devereaux had an assistant whose body washed up in Tanzania. I've been asked to locate his son. Pickstone thought he could be in Karonga but I've actually found him in Lilongwe.'

Again Martin was silent. 'Okay, Tim, give her the son's address,' he said finally. 'What harm can that do?'

'We *weren't* involved were we?'

'No,' Martin said emphatically. 'It had nothing to do with us. I'm not hiding anything, Tim. The whole Devereaux incident was certainly suspect but the police had other things on their minds. There was a tobacco farmer involved, I'm sure of it. Karl someone. Look in the file. I snooped a bit but . . . you know how it is.'

'Could the daughter be in danger?'

'Definitely. As I said, best to steer her off it.' He

changed the subject abruptly. 'And how is the other matter progressing? I know you've only been there two weeks. What's happening?'

'Hang on.' Tim had risen and closed his office door. He returned to the telephone. 'Getting to Likoma isn't easy. It will raise questions. There's absolutely nothing there to justify a visit.'

'I know but you must get over there quickly. I was going to contact you. Our friend Frederick Hamilton has booked a flight to Lilongwe via Nairobi for Saturday week.'

Tim sat up straighter in his chair. 'What's he up to? Why come back now? Do you think he's found another buyer for the documents?'

'Jesus, Tim, don't even suggest that.'

'Well, what would you do? He's after money and it's been over a month since he first approached us. The Argentineans would love to get their hands on those pieces of paper.'

'I know,' Martin said gloomily. 'So would Spain. Hamilton's no fool. If the documents are there and he's read them as he claims . . .' He stopped. 'If he gets to Malawi, Tim, you might have to . . . ah . . .'

'Forget it,' Tim said sharply.

'It will be an order,' Martin said, just as sharply.

Tim changed the subject. 'Does anyone other than the old man know why I'm *really* here?'

'Have some respect! The High Commissioner is hardly an old man.' Martin understood why Tim had asked the question. 'Do your best, Tim. No-one else knows why you're there. Try not to blow your cover unless it's absolutely necessary but you may have to go missing for a couple of days.'

'Thanks,' Tim said drily. 'I'll do what I can. Do *you* think Hamilton's planning to retrieve the documents?'

'That's my guess. He came to see me last week. I stalled of course, said these things take time to arrange, but if he's returning to Malawi maybe he's getting suspicious. We can't afford to let him remove them, Tim. They could go anywhere. You've got to find them before he gets there, otherwise –'

'I've got eight days then,' Tim cut him off.

'Do whatever you have to. I mean it, Tim. He cannot be allowed –'

'If they're on Likoma I'll find them,' Tim cut him off again. He knew the alternative and it didn't sit well with him. He sometimes wondered, if the order came, whether or not he could bring himself to obey it.

'I'm certain they're there. Hamilton isn't a criminal, just a greedy little man. He's hidden them on the island, you can bet on it. Probably buried them somewhere.' Martin let him off the hook, knowing Tim's reluctance only too well. Martin sympathised but, as Parker-Brown had said to him many years before, 'Every job has its down side'.

As soon as the conversation was over, Tim went looking for the file. He found it without trouble, a fact which surprised him, considering its age. The contents had been scant.

★

That was four days ago. What made him bring the file on this trip to Blantyre was the imminent arrival of Devereaux's daughter. Having read it, Tim was in two minds whether to disobey Martin's order to steer her off. He could imagine only too well the frustration of John Devereaux's family and, in the back of his mind, he was tempted to hand the few facts he had over to the daughter. Now that he had met Lana he was uncertain what to do. He liked her. He was attracted to her. He wanted to help her. But he did not want to place her in danger. From what he'd seen of Lana, she was more than capable of bulldozing her way into trouble.

He sat looking down at the file, thinking it a poor epitaph for a man like John Devereaux. A foolscap page torn from Martin's notepad stating that John Devereaux had registered with the High Commission on 5 March 1983 and asked about a colleague called Robin Cunningham who was missing. Martin had simply recorded the enquiry, its date and time and, for some reason, the name of a now retired French Intelligence Officer, Jean-Claude Bourquin.

The second sheet was a photostat of a report sent to the FCO in London which stated that Cunningham had drowned. Martin had pencilled in the words 'his assistant too?' at the bottom of the page. The next note, dated May 24th, recorded that a Sarah Fotheringham of Karonga had reported Devereaux missing. At the bottom, Martin had squiggled a large question mark and the name Karl

Henning which was circled several times. A copy of the coroner's report, dated 15 June, which had attributed the death of John Devereaux's assistant, a Mr Jonah Kadamanja, to drowning, was pinned to it with the word 'BULLSHIT' scrawled across the top in Martin's handwriting. The police report was succinct and lacking any detail. They had used words like 'exhaustive investigations' and 'mysterious disappearance' but the report was dated 6 June, just two weeks after Devereaux went missing. Martin had refrained from comment, or written comment anyway.

A faded and yellowing newspaper clipping showed Karl Henning and Minister Dick Matenje in deep conversation at, what appeared to be, a cocktail party. There was no covering editorial. Henning was clearly making a point, his right hand raised, forefinger just inches from the Minister's chest. Matenje had a politely determined look about him, as if Henning was annoying him but he was too well mannered to say so. Looking at the photograph Tim had the feeling that the two men knew each other well.

The last paper in the file was a chronological sequence of events and, reading through them, Tim could see why Martin had the idea that the tobacco farmer was, in some way, implicated. Henning had been in Blantyre at the same time as Cunningham and had stayed at the same hotel. He had been absent from his farm for four days, coinciding with the disappearance of Cunningham. From somewhere Martin had learned that Henning had reputedly gone sailing during that time. Henning had also been in Blantyre when Devereaux arrived. Once again, he had apparently gone sailing, this time coinciding with Devereaux's disappearance. For a tobacco farmer, Henning appeared to take a surprising number of days away from his farm, including numerous overseas trips, mainly to the Far East. His bank records, which Martin had somehow obtained, did not reflect the travel expenditure so the man obviously had money outside Malawi, or someone else was financing his globe-trotting.

Martin must have been tempted to give the Exchange Control authorities a tip-off. Their telephone number and a man's name had been scrawled on the page, then crossed through. Tim didn't blame him for not doing it. Getting involved in criminal cases brought unwelcome attention to someone in a position which required that they keep out of the limelight. Martin had, however, come up with the fact that Henning had a bank account in Hong Kong and another in Geneva.

Henning was not an employee manager, as were a lot of men who ran the large tobacco estates. He owned his farm outright, having purchased it in 1964. The farm appeared to be Henning's only source of income, subject to the pressures of inflation, foreign exchange fluctuations and demand from the world tobacco market, not to mention the unpredictability of the weather. While he was hardly on the bones of his arse, finances would be fairly tight. There had to be something else, something generating undeclared hard currency outside

Malawi. It had to be substantial, otherwise the risks were too great. Why did he continue to visit places like Hong Kong, Tokyo, Bangkok and Singapore? Not to sell tobacco, that's for sure. Farmers sold their tobacco at auction and the on-selling was left to brokers.

Tim folded the file and put it back into his brief-case. He was greatly troubled. There was nothing in the file to directly implicate Karl Henning – just a few coincidences. Tim's own enquiries about Henning had revealed that the man was regarded highly by those who knew him, ran a well-managed farm and no scandal had ever been attached to his name. He had been married but the union had ended in what appeared to be an amicable divorce ten years ago. Mrs Henning had left Malawi and not returned. There had been no children.

On the surface it appeared that Karl Henning was a man to whom coincidence attached itself. Sitting next to Lana Devereaux on the plane was a case in point. He could never have engineered that himself. And yet, Tim could not shake off the feeling that Henning would bear watching.

There was no point in worrying Lana with vague suspicions which could very well prove groundless. She was on a difficult enough visit as it was. Henning had admitted meeting her father. Had he done that because he had nothing to hide, or to entice Lana into his company for sinister reasons of his own?

And who was impersonating Tim? What possible motive could someone have for doing that?

Certainly the intention had been to frighten Lana Devereaux but why use Tim's name?

Tim didn't like it but there was nothing much he could do for Lana. He had to get to Likoma ahead of Frederick Hamilton and try to locate the documents – if they existed. Lana had already shown she could take care of herself. 'Jesus!' he thought, disgusted. 'It's all very well for Martin to tell me not to get involved. What if she's in danger? Shouldn't she be warned? Damn the woman. Why did she have to come here?' He shook his head, irritated with Lana Devereaux, himself and his job. 'A hell of a choice,' he muttered to an indifferent Queen Elizabeth on the wall. 'A woman's life or a government's downfall.' He glared at the photograph. 'I suppose *you'd* put duty first.' He had never been in this situation before, where his personal feelings got in the way of his professional life. He'd spoken to others who had found themselves in the same dilemma. Some had given in to their own conscience, others hadn't. Some regretted their choice, some didn't. There was no easy answer.

Lana spent the rest of the morning exploring Blantyre and its sister town, Limbe. Then, on impulse, she took the road to Mulanje, some eighty kilometres south-east, towards the Mozambique border. The strip road was in terrible condition. Parts had been ripped up in readiness for upgrading and were rutted and stony. Other sections were full of potholes, their partially tarred surface losing the

233

battle against weeds and makeshift maintenance. Driving was made extremely hazardous by the continuous stream of pedestrian traffic, some wheeling laden bicycles, others pushing carts, no-one interested in moving off the road for the occasional car, bus or truck. Goats played a kind of Russian roulette game with the traffic, miraculously escaping injury. Chickens were seldom so lucky. Lana passed several pathetically naked dead birds lying in the midst of what appeared to be the end result of a pillow fight, causing her to wonder why their feathers deserted their bodies in times of crisis.

The road took her through attractive rolling country for about twenty-five kilometres, with fields of sweet corn and, what she assumed to be, tobacco. Then abruptly it became another world, the endless slopes of tea estates, undulating away into the distance with occasional glimpses of sprawling white homes set amid a sea of rolling green. She tried to imagine the life of a tea planter here. The term, in her opinion anyway, was as colonial as District Commissioner or White Hunter. She envisaged portly men in Panama hats and wispy women in flowing floral, their every wish accommodated by a swarm of white clothed servants. Her vision was shattered somewhat by the sight of a khaki clad young man amid the plants, laughing heartily at something a Malawian next to him was saying. 'Oh well,' she thought, '*some* of them must be rotund.'

Everything was a lush green, industrious,

234

orderly and distinctly different to any form of agri-culture she'd seen before, Malawi seemed to be a country struggling yet determined to survive. The people had a peaceful look about them, gentle and happy. Children were plump, if rather shabbily dressed, and she remembered that the country was usually self-sufficient in terms of food production.

Just before the small village of Thyolo she began to look out for 'Mwalawanthunzi', a rock which was supposed to possess magical powers. The brochure had said that if appropriate offerings are made, clouds will form overhead to provide a hot traveller with shade. People passing would tap the rock with a pebble for good luck. She found it on a bend in the road and stopped to read the plaque, experiencing a flash of annoyance that someone, in their wisdom, had found it necessary to cement the magic 'rock of shade' into place and wondered, not for the first time, why the colonial powers of yes-teryear had felt morally obliged to imprint author-ity over everything they touched. Before setting off again she picked up a pebble and tapped the rock. 'I need all the good luck I can get,' she murmured to the inanimate piece of granite.

Thyolo was one long main street lined with square built shops, many in dire need of repair. It might have been uninteresting but for a distinctly Portuguese influence. It had an air of departed affluence but its bustling streets, filled with market stalls, people and vehicles, showed that while wealth may have fled, energy was there in abundance.

Beyond Thyolo the condition of the road

improved considerably. Mulanje was visible way before she reached it. The highest peak in Central Africa sat, craggy and huge, as if it had been gently lowered into a sea of undulating green. As she got closer, the mountain seemed to stay the same distance away, almost as though it were retreating from her. Suddenly however, it was right there beside her and Lana could see the vivid yellow plastic coats of plantation workers. The road took her around the base of the mountain through ancient forests nestling in deep shade below 3000 metres of Ice Age bauxite. The scene had a brooding, stormy appearance, the air intoxicating and heavy.

The Mulanje Country Club, a sprawling, whitewashed edifice at the foot of the mountain, had seen better days but, after a quick look at the village, Lana decided her digestive system stood a better chance of survival there than anywhere else. Golf fairways stretched away on three sides, dotted with bunkers and oiled sand greens. Finding a seat near the row of windows in the cavernous lounge, she sat looking out over the golf course, enjoying the sun which filtered down through large trees.

Waiting for her chicken-in-the-basket, the only thing on offer that day, she idly watched three men playing golf. One of them in particular drew her gaze, a tall man wearing a cap and sunglasses. 'Bloody hell,' she muttered in surprise. It was the bogus Tim Gilbey, large as life. 'Well now,' she thought. 'Perhaps we can find out who you *really* are.'

The men finished their round, shook hands, and strolled towards the clubhouse, caddies attending to their discarded clubs. Lana smiled grimly as they approached. She was looking forward to the encounter, wondering if she should call him Tim Gilbey in front of his companions. Just as the men entered the clubhouse the waiter arrived with her food. Diverted for a moment, she did not see the man's look of surprise, or his hurried departure from the club. When she looked back, he had disappeared.

'Damn!' She snapped off a chicken leg and bit into it. Then a slow grin spread across her face. 'Maybe not damn after all. This is where I get lucky.' Lana left her food and approached the other two who were punishing packets of crisps and bottles of beer as they relived, stroke by stroke, their game. 'Excuse me.'

They looked around.

Lana summed them up quickly. Open faces, relaxed smiles, eyes holding nothing more than frank admiration. Nice ordinary men with nothing to hide. 'That other man who was with you. I think he's someone I know. He's not Geoff Smith is he?' 'Oh great', she thought. 'Couldn't you come up with something better than Smith?'

'Tony?' one of them responded. 'Sorry, miss. That's Tony Davenport.' He looked genuinely disappointed he couldn't help her.

'My mistake.' Lana smiled and turned to leave. 'Sorry to trouble you.'

'No trouble at all. If we run into your friend who should we say was asking after him?'

Lana shook her head. 'It doesn't matter. I've just remembered he's away on holiday anyway. Thanks.' She turned and made her way back to the table. Now she had a name it shouldn't be difficult to find out more about Tony Davenport. The man must be a fool. Surely he should have realised his deception couldn't work. Malawi's white population was so small it was inevitable Lana would discover his real name. Still, his lack of common sense was reassuring.

She finished lunch and glanced at her watch, surprised to see it was almost 3p.m. The drive back to Blantyre would take a good hour and Tim Gilbey was picking her up at 6.30. That gave her time for a swim in the hotel pool, a leisurely shower and maybe thirty minutes' nap. Lana had trained herself to catnap, something she found useful on long flights, or on jobs where regular hours were impossible. She paid her bill and left, gazing upwards at the towering mountain, home of legends and superstitious beliefs, the subject of several books, including one by Laurens van der Post. So engrossed was she that she failed to notice Tony Davenport sitting in his car a hundred metres down the road.

Her map indicated there were two ways back to Blantyre. The way she had come, via Thyolo, or a mainly gravel road through Midima. The dirt route appeared shorter and she would see more of the country. About ten kilometres from Mulanje, Lana found the signpost and swung right. Dust instantly billowed up behind the car and she had to slow down. The condition of the road had not been improved by unseasonably torrential rain two weeks earlier but the four-wheel drive Subaru handled it well. She stopped once to enjoy the view back towards Mulanje and the Mozambique border. Dust hung in the airless afternoon like a fine red mist.

About halfway back she became aware of another vehicle keeping its distance behind her. 'Nothing strange in that,' she reasoned. 'No-one in their right mind would try to overtake through dust like this.' Still, she could not shake off the feeling that the car was tailing her. Twice, on long bends, Lana had looked back to see a red car sitting just behind the worst of her dust. On the last bend she looked again but saw no sign of it.

The land was rising. Farms stretched away left and right. She had passed no cars and the road was largely free of the pedestrian traffic which had been so prolific on the way down. Something made her glance in the rear vision mirror and she jumped with fright. The red car was no more than a metre off her bumper. 'He's insane!' she thought as the car swerved out suddenly and began to overtake. Lana slowed to let the maniac pass. Too late, she realised that the driver was Tony Davenport.

Glancing over as he drew level, she saw the grimly determined look on his face and, with a shock, she saw him wrench the wheel. He was deliberately trying to run her off the road. Her reaction was instinctive and immediate. On more than one occasion in London the sight of Lana on her Harley Davidson brought out bullying tactics from other road users. She had been harassed by bike riders – although not once had the aggressor been on a Harley – taxis and private cars. She had learned that counterattack was the most effective means of defence. With no hesitation, Lana swung the Subaru towards Davenport, at the same time rapidly changing down a gear.

Being permanently in four-wheel drive, the Subaru already had a good grip on the loose gravel road and responded well to the gear change. It side-swiped Davenport's red Ford with all the gusto of a Mac truck. The Ford's tyres slid helplessly, not having the traction to withstand the determined ramming from the smaller vehicle. Tortured metallic shrieks, over-revved engines and wheels spinning sending a spray of stones and dirt filled Lana's head as she grimly held the steering wheel and forced the red Ford further onto the wrong side of the road.

Davenport, perhaps preferring his chances if he was back in control of his own vehicle, wrenched the steering wheel violently and the two cars parted company suddenly – the Ford careering out of control down the grassy slope beside the road to come to rest wedged firmly between a tree and a fence post. The Subaru, with nothing to push, began to follow. Lana eased off on the accelerator and brought the car slowly back to the middle of the road. She pulled up as soon as she could and climbed shakily out. Dust billowed all around but did little to hide the damage. The Subaru's front right side looked as though it had been through a blender. 'Shit!' Lana shouted.

Furious, she got back into the vehicle and reversed rapidly to where Davenport was slowly getting out of his wrecked car, via a back door. He looked up, startled, when he realised it was her. 'You stupid bastard,' she yelled, getting out and striding to him. 'What the hell are you playing at?'

Wordless, he indicated his vehicle. Only the roof remained undamaged.

Lana's eyes flicked to the Ford, then back to Davenport. 'You got what you asked for,' she gritted. 'I intend to report you for this.' She took a deep, steadying breath. 'I'll be giving the police your real name, Mr Tony Davenport.'

Davenport's mouth was opening and shutting like a fish.

Lana, with one last venomous glare, turned away. 'Wait.'

She didn't wait. Instead she growled, 'To hell with you.' As she drove off she was hoping that Tony Davenport had a long, hot wait for someone to give him a lift – plenty of time in fact to ponder the wisdom of his deeds.

About three minutes later the shock hit her. 'You damned fool,' she said loudly, hitting the heel of her hand against the steering wheel. She was not berating herself for running Davenport off the road so much as for reversing back to yell at him. She conceded she'd been lucky. Tony Davenport had been too shaken by the crash to think of trying to harm her further. Even so, Lana scolded herself for her foolishness all the way back to Blantyre.

ELEVEN

Lana collected her room keys at reception and was handed a message. She read it in the lift. It was from Karl, asking her to call him back as soon as possible. Expecting more pressure from him to attend his lunch and go sailing, she delayed making the call for half-an-hour. By the time she dialled his number she had made up her mind not to be pushed into accepting.

'Karl Henning.' He answered the telephone like a man expecting bad news – gruff and brusque.

'Lana Devereaux.'

'Thank you for returning my call. Where have you been?'

'Sightseeing,' Lana told him shortly. *What business is it of yours?*

'I thought you were making enquiries about your father.'

Careful. 'I'm also on holiday.'

'I'm glad to hear you say that. Have you made up your mind yet?' When she said nothing, he added, 'About sailing?'

Whether she was still shaken from the encounter with Tony Davenport on the Midima

Road, or whether she simply resented being pushed, Lana didn't know. She did acknowledge to herself later, however, that she could not have been more ungracious if she had tried. 'As I told you yesterday, Karl, I'll let you know in a couple of days. The lunch is looking doubtful. If I go sailing with you I'll find my own way to your yacht.' She spoke crisply, hoping he would back off.

To her surprise, he chuckled. 'Oh dear. A failing of mine I'm afraid. When I get an idea I . . . Look, I'm sorry. I'll wait to hear from you.'

'I'd appreciate that.'

Perversely, he took offence. 'Don't put yourself out or anything, Miss Devereaux. After all, I'm only trying to help.'

Lana would not be intimidated. 'As much as I appreciate your offer, Karl, I would prefer it if I were not constantly being pressured into doing something I may not wish to do. I've told you already that I'm not sure of my movements. If that's not good enough for you, I'm sorry.'

His voice went deep – though whether from anger or embarrassment Lana didn't know. 'What plans have you made?'

'None.'

'None?' He didn't believe her and it showed.

Lana relented. 'I'm driving up to Lilongwe tomorrow. After that, I have no idea.'

'Are you going up to Karonga? After all, that's where your father was when he went missing.'

'How do you know that?'

'You mentioned it.'

243

Lana knew she had not. But this was the second time he had mentioned Karonga. She decided to do some pushing of her own. 'I might get up there. I'd like to see it, maybe talk to some people who could remember Dad being there.'

His throaty laugh sounded forced. 'My dear girl! Don't take this the wrong way but why would anyone remember someone they met briefly fifteen years ago?'

You did!

'Most of them will have moved away. Even Sarah . . . the expatriates don't stay up there very long.'

'Who is Sarah?'

'It doesn't matter. I've just remembered, she died last year.'

He sounded as though he regretted mentioning her. 'Then, who was Sarah?'

Reluctantly, he answered her question. 'Sarah Fotheringham. A sort of self-made missionary. She'd lived up there for as long as I can remember. She might have met your father. But as I said, she died last year.'

'A pity,' Lana said lightly.

Abruptly, he changed the subject. 'I know you're concerned about running out of time but the trip from Chilumba to Nkhotakota will only take a couple of days.'

'In a howling gale maybe.' Lana had looked at the map. He was talking 250 kilometres.

His voice went silky, as if he sensed victory. 'I can't spare more than three days away from the

244

farm. If we run out of wind I'll use the engine. You won't regret the trip. The lake is beautiful up north.' She heard him light a cigarette and blow smoke noisily. 'I'm not trying to influence your decision. I'll wait for you to call me. But you should know that I plan to set sail either Sunday night or Monday morning. Over to you.'

They said goodbye and Lana hung up wondering what the trip with Karl, if she made it, would reveal. She was very tempted. More so now than yesterday. Why did he keep mentioning Karonga? Did he know that Moffat Kadamanja lived there? And why did he back away from Sarah Fotheringham's name? Who had she been? Lana was fairly certain that Karl Henning knew more than he was saying. But did that implicate him in her father's disappearance? If it did, was Lana in danger? Why was he so insistent that she join him on his yacht? To keep an eye on her? To harm her? Or to help her?

Lana sighed. She had met three people since coming to Malawi. Tony Davenport appeared intent on either frightening her away or causing her harm. She was uncertain which. Karl Henning, she was beginning to think, was a wolf in sheep's clothing and would bear a great deal of caution on her part if she were to accept his invitation. And Tim Gilbey had information he was keeping from her. She knew that Davenport was not to be trusted but what about the other two?

She undressed and showered, letting the hot water flow over her. 'What am I doing here?' she

245

asked herself. The answer hammered back into her brain as she knew it would. 'Dad.'

Tim Gilbey knocked on her door at exactly six-thirty. 'Feel like a walk?' He was casually dressed yet managed to look elegant and masculine – a rare combination to which Lana was not impervious.

'After last night I'm not certain that's such a good idea.'

'Just around the corner.' His eyes approved the way she looked.

Lana had taken unusual care with her appearance. Khaki trousers impeccably cut and pressed accentuated her long legs and a teal blue blouse set off the colour of her eyes. No make-up but the hint of French perfume was unmistakable. 'Lead on, McGilbey.'

He offered his arm and she took it, liking the way he tucked it into his side. It was an old-fashioned gesture and he made it unselfconsciously, as though it was the most natural thing in the world.

Tim kept the conversation light and moved eas-ily. Under her fingers, however, his arm felt slightly tensed, and she noticed that his eyes probed every shadow. They walked from the Mount Soche to the Hong Kong restaurant, less than a hundred metres, encountering nothing more startling than a scavenging dog and a dignified-looking Malawian man who raised his hat as he passed.

Seated at a window table, Tim, at Lana's request, ordered for both of them. She was startled when he asked for 'Ants On A Tree' as an entree but, since the rest of the meal was standard Chinese fare, said nothing. When the waiter left, Tim asked what she'd done for the rest of the day.

'The man who came to the hotel and said he was you – his real name is Tony Davenport.'

He didn't ask how she found out but responded without hesitation. 'He's a tobacco farmer. Has a property north of Lilongwe and another one down this way. Quite well known. I think he was born here. Good family. Never married. Bit of a boozer.'

She grinned at him. 'Is that a computer between your ears, I have to ask? That's without even trying.'

'It's not much.' He frowned. 'From the little I know of him it's rather out of character.' The waiter brought their beers. Once the man had gone he added, 'How in God's name did he expect to get away with it?'

'Perhaps he thought I'd get scared and leave the country.'

Tim pulled a wry face. 'Not much chance of that is there?'

'None.'

'Didn't think so.' He smiled. 'I'm sorely tempted to lean on him a little.'

'Lean on him?' Lana raised her eyebrows.

'Very diplomatically of course.'

'Of course.' She sipped her beer, frowning. 'He tried to run me off the road this afternoon.'

Tim looked startled. 'Seriously?'

'Very.' She shrugged. 'At first I thought it was

some lunatic trying to overtake but he deliberately swung into me.'

'Good grief! What happened?'

Lana looked at him with a touch of defiance. 'I swung back.'

Tim was in the process of picking up his beer. He put it down quickly. 'You did *what*?' he asked in a strangely strangled voice.

'The advantage was mine. The car I've hired is in permanent four-wheel drive. Davenport was driving a Ford.'

Tim closed his eyes briefly.

'We were on dirt. I just shoved him off the road.' She smiled sweetly. 'His car is in intensive care.'

'And your car?' he enquired. His mouth twitched, as if he was trying hard to keep from laughing.

She frowned. 'Bleeding but drivable. I'll have some explaining to do.'

'The police?' he asked faintly.

'Ah, no actually.'

'Terrific!' His voice was heavy with irony.

'I'll report it if I get the time.'

'Did you really have to attack him?'

'He started it. I wasn't going to sit there and do nothing. What would you have done?'

He ignored that. 'Lana,' he said slowly. 'Are you sure you want to proceed with this? That's twice now – three times if you include Davenport's visit to your hotel.'

She looked him straight in the eye. 'Tony Davenport hasn't scared me off yet, Tim,' she said

248

softly. 'I have to do this, please understand.' He was nodding and she added, 'You lean on him as hard as you like. He's a bully. Bullies don't like leans.' Then she grinned. 'Very diplomatically of course.'

He inclined his head. 'Of course.'

She leaned forward and said pointedly, 'Except you can't do that can you?'

Straight-faced, he fobbed her off. 'Tell me exactly what happened.'

'You're doing it again.'

'What?'

'Answering a question with a question.'

Tim merely said seriously, 'You're a British subject. If someone is trying to harm you, it's my job –'

'Stop that.' She shook her head. 'Forget the diplomatic service for once.'

His lopsided grin was devilishly attractive.

Lana smiled back. 'That's more like it.' She sipped her Carlsberg Green, pulled a face and changed the subject herself. 'What happens to the beer here? Must they sell it before it's ready?'

'Can't have that.' Tim raised his hand and the waiter came to their table immediately. 'Two MGTs, Bambo, please.'

'What's an MGT Bambo?' Lana asked, mystified.

Tim laughed. 'An MGT is a Malawi gin 'n' tonic. Bambo is a polite way in Chichewa of saying mate, gov, pal, sir, or anything else that might mean a Malawian man.'

'It sounds terrible.'

'Wait until you ask for chambo, the lake fish.'

Lana burst out laughing.

He cocked his head, smiling. 'You're not bad at changing the subject either.'

So she told him of her encounter with Tony Davenport at the Mulanje Club and on the Midima Road. He listened in silence.

'Sounds like he panicked.'

She nodded slowly. 'Perhaps. He certainly made himself scarce when he saw me at the club.'

'There's no doubt that you're being warned off. The question still is why?'

'To protect others. It has to be.'

'You can't rule out serious crime, Lana.'

'Murder?'

He looked at her seriously. 'How would you feel if you discovered that your father had been murdered?'

She considered it, but only briefly. 'Murderous.'

'There's no point in asking –'

'None,' she interrupted firmly. 'I intend to find out if I can.'

'I rather thought you'd say that,' he said ruefully. 'To that end, and against all my better judgment, I have some news for you. Moffat Kadamanja moved to Lilongwe last year. I have his address.'

The waiter came back with their MGTs. Lana tried hers. 'Mmm – not bad.'

Tim looked horrified. 'Is that all you can say? The Malawi crowd take their gin very seriously. What you're tasting here is avidly sought from Cairo to Cape Town.'

She paid serious attention to her next sip. 'A touch of *savoir-vivre* undoubtedly,' she murmured.

She sipped again. 'Bloody good in fact,' she added, putting down her glass.

'Good girl. Louder next time. The people over there can't hear you.'

'Does Kadamanja know I'm in Malawi?'

'Yes. One of our chaps at the High Commission has spoken to him. He was a bit unhappy about being phoned at his office. The man who spoke to him got the impression he was worried about being overheard.'

'Was he told why I'm here?'

'Wasn't necessary. He said something about always knowing someone would turn up eventually.'

'Will he talk to me?'

'He's looking forward to it apparently, though not at his office. He asks that you go to his home.' Tim picked up his glass and looked at her over the rim. 'His caution is a bit of a worry. One has to ask why.'

Lana ignored Tim's obvious attempt to warn her off. 'How old is he?' It occurred to her that he could easily be a teenager – full of ideals and enthusiasm but with little or no interest in things past.

Tim cocked his eyebrow. 'I have no idea. And before you ask, I don't know if he's been circumcised either.'

Lana grinned. 'Damn! I'd hoped you'd know that too.'

The waiter came back with Ants On A Tree. Lana looked at it. Lettuce leaves sprinkled with crispy noodles and mince. It looked nothing like its name. 'This is how it's done.' Tim picked up a leaf, folded it around some of the noodle and mince mix and ate with his fingers. Lana copied him and found the combination delicious.

'What are you doing tomorrow?' Tim licked his fingers then grinned when he saw her watching him. 'Sorry. Old boarding school habit.'

'No problem.' Lana licked her own fingers. 'Although I always thought Glenalmond was slightly more upmarket.' She grinned back. 'Slight change of plan. If Kadamanja is in Lilongwe it suits me quite well. Tomorrow is Wednesday. I have no commitments until Saturday. If he's willing, I'd like to spend a couple of days talking to Moffat Kadamanja.'

'What happens Saturday?'

'Karl Henning has invited me to lunch. He's also invited me to fly to Chilumba on Sunday and bring his yacht down to Nkhotakota.'

'Don't you find that a bit *too* convenient?'

'Only if there's something you're not telling me,' she shot back.

His intensely blue eyes looked deep into hers. What she saw there briefly was anger. It was gone in an instant. Lana found it difficult to breathe suddenly. *Damn he's attractive!* Mutual attraction between them was close enough to reach out and grasp.

'Why Karl?' he asked softly.

The mood was broken. Reality pushed itself between them. 'He met Dad. He's a link. He's the only one I have. He also mentioned someone in Karonga called Sarah Fotheringham who knew Dad.'

Tim was busy with his food again. 'She reported him missing,' he said absently.

Lana watched him. His eyes blinked briefly in annoyance as he realised the slip. 'Did your boss in London tell you that or have you been the recipient of a little divine intervention?' she asked sarcastically.

'Uh . . .' he floundered and fell silent.

'What else does the file say?' Her voice had a steely ring.

'Nothing tangible. Just be on your guard.'

'Not good enough.'

'No.' He wiped his mouth with a napkin. 'Rather thought you'd say that.'

She watched him in silence for a few seconds. 'I tell you what I think,' she said finally. 'The file *is* in your office, not in London and it specifically mentions Karl Henning. I'll lay odds it speculates on what really happened to my father. You, however, are not in a position to enlighten me. Why? I'll tell you why. Because you, Tim Gilbey, are not what you pretend. You are no more a Commercial Attache than I'm a Persian Princess. You . . .' she stabbed a finger across the table at him, '. . . for whatever reason, can't get involved in case it interferes with the real reason you're in Malawi.' She smiled grimly. 'How am I doing?'

'Lana . . .'

'Forget it,' she snapped. 'Astonishing as this might sound, I actually understand your position. I don't like it, but I do understand it.' She pushed her plate away. 'That,' she grated, 'was delicious.'

'MGT or wine?' he asked gently.

'Wine,' she ground out. 'A dry white would be lovely.'

He ordered a South African Montagne Premier Grand Cru. 'I'm sorry, Lana. I wish I could help. I know how much this trip means – what you're hoping for.'

She stared him down. 'You have no idea,' she said sadly. 'No-one does.'

He put his hand over hers, warm and strong. 'I'm sorry,' he repeated.

Bitterness churned in her stomach. Not at Tim, she realised he was in a difficult position. Anger at the system. Frustration, disappointment and something else. Fear. How much danger was she really in? Would Tim tell her if she asked? She decided to find out.

He shook his head. 'If you were my sister I would beg you not to proceed.'

'I'm not your sister.'

'Okay, my wife.'

'I'm not your wife.'

'Don't go,' he said in a hard voice.

She removed her hand. 'Thank you,' she said softly. 'I know you're breaking rules.' *Breaking rules!* He had just told her far more than he should. He was breaking every rule in the book, she knew that. The look on his face told her he wasn't enjoying the experience. Lana tried to lighten the sudden wariness between them. She smiled suddenly. 'If it makes you feel any better, we can discuss the sex life of the red-legged earth mite for the rest of the evening.'

'I don't think so,' he replied straight-faced. 'They're hermaphroditic. We'd just go round in circles.'

'I know that syndrome,' she said lightly, then changed the subject. 'Why has the magic rock of shade on the Thyolo Road been cemented into place?'

He blinked, collected his thoughts and answered her question. 'Because the bloody thing kept on moving.'

'It's too big to be moved.'

'You know that; I know that; the people who built the road knew that; but someone forgot to tell the rock. The engineers had graders push the rock off to one side of the road. Next morning it was back in the middle. They pushed it off again but back it came. This went on for days.'

'Couldn't they have built the road round it? After all, it's hardly straight to begin with.'

'In the end that's what they did. Despite every effort, the rock kept moving back to its original position. The locals refused to work on that part of the road and the engineers finally gave up. The road went around the rock but they cemented it in, just in case.'

'Quite a story.' She wasn't sure she believed it.

'I'm not making it up. Ask anyone who's lived here a while, they'll tell you the same thing.'

'Is there much magic in Malawi?'

'Of the bone throwing variety you mean? No more or less than other parts of Africa. Witchdoctors are still pretty powerful. Some of the expatriates actually use them to put a spell on their house when they go on leave. Stops them being burgled they reckon. It seems to work too. I even heard about a chap the other day who got rid of a staff member by placing a blood-soaked white chicken feather in the man's desk drawer. Bit stupid really. Best not to dabble in what you don't understand.' He smiled at her. 'Do you believe in witchcraft?'

'I believe in the power of the mind, most certainly. If you want to call it magic, witchcraft or voodoo that's fine by me. Whatever it's called, I've seen it work before though if you look for a logical explanation you can usually find one.'

The conversation remained light and off the subject of Karl Henning. Lana knew that Tim could have told her more and, several times she thought he was wrestling with his conscience as to whether or not to speak out, but in the end, he said nothing about Henning. He did, however, inadvertently, and much to his regret, clarify Lana's plans for after she had seen Moffat Kadamanja in Lilongwe.

As they walked back to the hotel Lana was in two minds whether or not to invite him up to her room for a nightcap. She was not worried that Tim would take the invitation to mean more than a drink. What concerned Lana was her own behaviour. Alone, in her room with him, could she trust herself not to ravage him? The prospect of such a thing, she admitted to herself, was profoundly attractive. Tim solved the dilemma by asking, 'Your room or mine?' as they collected their keys, then added quickly, 'A drink.'

'Just one,' Lana replied, her heart hammering. 'I'm driving to Lilongwe tomorrow.'

In the lift, he took her key and put it with his behind his back. 'Which hand?'

Lana pointed to his left.

It was her key.

She raised her eyes from his hand. She could not read the expression on his face. She put out her hand for the key and he closed his strong brown fingers around it, drawing her closer. The electricity between them was so intense that Lana swayed towards him. His arms went around her, pulling her into him. Their lips met just as the lift stopped and the doors opened. Neither of them knew that two men waited to get into the left until one of them cleared his throat.

The depth of feeling was too new, too unexpected for either Lana or Tim to act naturally. They sprang apart embarrassed. Lana went past the men without looking at them, thoughts and emotions whirling out of control inside her. Tim gathered his wits sufficiently to give them a brief nod and a gruff 'Evening,' before he too left the lift, uncomfortably aware that both men wore broad grins.

The walk to her room seemed endless.

'I'm on the fourth floor,' Tim said, pointlessly.

'Really!' *Christ! He didn't just tell you he'd won the lottery.* Her over-reaction, in an attempt to get back to normal, increased her embarrassment. *This is not like you. Get a grip!* But she couldn't. The intensity was still there and she was thoroughly shaken by it.

They reached her room at last. Lana was acutely

conscious of his nearness. If she put out a hand, she would touch him. She risked a look at his face and found his eyes, serious and deep, were watching her. Lana knew that one move from the other, one lift of an eyebrow, one light touch, the smallest sign of intimacy, would result in them spending the night together. And she knew that Tim knew it too.

Each of them, for their own reasons, backed away from it.

Lana opened the door. 'What's your poison?' She was glad her voice was steady.

'Scotch.' His was too.

She indicated a table and two chairs in one corner, deliberately ignoring the sofa and making a conscious effort not to look at the bed. 'Take a seat.'

As she was pouring his scotch he said casually, 'I suppose you'll be going up to Karonga to see Sarah Fotheringham.'

She handed him the glass, relieved by his tone. 'No point. Karl said she died last year.'

Tim frowned. 'Then she makes a perky corpse. I spoke to her on the phone a few days ago.'

The desire which had been so strong in her so few moments ago, vanished. Lana picked up her scotch. She sipped it slowly before responding. 'Two questions. Why did you speak to her and why would Karl lie?' She crossed the room and sat in a chair by the window. 'Scratch the second question – her name slipped out and Karl went into reverse gear.' She looked at Tim. 'Which leaves me with the first.' Her stare gave his eyes nowhere to go.

'Okay,' he admitted. 'I've done some rummaging on your behalf. Sarah Fotheringham remembers your father very well. When he went missing it was Sarah who reported it. She also mentioned that Karl Henning's ketch was seen in the area.'

'Not conclusive.'

'It was in the area when the first two were killed.'

'Still not conclusive.'

'It had never been in the area before and hasn't been seen since.'

Lana put down her glass. 'What else is in the file?' she asked softly.

'Nothing much. Henning has an undeclared income but that's not a major crime. He makes a lot of business trips to the Far East. He was in Blantyre, at the Mount Soche, when your father stayed here and he was also in Blantyre, and guess what, also at the Mount Soche when the first two got here. Coincidence? Sarah believes he's implicated. She's agreed to talk to you.'

'You don't trust Henning, do you?'

'I wouldn't trust him with an onion.'

She smiled a little at that. 'How professional of you!'

'It's a gut feel.'

'There's got to be more. In the restaurant you told me not to go sailing with him.'

'Can't you see,' he said, sounding exasperated, 'that someone doesn't want you here? Who else knows who you are and why you're here?'

'You do,' she shot back.

'Don't be ridiculous.'

'I'm not being ridiculous,' she said, stung. 'If you're so worried about me, why don't you come to Karonga with me?'

She had no idea how much he wanted to. 'I'm too busy.'

Lana banged her glass on the table. 'Fine. I'll go on my own. And for that matter, I'll accept Karl's invitation. Maybe it's enough for you to make wild guesses. It's not enough for me. If he's involved I'll not find out by sitting on my backside. Now, if you wouldn't mind, I'm tired. Good night.'

After he had gone Lana drained her scotch. Then, as an afterthought, drained his as well. She could not believe how quickly the passionate vibes between them became so full of anger.

Tim went straight to the telephone in his room and phoned Martin Flower at his London home. 'Hope you weren't in bed,' he said, when his boss came on the line.

'I was watching television.' Martin sounded grumpy.

'Lana Devereaux is going sailing with Karl Henning. I can't talk her out of it.'

'Damn the girl!'

'I think she's in danger. She was attacked last night and today someone tried to run her off the road. That same someone, incidentally, impersonated me and threatened her with deportation.'

Flower chewed this over. 'It's none of our business. Don't let this get in your way, Tim.'

'It's already in my way,' Tim snapped. 'I can't sit back and allow her to run headlong into trouble.'

'There's nothing you can do.'

'I told her what was in the file.'

'I don't suppose it matters. Nothing was ever proved, it's all speculation.'

'True but I have a bad feeling about this one, Martin. What if Henning intends to get rid of her? A quiet word of warning in his ear might not go astray.'

There was silence while Flower considered the suggestion. 'Okay, Tim,' he said finally. 'But for Christ's sake, son, when you put the wind up him, make sure it's a gentle diplomatic breeze. A howling FCO gale is the last thing we need at the moment.'

'Trust me.' Tim grinned. 'Thanks, Martin.'

'Sod off,' Martin grumbled. 'I've missed the end of a splendid play thanks to you.'

Tim found Henning's number in the phone book and dialled, half hoping the man would be in bed asleep. But Henning came on the line almost immediately and was clearly wide awake.

'Karl Henning.'

'Tim Gilbey. British High Commission.'

'How may I help you?' Henning asked smoothly.

'Lana Devereaux is a friend of mine.'

'She's a friend of mine too.' If Henning was surprised he showed no sign of it.

'I hope you mean that.'

'What's that supposed to mean?'

'Accidents,' Tim said. 'Don't let one happen to her.'

Henning went silent for a moment. Then, 'Mr Gilbey did you say –'

'Yes,' Tim answered briefly, expecting anger.

'I don't know what the hell you're talking about.'

'I think you know what I'm saying.'

'Spell it out.' Henning sounded amused rather than angry.

'Our records go back a long way. It's interesting how often your name appears. What I'm saying, Mr Henning, is that if anything happens to Lana Devereaux while she's sailing with you, this office would be obliged to assist with any official enquiry.' Tim had his fingers crossed. 'It's in your interest to keep her safe.'

'Accidents do happen, Mr Gilbey. I can't be held responsible for her absolute safety. We're sailing to Nkhotakota. Yachts sink.' His voice was calm, as though he were reasoning with a child. Tim realised just how dangerous the man might be. He did not appear to have been thrown in the least by Tim's veiled threats to expose him. In fact, he seemed to be enjoying himself.

'You know what I'm saying, Henning,' Tim snapped. 'Don't play games. You've been lucky so far but don't push it.'

'I haven't the slightest notion what you're talking about,' Karl Henning said silkily. 'Now, if that's all I'm rather busy.'

'Just bear this in mind,' Tim growled, hating the

man. 'Your overseas connections are known to us. Your activities in Malawi just prior to the '83 coup attempt are also on record. You had some interesting friends back then. Oddly enough, they're all dead. Do you understand me?'

'Go to hell, Mr Gilbey.' The receiver was slammed down.

'Great!' Tim was thinking. 'A gentle diplomatic breeze! Christ, I just sent out a bloody tornado.'

Unable to sleep, he sat by the window staring out, thinking. There had been one or two moments earlier when the urge to touch Lana had been almost too strong to resist. It wasn't just the way she looked, though God knows, she was most certainly worth looking at. It was her fierce determination, coupled with one or two signs of vulnerability.

Tim never actually sought romantic interludes while on assignment, though he certainly didn't back off when they popped up. Lana was different. A night of passion with her would, he knew, lead to something deeper, more permanent and that was the last thing he needed until his job was over. He acknowledged that, as well as finding Lana the most attractive woman he had ever met, he also liked her. He admired her spirit and courage. He respected her intelligence. He liked her sense of humour. 'Dear God,' he was thinking. 'I even like the way she threw me out.'

Lana lay on her back, staring up at the ceiling. Dinner with Tim Gilbey had been pretty well what she expected – enjoyable. 'What else could it be?' she asked herself. He was sophisticated yet possessed an endearing homely quality. He was sensitive yet firm, with the quiet assurance that rests easily with peak physical condition. He was certainly something more than his official position would suggest. What then was the reason for his being in Malawi? 'Good conversationalist, good company, good-looking, good . . . God!' She sat bolt upright. 'What the hell is wrong with you?' She lay back frowning. 'He's just doing his job. Get your mind back on track.'

But she couldn't. Not straightaway. The way he looked, the feel of his arms, of his lips on hers, the passion in those deep blue eyes, this was a man she wanted to know better. This was a man, she admitted to herself, that had the words 'satisfaction guaranteed' stamped all over him. And Lana was not thinking about sex.

She forced herself to concentrate on Karl Henning. Tim had told her nothing. 'Don't go,' he had said. So what did that tell her? Not a damned thing. She was still irritated that Tim Gilbey obviously possessed knowledge about Karl, and possibly even her father, yet had done little more than warn her to be on her guard.

Karl, she admitted, did disturb her. She could accept coincidence – life was a series of them. But were there too many? He seemed nice enough. Why was he helping her? Because she was new in his country and he was just being hospitable? Her father had said there was more hospitality in Africa than anywhere else in the world. Did Karl have seduction on his mind? Seduction she could handle.

What about Tony Davenport? Tim was going to lean on Davenport but, if he found out anything, would he tell her? 'Would he hell!'

She turned onto her back again. Tony Davenport was trying to frighten her off. *How the hell did he know I was in the country?* Someone told him. It could only be Karl or Tim – no-one else knew. Frustrated, Lana stared into the darkness. 'This is ridiculous. Bernard tried to warn me. I wish I'd never come.'

But she knew she didn't mean that. Just being where her father had been would help. Her thoughts drifted to Moffat Kadamanja. He lived in a village on the outskirts of Lilongwe but it was not possible to contact him by telephone. He was expecting her and prepared to talk to her. That was all she knew. Had he made any enquiries of his own? His father's body had at least been found and the coroner's report stated accidental drowning. Perhaps there was no reason to suspect foul play. He might be a simple, rural Malawian with an African's stoic acceptance of death and no desire to take the matter further. He could be fifteen or fifty, she had no idea. She remembered Tim's comment and grinned into the darkness. Dammit! she didn't even know if he were circumcised!

Tim! Tonight something nearly happened, a chemistry of some kind, which, however fleeting, had been strong. But she had backed off. Why? Was it because she wanted nothing to complicate her real reason for being in Malawi? 'That makes sense,' she thought. 'I've waited fifteen years for this. I need a clear head, I can't have a man, no matter how attractive he is, clouding my judgment.'

The last man Lana had found attractive had been a Dutch drilling supervisor in Sumatra. More at ease planting dynamite in cliffs than bothering about political correctness, he had impressed Lana by shedding tears over the plight of a small, badly injured puppy. She was half in love with him when he casually dropped the fact that he was married.

The experience had left Lana with a legacy of deep suspicion about men. While her heart had not been seriously broken, it had been fractured enough to hurt for several months. She drew no comfort from the knowledge that he had not deliberately lied. She had *assumed* he was single because he was a willing participant in a relationship which deepened rapidly. Her shock, when he said he was married, astonished him. 'And that,' she conceded, 'is what hurt.'

Lana played fair. She expected others to do the same. Her first tentative step into love had slapped her in the face. While she was too honest within herself to turn one disappointment into bitterness, she nonetheless had retreated into cynical observation of men, rather than trying again.

It was three years since the Dutchman in Sumatra. Lana was over that hurt. She was probably over the mistrust too. Was she ready to try again?

'It's not simply physical, although, God knows, he's attractive enough.' It was a total thing. Tim

Gilbey fitted perfectly into her idea of the ideal man: modern enough to treat her as an equal yet old-fashioned and comfortable enough with himself to offer the courtesies which she believed had, by and large, been bludgeoned to death by the feminist movement.

She discounted the fact that she had literally thrown him out of her room. The unexpected rush of emotion had unsettled her, left her unsure of herself. 'Defence mechanism,' she excused her actions. 'It all happened too fast.' She felt her eyelids grow heavy.

'On a scale of one to ten,' she mused. She was getting sleepy. Her thoughts often rambled like this just before she dropped off. 'Tim might go a perfect score. And those eyes!'

Lana fell asleep.

TWELVE

In the morning, refreshed and eager to get going, Lana's mental meanderings of the night before fell into place.

Moffat Kadamanja was, for now, an unknown element. If he knew anything, if he could help, well and good. If not, she'd go it alone.

Karl Henning might be a very nice man trying to help. Okay, she'd let him help. He might also be a very nasty man trying to harm. There was only one way to find out. And in finding out, she might learn more about her father.

Tim Gilbey was undoubtedly the most attractive man she had ever met and probably one of the most provoking. Had he told her everything? What else was he hiding from her? Would she ever see him again?

Just where Tony Davenport fitted in she had no idea.

Over breakfast Lana reviewed her options. She concluded she didn't really have any. Not yet. What she had was a vague plan of action, an invitation she was uncertain she wanted to accept, a man who wanted to meet her in Lilongwe, a woman in

Karonga, and that idiot, Tony Davenport, who was going out of his way to make life as difficult as possible. 'I can do this,' she told herself. She was in Malawi doing what she always intended. She owed it to her father and to herself. 'And that,' she decided, 'is the bottom line.'

Satisfied and resolved, Lana drove north towards Lilongwe. She could have taken the new freeway and been in the capital within five hours. Instead, because it was the road she knew her father would have driven, she went via the old route, through Zomba, over the Shiré River and up the Dedza escarpment to the plateau. Shorter by far than the freeway, it should have taken less time than the new road. Unfortunately, the road was more pothole than tar but the views were worth the inconvenience. Beyond Zomba, once colonial capital of Nyasaland, the hilly country quickly fell away. Heat haze stretched to a blue infinity. The air became still and sultry as the highway swept down to lake level and crossed the swirling, chocolate brown Shiré River at Liwonde. The scenery Lana had admired from 30,000 feet did not let her down. The further north she travelled, the more diverse it became until she was high on the spectacular Dedza plateau, where mountains stretched away on all sides like monstrous waves. She wondered why more tourists didn't come to Malawi. Lakes, rivers, hills, mountains, open savanna, for such a small country it had so much. 'Except a healthy economy,' she thought, dodging some wicked potholes in the centre of the road. 'If only Dad *had* found oil . . .' But she knew he hadn't. The two reports he'd sent to PAGET indicated that oil under Lake Malawi was still a good five million years in the making.

Lana forced her mind back to the present. She had decided to allow herself two full days in Lilongwe before going on up to Karonga. Her intention was to spend as much time as possible with Moffat Kadamanja. He, more than anyone else, might be inclined to speak honestly.

It was early afternoon when she booked into the Capital Hotel. Clever use of wood, dark brick and tiles created a cool tranquillity. Tropical gardens planted close against floor to ceiling windows displayed their lush verdancy both inside and out. Her room on the second floor had an uninterrupted view of manicured gardens and Lana, who had never paid much heed to horticultural pursuits, found much to admire in the well-planned mix of mature palms and shrubs. She looked at her watch. Three o'clock. Might as well go and look for Kadamanja's village.

All she knew about Moffat Kadamanja was that he lived in Area 3, off Selous Road near the Civil Service Club. 'Old Town,' the original small town which existed before the new capital was built, she was informed by a man at the reception desk, 'is over the bridge.' She had no idea how to find it and decided to explore on foot.

She had no difficulty in locating the main shopping centre – it was a block away from the hotel and stunning high-rise buildings, towering up from the trees, showed the way. She took time out to admire the Reserve Bank of Malawi building, its golden colour and top heavy design intended to represent one of the traditional baskets used in Malawi to gather maize. The city centre was a strange mixture of modern Western style buildings – the design of some which defied gravity – side by side with markets, Indian trading houses, and squat, run-down African style shops. New buildings were being erected everywhere. Lana strolled from shop to shop, a growing band of hawkers displaying their wares behind her. She supposed that one day, when all the building was finished, Lilongwe city centre might have some sense of order. She found it messy and considerably different to the impression she'd got of it from the air.

Having explored, and becoming a little fed up by the persistence of some of the hawkers, she went to return to the hotel. As she walked up to the entrance, however, she noticed a sign on the opposite side of the road which said 'Japanese Gardens'. She crossed the road and found herself in a park. Of the Japanese Gardens, she saw no sign, unless a lone pavilion was supposed to be it, but she wandered on through the park and, ten minutes later, found herself on Capital Hill.

This was the new seat of government. Every Ministry had its own building, each identical to the other – a long white rectangle, three storeys high, with balconies running along the entire length of the first and second floors. Set in landscaped gardens, which were showing signs of neglect and recent drought, Capital Hill must still have been a pleasant place to work. Lana spent thirty minutes wandering in the park-like grounds until a man came out of one of the buildings and asked if she was lost.

'No,' she replied, smiling. 'I'm just looking.'

He smiled back. 'Are you a visitor?' He was watching her carefully.

'Yes I am.'

'You should visit the nature sanctuary.'

Lana took advantage of the man's knowledge. 'Where will I find old Lilongwe?'

'Old Town? On the road to Blantyre.' His gaze shifted to a point over her left shoulder.

'Really?' She was surprised. 'I drove up from Blantyre today and didn't see it.'

'Then you have been there.'

'I see. I thought that was the start to Lilongwe.'

'That is so. That is Old Town.' He turned to leave. 'If you have no business on Capital Hill you must not trespass. I'm sorry.'

Something was wrong. The man spoke softly, with no anger, yet his actions were almost aggressive. He was gesturing with his hands that she should leave. Lana couldn't see why she should. 'I'm not doing anything wrong. If you don't want people in here you should put up a fence.' *Cool it for Christ's sake, girl, you're not in England now.*

She half expected anger. Rules and regulations were rigidly enforced in most developing countries, especially when being broken by a white person. But when he turned back all she saw was

272

regret, though he was still waving his hands that she should go. 'There is a sign in the car park – did you not see it?'

Arguing would be a waste of time, she could see that. 'I'll leave immediately even though I think it's ridiculous,' she snapped. Then she relented. The rules were hardly this man's fault. 'Good day to you, sir.' *God! I don't believe I said that.*

'Yes, madam,' he replied soberly, walking away.

Leaving the grounds Lana did see a small sign which read OFFICIAL BUSINESS ONLY and remembered seeing it on the way into the complex. She had thought it referred to the parking area.

It was four-thirty when she returned to the hotel. Old Town must be about ten kilometres away if she remembered correctly. No point in going today. She bought a postcard in the lobby curio shop then sat outside with a cup of coffee and wrote briefly to her mother and Bernard.

Locating the original old town of Lilongwe the next morning was easy. Moffat Kadamanja's house was less obliging. Streets very often had no name – or none that she could find. It wasn't until she realised that every house was numbered and the numbers ran with a reasonable degree of consecutive order, that she was able to find it.

Driving through the labyrinth of old Lilongwe, Lana felt she had stepped back into an older Africa. There was no comparison with the new capital's wide and carefully planned street pattern. She wondered which the local people preferred. New Lilongwe was a meshing of a number of different cultures but it lacked an essential element, an African meander which, while not as orderly, had a village quality, a friendly, family feeling about it. The shops had a market look to them with a bazaar-style jumble of goods displayed and, outside each shop, tailors worked on ancient hand-wound sewing machines. Loud reggae music from hundreds of radios joined the shouted conversations. Stalls sold everything from fish to tin buckets – some stalls sold both – and venders thought nothing of running to the car displaying their wares in a friendly, smiling, but very persistent hard sell. Lana knew which she preferred. Old Town was the real Africa.

She reached Moffat Kadamanja's house a little after eleven in the morning. As houses went, it wasn't much to look at. Like most in the area it was set in the centre of about an acre of land. Around the plot a high chicken wire fence, with two strands of razor wire on top, protected the Kadamanjas from burglars. The red brick rectangular-shaped house was shaded by several huge mango trees. The small windows had curtains drawn. The corrugated iron roof, the sheets of which varied significantly in age and condition, had once been green. Mealies grew down one side of the house and on the other a woven straw wall shielded a flourishing vegetable garden from the worst of the sun. A goat was tethered in the shade near the house. An old and battered child's tricycle lay on its side on the hard-baked red earth. The rusted cab of a Bedford truck gave purchase to vigorously healthy busy lizzies, while a few arum lilies competed gamely with their colourful display. Lana parked in the street, went through the gate and knocked on the front door.

After nearly half-a-minute, just as she was about to knock again, a woman's voice called something in Chichewa. Feeling somewhat foolish, Lana shouted her name, then added, 'I come to see Mr Kadamanja.'

'You wait,' the voice said in English.

Lana heard footsteps, then silence. She waited. Nothing happened. She stared at the front door as if it were to blame for the inactivity. Feeling she was being watched Lana glanced sideways just in time to see a small head pop back behind the house. Deciding to investigate, she stepped quietly to the corner and discovered three giggling children who, at her appearance, fled shrieking with laughter. A woman appeared from the back, smiling and beckoning. 'Excuse. My English not good.'

Lana shook her head. 'My Chichewa is none.' Unconsciously, she was speaking pidgin English, something she always tried very hard not to do but, under the circumstances, simplifying the conversation was the only way to go. She placed her hand against her chest. 'I am Lana Devereaux. I come to see Mr Moffat Kadamanja.'

'Yes.' The woman smiled widely. 'He is my husband.' She was young, perhaps in her mid-twenties. Her peppercorn hair had been braided into dozens of tiny pigtails, each held by an enormous ribbon. The cornflower blue of them matched a cotton dress which strained over the bulge of advanced pregnancy. She was barefoot. Her smile revealed very white teeth and dimples set in one of the sweetest faces Lana had ever seen. 'My husband will be here very soon, you come inside.'

Lana followed Mrs Kadamanja into the house. It was obvious that the Kadamanjas had little money to spend on luxuries but everything inside was scrubbed scrupulously clean. Brightly coloured cotton curtains added a cheerful look to the drabness of unpainted cement-rendered walls. The linoleum floor was almost invisible under an array of coir and reed mats. 'You sit.' The woman pointed to a sofa.

Lana sat. The three small children, the eldest of whom, a girl, couldn't have been more than five or six, hung around their mother's skirt and gazed at Lana with wide-eyed curiosity. Under this unwavering scrutiny, Lana tried to make conversation. 'Is Mr Kadamanja at work?'

'Work?' The woman seemed puzzled by the question.

'Yes, his job.' It occurred to Lana that if Moffat Kadamanja was at work she might have to wait hours for his return.

The woman's face brightened. 'My husband no work today.'

Lana nodded encouragingly but nothing more was forthcoming. 'My name is Lana,' she said slowly. 'Lana.'

The woman repeated it, stretching the first syllable attractively.

'What is your name?' Lana asked.

'Frances,' the woman said shyly. Lana suspected she would also have a tribal name but decided not to ask. It was hard enough making simple conversation.

'That's a very nice name.' She looked at the older girl. 'And what is your name?'

Frances shook her head and answered for all the children. 'She not speak English. She will learn it at school.' She pointed to the smallest, a girl about two. 'This one Betty.' Frances turned to her only son and pushed him forward. 'This one George. Same as Moffat's grandfather. Same as old King of England.' The pride in her son was evident and Lana remembered that Africans regard sons with special affection. The older girl was then introduced. 'This one Ruth.'

'Does she go to school yet?'

'No.'

Well, that's another subject down the drain. Lana wracked her brain. 'When will Mr Kadamanja be here?'

'Soon.'

Lana was getting desperate. She couldn't sit and say nothing. She patted her stomach. 'Another baby?'

Frances giggled and nodded.

'When will it come?'

'I do not know. One month, maybe two.'

A car pulled up outside and Lana prayed it would be Moffat Kadamanja, adding a mental postscript that he could speak reasonable English.

The tall, good-looking and well-dressed man who walked into the house came as something of a shock. He was the same person who had asked her to leave the gardens of Capital Hill.

Moffat Kadamanja dominated the small room, not so much by his physical size as by his bearing. He was a man of obvious confidence, whether from arrogance, ability, or something else, Lana had yet to find out. Whatever it was, he was an authoritative figure, something she had sensed yesterday. 'Miss Devereaux.' He extended a hand. 'Moffat Kadamanja. I thought it must have been you yesterday. Did you know you were being followed?'

'Are you sure?' A chill went through her. Surely Tony Davenport wouldn't dare.

He nodded. 'Two men were watching you from the car park.'

'White men?' She could have kicked herself. 'I mean . . . it's just that a white man has been following me.'

Moffat Kadamanja ignored her sudden embarrassment. 'They were African.'

'Are you sure?' she asked again. Who would follow her? Perhaps he was mistaken.

He permitted himself a small smile. 'I believe I know Africans when I see them, Miss Devereaux.'

Lana stared at him, suddenly afraid. What the hell was going on? Who would be tailing her?

'We must talk, you and I,' Kadamanja said. 'Not here. I don't want my family involved in this.'

'Of course.' She rose quickly. 'Where do you suggest?'

278

He smiled again. He had a small gap between his front teeth. When he smiled his face became boyish, as though he had just shed a good ten years. 'My bar,' he said. 'I have friends there. Come.' He turned and walked outside. He had not said one word to his wife or children.

Lana went to Frances. 'Thank you,' she said. 'I hope your new baby brings you much happiness.'

Frances looked at her as though she were mad.

'We will take your car,' Kadamanja said when she joined him outside. 'What happened to it?'

'I have no idea. It happened while it was parked.' No point in worrying this man with the truth – at least, not yet.

He eyed the damage. *'Pepani,'* he said shaking his head. 'Sorry,' he repeated in English. He walked to the passenger's door and opened it. 'You drive,' he ordered.

Yes sir! She knew he was not being rude, he was simply used to making all decisions when women were involved. She grinned inwardly at her about-face. If a white man had issued orders she'd have challenged them. *This man barks out two words and I scamper to obey.* She supposed it was because she knew it wasn't arrogance on his part, just a masculine assurance that his decision was the right one. It was the African way, the traditional way, and she found it easy enough to accept.

She was glad he was in the car with her. She would never have found the bar on her own. It was less than two kilometres from where he lived but the network of potholed tracks they traversed to get there left her totally lost. Apart from giving directions, he made no attempt at conversation. He said but one word when they arrived. 'Lock.'

Lana locked the car.

The bar room had no pretensions of grandeur. A square, with curtainless, burglar-barred windows at the front, the bar along one wall, a jukebox halfway down another, and some cheap metal and formica tables with vinyl-covered chairs placed randomly around the room. Ashtrays were the metal floor type, half-filled with sand. Cigarette and beer advertising plastered the walls. Whoever laid the black and white floor tiles had completely lost the plot about halfway up the room as their neat synchronisation went haywire, never to be found again.

The barman greeted Moffat like a long-lost brother. Half-a-dozen women eyed him invitingly. One of them sauntered over and, although she spoke Chichewa, Lana recognised two words. 'One hundred Kwacha.' Moffat simply laughed, slapped her behind and, without asking what Lana wanted, ordered her a beer. 'We can talk here.'

He led her to a table at the back of the room. 'Hey, Bambo, who is your friend?' one of the women laughingly called in English.

Moffat replied in his own language and, in response to Lana's querying look, explained. 'They work here.'

'All of them? What on earth is there for them to do?' She blushed suddenly at the stupidity of her question.

Kadamanja saw her realisation and smiled. 'It's our way,' he said, with no embarrassment. 'Every bar has hostesses.'

One of the girls brought over two ice-cold Carlsberg Greens. There were no glasses and no money changed hands.

'Don't you worry about AIDS?' Lana couldn't help but ask, knowing the disease had reached epidemic proportions in central Africa.

'Of course. They are checked every two months.'

Fat lot of good that does! But Lana said nothing. Death, by any means, was treated with fatalistic acceptance in Africa. A very old person who had run the gauntlet of disease, wild animals, poverty and political instability was always well-respected. A winner in life's game of chance. AIDS was simply the most recent Russian roulette of Africa and Lana knew she'd be wasting her breath.

She looked at this man sitting across the table. Did he have any answers for her? Would he tell her if he did? His father and hers had been together fifteen years ago. Both had died in unexplained circumstances. This fact alone made her feel connected to him, as though he were a distant relative. Would he feel the same way? 'Was I *really* trespassing yesterday?' As opening gambits went, it wasn't much but Lana wanted to get a feel for Kadamanja before saying more.

He smiled. 'Technically, no. I saw you out there and thought you were trying to make contact with me.'

'I was told not to. In fact, I had no idea where you worked. How did you know it was me?'

His eyes were deep and unreadable. 'The man who contacted me said you were beautiful. You are.'

Lana nearly blushed again. The compliment was given with absolute sincerity and not a shred of innuendo. 'Thank you,' she managed.

'I was going to ignore you but then I saw the men following you.'

'I had no idea they were there.'

'Yes. That was obvious.'

'Why *did* you come out?'

He seemed to reach a decision. 'May I speak frankly?' When she nodded, he went on. 'I do not know many white people. I work with a few but that is all. What I have seen of them – please do not be offended – there is a kind of arrogance with them.'

Lana squirmed inwardly, remembering her attitude yesterday.

Kadamanja saw her discomfort. 'Do not worry please. You were right to be angry yesterday. I expected it. We were being watched. I did not wish to appear friendly.'

'Why?'

'I'll get to that. First I must say what is in my heart. It is this. If you come to seek vengeance then I cannot help you.'

'Vengeance!' The thought startled her. 'No, Mr Kadamanja, I do not wish to get even. All I have ever wanted was to know what happened.'

He was watching her closely. 'A great injustice was done. It would be normal for a white person to want to punish those who were guilty.'

'Don't you?'

He shook his head, smiling. 'Africans are different.'

Lana said quietly, 'I don't believe you,' and was totally unprepared for his reaction. He threw back his head and laughed heartily.

'Miss Devereaux,' he said finally. 'The things I saw in you yesterday are still here today. That is good.'

'What things?'

'Honesty and determination,' he told her promptly. 'Bravery and caution. Yesterday I went to see you because I was afraid you would be arrogant. If you had been then we would not be here now. Yes, I want to know what happened. Yes, of course I want whoever was responsible to be punished. But, Miss Devereaux, not at my own expense or that of my family. If you want my help we will do it my way, the African way. That is what is in my heart. What do you say to it?'

Lana knew she was being tested. She tried to work out what it was that Moffat Kadamanja expected of her. Then she thought, 'To hell with that. If it's honesty he's after, he might as well have it undiluted.' Besides, she realised Kadamanja would quickly spot any attempt on her part to be anything other than completely up front.

'Mr Kadamanja, I do not know the African way. I only know my way. I won't be satisfied until I know what happened to my father. When I find that out I'll deal with the rest of it. Whoever was responsible for what happened to both our fathers is clever and dangerous. If your way is better than mine then we'll do things your way. If not, well . . . I suppose we'll just have to argue. That is the best I can say.'

He was nodding. 'The truth shines from your eyes. You have spoken well.'

'I speak from my heart. And I'll tell you something else. You and I are connected, I can feel it. We are after the same thing. I would like to work with you on this.'

'We may only learn some of the truth. The rest may be lost to the passing of the years. It will be enough for me, but will you be satisfied?'

'I don't know,' Lana said soberly. 'For as you have already observed, I have a need to understand. I believe you called it arrogance.'

'Is it not arrogant to expect to know everything, as if it is your right?'

'Mr Kadamanja, it *is* my right and it is yours too.'

'No,' he shook his head. 'The truth has many moods. You can never know the whole truth for, as hard as you try, you will find you are running in circles around a ball which spins faster than you can run. You should be content with the truth as you know it.'

'You know,' she said, smiling, 'that makes more sense than just about anything else I've heard.'

Her comment surprised him. 'I did not expect that from you.'

'Because I'm white?'

He nodded, saying nothing.

'Our fathers . . .'

He nodded again. 'Yes, our fathers.' He glanced away briefly. 'In Africa we call our friends brothers and sisters. We will become brother and sister, you and I. I feel this strongly.' He smiled suddenly. 'It is not so strange that we should.' Then he laughed. 'Although your mother and mine might be surprised.'

Lana laughed with him. This man was nothing like she expected and everything she had hoped for. 'Please call me Lana,' she said. 'I know Malawians are formal but, under the circumstances . . .'

He nodded. 'I am Moffat.'

'It's an unusual name. Scottish?'

He was delighted. 'Yes. My father chose it. He was very fond of reading about David Livingstone. He called me Moffat after Livingstone's wife.'

'Why didn't he call you David after Livingstone himself?'

Moffat regarded her gravely. 'My father was born in the Zambezi Valley at a place called Shupanga. That is where Mary Livingstone is buried. The old people tell of her gentleness. The stories are passed down. Mary Moffat-Livingstone was buried under a huge baobab tree. It is still there.'

'That's lovely.' Lana felt she had been handed a precious memory. 'Your father was Jonah.'

'Yours was John.'

The glance which passed between them ran deep. Friendship and kinship. Bonded by tragedy, they were partners in their quest for the truth.

Their hands touched and held. His hand was warm around hers. 'I will tell you everything I know. It is not a story which has an ending. It has no real beginning either, since I do not know some things – they died with my father. It is always so, is it not?'

Lana did not need to respond.

'I am my father's only son,' Kadamanja began. 'He died when I was sixteen. From the time I was ten my father expected me to be a man. Nothing too big you understand – he was a very fair man. Cutting wood for my mother, tending the goats, protecting my sisters, just small things like that. He was often away but saw how proud I was to help and one day began to tell to me of his work. Some of the things I speak of now are things my father told to me. I expect you to honour the confidential nature of them please.'

Lana nodded.

Moffat took a long haul on his beer, wiped his mouth with the back of his hand and called out for two more beers. 'My father worked in government for fifteen years. He started as a clerk with Trade, Industry and Tourism, became a financial assistant in the Education Department and was finally promoted to administrator with Local Government. He served this country proudly and never, not once, gave the old Congress Party any reason to be dissatisfied.' Moffat finished his beer in one swallow and clicked his fingers impatiently for the next two bottles. Lana hastily took a swig of hers, offered to pay for the second round but backed down immediately when she saw the look on Moffat's face.

'When a man who worked for someone very high up in the government made contact with him early in 1983 my father became quite worried.'

'Who? A Minister?'

Moffat shrugged. 'That is one of the things which died with my father. Perhaps he did not know himself.'

Lana frowned. 'Surely his concern indicates that he did.'

Moffat nodded. 'That is what I think too. I only know one thing for certain. The name of the man who approached him.'

'Did your father tell you?'

'He told me some things, yes. But now I am a man I realise he did not tell me everything. I was sixteen then. It is possible that my father did not trust me with all he knew.' Moffat looked unhappy at the thought. 'Those were very difficult times in Malawi. A lot of unexplained things happened – people were frightened.'

Lana squeezed his hand. 'I understand that. Can you tell me what you know?'

'I have always regretted that I did not pay more attention.' Moffat broke their hand contact abruptly and picked up his beer. 'I was sixteen. What did I care?'

She watched him tip the bottle and swallow with obvious enjoyment.

'This is what I remember,' he said, picking up her hand again. 'My father was instructed to assist with PAGET's geological survey of the lake. He was to report back only to a Mr Edward Phiri.'

'The man who approached him?'

'Yes.'

'What kind of things did he have to report?

'Edward Phiri was not interested in the survey as such. It was who your father spoke to that concerned him.'

Lana nodded slowly. 'I see. That work was supposedly top-secret. President Banda had not been informed. The reason given was that he wanted nothing to spoil Lake Malawi. We, that is PAGET, assumed that if anything were found then the President would have to be told. No-one in London was happy about the secrecy. There must have been a leak somewhere.'

'That explains something which has worried me for years. I could never understand why my father was sent to spy on yours.'

'He didn't tell you?'

'I don't think he knew. He was just following orders.'

'So did he report back as instructed?'

Moffat looked happier. 'No. Not once.'

'Are you sure of that?'

He nodded. 'Positive. He told me he wouldn't. My father was a very honourable man. I believe he spoke the truth. However, a few years ago I came across something which, as far as I'm concerned, proved he didn't.' He eyed her soberly. 'Malawi is a different country now. Life is free and people can say what they like. It was not always so. But who knows,' he shrugged eloquently. 'There are those who would have us go back to the old ways. If

what I am about to tell you gets out . . .' He left it
hanging between them.

'I am only interested in the truth about our
fathers. If you help me I will never betray your confidence.' Lana spoke so vehemently that he smiled.

Then he seemed to change the subject. 'When
my father died, one of his brothers came to take
my mother to his home. That is what happens in
our society. The living brothers carry on having the
dead brother's children for him.'

'You mean, your mother married your uncle?'

'Yes. Does it shock you?'

Lana went silent, thinking about it.

'The truth. If you lie, I will know,' Moffat said
relentlessly.

'Did she have a choice?'

'No.' He said no more, offering no alternative
but to tell the truth.

'It doesn't shock me.'

'Why not? It shocks most whites.'

'It would only shock me if it happened to me.
This is not my way. I accept that your customs are
different. However, I would hate it.'

Moffat laughed, delighted with her frankness.
'But you would be cared for.'

'I can care for myself.' She leaned towards him. 'Let
me ask you something. If you were a woman, would
you try to find out what happened to your father?'

He shook his head slowly.

'Do you disapprove that I am trying to do just
that? The truth. I'll know if you lie.' She grinned at
him.

289

He was more than a match for her. 'If you were black, yes. It is not our way. But your customs are different.'

Lana sat back, satisfied. This man was not only on her side, he was on the same wavelength and, more importantly, the difference in their colour did not seem to bother him. 'You were telling me that you found proof that your father did not send reports back.'

He wagged a finger at her. 'I still am. Tch! I see you must be taught.'

She knew immediately what he meant. 'I apologise.' Then added wickedly, 'Take your time.'

Moffat shook his head, smiling. 'We have a saying in Malawi: *Anyamata akwathu buleki ndi pachulu*. It means that the impatient reduce their speed by running up a steep hill while the wise go faster by slowing down.'

'We have a similar saying. More haste, less speed. Unfortunately, most of us forget.'

'In Africa, to rush is not only unwise, it is also bad manners. This is our way.'

'Okay. The African way it is.'

Moffat gave her an approving look. 'When my mother died my uncle contacted me. He was greatly troubled. It was 1992, the Catholic Church had dared to criticise Banda's regime and the people were rioting. The Malawi Young Pioneers – they were the armed section of the Congress Party – were intimidating everyone and raiding houses in search of incriminating evidence.'

Lana put up her hand. 'Can you explain that?'

290

'Not really. I think they were doing everything in their power to disrupt the first multi-party general election. Anything they found that was even remotely contentious was taken as a sign of treachery. My uncle had found a file among my mother's belongings. It was a file belonging to my father. I have no idea how my father got hold of it.'

Moffat waited for Lana to interrupt, then when she didn't, and with a note of approval in his voice, went on. 'In the file was a photocopy of a letter PAGET sent to Minister Matenje accepting the terms and conditions of the survey and agreeing that the survey would be conducted in secret. There was also a handwritten note to Edward Phiri. I have memorised it.' Moffat finished his second beer. 'You don't drink much do you?'

Lana pushed an untouched bottle over to him. 'Not as fast as some. Here, you have it.'

He made no comment, went to drink then set it down. 'The memo said: "*They're at it again. Replace the assistant Matenje has assigned with one of ours. Make sure he's reliable and knows nothing. The new PAGET geologist flies in Thursday. John Devereaux. Have our man meet him in Lilongwe. Devereaux is seeing Matenje in Njuli Friday. I want regular reports, same as before.*"' Moffat looked at Lana. 'The memo was unsigned.'

'That doesn't prove your father sent no reports.'

'There was a second note: "*To date I have received no word. Are you sure the new man is reliable?*" I knew my father well. If he'd taken the trouble to get hold of that file he would also have placed in it any reports he sent. You have to trust me on this. He did not send one.'

'Who do you think wrote the notes?'

'I have no idea. Someone in a position to know about the survey, someone trying to discredit Matenje, therefore someone highly placed. Dick Matenje was a high flyer back then. Whoever wrote the notes would have to be similarly placed to be worried about him.'

Lana was chewing the inside of her mouth. 'So,' she said softly. 'It *was* political.'

'As far as the survey was concerned, yes.' He looked grim. 'But perhaps not a reason for our fathers' deaths.' He waved and called a greeting to a man who had just come into the bar. The man waved back, nodded, then turned to face the bar. 'Why would those men be following you?' Moffat asked suddenly.

Lana told him everything that had happened since her arrival. 'This Tony Davenport thing is worrying,' she concluded. 'As far as I know, only two people know who I am and why I'm here. Tony Davenport *must* be working for one of them.'

'Not necessarily. Your name is unusual. Immigration records could have been seen by a number of people. Someone could easily have made a connection between you and your father.'

Lana looked grim. 'I never thought of that. This widens the ball park considerably.' She shook her head. 'I'm not sure if it's a good or bad thing.'

'It's bad.' Moffat looked worried. 'Like you, I have been warned. I will speak of that in a minute.'

He hunched towards her and lowered his voice. 'Someone knows what happened fifteen years ago. They are trying to frighten you. If they fail . . .' he shrugged, leaning back again, '. . . I do not think they are going to leave it at that.'

Lana had gone cold. 'Kill me?'

Moffat's eyes were unreadable. 'They've killed before. Whatever reason they had then they have now. It is a dangerous path we take.'

'I didn't expect this. I thought I could come here and maybe speak to some people who met Dad. It never occurred to me that . . .' her voice tailed off.

'Are you having second thoughts?'

'I won't lie to you. These scare tactics are working, especially if they're being orchestrated by someone in government.'

Moffat nodded. 'Your fear is a good thing. I too am scared.'

'But you'll go ahead?'

'Yes.'

Lana reached her decision. 'So will I.'

'Good. Tell me, the two men you have met, have you any reason to suspect either of them?'

She thought about it. 'Not really,' she said slowly. 'Tim Gilbey is the Commercial Attache at the British High Commission. Unless the Brits are covering something up, he's not likely to want to scare me off. Besides, Davenport is hardly going to impersonate Tim . . .' she broke off as a thought hit her.

'Unless it was assumed you would heed the

293

warning,' Moffat finished for her. 'Why wouldn't he?'

Lana frowned. 'I was handed to Tim Gilbey on a plate. If he, or the High Commission, have a reason for scaring me off it would have been terribly easy to arrange. And he was there when I was attacked. That's pretty coincidental wouldn't you say?'

'Doesn't make sense,' Moffat stated flatly.

'Nothing makes sense. Why am I being followed? Who wants to know where I go? Is it Davenport himself? Tim? Karl Henning? God, Moffat, what exactly have I stirred up?'

'How did you meet Henning?'

'He sat next to me on the flight from Johannesburg.'

'Mmmm.' Moffat looked thoughtful. 'That would have been impossible to arrange.'

'He had no idea who I was.' Lana frowned. 'Mind you, when he did discover my name it seemed to throw him.' She told Moffat of Karl's invitation to lunch Saturday, and to go sailing. 'Meeting Karl on the plane was pure coincidence but there's something about him that bothers me. Whether I accept his invitation . . .' she shrugged. 'I really can't decide.'

'We must both be careful. It is best we are not seen together.'

Lana nodded, then looked worried. 'What if I was followed here?'

'You were not.'

'How do you know?'

'I expected you today. I have friends. The man

who just came in here is one of them. You were followed when you left the hotel but . . .' he grinned. 'Those men had a little car trouble.'

Lana laughed. 'Good stuff.'

'It was not for you alone that this was arranged. I must also protect my family.'

'Why are you worried about your family?'

Moffat drummed his fingers on the table, thinking. 'I do not wish to worry you further but I think you should know this,' he said finally. 'When I found that file I tried to make enquiries. I got absolutely nowhere. At the time I thought it was because I was asking questions about the late Minister Matenje.'

'That makes sense. Was Banda still President?'

'Yes. I know what you're thinking but I have my doubts. Banda was in trouble and on the way out. He had just called a referendum on multi-party democracy and two thirds of the population had voted in favour of it. The mood in government was suddenly more democratic than America.'

'Did you find out anything at all?'

'Yes,' Moffat said soberly. 'I found out that someone, and I have no idea who, got to hear I was asking questions and decided to warn me off. My wife was followed. Two men tailed her everywhere. They made no attempt to hide from her – they wanted her to see them. It was enough for me. I stopped asking questions.'

'And you've been left alone?'

'Someone slit the throat of our last goat. After that we were left alone.'

'Why did you agree to see me then?'

'I wanted to meet you. I too feel that we are somehow connected.'

'There's a woman up in Karonga who knew our fathers.'

'Who?'

'Sarah Fotheringham. She reported them missing.'

'How did you learn this?'

'Karl Henning let her name slip. Then he tried to cover up by telling me she was dead. It was Tim Gilbey who told me she was still alive.'

'I lived in Karonga but I never spoke to Miss Fotheringham although, of course, I know of her – everyone does. This is the first I've heard that she knew our fathers.' Moffat thought for a moment. 'The answer is in Karonga, I'm sure of it.' He was drumming his fingers again. 'I know I said we must not be seen together but this is too important. I will go there with you.'

'What about your family?'

'They will go to my uncle's village. It is safe there.'

They locked eyes. 'God I hope we can find something. Someone should pay for this.'

He squeezed her hand. 'Stop running around the ball.'

THIRTEEN

There was a fair number of heavy, tobacco laden trucks on the road north of Lilongwe and Moffat, who was driving, was unusually silent as he concentrated on the road. Lana's mind kept wandering back over the past two days. They had been extraordinary days. She was no longer alone in her quest. Moffat was completely on her side and at her side. Not only had he insisted on coming to Karonga with her, he had also convinced her to attend Karl Henning's lunch party. As he put it, 'We will say I am your driver. That way, I will be sent to sit with the servants. It is interesting how many secrets servants know about their master.'

When Lana expressed doubt, worried that Karl would recognise Moffat, he had said, 'Karl Henning doesn't know I exist, let alone what I look like.'

'Are you sure of that? What about your goat?'

His reply worried her. 'I believe there are two issues here. It is as I said before. The secrecy and spying about the survey was political. I believe, however, that our fathers' deaths was something quite different.'

Which left Lana wondering just how many enemies they had out there. She was glad Moffat was with her. He was as committed as she to finding out what happened to their fathers and would do everything in his power to help. It was a sense of togetherness, a feeling of unity, that two heads were better than one, that was not only reassuring, it was profoundly moving. As an only child, Lana had never experienced sibling kinship. She rather felt now that this is how it would feel.

It seemed impossible that it was only two days ago that she and Moffat had met. They had left the bar and gone back to his house. Somehow, in the magical way news has of travelling in Africa, a stream of visitors came by to greet her. Smiling, friendly faces, caring, gentle people, polite and interested, their sincerity worn on open faces, there to read, like lines on a page. They all had questions, they all had stories, and as she sat surrounded by these people, Lana thought how easy it would be to throw off her Western way of life.

The day ended far too soon. At Moffat's insistence she returned to the hotel well before dark. 'There will be those watching for your return,' he warned.

And there had been. Lana wondered how she had failed to notice them the day before. They were waiting in the lobby. Two men. Bored indifference suddenly replaced by too quick movements and furtive glances as both sauntered casually closer to where Lana waited for her room key. 'I think these gentlemen were before me,' Lana said innocently to the receptionist. Their obvious embarrassment and hasty departure gave her great satisfaction.

She had arranged to meet Moffat in the morning about thirty kilometres west of Lilongwe, on the Namitete Road. 'Do not worry about being followed,' he had said, after giving her directions. 'It will be taken care of.'

And it had been. The car behind was obvious as she left the hotel but, minutes later, it fell quickly behind and stopped, steam billowing from under the bonnet.

The Namitete Road was quiet and Moffat had assured her they wouldn't be seen. She wondered what he was planning. All he would say yesterday was, 'When in Africa, do as the Africans do.' Rounding a bend there was his car. Lana slowed and began to pull in behind but he'd been watching for her and drove off, waving that she should follow.

They drove another fifteen kilometres before he turned onto a barely discernible track and cut across country. Dry, brown grass grew nearly as tall as her car. Ten minutes later the track opened into a shaded clearing and Moffat stopped. Lana pulled up behind and got out. His wide smile of greeting, and the bear hug that went with it, said it all. The sense of kinship was still real. 'I understand two of our friends developed a little more car trouble,' he said, grinning.

'I felt so sorry for them,' Lana said, pseudo serious. 'Poor things.'

Moffat laughed. He looked keyed up, excited and a little nervous. 'We walk from here. But first, I have things to tell you.'

This was a different Moffat to yesterday. He had been confident and in charge then. Today he had an air of apprehension.

'You and I, we are of one heart.'

She nodded.

'But we are from different worlds.'

Lana remained silent, sensing he was groping his way.

'In Africa our ways will often be strange to you.'

She watched his face, wondering what he was building up to.

'Some things are hard to explain. This does not make them untrue. There is truth, even when you cannot see it. Do you understand that?'

'God?' *Was this what he was planning – some kind of church meeting?*

Moffat shook his head. 'Not God. People with magic powers. Once there were many in Africa but now there are only a few. Their ways are strange. We are going to see one such man. He is the Nganga.'

'Nganga?'

'That is how we call him.'

The penny dropped. 'Do you mean a witch-doctor!'

Moffat simply smiled. 'Do not worry. I am told that in your country people also go to see those who can predict their future.'

300

'A *witchdoctor!*'

He put his hands on her shoulders and looked into her face. 'He will do you no harm. If we are lucky, he will help us. You must do exactly as I say and you must not speak. Do you promise?'

Lana's heart stepped up its rhythm slightly. This was not something she had bargained on. 'This won't work, Moffat. Witchdoctors rely on the beliefs of others, that's their power. How can he help me?'

'All I ask is that you keep an open mind. Will you do that?'

He looked so earnest. Lana could not believe that someone who had worn a business suit the day before could today be pleading with her to believe in witchdoctors. 'I'll do it for you but I have to tell you, Moffat, that I find the concept of witchdoctors a bit bizarre.'

He smiled. 'I am looking forward to discussing this after we have seen the Nganga.'

She left it. The experience would at least be memorable. 'How far do we walk?'

'Not far.' He pointed. 'See those trees? He lives there.'

Lana looked. The trees were about three kilometres away. 'Why not drive?'

Moffat laughed. 'What is this? Are you too lazy to walk?' He turned towards the distant trees. 'We cannot drive. It is a sacred place and must be treated respectfully. Our cars would disturb the spirits. Come. You will enjoy the walk.'

He was right. The morning sun was warm on

her shoulders but had not burned off the last of the night chill. Dew sparkled on the grass and the dampness of it raised a smell of pleasant earthiness from the sandy track. The wide blue sky carried no clouds and the air was like champagne, sharp and effervescent. Moffat commented periodically on the sights and sounds of the bush. 'Listen,' he said, 'do you hear that bird? It's a Mokoe. He's saying go-way, go-way.'

She listened and could hear it quite distinctly.

'Hunters hate them. They only make that sound when they're disturbed. It warns other animals.'

'Good for them.'

Moffat shook his head, smiling. 'You have much to learn about Africa, Lana. Not all hunting is a bad thing.'

'For food and clothing, like in the old days, certainly. Not for sport though.'

'Why not?' He sounded genuinely puzzled.

'It can only be called sport if hunters challenge their prey with no more than the animals have for protection. Otherwise, it's one-sided. Bit like expecting the local lads from the pub to take on Manchester United.' She could see he didn't understand. 'It's not sport if there can only be one outcome.'

'Okay, I agree with that. Africans don't hunt for sport anyway.' He looked at her. 'What about protection? What would you suggest using against a leopard?'

'Why not leave him alone,' she said succinctly.

'And if that leopard had been stealing your cattle

and goats? Or worse. What if he had killed someone in your village, maybe even your own child?'

'Then,' she said soberly, 'the leopard should be despatched without delay.'

'With kitchen knives? That would make it fair wouldn't it?'

'No. With a bloody great gun.'

Moffat stopped and looked at her. 'You're not making sense, Lana Devereaux.'

'I am,' she said. 'But you have to be white and not of this continent to understand it. Most Europeans have double standards. One is the ideal, the other is real. They're rarely the same.'

He shook his head. 'In Africa there is only the real. We know nothing else.'

She couldn't resist it. 'Like seeing a witchdoctor?'

'That's real,' he said sincerely. 'You wait and see.'

He set off again, walking with long, easy strides, comfortable in shorts, a loose shirt and sandshoes with no laces. She thought he looked quite at home. 'Do you spend much time in the bush?'

'Not as much as I'd like. Frances grew up in the bush. She prefers city life now.'

Lana stepped over the droppings of an animal then stopped dead. 'Moffat, look at this. Is that lion spoor?'

He squatted down and looked at the ground, shaking his head. 'Lion are rare in Malawi. Today most are in the game reserves. This is a serval.'

'How can you tell?'

He was studying the spoor. 'Mainly size, but also shape, depth of indentation.' He grinned up at her.

'Oh yes, and a friend in Game Department told me there are several families of servals in this area.'

She smiled, shaking her head at him. 'For a moment there I was impressed. I'd love to see one.'

He rose, brushing sand from his hands. 'You won't. They sleep during the day. Probably down an old antbear hole.' He set off again. 'Come, we are expected. We must not keep the Nganga waiting.'

'You mean he knows we're coming?' She didn't think Moffat could have got a message to him since last night.

'Oh yes. He knows.'

'How?'

'He is the Nganga,' Moffat said. 'Not only will he know we are coming, he will know you are white and why we come. You wait and see.'

Lana doubted it. Moffat must have got a message to him somehow. And yet his belief that the witch-doctor could predict their visit was obviously sincere. There was something else as well. From somewhere, she had heard or read that women were not regarded highly by medicine men. In that she was a stranger, white to boot, as well as female, she had grave misgivings that this Nganga would be overjoyed to see her. She mentioned it to Moffat.

'Normally he would refuse to see you. Others have tried, journalists mainly. The Nganga is not interested in speaking with them. I'm hoping he will see you because you are with me. You must say nothing. I will translate if he agrees, otherwise you will have to wait until we leave for me to tell you what he has said.' Moffat hesitated, looking worried. 'If he gives you something to drink, you must swallow it immediately. Take my advice. Don't smell it. Just drink it straight down and hand back the container.' He looked at her seriously. 'And try not to vomit.'

Lana's misgivings had grown somewhat. 'What's it likely to be?'

'Nothing that will harm you. I have no idea, the Nganga uses all sorts of things for his medicines.'

'I'm not sure about this, Moffat. I have no business going to see a witchdoctor when I don't believe in them. What if he realises? It might make him angry.'

He stopped and looked her squarely in the eye. 'Do you trust me?'

'Yes.' She didn't have to think about it. She trusted him completely.

'Then do as you are told.'

There was the red rag, fluttering in her face. Years of questioning that which made no sense, years of authority challenged, a lifetime demanding explanations, all scuttled aside like cowardly wraiths and remained in hiding. 'Okay,' she said in a small voice.

'Good girl. Just think of it as an honour – it *is* an honour – and you'll be fine. The Nganga will only be trying to help.' Blissfully unaware of how close he had sailed to the edge of Lana's sense of fair play, Moffat used the rest of the walk as a nature ramble, imparting both knowledge and stories of tradition.

'How do you know so much about the bush?' she said as they finally reached the trees.

'No more than anyone else. Live in Africa and you are as one with the animals who share it. They are as much a part of life as the trees and flowers. It has always been so. Come, this is the way.'

He led her around the dense stand of trees. At first, Lana thought they were walking on the edge of an impenetrable forest but, going further, she could see that growth was actually a crescent shape. In the centre, hidden by the trees except for one small opening, huge boulders were strewn, like great grey marbles. Some balanced precariously on others. Some clustered together, others stood alone. It was as if the ancient gods had grown bored with their game and had simply abandoned them.

The area within the crescent was no larger than a football field. There was a strange stillness about the place and, although shade from the surrounding trees did not reach far, the temperature seemed to have dropped considerably.

Lana stopped. 'Wow!'

'Something else isn't it?'

She grinned at the expression. Sometimes Moffat seemed so Western in his ways yet deep inside him lay ancient African traditions which he never questioned. He was a man, as she supposed most Africans were these days, poised between two worlds. She thought it sad in many ways that one must ultimately give way to the other. So much was already lost. Africa had changed a great deal in the past hundred years. The momentum now was simply too great to stop. Perhaps Moffat was one of the lucky ones. Or did it confuse him? She filed the thought away to ask him at some other time.

They reached a jumble of boulders and Moffat, with no hesitation, walked straight towards the largest. 'Through here.' He led her through a crack between two enormous rocks. Lana had not even noticed it – so well concealed was the opening.

'Been here before have you?'

His answer surprised her. 'Never.'

'Then how did you know . . .'

He silenced her scepticism with a look.

Once through the crevice, Moffat stopped. 'Now we wait. No more talking please.'

They were in a clearing, completely hidden from the world beyond. At the far side, set against and under the overhang of a large grey rock, was a hut. She hadn't known what to expect but she hadn't expected anything as run down and basic. An Nganga would, she'd have thought, have a grander dwelling. An oblong shape of grass and cracked dry mud, two squares left for windows, a doorway with no door and a verandah which had a thatched roof supported by four spindly and twisted branches. It sagged at one end, the reed thatch hanging forward and down like a waterfall of dry grass. The floor beneath was swept earth. To stand upright, a person could be no taller than 120 centimetres.

There were pots and pans, several blackened stone circles where fires had been lit, gourds, the complete skeletal remains of animals, masks, spears, sticks, pouches made of animal skin, and, looking rather out of place, an old refrigerator, rusted and leaning on its side. Chickens, goats, pigs and three scrawny dogs scavenged half-heartedly on the bare earth of the compound. The area smelled of old cooking fires, animal dung and rancid fat.

She stood next to Moffat, wondering what happened next. He said quietly, 'There has been an Nganga here for as far back as the storytellers remember. Two hundred years at least. The strength of their spirits remain. It is this which makes the Nganga so powerful.'

As if on cue, the Nganga materialised in the doorway. He was tiny and of immense age. The delicate bones of his small body pushed against creased and leathery skin, stretching it taut to near breaking point. He had a small pot belly and wiry legs. Lana could not help but wonder how Moffat held this delicate old man in such awe. As the Nganga shuffled slowly towards them she could see that he was unable to stand erect, bent slightly forward, as if years of living in his too-small hut had caused him to be permanently folded from the waist. He was barefoot, wearing a loin cloth of animal skin. Feathered armlets and anklets were so tight on his limbs they were in danger of cutting off his blood supply. A string of old cowbells hung from his waist. On his torso, painted in white, was his own skeleton. Human and animal teeth, bones, small pouches and several coins were strung on leather thongs around his neck. Draped over one shoulder and dangling in folds down his back and chest, a leopard skin thumbed its nose at world opinion.

To look at them, the Nganga had to lean backwards. When he did, Lana was able to see his face clearly. The skin was like old parchment, crinkled and worn. He had only one blackened tooth jutting upwards and out from his lower jaw like a defiant tree stump after a bushfire. But it was his eyes. They were the eyes of a young man. Clear and deep, they burned with life. They flicked over Lana, assessing and knowing. Great wisdom and compassion swam in those dark pools but ruthless calculation swam with them. A shiver ran through Lana as the Nganga's eyes cut through her mortal skin and bone, penetrating to the soul within. That one look seemed to expose her entire life.

When the old man spoke, his voice was thin and frail. Moffat listened respectfully, only responding when the Nganga stopped. The medicine man's eyes roved Lana's face and then he nodded abruptly, turned and indicated that they should follow.

Moffat spoke to her softly. 'It is all right for me to translate. He doesn't usually allow anyone to speak but on this occasion he'll make an exception.'

They were led crouching low into the Nganga's hut. It was gloomy and smelled of alien things, the hard earth floor partly covered with animal skins. There was no furniture as such but an assortment of boxes, tins and bottles were stacked against every wall and a pile of skins formed a couch of sorts.

'Sit down after he does and cross your legs. Just do what I do.'

Lana nodded silently. She had been told not to talk and found she didn't want to anyway.

The Nganga folded himself to the floor with surprising agility. Moffat waited until he was settled, then did the same. Lana followed. When they were completely still, the Nganga spoke again. 'The woman doubts me,' Moffat translated. 'Tell her this. I see a door. It has this writing on it.' Each individual hair on the back of Lana's neck had a simultaneous erection as she watched, with ever-increasing disbelief, as the Nganga wrote 251 on the dirt floor with his finger. It was her room number at the Capital Hotel, not known even to Moffat.

The witchdoctor watched Lana's face. Then, with no outward expression, his eyes smiled and were satisfied. He took a pouch from around his neck, rattling it and chanting before spilling the contents on the ground between them. Lana knew what to expect but the hair on her arms joined those on the back of her neck as the age-brown bones fell to the ground. She guessed they would be human bones. The Nganga studied them for a long time.

Finally, he reached over and picked up Lana's hand. He closed his eyes and began to croon, an eerie and monotonous sound which went on and on. Lana was beginning to feel a little foolish. She was sitting in a tiny ramshackled hut in the middle of nowhere with a witchdoctor holding her hand. But, just as the thought crossed her mind, the crooning stopped abruptly and her hand was released. The Nganga spoke to Moffat who then translated for Lana.

310

'When isi-Kombazana no longer calls over the great water and the silent ones gather where witches burn, the drums of retribution will stop beating and music of the spirits will be heard.'

Judging by the look on Moffat's face, he didn't know what it meant either.

The Nganga took one hand from each of them in his and spoke again. Moffat translated.

'Great Mother's shame lies hidden, two men seek her secret and the eyes that cannot see will lead the way.'

The witchdoctor sprinkled some liquid over the bones on the earth.

'Two are from one womb and yet they are not.'

He leaned forward, his face almost touching the bones.

'The one who fears all eyes and ears will find the jaws of silence.'

The Nganga let go of their hands and collected up the bones, running his thumb over each in turn, his eyes closed.

'One will speak yet say not a word.'

The Nganga opened his eyes and stared directly at Lana. Spittle flew from his mouth as he spoke again. Although she had to wait for Moffat, Lana knew the Nganga was speaking directly to her.

'There is fear and sorrow for this woman and she is in danger. Beware. The grave has three mouths and one is hungry.'

The Nganga threw the bones and picked up their hands. His eyes were closed again and he rocked silently, as if in sorrow himself. Lana felt her concentration focus on that wrinkled face. She

311

could not have looked away, even if she tried. The medicine man's eyes flew suddenly wide, glazed with a trance-like haze of venom.

'Fisi feeds on the skill of others but takes the young and weak for himself. There is power in the old arts which can be summoned through belief.'

Silently, he produced two earthenware cups and handed one each to Moffat and Lana.

'The spirits have been called. Drink.'

Following Moffat's example, and feeling her stomach churn at what might be in the watery-looking liquid in the cup, Lana swallowed hers immediately. The taste wasn't unpleasant, it had a mild mint flavour, yet she felt a warmth take over her body.

The Nganga rose and left the hut. Although she tried hard to fight it, Lana could not keep her eyes open and a woolly drowsiness crept into her head. Beside her, Moffat toppled silently to the floor. A few seconds later, Lana did the same.

It was midday when she regained consciousness. Of Moffat there was no sign. She rose, remembering to stoop, and stepped quickly from the Nganga's hut, aware that she had never felt so alive, so vibrant, as she did right now. Moffat was sitting outside, playing with one of the sorry-looking dogs. When he saw her he jumped to his feet, smiling. 'Come, it is time to leave.'

Lana contained her questions until they were out of the protective ring of boulders. 'Can I speak now?'

Moffat nodded.

'Where did the witchdoctor go?'

'I have no idea. I woke just before you. How do you feel?'

'Marvellous.'

'Me too.'

'Have you ever done this sort of thing before?'

Moffat slowed his steps and she adjusted her own until they were walking side by side like two people without a care in the world. That was exactly how she felt. Whatever was in that cup had left her relaxed, confident and full of energy. 'The Nganga has many faces. He uses his powers sparingly. He is as capable of harm as he is of good and beware those who ask his help lightly. No. I have never been to him before.'

'It's just that you seem to be taking this in better than me. What happened back there?'

Moffat smiled. 'What happened back there is as old as Africa. Power, magic and secrets. He knew we were coming, he knew why, and he helped us. I believe he did anyway, the Nganga is part of my heritage. How about you? Still a disbeliever?'

'I really couldn't say. He knew my room number at the hotel, that surprised me. As for the rest of it, I couldn't make head or tail of anything. Did you make any sense of what he said?'

'Some. He spoke in riddles but a little made sense.' Moffat stopped, listening. 'Hear that bird?'

In the distance a wood dove was calling *du du du du du du* in a long descending series of notes.

'That's isi-Kombazana. The wood dove. We

313

believe he is saying, "My mother is dead, my father is dead, all my family is dead and my heart goes du du du du du du".'

'What did the Nganga say? *When isi-Kombazana no longer calls over the great water.* Is he referring to us? To our fathers?'

'Could be.' Moffat looked approvingly at her. 'You're beginning to think like an African.'

'How's that?'

'Laterally.'

Lana laughed. 'Was his whole message an exercise in lateral thinking?'

'I have no idea. The true meaning is shrouded in parables and symbols. We cannot take his words literally.'

'What do you think he means then?'

Moffat looked thoughtful. 'The first part seems pretty clear. The wood dove never flies over large expanses of water but the Nganga can hear it calling for its family over the great water.'

'What's the great water?'

'Lake Malawi. The people who lived near the lake before the white man came and named it Lake Nyasa simply referred to it as the great water.'

Lana nodded. 'But when he says *over the great water* does he mean that literally or could it be on the far side of the lake?'

Moffat shrugged. 'Don't know.'

'Okay. Try this. You and I are calling for our fathers over Lake Malawi but then stop. Why?'

'Because the mystery of their deaths becomes clear.'

314

She nodded again. 'That makes sense. It's the only thing, other than following their footsteps to the same end, which will stop us wondering.'

'Don't even think that, you can make things happen just by thinking them.' He gave a superstitious shudder. 'Be positive.'

'Okay. What was the next part?'

Moffat raised his eyebrows.

'Give me a break,' she said. 'I'm keeping an open mind.'

He grinned. 'Admit it. You're impressed.'

'That too,' she conceded. 'Now, what was that bit about witches?'

'*The silent ones gather where witches burn.* Don't ask. I haven't got a clue what that could mean. Silent ones might be spirits.'

'And the witches?'

'Witches were always put to death. They were either poisoned or burned. Every village had its burning place.'

'Okay, let's move on. *The drums of retribution will stop beating.* That seems pretty clear. The call for revenge will cease at last. That's positive.'

'Not necessarily. Drums send messages or make announcements. They are also used in ceremonies. If they stop beating we might assume they have no message, but why? Is there no message to send or is there no need to send it any more? If the Nganga meant a ceremony, did the drums stop because the ceremony is over or because there is no ceremony?'

'Ouch!'

'See what I mean?'

'What about the next bit?'

'*Music of the spirits will be heard.*' Moffat looked at her blankly.

Lana stared back at him. 'Not a clue, huh?'

He shook his head. 'The next bit makes some sense. *Great Mother's shame lies hidden.* I don't know what the shame is or where it's hidden but great mother is how Queen Victoria used to be called. In this case I believe the Nganga could mean England.'

'So England has something shameful which is hidden.' Lana let out an explosion of disgust. 'Nothing new in that but what the hell does it have to do with us?'

He wagged his finger at her.

'Sorry. *Two men seek her secret.* Which two?'

'There are ten million people in Malawi. Take your pick.'

'As clear as that is it?'

'Your mind is closing.'

She ignored that. 'What was the next thing he said?'

'*The eyes that cannot see will lead the way.*'

'Any ideas?'

'It might mean innocence, it could be an image or statue, a place of darkness even.' Moffat sounded doubtful. 'Perhaps a blind man.'

'Okay. *Two are from one womb and yet they are not.*' Lana grinned at him. 'You and me.'

'You and I,' he corrected her.

'Sorry. Just getting excited. It's like cracking a code.'

'Don't get too carried away. What about, *The*

one who fears all eyes and ears will find the jaws of silence. One will speak yet say not a word.' He shrugged. 'We might leave those for the moment. I've no idea.'

'The next bit was directed at me.'

'Yes. *There is fear and sorrow for this woman and she is in danger. Beware.*' Moffat looked down at her seriously. 'That was good advice.'

'I know.'

'Still going on with it?'

She nodded. 'Can't stop now. I'm too close. I can feel it.'

His fingers locked on her arm. '*The grave has three mouths and one is hungry.* I didn't like that. One of us could die.'

'You told me to be positive.'

'Yes.' He looked gloomy. 'It was the word "grave" that got to me.'

'Could it have another meaning?'

'What?'

He had a point. A grave was a place of death — nothing more or less. She didn't like it any more than Moffat. 'Let's not dwell on it.' She linked her arm through his. '*Fisi feeds on the skill of others but takes the young and weak for himself.* Fisi is Swahili for hyena, I know that much. He eats carrion, mainly leftovers from lion kills but is more than capable of killing for himself, especially if something is vulnerable. That sounds like a warning.'

Moffat agreed. 'It does. But the Nganga gave us hope too. *There is power in the old arts which can be summoned through belief.*'

317

'The potion?'

'No. That was one of his tricks. The feeling will stay with us for a while. It's the sort of thing they do to make you believe in their powers.'

'Do you really believe?'

'Yes,' he said simply. 'The trick is to get you to believe too.'

She wasn't sure she could. 'What was in that potion?'

Moffat looked shifty. 'I don't know.'

Lana stared at him. 'You must have some idea.'

He looked miserable.

'Well?'

'Ah . . . they tend to use natural ingredients.'

'Like?'

'All sorts of things.'

'Moffat!'

'I don't know, really I don't. Herbs, animal parts, uh . . . excreta and urine, blood, ground-up bones, that sort of thing.'

Lana digested the information with about as much enthusiasm as she had the potion. 'Thank you very much, Moffat,' she said finally. 'I am truly, truly sorry I asked.'

They said goodbye at the cars. Moffat was going home to pick up his family and take them to his uncle's village.

Lana returned to the hotel, her mind turning over the Nganga's words. She was still feeling more refreshed, more energetic than she could ever remember. But that was all. The things the witchdoctor had said were too broad, too general for her to take seriously. He was clever, she'd give him that. Maybe, she had to concede, he possessed some second sight. That business with her room number was strange. As for the rest of it, what had he told them? It was a bit like reading your horoscope – it was always possible to relate it to one's own circumstances.

Her two faithful tails were in the lobby. Lana gave them a cheery wave. There was a message for her to call Tim Gilbey but, when she tried his number she was told, 'Mr Gilbey will be away until Monday week.' She wondered where he had gone.

Then she called Karl Henning. A servant told her that Mr Henning was not at the farm so she left a message that she would be coming to lunch.

That was yesterday. This morning she checked out of the hotel and drove to Old Town to pick up Moffat. She saw no sign of the two men tailing her and presumed that whatever it was that Moffat's friends had done to their car had been terminal.

Moffat travelled light. One small handgrip. He threw it into the back seat and walked to the driver's side. 'I'll drive.' It was an order, not an offer.

'It's fine,' she said, a touch of steel creeping into her voice.

'I'm supposed to be your chauffeur.' He opened her door. 'In that obstinate white head of yours, you know I'm making sense.'

'I hate it when you're reasonable,' she grouched, but got out and walked around to the other side.

319

He was watching her, grinning. 'How can you call *me* obstinate when you get your own way all the time?' she challenged across the roof of the car.

'I am a man,' he said simply. 'Now get in before I beat you.' He disappeared into the car.

Lana got into the passenger seat. 'You wouldn't dare.'

'Into the back.'

Lana folded her arms. 'No. I'm not sitting in the back like some bloody white madam.'

Moffat leaned on the steering wheel and looked across at her. 'You are *supposed* to be a bloody white madam.'

Her nose went in the air. 'Fine. I'll be a bloody white madam when we get to Kasungu.'

'Do you *ever* do as you are told?'

A small smile crept out. 'I often react favourably to suggestion.'

Moffat laughed. 'Are all white women like you?'

Lana thought about it. She had once stated bluntly to friends in London that she'd much rather be hit over the head by a lusty, club-wielding cave man than be met at the door by a new age guy – she thought of them as NAGs – wearing her best apron. By way of response, her friends challenged her to marry a hairy-chested Neanderthal, have his kids, clean his house, cook for him and wait on his every wish and command. She had argued that the problem was not what women had fought for and won, it was what they had become as a result, and the effect it was having on men. This argument fell on deaf ears, leaving the uncomfortable suspicion that she was horribly out of step. Moffat was patiently waiting for a reply. 'No.'

'A pity.' It was lightly said. He turned on the engine. 'And now we go.'

Lana stirred from her thoughts. 'We must be nearly there.'

Moffat glanced at the gauge. 'Another thirty kilometres. We're getting into tobacco country. Would now be a good time to suggest that you get into the back?'

Karl's home was a low, Spanish-style building with immaculate gardens, a sparkling blue swimming pool and an all-weather tennis court. The setting was beautiful, overlooking a large, artificial lake. He heard the car and came outside, several Doberman pinschers running excitedly beside him. 'Lana, how delightful. I'm so pleased you decided to accept my invitation. What on earth happened to your car?'

'Some fool tried to run me off the road.'

'The locals aren't very good drivers.' He surveyed the damage, ignoring Moffat. 'Looks like you were lucky.'

'That's why I have a driver with me. He is familiar with the roads north of here.'

'Good idea.' Karl pointed for Moffat's benefit. 'Park over there. Go around the back to the kitchen. My staff will give you something to eat.'

Moffat said, 'Thank you, master,' and drove to where Karl had indicated he should leave the car.

Karl led Lana into the house. It was furnished with heavy, masculine pieces with a clever blending of shape and contrast. Lana was drawn to a large, hand-carved chiffonier. 'This is magnificent.'

Karl joined her in front of the cabinet. 'It is, isn't it? A lucky find.'

'Where did you get it?'

'In a small village near Karonga. It was in an old shed.'

She ran her hand over the gleaming wood. 'If only it could speak,' she murmured. 'What tales it could tell.'

He smiled. 'This particular piece has a nefarious history. It belonged to an Arab slaver called Mlozi who was hanged in 1895.'

'How do you know?'

Karl bent and pulled out a drawer which was empty. He reached to the back and pressed a spring. A section of the base slid back, revealing a secret cubbyhole. 'I found a sort of ledger in here. It was undoubtedly Mlozi's. It contained details of cargo and sailing dates for the Arab dhows which took slaves down to Losefa. Pinned to each sailing was a receipt. They were all made out to Mlozi.'

'Where is the ledger now? I'd love to see it.'

'It was an important piece of Malawi's history. It's in the museum in Lilongwe.'

'I wonder how this came to be in a shed.'

'I don't know the answer to that but I can hazard a guess. Mlozi's stockade was shelled to the

322

ground. Mlozi himself was found hiding in a cellar under his house. He was tried, then promptly dragged off and hanged from a tree. I imagine a great deal of looting took place. The man I bought it from had no idea how the cabinet got there. It had been there as long as he could remember.'

'That's fascinating.'

'You like old furniture?'

'Love it. Our house in England is full of old stuff. My mother has been a collector for years.' Lana looked around the room. 'No woman's touches?'

'I was married once. We're divorced.'

'I'm sorry, I didn't mean to pry.'

'Pry all you like, my dear. I don't mind. Now, perhaps you'd like to freshen up before the guests arrive.'

She found Karl outside on the terrace deep in conversation with another man. 'Ah, Lana,' Karl said when he saw her approaching. 'Come and meet a friend of mine. Ramón Alzaga from Buenos Aires.'

The stranger rose and regarded Lana with frank admiration. He was slightly taller than her and thickset. His tanned body was powerful and fit. He wore his dark hair slicked straight back and had the kind of five-o'clock shadow she suspected would never quite go away. An aquiline nose lent a slightly aristocratic look to his face. He was not unattractive in a swarthy kind of way. Dressed as he was, in khaki shorts and white short-sleeved shirt, he had the appearance of someone who lived permanently in Africa rather than Argentina.

Karl was saying, 'My friend, allow me to introduce Lana Devereaux.'

Ramón put out his hand and Lana, thinking he wanted to shake, responded with her own. Instead, he raised her hand to his lips, brushed them lightly over the back and then, turning her hand over, kissed the palm. 'Charmed,' he murmured.

Lana retrieved her hand feeling somehow that she had been undressed in public. 'How do you do,' she said formally. Her hand had been kissed before but never with such slow and sensual innuendo that was both disturbingly intimate and deliberately provocative.

Ramón turned to Karl. 'Where did you find such a delightful flower, my dear friend?'

Karl smiled at Lana. 'I had the good fortune to sit next to her on a flight from Johannesburg to Lilongwe,' he said lightly.

Lana went to sit at the table and Ramón, with an excessive show of good manners, fussed over her chair until she was settled. Karl was still smiling but Lana noticed that his eyes were rock hard. He was not pleased at the presence of the Argentinean and was unable to hide it.

His next words confirmed that Ramón's visit was unexpected. 'Such a surprise,' he told Lana. 'Ramón called me from Blantyre. He's been doing business in South Africa and Zimbabwe and, since he needed to see some people in Malawi, decided to surprise me with a visit.' Karl laughed. 'Mind

324

you, his surprise was conditional. Typical Ramón. He'd managed to get a lift to Lilongwe but I had to fetch him from there. That's why I wasn't here when you called.' He looked at Ramón. 'It must be . . . what . . . two years since we last saw each other? Too long my friend, too long.' While his words were warm, his eyes retained the consistency of granite.

Ramón inclined his head and glanced coldly at Karl. Lana could see that the two men did not like each other and were making very little effort to conceal their feelings. When Ramón turned back to Lana, however, his eyes held nothing more than admiration and interest. 'I was too close to Kasungu to miss the chance of catching up with Karl. He tells me you are going sailing together. I hope you don't mind but Karl has invited me to join you.'

'It's not up to me to mind, I may not be able to make it myself,' Lana said. She wondered what the hell was going on. She was fairly certain that Karl had not invited the Argentinean to join him, or, if he had, he had done so against his will. That meant that Ramón had probably invited himself. Why? He didn't seem to like Karl any more than Karl liked him. 'Interesting,' she thought. 'There's something more than masculine dynamics happening here.'

Guests began to arrive as early as 11.30. Two hours later, the lunch party was in full swing. Tobacco farmers, teachers, a doctor and his wife, pilots, a couple of tobacco buyers and an assortment of others. Maybe it was because they lived in such a remote area, perhaps because they had to rely on each other for company, but Lana mostly found their open and good-humoured conversation refreshingly stimulating. There were no pretensions with these people.

One was open to the point of rudeness. A woman in a white dress commented loudly, 'The trouble with little children is that no-one knows how to cook them any more,' as three small boys, wet from the swimming pool, brushed past her. She looked across at Karl. 'Do stop them running through the guests, they're an absolute pain.'

When Karl went off to speak to the children, the woman sat next to Lana. 'I'm Stella.'

'Lana Devereaux.' Lana was wary. There was something hostile about the woman.

Stella stared at Lana. 'So,' she said softly. 'Where did you spring from I wonder? Karl *is* a dark horse.'

'I met him on the flight to Lilongwe. He's been most kind.'

Stella gave a hard little laugh. 'Karl is never kind, darling. Not where pretty women are concerned.' She rose and looked down at Lana. 'I hope you like the missionary position, my dear. It's the only one he knows.' She left before Lana could think of a suitable reply.

As she watched Stella walk off Lana wondered what on earth had provoked her. 'What a vulgar creature,' she thought, more amused than offended.

Karl rejoined her. 'Don't mind Stella,' he said, as if he'd read her thoughts. 'She's had too much to drink.'

'She did seem a little out of sorts.'

He smiled wryly. 'Stella opens the gin bottle at 11.30 every morning. Throws the top away. She manages to upset most people by midafternoon.'

'But why?'

He smiled. 'She's a very nice woman. Just unhappy. How's your drink?'

'It's fine. She doesn't seem to like you very much.'

He smiled absently then waved to someone. 'Excuse me, Lana, more guests.'

Left alone, Lana watched the ever-swelling crowd on the patio, or *khonde* as she had been told it was called. Men and women, casually dressed, tanned and carefree, everyone knew everyone else. She looked around. Apart from the servants, not a black face among them.

Talk flowed over and around her. Lana sipped white wine slowly and generally refused topping up, noticing that the same inhibitions did not afflict most of the guests. Conversations became louder and more raucous as the afternoon wore on. Men flirted openly with other men's wives and no-one seemed to think it strange. Faces flushed and unsteady on their feet, some found the swimming pool while others departed in an alcoholic haze. It struck Lana suddenly that this was how these people compensated for their isolation.

Ramón Alzaga appeared at Lana's side at regular intervals. She found his flamboyant displays of attentiveness both false and annoying. It may have been the Latin way, but his constant touching her bordered on mauling and his body language sent a clear message that she was his for the taking – if he could be bothered. His conversation was full of innuendo and his eyes full of contrived smouldering passion.

Lana, who had always detested public displays of passion which she firmly believed belonged behind the closed door of the bedroom, did not take long to register the fact with him that his attentions were unwelcome. 'If you don't mind, Mr Alzaga, I'd appreciate it if you would keep your hands to yourself.'

He reacted predictably. Throwing both hands up, he said loudly enough for those close to them to hear, 'You are a beautiful woman. Have pity on a man who cannot help himself.'

Lana smiled at him sweetly and said, just as loudly, 'You have been helping yourself, Mr Alzaga. I don't like it.'

His eyes still smouldered, but not with admiration or desire. 'You English,' he hissed at her. 'You have no emotion, no hot blood.'

Lana stepped closer and put her face a few centimetres from his. 'We were hot-blooded enough for you in the Falklands, Mr Alzaga,' she said softly. 'That should have taught you *something*.' She stepped back and her tone returned to normal. 'Now keep your bloody hands to yourself.'

She turned and left him standing there, fury and embarrassment clear on his face. Several people who had been close enough to hear the encounter glanced at her with approval but Lana was troubled. She had made him her enemy which was stupid of her. She couldn't care less about his feelings – he'd got what he'd asked for – but, if she joined Karl and Ramón on the yacht, it could be awkward. Ramón was a further complication in a situation which was already complicated.

At three, Lana said goodbye to Karl. A strangely subdued Stella, who had disappeared for about an hour, presumably to sleep off the gin, was with him, her hand possessively on his arm. She accompanied Karl and Lana to where Moffat waited in the car. The expression on Stella's face told Lana that the woman regarded her as a threat to whatever relationship she had with Karl. It went hard with dislike when Karl restated his invitation for Lana to join him on the yacht.

'I'll get there if I can,' Lana promised.

Just after they pulled away, Lana leaned forward and asked, 'Did you learn anything?'

Moffat glanced into the rear-vision mirror. 'He's away a lot. When he's here he's a tough man to work for. He's having an affair with that woman, Stella. Broke up her marriage apparently. And he keeps a loaded pistol in a drawer beside his bed. That's it. How about you?'

'One of his guests, a Ramón Alzaga, is also going sailing with Karl. He's a right royal pain in the arse. He and Karl call each other friend but there's no love between them. And Stella doesn't like me.'

Moffat laughed.

'Pull up. I want to sit in the front.'

The car swerved to the side of the road. 'Damn!' Moffat said. 'Just when I was getting used to a bloody white madam.'

As the Subaru drove off Stella murmured to Karl, 'Another conquest, darling.'

'Have another drink, Stel.'

'Naughty boy. Just when I had something to tell you.'

Karl looked at her with barely concealed impatience. 'Don't start your games, Stel. I'm not in the mood.'

'Turned you down flat did she? Poor old you.'

'Give it a rest, Stella. You know why I want to keep an eye on her.'

'I know why you *say* you want to.'

Karl looked exasperated. 'She's after information about her father. She might stir up trouble.'

'Why? It's nothing to do with you. It's not your fault those men died. I don't understand why you're so worried.'

Karl patted her arm absently. 'It looks bad, that's all.'

Stella's eyes gleamed with malice. 'Poor darling Karl. Don't worry, I'll cover for you as usual.' She turned into him expecting a kiss. When he didn't oblige, she pouted. 'I don't think you deserve it but

I'll tell you anyway. When I was in the bathroom I overheard her driver talking to the servants. He seemed to be very interested in you.'

'Servants always gossip.'

'Mmmm! But this one has an unusual name. Lana Devereaux's driver is called Moffat Kadamanja.'

Karl's eyes went like granite as he stared after the departing car.

FOURTEEN

Tim Gilbey slammed down the telephone, irritated. 'Where is the bloody woman?' He glanced at his watch. Two–fifteen. He had no choice, he *had* to leave now in order to reach Monkey Bay in time for his lift to Likoma Island.

The receptionist looked up startled as he rushed past her. 'I'm off,' he said, not bothering to stop. 'If Lana Devereaux returns my call tell her . . . tell her I'll be back Monday week.' He wanted to say more but knew he couldn't. He also had no idea when he'd be back but that was the least of Tim's worries.

'Have a nice tour,' the girl called after him, wondering why he was in such a hurry. After all, Malawi wasn't going anywhere. He was only doing what they all did – a familiarisation tour of the main centres. His secretary had offered to set up meetings with major businesses but he had declined, saying he'd rather play it by ear. The receptionist thought that was strange. Most of them wouldn't dream of fronting up unexpected.

Tim reached his car, unlocked it, threw his briefcase into the back seat, pulled off his jacket and tie which he flung on top of the briefcase and climbed in. He felt frustrated that he'd been unable to reach Lana, anxious he'd miss the trawler which left the wharf at Monkey Bay at four-thirty promptly, pissed off with that idiot Hamilton who was clearly returning to Likoma to retrieve the documents and convinced now more than ever that Karl Henning was a clever and very dangerous man indeed.

Once out of the city limits he drove at a furious pace. If he missed the fishing boat he'd not get another chance to reach Likoma for several days. Flying there was an option but he wanted to avoid his visit becoming known at the High Commission. There was no way he could justify it without raising suspicions. Not that it mattered, he supposed. It was just that the bloody FCO were so paranoid about secrecy they didn't even trust their own High Commission staff.

Lana Devereaux was in more danger than she knew. Tim had just spent two hours grilling Tony Davenport – the outcome of which convinced Tim that Karl Henning was not above getting rid of Lana if he believed her to be a threat. Davenport had tried bluster at first but finally admitted that he had gone to the hotel posing as Tim Gilbey on the instructions of Henning.

Tim had asked him why.

Davenport told him – reluctantly at first but with increasing enthusiasm as he went on, almost as though it was a relief to be finally getting some things off his chest. 'He's a friend of mine.'

'Not good enough.'

Tony Davenport shifted uncomfortably under Tim's unblinking stare. 'I owed him a favour.'

'What kind of favour?'

Davenport would not meet Tim's eyes. 'He helped me once.'

'He's blackmailing you.' It was not a question. Tim's voice was hard.

The statement seemed to startle Davenport. 'No, nothing like that.'

'What then?'

'Look, if you don't mind, it's a private matter between Karl and me.'

'I do mind. We'll sit here all day if necessary. I'm warning you, Davenport, you may have been born in Malawi but you're still a British subject. Life could be made very difficult if your work permit is not renewed.'

The threat worked. Davenport seemed to reach a decision and leaned towards Tim. 'Just between you and me then.'

Tim threw his pen down and folded his arms. He had him. 'I am not a policeman, Davenport. Lana Devereaux was attacked in the street and threatened by you at the hotel. She has declined my suggestion that she go to the police but she *has* made an official complaint. It's my job to find out what you're up to. I would anyway. As well as being British, Miss Devereaux is a friend of mine.'

'It won't go any further?' Davenport asked, reassured.

'No.'

'It's nothing much. I got into financial trouble a

few years ago. Couldn't go to the family, they'd bailed me out before. Karl helped me.'

'How much?'

'Do you mind, old man? That's my business.'

Tim let that go.

'He's been very understanding. Never asks when I'll pay the loan back. Something always seems to come up. I've paid back a bit, but . . .'

'Okay, so you owe Henning a favour. Threatening and frightening Lana Devereaux seems a little over the top.'

Davenport looked uncomfortable. 'It's the first time he's asked me to do anything like that.'

'You've helped him before?'

'Little things. Like . . . well . . . when tobacco goes out of the country, sometimes Karl asks me to find a little space in the middle of the load.'

'What for?'

'I don't know.'

'You help him to smuggle and you don't know!'

'Yes,' Davenport admitted reluctantly.

'So, he's got you by the short hairs. I suppose he's threatened to report you.'

'No, no,' Davenport said hastily. 'He just kind of mentions the loan . . . you know,' he added lamely.

'So, Henning just kind of mentioned the loan and then told you to impersonate me and frighten Lana Devereaux out of Malawi.'

'No. He left the arrangements to me. He just told me to frighten her off. I used your name because I'd seen a bit about you in the paper. I figured since you'd only just arrived not many people

335

would know you.' Davenport took a deep breath. 'Karl said he'd met this girl on the plane who could end up in trouble because she was trying to dig up something to do with the disappearance of her father in Malawi fifteen years ago. He said it would be best for her if she was scared off. He didn't actually say so but he implied that whoever was responsible was still around and if they got to hear of her asking questions she might well disappear herself. You're new here, Gilbey. You don't know how it was back then. If Karl is worried for Lana Devereaux's safety then he has good reason. He's a pretty influential man – knows just about everyone. He said she wasn't to be harmed but I had to lay it on thick enough to get rid of her.'

'It didn't occur to you I suppose to question his motives?'

'Good God, no! Why would I? I've known Karl Henning nearly all my life. He's as straight as a die. To be perfectly honest, I rather got the impression he had taken quite a fancy to Miss Devereaux. She's exactly the kind of woman he needs, I realised that the moment I met her.'

'What do you mean?'

'Strong-willed. I didn't get to first base trying to frighten her.'

'So you had her attacked in the street?'

'I'd set it up before going to the hotel. Just in case. They wouldn't have harmed her, just roughed her up a little. Their instructions were to let her know that she wasn't wanted in Malawi.'

'Did Henning know your plan?'

'I didn't tell him. I don't think he would have allowed it.'

Tim rather thought he would but said nothing.

'The attack might have worked but you happened along.' Davenport gave a small grin of admiration. 'Mind you, she put up a good fight on her own. Both men got more than they bargained for. They refused to have any more to do with her and I had to find others to watch Miss Devereaux in Lilongwe.'

'You're having her tailed? In God's name, why?'

'I called Karl and said the scare tactics didn't seem to be working. He asked me to keep tabs on her movements. I think he wants to protect her.'

Tim was suddenly worried. 'So she's been tailed all over Lilongwe?'

Davenport looked miserable. 'No. My men developed car trouble. They lost her twice.'

Tim hid a grin. Lana Devereaux seemed to lead a charmed life. 'Okay, now we're going to talk about the Midima Road.'

Tony Davenport had the good grace to look shamed. 'That was stupid, I admit. I saw her at the Mulanje Club and panicked. She went over to the men I played golf with and spoke to them. I didn't know what to do. I realised that Lana Devereaux must have discovered who I really was. I had this idea of running her off the road and then threatening her.' He took a deep breath. 'It backfired. The bloody woman ran *me* off the road. My car's a wreck.'

Tim was hard pressed not to laugh out loud.

337

'I know it was a dumb move. If Karl found out he'd tear a strip off me.' Davenport shook his head and added plaintively, 'She's not like ordinary women. Lana Devereaux's got balls. Anyone else would have run away by now.'

Tim looked across his desk at Tony Davenport. The man was weak, not terribly intelligent and putty in the hands of Karl Henning. Tim was not convinced that Henning's motives were as pure as Davenport believed them to be. Lana Devereaux was, in Tim's opinion, still very much at risk.

As soon as Davenport left his office, Tim put in a call to Lana in Lilongwe. He intended to warn her. But she was out so all he could do was leave a message for her to call him back. Tim delayed his departure for Monkey Bay for as long as possible but, after trying to reach Lana one last time, could put it off no longer. As he drove he wondered if her luck would hold. Or would she find, like her father fifteen years before, that luck was a fickle friend.

Monkey Bay boasted a naval base, a number of fisheries projects and a small scatter of assorted buildings and dwellings in a kind of lazy and disorderly sprawl. A great deal of the harbour was off-limits to tourists in an attempt to preserve whatever secrets the Malawi Navy had to hide. Tim rather suspected that the navy's past was more glorious than its present or future. He knew that a British gunboat HMS *Gwendolen,* commonly referred to as *Gwen*, had not only fired the first naval shots of the First World War, but had also won the first naval engagement. The fact that Germany's one and only gunboat on the lake, the *Hermann von Wissmann,* had been high and dry on a beach undergoing some repairs when the *Gwen* opened fire by no means diminished the victory. Nyasaland had won its place in the history books.

Tim, through a network set up by preceding operatives, had made contact with a Captain Manuel Santos and been told, 'You come 4.15 Friday afternoon. You not here, I go.' It was closer to 4.30p.m. by the time he arrived. Much to Tim's relief, the fishing trawler *Katembe* was still tied up at the wharf. He hurried down the sloping ramp and up the gangplank onto the trawler. Despite an urgent need of a coat of paint, the decks were neat and scrubbed down.

'You Gilbey?' a guttural voice asked.

Tim turned around. 'Yes.' He put out his hand. 'Sorry to keep you.'

The man ignored Tim's outstretched hand. 'You did not keep me,' he growled. 'Santos wait for no-one.'

He was a short, stubby man. Grizzled grey hair escaped from under a woollen cap. He had not shaved for at least three days. Bushy grey eyebrows sprouted above dark, unreadable eyes. He had a fleshy nose, thick lips and his swarthy skin was pitted with old acne scars. He wore faded blue overalls and the toe of one old boot gaped open. Portuguese-African ancestry was evident and pleasantries appeared beyond him. 'You pay, we go.'

Tim followed him into the cramped wheel-house. Stained enamel coffee mugs and empty bottles of rum cluttered every surface. Behind a brass compass binnacle and spoked teak steering wheel – which, had the man but known, would have fetched several thousand pounds at Sotheby's – a statue of the Virgin Mary and a yellow oilskin jacket competed for space on the chart table. An unmade bed along the back wall and several dirty plates on the floor indicated that Captain Santos slept, ate, drank and worked from the wheelhouse. 'Three thousand Kwacha,' he said, his hand out.

'I was told half that,' Tim protested.

Santos shrugged. 'Take or leave. No matter.'

Cursing the man, Tim paid him.

Without bothering to count it, Santos put the money under his mattress. 'Follow me.' He took Tim to a forward cabin. It was small but, after the mess the captain appeared to thrive in, surprisingly neat and clean. 'We go soon. Wait for someone else.'

'Who?' Tim was alarmed. Who else would be wanting to go to Likoma? Not Hamilton, he hoped.

The captain leered and made an obscene gesture, cupping both hands over his genitals. 'Fuka fuka,' he said, giving a grin of sorts. His two front teeth were gold. 'She come soon.'

'God!' Tim thought, after the man had gone. 'Who the hell would want to go with him?' He found out soon enough. A young African girl was ushered up the gangplank by a much older man. Captain Santos counted out some money and paid the man who left without a backward glance at the dejected and frightened girl.

Tim was disgusted but not unduly surprised. Daughters were not highly regarded by many fathers. This one had obviously been sold to the obnoxious Santos. By the look of her swollen belly, Santos wouldn't be the first to take her. As sorry as he felt for the girl there was not much Tim could do to help her.

The trawler got under way almost immediately. Tim left his cabin and went on deck, watching the sheltered harbour of Monkey Bay grow smaller as the *Katembe* gathered speed and cut across the mirror surface of the lake, skirting Cape Maclear and heading north towards deeper Mozambique waters and the tiny island of Likoma. The trip, he had learned, would take approximately sixteen hours – give or take weather conditions which Tim had been told should remain calm – and, sorry as he was that most of it would be during the night, at least it relieved him from trying to make conversation with the captain.

There were only the three of them on board – Captain Santos, the girl and Tim. Santos crewed his trawler with fishermen from Likoma, picking them up on his way north and dropping them off once his hold was full before heading south to Monkey Bay. That way he saved a good four days' wages and had the added advantage of the occasional passenger who wished to travel to or from Likoma. These he fleeced unmercifully, knowing that his price was still far less than by air charter, or the commercial cruise ship, the MV *Ilala* which claimed to circum-navigate the lake on a regular basis but which, in point of fact, spent most days at anchor or in dock while engineers tried to coax life back into her ageing engines.

'Hey, Gilbey.'

Tim looked up at the wheelhouse. Santos had a bottle of rum in his hand. 'You like drink?'

Tim made his way up the short ladder. There was no sign of the girl. Santos handed the bottle over. 'Fifty Kwacha a glass.'

Tim handed it back. 'Don't drink rum,' he said pleasantly.

Santos regarded him suspiciously. 'Beer in galley. Fifty Kwacha each. Or I make you katembe. Same price.'

'What's katembe?'

'Half red wine, half Coke. Is good. I name boat after it.'

'I'll stick to beer, thanks.'

The price was highway robbery but there wasn't much Tim could do about it. He went to the galley and found a beer. He also located the girl who was sullenly preparing a meal. 'Hello,' he said. But she ignored him and he returned to the wheelhouse.

'You pay first.'

Reluctantly, Tim handed the man fifty Kwacha. The captain belched, pocketed the money and made a show of studying the charts.

'You want fuka fuka?' he asked slyly.

'No,' Tim answered shortly.

Santos scowled at him. 'Cheapa cheapa. For you, two hundred Kwacha.' He rubbed his hand over his stubbly chin. 'Very clean girl.'

'Look,' Tim said conversationally. 'I've said no, I mean no. Okay?'

Santos looked knowingly at him. 'You a sissy man? Bum fuka?'

Tim carefully placed his bottle on the chart table, took two steps towards the captain, gathered up a fistful of overall and lifted the man off the floor. With his face just centimetres from the captain's, he said calmly, 'I've paid you to take me to Likoma. Shut the fuck up and do it. Do I make myself clear?' He let the captain go.

The man wasn't expecting it and, although it wasn't a long drop, landed heavily. 'You breaka my leg,' Santos yelled.

'No,' Tim said quietly. 'But I'm always happy to oblige.' He picked up his beer. 'I'll be on deck.' He left the wheelhouse and the repulsive Captain Santos and found a quiet spot on the deck where, leaning over a rusted railing, he contemplated where such a sub-species might have originated. The man belonged under a rock.

His mind drifted to Lana Devereaux. 'I hope she's all right,' he thought. 'I wish I could have spoken to her.' He remembered Tony Davenport's words about Karl Henning. *He can say what he likes. Henning is trying to scare Lana off for reasons of his own, I'm positive of it.*

The captain began singing lustily. He had a surprisingly good voice. Tim tried to focus on the task at hand. Martin Flower had telephoned yesterday. 'Word's just come in – there's some excitement in Argentina. Might be a coincidence, might not. I don't care what excuses you have to give, you've got to get to Likoma before Hamilton.'

Did Frederick Hamilton intend to retrieve the documents? Seems likely. Why? Because he's suddenly nervous about leaving them on Likoma or because he's found another buyer?

Tim didn't like Hamilton on principle. He had only been back in London for a few months after a gruelling four-year stint in Afghanistan. Anticipating a two-year home posting, he was halfway through renovations to his lounge and kitchen and just entering into a relationship with an enchanting and gifted graphic artist when Martin sent him to Malawi. As a result, his flat resembled a bomb-site and would have to stay that way until he returned. The graphic artist regretfully told Tim, 'If we were further down the track I'd wait for you, but don't count on it.' Tim understood. She was far too attractive to sit alone, waiting for a man who might, or might not, become a fixture in her life.

'I've got to get out of this business,' he was thinking as he watched the heavily timbered shoreline slide past. Afghanistan had soured him. Politics didn't care about people – real people suffering real hardships. Countries like Iran, Pakistan and Saudi Arabia, indifferent to a decade of war which killed a million Afghans, began jockeying

344

for position in the new government almost immediately the Soviets withdrew. The warring Mujaheddin groups, already divided for ethnic reasons,
were encouraged to carry on the fight for freedom
and peace. Under the guise of financial assistance,
the different groups were armed. As a result, once
beautiful and historical cities like Kabul, Qandahar
and Herat were shelled beyond recognition. Tim
himself had come under fire from the Uzbek in the
north. All he had been doing was driving along the
dead straight road between Kabul and the Uzbek-
istan border to meet a colleague. It seemed to Tim
at the time that the Mujaheddin were dispassionately practising their rocket-propelled grenade
launchers, and a moving target – any moving target
– would do.

Tim had joined the Foreign and Commonwealth Office driven by ideals formed at university.
Now, after less than ten years in the field, those
early illusions had given way to the realities of
power and politics. He had a degree in Business
Administration and Economics, spoke French,
German and Russian fluently, Spanish and Italian
not so fluently and Portuguese badly. Coming so
quickly after the disillusionment of Afghanistan,
the gamble being taken with Lana Devereaux's life
in the interests of national secrecy finally tipped
the scales. Tim wanted out. But for now there was
a job to do and do it he would, to the very best of
his ability.

It was getting dark. The deep throb of the
trawler's 340 horse power Cummins diesel engine

was solid and steady though Tim would have liked to experience the total silence. The last of the sunset had stained the water pink. Bow waves creamed crisply behind, slapping together in the middle and flattening out, leaving an outraged ripple as evidence of the invasion. On the eastern shore, a large fire flared briefly – proof that mankind was out there, that Tim was not alone on this boat with a drunken lout of a captain and a sullen enslaved cook and concubine.

'What of Lana?' he thought, his mind wandering sideways again. He found it hard to recall the girl in London. Lana Devereaux's deep blue eyes, her fierce determination, got in the way. He admired her courage but it was more than that. Like the fire on the shore, mutual attraction had flared bright for a moment. And, like the fire on the shore, it had died just as quickly. But it was still there, smouldering beneath the surface. He knew why Lana had backed off – he would have done the same. She was already on an emotional seesaw. *And when she comes off it?* When she came off it, Tim would be there – it was one of the few things he knew for certain.

Night fell with the lack of subtlety that was so quintessentially African. Before Afghanistan, Tim had worked for three years in what was then Rhodesia. The no-nonsense approach of nature in that country always impressed him. Nothing coy or teasing about it. Nature was what it was. No apologies. Achingly beautiful one minute, deadly the next.

His mind drifted again. It seemed to Tim that people were influenced by the forces of nature. *Look at the Swiss.* Their narrow-mindedness was legend. Was that because they lived in a country hemmed in by mountains? *What about Australians?* Was their personality broad and brash because their country was?

The captain had forgone his haunting Arab song for something which sounded like an Irish sea-shanty. What forces formed a man like that? The song broke off suddenly and Santos bellowed, 'Girl, where's my food? *Chakula pesi pesi!*'

The girl replied in her own language. Whether the captain understood or not Tim did not know. The man simply resumed his song.

Tim went into the galley and helped himself to another beer. 'Fifty Kwacha,' Santos yelled from the doorway of the wheelhouse as Tim went back on deck.

'Fifty Kwacha buys three beers, you old rogue, and even then you're well into profit.'

The captain muttered something and disappeared. Pretty soon he was bellowing out another song.

Dinner was a delicately spiced stew of lake fish accompanied by a kind of wild spinach. The girl, having set the plate in front of him, took the captain his plate and stayed in the wheelhouse. Tim washed the meal down with yet another beer, called 'Good night', to the now silent Santos, and

347

went to his cabin. He undressed quickly and, having placed his wallet and Browning automatic pistol under the pillow, rolled onto the narrow bunk and switched out the light. Within minutes he was lightly asleep, his senses dimmed but not out. If the captain decided to help himself to the cost of the two extra beers, he would be in for one hell of a shock.

Eight hours later, as the first shards of light appeared in the eastern sky, Tim was wide awake. There was hot water in a curtained-off shower recess and the hand-pumped heads were surprisingly clean. Refreshed and ready for what the day would bring, Tim emerged on deck before the sun was truly risen. They were travelling close to the Mozambique shore. To the west, Malawi had all but disappeared. The air was crisp, almost cold. 'You make coffee,' Santos shouted to him. 'Strong, black and sweet.' He threw back his head and laughed heartily. 'It is a beautiful day. I am in love.'

The girl came down the steps and made her way towards the galley. To Tim's surprise, she was smiling. The captain must have his good points after all. He greeted her and she responded. 'Eh heh.' He followed her into the galley. 'You sit,' she said. 'Me fix coffee.'

Santos was singing lustily again. The girl glanced up at the wheelhouse, shook her head, smiled and bustled around the galley as if she had been on the trawler all her life. 'What a difference a night makes,' Tim thought. But he was pleased for the girl. If Santos could bring about such a change in one night then her future may not be as bleak as it first appeared.

The island of Likoma, and her more westerly little sister, Chisumulu, were visible from the trawler just before eight in the morning. Until then, with the backdrop of Mozambique behind them, they had been indistinguishable from the mainland. The tin roof of St Peter's Anglican Cathedral dominated the larger island, reflecting the morning sun with almost painful ferocity. As they drew closer, the cathedral came into focus. It was an impressive sight, similar in size to Winchester Cathedral and built, as far as Tim could see, from granite. Stained glass windows glinted in the sunlight. As the *Katembe* rounded the point into the small harbour, villagers ran down onto the sandy beach, waving and shouting a greeting. Santos, brandishing another bottle of rum, waved and shouted back. He appeared to be immensely popular with the fishermen.

'Here, Gilbey,' Santos yelled. He was in excellent humour. 'I promise Likoma. Here is Likoma.' He looked over his shoulder and said something to the girl who had rejoined him, then called out to Tim. 'Santos very happy you say no. If you say yes then Santos have to kill you.'

Tim just shook his head and watched the view. The man was a little mad, a little bad, with no scruples and no redeeming features. But in that hard rock of a heart of his there must have been one small tender spot and the girl had found it. He wished them both well.

The *Katembe* anchored in the little harbour. There was no wharf but a boat, loaded with men, immediately left the shore and headed towards the trawler. A tall black man wearing the white surplice of his calling stood at the stern, smiling.

As they drew closer, Santos bellowed out a greeting. 'Hey, Father. You marry me today.'

The priest waved and smiled. 'When you bring the same girl twice, Captain Santos, then I'll marry you.' The African's English was impeccable. The boat drew alongside and the priest looked at Tim. 'Who do you bring to our island today?'

'Gilbey.' Santos deftly caught the rope thrown and tied the boat fast. 'This girl I love, Father.'

The priest joined Santos on the deck. 'Good. Bring her back next time.' He was still looking at Tim. 'What brings you here, Mr Gilbey?'

Good question. I'm looking for secret documents. If necessary, I'll kill someone for them. How does that grab you? 'I'm new in Malawi. I've been told about Likoma. I wanted to see it,' Tim lied with no discernible prick of conscience.

'What is your occupation, Mr Gilbey?' The priest had shrewd eyes.

'I am the Commercial Attache at the British High Commission.' Tim held up both hands. 'I know, I'm a little out of my way but I've read about this place and was determined to see it. The opportunity came along and . . . well . . . here I am.'

'Welcome then, Mr Gilbey. We are a small

350

community, as you will see. I hope your visit will be worth it.'

'Off,' Santos suddenly bellowed. 'You get off. Crew here, I go.'

'Don't mind the captain.' The priest smiled at Tim. 'His English leaves a little to be desired, his manners are atrocious and his personality could do with a little work but he's a good fellow at heart. The wages he pays bring much-needed money into our community.'

'Your English is excellent,' Tim commented.

'Thank you. The island has one hundred per cent literacy. The early missionaries built schools here. It is an honourable legacy is it not?'

'What is here other than the cathedral?'

'A few shops. Several small villages. A hospital, post office, community entertainment centre, three schools and a couple of rest houses.' The priest pointed to a building which perched, like an eagle in a tree, on top of a hill. 'The police post.'

'Perhaps you could recommend somewhere to stay? If you'll just hang on I'll get my bag.'

Tim went below and grabbed his rucksack. Santos was on deck speaking to the fishermen. When Tim said goodbye the only response the captain gave was, 'Yeah.' Tim joined the priest in the boat.

'I am Father Smice by the way,' the priest said, holding out his hand.

Tim shook it. 'My name is Tim,' he said.

'Tim.' The priest squinted at him. 'Timothy. A very worthy name. Did you know it is Greek? It means "honouring God".' He smiled. 'Don't mind me. It's a hobby of mine.'

The boat deposited them right up onto the beach. Father Smice pointed to a low, tin-roofed building just in front of the cathedral. 'Akuziki Private Rest House. You can stay there for forty Kwacha a single per night. They do meals, or you can buy food from the little shop next door.'

Tim looked at it doubtfully. It was smack in the middle of a small marketplace. He had hoped for something a little less public.

Father Smice took his arm and pointed to a cove further along the shore. 'Wilderness Safaris have just put up a tented camp behind that line of trees. Camp Likoma. It's more expensive but the food is good. If you go there, tell the manager I sent you.'

'I will. Thanks.'

'How long will you be staying, Mr Gilbey?'

'Couple of days,' Tim said evasively. 'I'd like to see Chisumulu too.' He looked around. The island did not have the lush, tropical island look he would have expected. 'Not many trees close to shore are there?' he commented.

'We have plantations on the far side. Alas, it will be some years before they can be harvested.' He indicated smoke rising from behind a couple of large baobab trees back from the edge of the beach. 'That's why. The people use wood in their kilns for smoking fish.' Father Smice turned and faced Tim squarely. 'I don't wish to appear rude, Mr Gilbey, but I'd like to ask you a fairly direct question. We hear rumours that a tourist lodge is to be built on the island. Can you tell me if this is so?'

Tim did his best to look mysterious.

'Ah, quite so, Mr Gilbey. You are not at liberty to say. Forgive my question – it is asked with the best interests of the islanders at heart.'

Tim lowered his voice. 'I will tell you only this, Father. I will be having a very good look at the island. I cannot say any more.'

'Of course.' The priest could not keep the joy from his voice. 'It would be a very good thing for our small community.' He turned to go. 'Come to Evening Service while you are here. We would be honoured to receive you.' He strode away, a tall imposing figure in white. Tim watched him go, his conscience very busy with its pitchfork on his shoulder.

He made his way towards the tented camp. It sat on a slight rise in the land, overlooking the harbour. Permanent tents had been erected over cement slabs and each had a wooden deck in the front giving uninterrupted views of several bays, a couple of small islands and the Mozambique mainland. At the back, accessed through a breezeway, each tent had its own private bathroom and toilet. The manager was delighted to book him in and overjoyed that he was staying more than one night. They could provide him with breakfast and dinner, the former at 6.30a.m., the latter at 5.00p.m. 'We have no electricity,' the manager told him in the same oddly formal English as Father Smice. 'That is why you must take your meal early.'

Tim assured him it would be fine, asked if there

was a map of Likoma, smiled and said it didn't matter that there wasn't and, having dumped his rucksack in his luxurious tent, told the manager he was off to explore the island.

'Do you like scuba diving?' the man asked. 'We have some of the best on the lake.'

'Perhaps tomorrow,' Tim replied. He noticed that equipment was available for hire on request.

'If you want to see the island better you must climb up Macholo. It is the highest point. You will like the view.'

Tim thanked him for the advice.

'You have to see the cathedral too. It's very beautiful.' The man's pride was evident. 'The choir stalls have been made from soapstone.'

'I do want to see the cathedral.' Tim took advantage of the manager's willingness to talk. 'How many priests work there now?'

'Not as many as we would like. I don't know exactly. Some are not priests, they are missionaries and doctors.'

'Are they all from the island?'

'Oh no. Only Father Smice and the Canon.'

'Are they all Malawian?'

The man shook his head. 'They come from many parts of the world. Several are from your country.'

Tim decided he'd asked enough questions. He didn't want the man to think him overly interested in the cathedral and its resident clergy. All he said was, 'They are lucky to live in such a beautiful place.'

★

Once, Likoma had been the missionary headquarters of the Anglican Church in Central Africa, established in such an out-of-the-way place as a refuge from attacking Ngoni and Yao tribes on the Portuguese-controlled mainland. The cathedral was a grandiose idea of the first Bishop of Likoma, one Chauncey Maples, who unfortunately drowned near Monkey Bay and never saw his dream realised. Tim supposed that Bishop Maples was preferable to that other breed of evangelists who arrived in Africa around the end of the nineteenth century, with a Bible in one hand and a gun in the other, yet he wondered how the Bishop had managed to get the Oxford and Cambridge Universities' Mission to central Africa to build such an edifice. It was completely over the top for such a small place. No-one was going to travel thirteen kilometres by boat to attend services, no matter how imposing the venue.

The roads, if you could call them roads, held no traffic at all. Come to that, Tim didn't see a single car on or off the road. He thought about Hamilton. Where would the man hide documents? Somewhere in his house or room? With a friend? Buried on a beach? Hamilton had arrived in Malawi today sometime. Would he fly directly to Likoma, would he overnight in Lilongwe or even, would he wait and catch the *Ilala* in a few days' time? Tim stopped and looked around. He had scrambled up Macholo and, as the camp manager had promised, it was a beautiful view. On all sides, the lake lapped at white, sandy beaches. The feeling of isolation was strong.

'What must it be like to spend your life here?' he wondered.

Coming down from the hill, Tim set off almost due north. On a peninsula ahead he could see one of the villages Father Smice mentioned. It looked idyllic – a place preserved in a time warp. If Father Smice was right, if there were plans to open the island up to tourism, Tim wondered if the benefits would not be suffocated by the down side. Tourists would bring capital to the island certainly but at what cost to the islanders?

Fifteen minutes later he reached the small cluster of houses. Children ran up to him laughing. Men smiled at him and raised their right hand, palm out. Women giggled. A small boy strolled by playing a penny whistle which appeared to be made of ivory. Tim walked to the far side of the village and stopped to admire the view. Set back from the dusty track, a man sat outside his hut, carving another penny whistle from wood. He had set up a stall of sorts against the wall of his hut. His work was quite good. Wood and ivory statues, candlestick holders, bowls and small carved animals were displayed but, by far the most prolific item was the musical instrument. Tim watched the man's deft hands shaving the whistle into smooth perfection. He was completely absorbed by what he was doing.

There was something strange about the man. His skin was deeply bronzed but not black. Hair matted his bare chest and shoulders. Not sparse and peppercorned, this man's chest hair was long and straight. Thick hair on his head was greying and curly, not frizzy, and grew almost to the man's shoulders. Tim realised suddenly that the craftsman was not African.

Perhaps he sensed he was being observed or maybe he just wanted to stretch his neck muscles but the man glanced up at Tim. His features were pure European. His face and eyes wore a peaceful, almost vacant expression and the smile on his lips was not one of greeting, rather one of the pleasure he was taking in his task. Tim went cold. The shape of his dark brown eyes was startlingly familiar – Tim had deep blue ones just like them in his dreams. The family resemblance was unmistakable. At that moment Tim Gilbey knew, with no doubt in his mind, that he was looking at Lana's father, John Devereaux.

FIFTEEN

Tim stared at John Devereaux. The man looked back, curious. Then he held up a penny whistle. '*Ndalama zingati?*'

Tim's Chichewa was rudimentary but he understood that John Devereaux had asked him, 'How much?' Perhaps he meant how much would Tim pay for it, Tim couldn't be certain. It seemed a strange way to put it and it was obvious that the words did not come easily. There was a stiffness to the way he moved his mouth. Tim walked to where he was working and dropped to his haunches. 'Very good work, where did you learn to make these?'

Devereaux shrugged. Not the slow, typically French shrug using shoulders, hands and mouth pulled into wryness, Devereaux's actions were those of a small child caught out – a quick, almost defiant, up and down of the shoulders. Tim would have expected more eloquence from a man like John Devereaux. Was he putting on an act? He looked deep into Devereaux's eyes. Tim saw neither fear nor furtiveness, cunning nor duplicity. What he did see was emptiness.

He wanted to hear Devereaux speak again. 'I heard a boy playing one of these as I walked through the village. Do you make lots?'

John Devereaux just stared blankly at Tim.

A woman came out of the hut behind them. 'He does not speak English,' she said, putting her hand on Devereaux's shoulder affectionately and patting it. 'He is the only one on the island who does not.'

Tim stood. 'He is not African.'

'No.' She looked down at Devereaux and smiled. He smiled back, like a pleased child. 'He does not know where he is from.'

'Are you his wife?'

The woman laughed at that. 'He has no wife. We all look after him. Without our help he would not be able to live.'

Tim looked at Lana's father with sympathy. Devereaux had gone back to his carving. 'Can you tell me any more about him?' Tim asked the woman.

She fidgeted a bit. 'I do not know. It is not for me to decide. Wait here please.' She set off down the track at a fast pace, looking back once or twice to see if Tim was still there.

Tim stayed where he was and watched John Devereaux, who was working with intense concentration. 'John Devereaux,' Tim said loudly enough for him to hear. But Devereaux did not react.

Ten minutes later the woman came back with an elderly man. 'This is my father. He is the Chief. He will speak with you.'

Tim looked at the Chief and the only word he could think of to describe the man was 'beautiful'. His hair was snowy white and, from the little Tim could see of it, worn longer than most African men. By Malawian standards, the Chief was tall. Nearly as tall as Tim. His skin was the colour of burnished bronze. On his face, it stretched taut over a high bridged nose and prominent cheek-bones. He held himself proudly erect and, if the dusty and baggy Western-style trousers and old tennis shoes let the side down somewhat, the leopard skin across the old man's shoulders and the feathered and beaded headdress more than made up for them. His dark eyes were shrewd and his lips might have been chiselled for a statue in a Pharaoh's tomb. He was one of the few remaining full-blooded Nkonde tribesmen and he bore his Egyptian heritage with dignity and an air of self-esteem which was both regal and confident. When he spoke, his voice was rich and deep. 'You ask about this man. Why?'

Tim felt the full force of the Chief's undisputed power and, fleetingly, thought it a pity that such a prince of a man ruled such a small and isolated community. He should have been leading a nation. 'I believe I know who he is.'

The Chief beckoned. 'Come, we will walk.'

Tim joined him and, side by side, they went slowly down to the small beach where several men were bathing. 'How are you known?' Tim asked.

'Chief Mbeya,' the Chief said briefly. 'How are you known?'

'Tim Gilbey.'

'Timgilbey,' the Chief repeated slowly. Then he smiled. His teeth were yellowed with age but, unlike many, he had a full set. 'At least it is easy to say.'

Tim knew the rules. To get the answers he required there would first be a lengthy discussion on other matters. 'Your island is beautiful.'

'Yes. It is also very small.'

'Then the problems must be small also.'

Chief Mbeya produced a pipe and lit it. He puffed slowly, allowing the smoke to escape from the corners of his mouth. 'It was not always so,' he said eventually. 'The Chiefs before me were great men.'

'From where did your people come?'

'Unlike the English, our history was not always written down. To go back more than several hundred years is not always possible. I know only what the storytellers relate.' He removed the pipe from his mouth and looked at Tim. 'Would you like to hear it, Timgilbey?'

As keen as he was to learn more about John Devereaux, Tim appreciated the compliment. 'If you don't mind telling it, Chief Mbeya, I would be more than honoured to listen.'

The Chief glanced at him in approval. His contact with the white race was spasmodic. Generally he found them impatient, brash and rude. This man was different. 'We will sit over there,' he said, pointing to the deep shade of a mango tree. 'Come.'

Once settled, the Chief began to speak. 'One

361

hundred years ago a great tragedy occurred among my people. It scattered the Nkonde into neighbouring tribal areas. They went north to the other great water [Tim surmised he was referring to Lake Tanganyika], they fled east to the high mountains and they came south as my village did. Some followed the setting sun and were never seen again. So far did our people flee from each other that they never regrouped. Those who remained where they were, who did not flee, suffered an evil fate.' Chief Mbeya paused to collect his thoughts. 'My father was Chief Mbeya but his father was not. The brother of my father's father was Chief Mbeya then.'

Tim knew that the storyteller's words could become rather convoluted. Africans seemed able to follow the complexities of historical relationships, often leaving Tim trying to sort out in his own mind the exact connection between people. On this occasion, however, he understood that Chief Mbeya was referring to his own great-uncle.

'That Chief was murdered by Mlozi.'

'The slaver?'

Chief Mbeya spat. 'Exactly so.'

Tim spat too. 'There was much evil in this land.'

The Chief hawked and spat again, further this time. Tim left it. He was no match for such a gifted expectorator. Slightly disappointed at such an easy victory, the Chief continued his story. 'Nkondeland was a peaceful place. Chief Mbeya ruled as many as 5,000 people. The villages were scattered so he appointed elders for each. My father's father was one such elder. He was the brother of Chief Mbeya. Do you understand, Timgilbey?'

'Yes I do. They would be his representatives.'

The Chief nodded. 'Exactly so. Four times a year the Chief met with his elders. That was how he ruled.'

One of the bathing men strolled, naked and unconcerned, out of the lake. Water beaded on his black skin, emphasising powerful muscles. He was a magnificent specimen, in the prime of life, and as natural as his surroundings. 'My nephew,' the Chief said, following Tim's gaze. 'I have no sons. He will be Chief Mbeya when I am gone. That is how it works with us. He will be a good leader. His heart is as strong as his body and every bit as good.'

'A fine-looking young man,' Tim replied. 'You must be proud of him.'

'Indeed,' the Chief agreed. He puffed on his pipe in silence for a few moments before continuing his story. 'My father's father went to the village where Chief Mbeya lived. He was very worried. The drums had spread a warning of Mlozi but the drums also told that Chief Mbeya wanted his people to stay, not run. When my father's father arrived at Chief Mbeya's village he was too late. Mlozi and the ruga-ruga had already been. My father's father found the body of his brother among the dead. This meant that he was now the Chief of Nkondeland. Knowing it would not be long before Mlozi raided his own village, he sent a new message on the drums. It told of the carnage and destruction he had seen. He said the Wankonde should not sit like cattle, waiting for slaughter. Every elder was to be responsible for the fate of his people. Entire villages moved in whatever direction their elders chose. My father's father took his people around the top of this lake and down the other side. He took them as far away from Mlozi as he could.' The Chief pointed to the Mozambique shoreline. 'They settled there and became as one with the Nyanja people. My father was born there.'

'But that was not the end of these troubles was it?' Tim asked. 'Many fled to this island to get away from other enemies.'

The Chief nodded in approval. 'Indeed. The Yao and the Ngoni were enemies of the Nyanja.' He puffed on his pipe. 'How is it you know this thing?'

'Before I came to Likoma I read a little of this island's history.'

The Chief puffed and nodded again. 'It is good. More should follow your lead. White people *should* know of our troubled history.' He smiled briefly. 'At least now we live in peace, although, as you have already observed, Timgilbey, peace and beauty was traded for greatness and that is a sad price to pay.' He went silent, staring reflectively out across the water. Then, 'I will tell you what I know about the music man in our village.'

Tim had passed some kind of test.

'It was in 1983,' Chief Mbeya began. 'My nephew found him on this beach. We thought he was dead. He had a terrible injury here.' The Chief touched the side of his head. 'And another here.' Chief Mbeya raised a hand to the back of his head.

'His skin was very white and wrinkled. He must have been in the water for a very long time. We did not think he would live. The women cared for him. He was sick for many, many weeks.'

'Can you tell me of this sickness?'

'He was like a baby. He could not walk. He spoke not a word. He would soil himself as an infant does. The spirits had taken his memory. He had to learn everything again, how to walk, to talk. In some ways he is still helpless. He is a little . . .' the Chief hesitated, 'a little like a boy of five years. He cannot concentrate for very long. He is happiest making his music pipes.'

'He uses ivory and wood. Where would the ivory come from?'

'I do not know,' the Chief said evasively.

'Why does he not speak English as the rest of you do?'

The Chief shook his head. 'We are taught by the men of God but only speak it when they come here. That man – we call him *Mpasa* – knows only my people. For fifteen years he has heard only Chichewa but, even so, he speaks the language like a child.'

'Why do you call him Mpasa?'

The Chief chuckled. 'He came from the water. We have a fish by that name. It is a fighting fish and very large. Mpasa must have been fighting to be so badly hurt.' He pulled on his earlobe. 'What name does Timgilbey have for Mpasa?'

'John Devereaux.'

'John Deborie,' the Chief repeated.

It was close enough. 'There is a problem,' Tim told the Chief.

'Why is this?'

'Mpasa has a daughter. She has come to Malawi to try to find her father.'

The Chief closed his eyes. 'She will find him,' he said quietly. 'And she will also find that her heart has broken in two.'

'You may well be right,' Tim agreed. 'He might not know her.'

Chief Mbeya sighed and rose. 'My heart weeps for such pain.'

Tim stood as well. 'As does mine.' He hesitated, then added, 'I have feelings for his daughter, Chief Mbeya. I would spare her this pain if possible. However, it would be wrong to keep from her the very truth she seeks.'

'You have a good heart, Timgilbey, and you speak well.' They began walking back towards the village. 'We are not God,' the Chief added. 'We can only stand and watch.' He stopped suddenly. 'She will not be able to take him away.'

'Why not?'

'He becomes confused and frightened. This is his home now. He knows nothing else.'

Tim had a thought. 'Do the missionaries know he's here?'

'This is a small place, Timgilbey. Secrets do not stay that way for very long. The priests from this island know of Mpasa. I do not know if the others do. Perhaps not. Mpasa is not seen by many. Today is one of his good days. There are many when he shuts himself away and makes tears of great sorrow. We ask why he is crying but always he tells us, "Sindikumva" – I do not understand – and we can see he speaks the truth. He lives with that which he does not know.'

'Perhaps he can be helped.'

'Perhaps.' Chief Mbeya did not sound convinced.

'Would you have any objection to my trying?'

'No,' the Chief said soberly. 'But you will see. Our own medicine men have tried to help him. It is no use. Inside Mpasa's head there is only Mpasa. The John Deborie who once was there is gone. I have known Mpasa for fifteen years. The only spirit left is that of Mpasa.'

Tim made his way back to the tented camp, deeply disturbed. The post office must have a telephone. He could contact the High Commission and ask them to get in touch with the hospital and arrange for someone to fly here and examine Devereaux. Tim had met one of the doctors only last week – a young Swede who was on two years' sabbatical leave and donating his services for very little remuneration. What John Devereaux needed was to be treated gently – not bundled up and rushed into some hospital or worse, asylum, to be treated like a specimen in a bottle.

And what about Lana? What earthly good would it do for her to see her father like that? Tim decided to postpone telling her until a suitably qualified doctor could be found. Then at least, if there was no hope that John Devereaux could be helped, Lana would be pre-warned. Even so, Tim knew Lana's life was about to be torn apart.

Were there other family members? She had mentioned her mother. With her father declared officially dead, her mother might have remarried. *God! What if she has? What if the sight of his daughter was the catalyst for Devereaux's recovery. What a mess that would be.* Tim briefly considered not telling Lana anything at all but, just as quickly, discarded the thought. A mess it might become, but the family had a right to know.

He glanced at his watch. Nearly one o'clock. The High Commission didn't open on Saturday but Tim knew his secretary's home telephone number. He could at least make some enquiries about finding help for Devereaux. It would mean revealing his whereabouts but to hell with that. He'd face Martin Flower's disapproval when the time came. Lana should, this very minute, be at Henning's lunch party at his farm near Kasungu. 'Better not try and contact her there,' he thought. 'She might let something slip to Henning. I'm not certain that he'd take the news too calmly.'

The tall figure in white coming towards him was Father Smice. 'Good afternoon, Father.'

'Good afternoon, Mr Gilbey. I was hoping to find you.' The priest slowed and stood, waiting for Tim to join him. Sunlight glinted off his gold-rimmed glasses and a slight breeze ruffled his surplice. With a backdrop of deep blue lake behind him, he looked like a painting.

'Well here I am,' Tim said, stopping in front of the man.

'Not wasting any time I see. Do you find our island to your liking?'

'It's very beautiful.' Tim glanced around. 'Is that your airstrip?' It was rustic to say the least. Gravel which had been levelled by hand and, Tim suspected, its length would be on the borderline of any legal requirements. Grass grew in clumps and cattle and goats grazed on it. Children were playing at the far end and, every now and then, people crossed from one side to the other.

Father Smice smiled. 'It lends a certain excitement to landing and taking off.' He pointed to a large tree. 'See that baobab? That's the departure lounge.'

Tim laughed. 'It's a lot nicer than some.'

'Yes,' the priest nodded. 'But not when it's raining.' He turned and they began walking. 'Where are you going?'

'Following my nose I suppose. I've seen the north, now I want to look at the south. Tell me, Father, does the island have a telephone?'

'Several. Not all of them work but you should find at least one that does. You have to go through the operator. There's a pay phone outside the post office but I understand it is not working at the moment. If you run into difficulties let me know. You can use ours at the cathedral.'

'Thank you.'

'Who would you want to phone so soon after arriving I wonder?' the priest teased. He glanced at

Tim. 'Do you mind? When one lives on a place like Likoma even the smallest item of news is interesting.'

Tim thought there was hardly much point in hiding his discovery of Devereaux from Father Smice. If a doctor came in to examine the man the entire island would hear of it. 'Did you know, Father, that a white man lives in Chief Mbeya's village?'

The priest stared straight ahead. 'Mpasa. Yes, I know of him.'

'What do you know of him?'

'What is your intention?' the priest countered. Then added, 'Why is this of concern to you?'

'I mean him no harm.'

Father Smice stopped walking. 'There is a good view of the bay from here. We will sit.' He moved off the track, folded his surplice neatly around him and sat on the grass. 'Is he the reason you are here?'

Tim shook his head. 'I found him quite by accident.'

'What is your interest in Mpasa?'

'Quite a coincidence really. His daughter has just come to Malawi to try and find out what became of her father. He was a geologist. He disappeared here fifteen years ago.'

'What makes you think that Mpasa is this girl's missing father?'

'Two things. The family resemblance is very strong. They are undoubtedly related. That, and the time Mpasa has been here. It coincides with the time her father has been missing. The daughter believes he is dead.'

Father Smice looked thoughtfully out across the lake. 'And so he is,' he murmured. 'If Mpasa is her missing father then the man she knew in his body is long gone.'

'I know,' Tim agreed. 'But his family still have a right to know.'

The priest sighed. 'I have long pondered the ethics of hiding this man. When he first came to us . . .' Father Smice's voice trailed off. He shook his head and came to a decision. 'He had been shot. I have never seen a wound like it. A part of his head was blown away.'

'Why didn't you contact the mainland and get help?'

'We expected him to die. Try to understand, Mr Gilbey. When Mpasa arrived, no-one thought he would last the day. He had been in the water for a very long time and his injuries were terrible. The villagers did what they could, made him comfortable, and waited for the end.'

'Which never came.'

'Each day we thought that today would be the one when he would die. For weeks Mpasa lay in a semi-coma. When he was lucid he was in great mental torment. Shaking, crying, displaying much fear. By the time Chief Mbeya's people realised that he would probably live, he had been with them for almost two months. The Chief held a meeting of elders. They voted to keep Mpasa a secret. You see, Mr Gilbey, it was feared that we would all be in great trouble with the law if it became known that we had hidden a white man for so long.'

'Especially since nothing was done to make him better,' Tim said sharply.

Father Smice fiddled with his glasses. 'That is not so, Mr Gilbey,' he said finally. 'It is because of our own medicine men that Mpasa lives. You see, once it became apparent that he wasn't going to die immediately, our people used traditional methods to cure him.'

'Don't you see?' Tim said. 'If he had got help immediately he might not be so injured now.'

'Mr Gilbey,' the priest said patiently. 'If he had been moved off this island he would have died.'

Tim didn't argue. It was fifteen years ago. No-one could prove otherwise now. Still, it was a sore point between the two of them. 'I can understand the villagers' concern. I find it hard to accept yours. Surely the moral issue alone should have told you that Mpasa came from somewhere and that others would be looking for him?'

Father Smice looked unhappy. 'I am a priest and have taken certain vows. But, Mr Gilbey, I am also one of Chief Mbeya's people. He is my Chief and when he orders me to do something, I am obliged to do it.' Father Smice folded his hands in his lap and looked down at them. 'There is something else,' he said. 'Whatever trouble Mpasa had been in, we did not wish it to visit this island. We are a peaceful people.'

'This trouble you speak of. Do you know what it could have been?'

'I wish I did, Mr Gilbey. All I can tell you is whatever it was, it still causes Mpasa anguish.'

'If that is the case, Father, couldn't there be something left of the man Mpasa used to be?'

'I do not think so.' Father Smice was still looking down at his hands. 'Mpasa must have swum to Likoma and yet, when he began to recover, he could not even remember how to walk or talk. I think his swimming here was instinctive. His fear is also instinctive.' The priest raised his eyes to Tim's. 'There is nothing left of the one you seek, only the one you see remains.'

'But I must try and help him.'

'You cannot. If his routine is broken he becomes terrified.'

'I don't want to take him away. I can arrange for a doctor to come here. If we get Chief Mbeya's cooperation there is no need for Mpasa to leave.'

'And why would you be doing this, Mr Gilbey?'

'For his daughter's sake.'

Father Smice nodded. 'Will we be in trouble?'

'I shouldn't think so. It was too long ago and it is clear that you have taken great care of him.'

The priest looked relieved. 'Then, Mr Gilbey, if Chief Mbeya and the church speak as one, the people of Likoma will undoubtedly cooperate.' He scrambled to his feet. 'And now, the reason I was looking for you. The Bishop sent me to ask if you would care to come to dinner this evening. He wishes to meet you. We manage quite a good table.'

'I would be delighted to accept.' Tim rose as well.

Father Smice smiled. 'We cannot compete with

373

the meals where you are staying but our food is all home grown. Simple but good.'

'I'll bring a bottle of wine.'

'Do not bother, Mr Gilbey. We make our own.'

Father Smice left Tim to continue his walk to the southern tip of Likoma, having warned him to keep well away from several small beaches. 'We still practise segregated bathing on Likoma,' he told Tim. 'If you go near to where the women bathe . . .' he smiled and spread his hands. 'Let's just say that not even God could protect you.'

Tim enjoyed the walk. The islanders were certainly industrious. Evidence of their farming skills filled every available pocket of arable land. Out on the lake, Tim could see the dugout canoes of island fishermen. On one beach a net was being hauled in. Women, bent at the waist, were washing clothes. Men and women carried produce to market. He passed a mission school and listened to the children singing in English. It was idyllic, yet strangely odd that such a remote community spoke almost perfect English. Likoma was a relic of the past, a place where little had changed in the last hundred years, the legacy of missionaries who blundered through Africa dispensing religion and morals. Despite their best intentions, so much had been lost. Winchester Cathedral belonged in Winchester. Perfect English belonged in England. Although the islanders seemed proud of their ability to speak English, Tim noticed that they rarely did amongst themselves.

A woman in a small shop amid a sprawling clutter of huts cheerfully sold Tim a couple of bananas, an orange and a bottle of lemonade. Tim finished his brief tour of the island and made his way back to Chipyela, the main village. He wondered, as others probably had before him, what kind of macabre sense of symbolism caused the missionaries to build their cathedral directly over 'the burning place', which is what Chipyela translated as in English.

It was past four by the time he arrived back at the camp.

The manager greeted him – 'I am most rude, Mr Gilbey. My name is Wireless, I am the manager.' He was disappointed that Tim would not be having dinner there but cheered up when he learned that his one and only guest had been invited to dine at the cathedral. 'They don't do that very often.'

Tim, still trying to come to terms with the proprietor's name, responded absently, 'Do you have a telephone?'

Wireless looked crestfallen. 'You must be an important man,' he reflected aloud, determined to learn why his guest had been invited to dine with the priests.

Realising the man was desperate for gossip which would undoubtedly find its way to every corner of the island by tomorrow, Tim gave him what he sought. 'I work for the British High Commission. I think the Bishop wants to know why I'm here. Father Smice seems to think I have something to do with a tourist lodge proposed for

375

Likoma.' It was a fair enough response. Tim had provided the man with hardly any information, but he had done it in such a way as to invite speculation. He wondered, by the time the gossip extended to both ends of the island, what rumours would be spread.

Wireless was satisfied. 'The telephone is through here, Mr Gilbey. It is working today I think.' Then he looked sorrowful. 'But, Mr Gilbey, so sorry, the post office is closed now. The telephone operator will not be there until the day after tomorrow. Unfortunately, the pay phone is broken. I am sorry.'

There was nothing Tim could do about John Devereaux until Monday.

Dinner at the cathedral had been a pleasant and somewhat informative affair. Father Smice, who appeared to regard Tim as his own personal property, insisted on a guided tour before taking him to meet the others. The cathedral itself was indeed magnificent, bathed in the most spectacularly red sunset Tim had ever seen. Father Smice proudly showed Tim the crucifix above the altar. 'The wood comes from the village where Dr Livingstone died,' he explained.

'I thought David Livingstone died in Zambia.'

'So he did. Chitambo. But, Mr Gilbey, that was just an accident of time. Dr Livingstone belonged to Nyasaland. He discovered the Lake of Stars.'

'Where's that?'

Through the stained glass window shimmering

waters reflected the last rays of sunset. Father Smice chuckled. 'You are looking at it now, Mr Gilbey. That is how the good doctor described Lake Malawi.'

'Lake of Stars. He must have loved Nyasaland.'

'We believe he felt more at home here than anywhere else in Africa. Indeed, his writings would indicate that he did.'

The priest's reverence for the legendary missionary was evident. 'A truly remarkable man,' Tim offered.

'Not always easy to get along with,' Father Smice admitted, proving that, while he was prepared to hero-worship David Livingstone he was not blind to the man's many faults. 'In the end, though, he mellowed. We believe he became truly a saint on that last journey.'

They left the altar and went outside. The sunset was almost garish. 'If a painter represented the true colour of this it would not be believed,' Tim commented.

Father Smice agreed. 'I feel very close to God at this time of day.' He turned to Tim. 'Tell me, do you believe in God?'

'Yes I do,' Tim said with no hesitation. 'But not to the extent that I would make worshipping Him my life.'

Again, the priest chuckled. 'Do not worry, Mr Gilbey. I am not trying to convert you.' He took Tim's arm. 'This way. I want to show you something.' Signs of an attempt to tame some of the overgrown garden were in evidence. Father Smice led Tim to a wooden trapdoor set into the ground close behind the cathedral. 'This was discovered recently. We had no idea it was here. We think it was built centuries ago. Some say it's part of the cathedral but there does not appear to be any way through from inside. Certainly, earlier inhabitants knew of it. I have been looking through our archives. It was sealed in 1942.'

The trapdoor was solid and showed no undue stress at having been concealed under shrubbery for many decades. A rusted staple and hasp with a very large padlock, which, in contrast, looked brand new, prevented the trapdoor from being lifted. 'If it was part of the cathedral you would expect there to be another way in,' Tim said.

'We have looked. There are no signs of a sealed entrance anywhere inside. Our head office archivist has examined the original plans and this crypt does not appear on them.' Father Smice grinned. 'It's a delicious mystery which has us all guessing.'

'The padlock is new.'

'Yes. Unfortunately the man who found this could not contain his curiosity. We have locked the door in case others are tempted.'

'Who found it?' Tim asked, probing for a name. Father Smice had to use Hamilton's name before Tim.

'One of the Brothers.'

'He must have been excited at such a discovery,' Tim pushed further.

'He was too excited,' Father Smice said soberly. 'The crypt was obviously sealed. He broke the seal.'

'Why wouldn't he?'

The priest led Tim away. 'Crypts have been sealed before. Usually to hide a dreadful secret. Whoever sealed this one did so for a good reason. Brother Hamilton should not have opened it.'

'It's only a room,' Tim protested. *Good! That gets that out of the way.*

'If the crypt is part of the cathedral then this is consecrated ground,' Father Smice explained. 'To open the crypt requires a long process. It can only be done by one who is trained for such things. None of us here has the training. Brother Hamilton should have known better.'

'Is he still here?'

'No,' the priest said sadly. 'Unfortunately, he was recalled to England. I believe he is no longer with the Church.'

'Did he find why the crypt had been sealed?'

'He said it was empty. It is not for us to know.' Father Smice indicated a low wing of the cathedral. 'Come. The others wait to meet you.'

Tim was introduced to the assembled clergy. The Bishop, an immensely charming and serene man from America, asked a number of probing questions about Tim's visit. The rumours of a tourist complex had been circulating Likoma for several years. The Bishop wanted to know if they were true. The more Tim dodged around his enquiries, the more they all became convinced that the real reason for Tim's visit had something to do with development of their island. It suited Tim to allow them to believe that, though he was unhappy that he might be building up false hopes.

They were a mixed bag around the table. Some were fully ordained priests, others missionaries with specialised training. One man – and Tim was unclear what he did on the island – was from the Basque Provinces and his swarthy face was almost obliterated by a huge and luxuriously bushy beard. He appeared to be suffering some kind of throat disorder. A gauze bandage covered his Adam's apple and his voice was a quiet growl.

Two of the men were from Belgium and Tim mentally dubbed them Tweedledum and Tweedledee. Both were painfully thin, with soulful, fatigue-smudged eyes, overlong noses and down-turned mouths. They reminded Tim of a breed of sheep, though he couldn't quite recall which one. He was not surprised to learn later in the evening that they were twins.

They were a jovial lot, well-read and travelled and prepared to discuss just about anything. A couple of them were also remarkably fond of red wine which flowed freely from what Tim thought must be a bottomless barrel in an adjoining room. The meal was roast chicken from the island which was both succulent and delicious. 'Corn-fed,' a quietly spoken Malawian priest from Lilongwe explained. Vegetables accompanying the chicken were home grown. A variety of cheeses made on the island followed.

Port was passed clockwise around the table. Replete and relaxed as they seemed to be, Tim thought it a good time to raise the subject of the crypt.

'We warned him,' the Frenchman rasped softly. 'Where did it get him? There was nothing in there.'

'Why would it be sealed if there was nothing there?' Tim asked.

The swarthy features of the Frenchman scowled as he leaned towards Tim, and port spilled, unnoticed, on the snowy tablecloth. 'Who knows? Perhaps something dreadful happened in there.' He leaned back again. 'There are always reasons.'

'Frederick is a strange man,' the Bishop volunteered. 'Solitary sort of person. Secretive too. I think he's an unhappy man. We cleaned out his room after he left us. He'd occupied it for nearly twenty years. No pictures, no rug, nothing to make it more comfortable. Sad isn't it? We tried to involve him more but,' the Bishop shrugged, 'he just kept to himself.'

There was general agreement around the table that Frederick Hamilton had made no friends, rarely went on home leave, was a diligent worker and generally not liked either by his colleagues or the island people. Tim got the impression that the Bishop felt, in some way, that by failing to get through to Hamilton, the Bishop had somehow failed the man.

The subject died and Tim didn't bring it back. The evening ended abruptly, just after nine. Father Smice loaned Tim a torch and he made his way back to the camp. As tempting as it was to pick the lock and have a look in the crypt on the way past, Tim left it. He doubted very much that the documents would still be there and besides, Father

Smice's explanation about consecrated ground made the idea less attractive. If the occasion warranted it, Tim would not hesitate to enter the crypt but there was little point in upsetting the priests for no good reason.

The little he had learned about Frederick Hamilton during the evening gave rise to a few problems. No obvious friend with whom the documents might have been left. An austere room which had been cleaned, no doubt thoroughly, and which probably offered no hiding place. No regular activity which might have pinpointed a place where the documents might have been secreted. 'About all I can do,' Tim decided, 'is to wait for Hamilton and follow him.'

At around midnight, the man who was known as Mpasa slipped into a deeper sleep – a sleep so deep that images from the past crowded together in a jumble of unrelated incidences – memories which had the man twitching and sweating and flinging his head from side to side. It was always like this. The nightmare which drained his energy, confused and frightened him, leaving him weeping and shaking for days after. In this level of consciousness, people spoke a strange language but he had no trouble understanding it. Only afterwards, once he'd woken, did the words become meaningless.

There was fear – a great fear – and pain and cold and arms which felt too heavy to move. A little girl was in front of him, laughing and swimming, always out of reach. He had to catch her but when he got to where she was, she had moved again. A great evil was behind him. He did not know what, just knew he had to get away from it. He was falling, falling, down and down.

As always, once the nightmare gripped him, John Devereaux began to shout. As always, someone came quietly to him to wrap him in their arms and comfort him through to wakefulness. As always, as the nightmare faded away, John Devereaux was left with nothing but fear and the sobs which shook his body for days. And, as always, along with the fear, an abiding sadness – a sense of having lost something precious.

Tim was just finishing breakfast the next morning when he heard the aeroplane. Leaving his coffee, Tim made his way, along with other curious inhabitants of Chipyela, to the airstrip and arrived just in time to see a lone passenger alight. He recognised him from photographs Martin Flower had sent in the diplomatic bag a few days ago. Frederick Hamilton had arrived.

SIXTEEN

Lana and Moffat were beginning to believe they would never reach Karonga. The 350-kilometre stretch between Kasungu and Mzuzu took a little over four hours and it was fully dark when they finally stopped in Mzuzu for something to eat. By 8.30 they were on the road again, heading south-east towards the lake and then north on the lakeshore road through Livingstonia and on up past Chilumba where Karl's yacht was moored.

The condition of the roads ran the gauntlet from excellent to suicidal. Once they reached the lakeshore road they spelled each other at the wheel every two hours while the other tried to sleep in the back. Lana had managed several catnaps. Moffat didn't sleep at all but lay with his eyes shut, resting, periodically making comments which – for the most part – were so vague that Lana felt he might as well be asleep.

She drove through Chilumba, not stopping to locate the harbour. Just outside the town, she pulled to the side of the road. 'Your turn.'

Moffat sat up. 'Only about seventy kilometres to go,' he mumbled.

384

'Want me to keep driving?'

'No. Let's just take a break. I'll be fine in a minute.' He opened his door and got out. 'Come on, out you get. Stretch those legs.'

'Thank God!' Lana walked around the car, trying to ease cramped muscles. She had been at the wheel as they climbed away from the lake just before Livingstonia. She lost count of the tight, hairpin bends, and Moffat's comment, 'Just be thankful you can't see the drop,' hadn't done much to help.

They stood together, sipping from cans of soft drink, the darkness and silence engulfing them. The night was almost uncomfortably warm.

'Karl Henning is guilty. I can feel it in my bones,' Lana said suddenly. She heard the rustle of clothing as Moffat moved beside her and put his arm around her shoulders. She leaned her head against his arm.

'What would the white way be if we find out it was him?'

'Report him to the proper authorities. How about you?'

'The African way you mean?' His voice held a note of anger. 'He would find that his crops had failed. His machinery would break down all the time. His servants would become troublesome. His house would burn down. If he had children, they would become sick and die. If he had cattle, they would die.'

'And how would you organise all that?' she teased him. 'The Nganga?'

'Do not mock his powers, Lana. These things are possible.'

'Only if you believe.'

'Not necessarily. Many whites in this country use a witchdoctor. They only half believe.'

'How strange,' she murmured. Tiredness washed over her. The strong warmth of Moffat's arm was comforting. He seemed so solid, so . . . there. 'Moffat?'

'What?'

'What's it like for you? I mean, you seem to be stuck in the middle of two cultures. I don't have that problem. I am what I am. But you . . . old African ways are just as strong in you as the more recently acquired European ways. Doesn't it confuse you?'

He moved slightly, shifting the weight of his arm around her shoulder. 'Sometimes,' he admitted. 'It will be even worse for my children.'

'How do you cope?'

He grunted, amused. 'What makes you think I cope?'

She turned her head in his direction. 'You cope, of course you do. You're one of the most laid-back people I've ever met.' She hesitated, not sure if he would be offended by her words. 'What's more,' she said eventually, 'you manage to combine your own traditions with mine with little or no effort. You keep your African identity while, at the same time, you move effortlessly through mine. I think it's wonderful but – and I have to ask – do you resent it?'

He was silent for almost a minute. 'Yes,' he said finally.

'Because of our arrogance?'

'Because in your arrogance you *expect* me to cope.'

'Ouch!' she said softly.

He moved again so that he faced her, both arms draped casually over her shoulders. 'You are very different.'

She could just make out his silhouette in the darkness. 'My mother is South African. She went out of her way to teach me that the policies in her country were wrong. It's a lesson I learned well and, I guess, because we were always visiting South Africa, I had plenty of opportunity to see for myself what she was trying to teach me. Thank you for saying I'm different.'

He moved away abruptly. 'We should not stand like this, you and I.'

'Why not?' She was surprised. 'We're friends.'

'Do you really want me to tell you?' His voice was serious in the dark velvet night.

She understood suddenly. 'That was stupid of me, Moffat. I apologise.'

He was silent for a moment. When he spoke again, he did so in a lighter tone. 'I have never met a white person like you.'

'Why do you keep drawing that comparison between us?'

'I don't believe you are blind to the differences.'

'Can't we just judge each other as humans?'

'Aren't we doing that already, you and I?'

'I suppose so,' she said slowly. 'Even so, the differences between us make us look at each other more closely.'

'Is that what you think?' Moffat thought for a moment. 'You could be right. My culture dictates my behaviour. It is deeply ingrained.' He moved near to her again and leaned against the car. 'Look, you are very attractive but I have seen many beautiful white women. It's your *attitude* that's got to me. You intrigue me. If I didn't know better I'd say I was falling in love with you. That is strictly taboo. For many, many years Malawians were actively encouraged to have as little as possible to do with whites socially, but it's more than that. In our culture it is okay for a man to have more than one wife. In our culture it is okay for a man to go with the hostesses in the bars. But, Lana, it is not okay for a man to have an extramarital affair and it is especially not okay for a man to have one with a white woman. Now do you understand?'

Lana understood how difficult it must have been for Moffat to say those things. She wanted to hug him but knew it would be unwise. What he needed from her, as he struggled with his emotions, was help. 'Moffat,' she said gently. 'You have told me about your culture. Let me tell you about mine. It is not okay to have an affair although many people do. But deeply ingrained inside me, that's *me* and not wholesale whites in general, is that I would never go with a man I knew to be married. I want us to be easy together but if that's hard for you I'll understand.' *Have I said the right thing?*

'I want us to be easy together too. I'm sorry. I'm ruining everything.'

'No. Truth between friends is better out in the open.'

'Come here.' He wrapped her in his arms. 'Experimental hug.' She felt his lips on her hair, then her cheek and finally, on her own lips. It was a light kiss and Lana made no move to either respond or pull away. 'Thank you,' he whispered, moving back from her. 'That will not happen again.'

'That bad was it?' She desperately wanted to lighten the atmosphere and it worked.

Moffat laughed.

'Come on,' she urged him. 'Only an hour to Karonga.'

He seemed relieved to be talking about something else. 'An hour! A bicycle can get there faster than us. Wait till you see the road.'

He had not been wrong. The journey took just over three hours. Lana gave up trying to sleep in the back, it was too bumpy. She climbed into the front seat and hung on grimly.

It was an hour before dawn when they finally drove through the deserted and dimly lit town of Karonga. Lana looked around with interest. It was larger than she expected. Shops of all descriptions – bottle shops, grocery stores, hairdressing salons, clinics, bars, general stores – all set well back off the road, most of them squat rectangles with barred windows and wooden verandahs. By contrast, a large Bata shoe wholesale depot and a very grand post office, both made from home-fired bricks, dominated the area near a newly built bus depot. At this hour, the only thing moving on the road were grazing hump-backed zebra cattle.

They reached a large roundabout. 'That was Old Town we passed through,' Moffat told her. 'The newer parts of Karonga are closer to the lake.'

'Where will we sleep?'

'Friends,' he said briefly.

'At *this* hour?'

'At this hour.' He pointed right. 'See that place?'

Lana could just make out a solid, two-storey building.

Moffat slowed the car. 'That's the old District Commissioner's office. See the cannon? It's one that was used to shell Mlozi's stockade.'

'The slaver?'

Moffat speeded up again. 'The lake is at the end of this road. We'll come back in the morning. Your father and mine camped there.' He turned left onto a sandy track. 'Nearly there.' He stopped finally outside a neat brick house. 'Come. Let's go and wake them up.'

Feeling somewhat intrusive, Lana followed Moffat to the front door where he banged and shouted loudly. She needn't have worried. A light went on inside and a man appeared sleepily at the door. When he saw Moffat, his face creased into a huge grin and the two of them spent some time thumping each other and laughing. Lana hung back but Moffat beckoned her forward. As she came into the light the other man's face was a picture of consternation. *'Mzungu!'* he gasped, and let forth a stream of Chichewa.

Moffat was laughing and shaking his head. 'He is horrified I bring a white woman here,' he told Lana, raising his voice over the barrage of words. 'When he calms down, I will explain.'

The man's wife appeared, clutching a robe around her ample frame. Like her husband, she was delighted to see Moffat and aghast to see Lana. However, she politely indicated they should come inside, showed Lana to a chair and sat opposite her, staring and occasionally shaking her head.

Moffat said to Lana, 'We will all speak English for your benefit but, first, let me tell them quickly why we are here. It will be easier in Chichewa.'

Lana watched their faces closely as Moffat explained. Their obvious relief, as the situation became clear to them, told Lana far more than Moffat had been able to about Malawi customs and taboos. Once they understood, Moffat reverted to English. 'These are my best friends. They are like brother and sister to me. This man is Daniel and his wife is Dorcas. They are the Namoko family.' Moffat turned to his friends. 'This woman is also our sister. Her name is Lana.'

Daniel Namoko rose and approached Lana. 'You are most welcome.' He put out his hand and Lana was only just able to manage the palm, thumb, palm clasp. Daniel's eyes twinkled. 'You will learn,' he told her kindly. He clapped his hands. 'You will be thirsty.'

Dorcas Namoko rose quickly. 'I will bring beer.'

Despite having been woken so early, the Namokos insisted on preparing food for Lana and Moffat and, while they were eating, Dorcas had quietly gone into her bedroom, changed the bed linen and then insisted that Lana sleep in the main bedroom. When she said she couldn't possibly put them out to that extent, Lana was left in no doubt that if she refused their hospitality they would be mortified. As she stretched out between cool sheets she could not help but reflect what her own reaction might have been had a friend arrived unannounced, in the middle of the night, with a stranger in tow.

In the morning Lana and Moffat drove to the spot where Moffat thought their fathers might have been camped. Lana was doubtful. 'The water must be half a kilometre away. Surely they would have camped where they had access to it.'

'The water is very low now. In 1983 the lake rose to its highest level in living memory. This bank would have been right on the edge.'

Lana looked out across the undulating white sand to the shimmering silver brilliance of the lake. It was a beautiful sight. The Livingstone Mountains some fifty kilometres away in Tanzania appeared to rise sheer out of the water. Fish eagles called their high and wild cry from the tops of trees. Whitecaps flared briefly in the shallow water. Further out, about a kilometre away, a line of darker blue showed where the lake bed shelved down. To the left, the beach curved out to a spit of land. To the right, far in the distance, the high plateau of Nyika dropped abruptly into the water. Moffat's guess had been correct. They were standing on the very spot where John Devereaux and Jonah Kadamanja had pitched their tents when Jonah became ill with malaria.

Half an hour later they pulled up outside a neat whitewashed house set in a well-tended garden. The sign on the gate simply said SARAH FOTHER-INGHAM. Several women, with babies snug in blankets on their backs, were sitting on the steps leading up to the front door. They glanced shyly at Lana and Moffat, then giggled when Moffat spoke to them. One of them replied, her eyes lowered in what, Lana had learned, was a mark of respect.

'She has someone with her,' Moffat translated.

Ten minutes later, a very old man appeared from inside the clinic. The waiting women jumped up, went to him and helped him down the steps. They bore him away with such tender solicitude that Lana thought he must be their Chief. 'Next,' a voice called from inside.

Lana and Moffat went into the clinic. It was a single room, about five metres long with a desk at one end and cupboards behind it. A table along one wall carried an old-fashioned set of scales. A small white blanket folded in the metal dish told Lana that it was used for weighing babies. Several chairs were at the other end of the room with some magazines stacked neatly on an old tin trunk which served as a coffee table. A tiny woman was seated behind the desk writing something on what looked like a patient's record card. 'Take a seat please,' she said in English, not looking up.

Lana and Moffat went to the chairs and sat down. Lana watched Sarah Fotheringham. Her hair was snowy white and caught up in a bun. Strands escaped and fell in wisps around her face. She kept pushing round wire glasses impatiently back up her nose. She was wearing a loose white blouse and, under the table, Lana could see white socks and old tennis shoes on her neatly crossed feet. She wrote slowly and held the pen awkwardly, as if arthritis had crippled her hand.

Suddenly Sarah Fotheringham looked up and smiled. 'And what brings you here today, Mr Kadamanja?' Without waiting for his reply she addressed Lana. 'Did you know that Kadamanja means "dirty hands"? Probably a most unsuitable and inaccurate name for Jonah Kadamanja's son if he is anything like his father.' Her face, when she smiled again, was like a beautiful etching. The fine features had not suffered unduly from age and her eyes were clear and full of wisdom. They also held a trace of impish naughtiness. 'I see I have taken your breath away, Mr Kadamanja.'

Moffat cleared his throat. 'How did you know?'

Miss Fotheringham ignored the question. Instead, she looked at Lana and Moffat for a long time. 'Come here, children.' She waved her hand.

'Bring chairs with you. I keep telling them not to stack them over there as if I am a performer and my patients an audience, but to no avail. They do not wish to appear rude by sitting too close. The result, I'm afraid, is that I believe I am suffering from terminal laryngitis.'

They took chairs and sat opposite Sarah Fotheringham. She waited for them to settle. 'To answer you, Mr Kadamanja, I received a message from someone at the British High Commission.'

Lana found her voice. 'Tim Gilbey. He said he'd spoken to you.'

'He was making enquiries on your behalf. I thought you'd be along sooner or later. This morning I learned you were in the company of Mr Kadamanja. I have been expecting you.'

Moffat was nodding. 'Drum talk.'

'Quite so. All the way from Lilongwe.' Piercing grey eyes roved Lana's face. 'You look exactly like your father, Miss Devereaux.'

'Please call me Lana.'

The eyes twinkled. 'So I shall, yes indeed, so I shall. What a delightful name.' Sarah Fotheringham brushed hair back from her forehead. 'He spoke of you once. He loved you very much.'

Tears sprang unbidden to Lana's eyes. Sarah Fotheringham's words had been unexpected. 'Did you talk to him often?' she asked, her voice not as steady as she would have liked.

Miss Fotheringham regarded her with compassion. 'Come.' She rose. 'There is somewhere much nicer we can talk.' She led them through a door and they were in a tiny kitchen. A small, enclosed courtyard was visible through the open back door. 'Out here, my dears. We all spend far too much time indoors. You sit, I'll make some tea. No, no, I don't need help. I'm not *that* old yet. You talk to Rosalind. She's just had a litter of kittens and is feeling sorry for herself.'

Lana sat in a cane chair and a large, cream coloured cat jumped immediately into her lap and began to purr. 'There, I'm never wrong. If Rosalind likes you then you must be nice. Thought so when I saw you. Never you mind pretending, Moffat Kadamanja. I know you don't like cats. I won't hold it against you.' She turned to Lana. 'Cats are for rats, not laps eh, Mr Kadamanja? That is what the Africans say of us and our love of them.'

'Moffat, please.'

'Tut!'

Moffat rolled his eyes. 'I have spent days telling Lana to do things the African way. In this case, I am outnumbered.'

'Very sensible of you, I'm sure.' Miss Fotheringham smiled. 'Your fathers enjoyed a good relationship. I can see you do the same. Excuse me.' She went into her kitchen but kept up a running commentary through the open door. 'Now where did I put the biscuits? I only bought them yesterday. Do you like shortbread, my dears? Damn! There's a chip in this cup. The family resemblance is remarkable, quite remarkable. Fine-looking man your father. Nice too. You must take after your mother. Lovely up here at this time of year. Not so much sickness. Don't let Rosalind bully you. Oh dear, I don't have any fresh milk. Will powdered do? How long will you be staying in Malawi?' Short, sharp sentences, mostly unrelated, never waiting for an answer and never giving any clue as to which of them she was referring.

As she went on, Lana's earlier excitement at meeting this woman subsided. What would she remember?

Finally, Sarah Fotheringham appeared, carrying a tray. She bustled around, pouring tea and passing them a plate of biscuits. When she fell silent at last, gazing at them with disconcerting candour, it was as though she had run out of steam. Lana looked back at her, saying nothing.

'You have his calm.' Miss Fotheringham pushed impatiently at her glasses, still staring at Lana. 'I suspect you also have his fire.' She smiled wickedly when she saw the look which passed over Lana's face. 'Now, now,' she admonished gently. 'That's *not* what I meant.'

Lana laughed.

'That's better.' Sarah Fotheringham sipped at her tea. 'Forgive me for talking so much. I don't see many English people.'

'Miss Fotheringham.' Lana leaned towards her. 'Please can you tell us about our fathers?'

'I can and I will. But first, what are you doing with Karl Henning?'

The question took Lana completely by surprise. 'I met him quite by chance on the plane to Malawi. I'm not *with* him exactly. He's very keen for me to join him on his yacht. I don't think I will, there's something about him . . .' She stopped, then went on. 'It was Karl who mentioned you. I don't think he meant to. When I showed interest he said you had died last year.'

'Did he indeed,' mused Miss Fotheringham. 'Interesting. Very interesting.' She nibbled the edge of a biscuit. 'As you can see, I'm very much alive, although I can understand why he would say that. Mr Henning has good reason to fear me.'

Moffat said, 'I knew it! You have proof?'

Miss Fotheringham glanced at him kindly. 'Knowing it, Moffat, is one thing. Proving it, quite another. Karl Henning is clever and dangerous.' She placed her cup carefully back on its saucer. 'We'll leave Mr Henning for the minute. Let's talk about your fathers, I can see you are both dying to. Let's see . . . hmmm . . . I heard they were here of course, everyone knows everything in this place. They were working about half-an-hour's drive north of here. Jonah Kadamanja came down with a terrible bout of malaria. I heard about it of course, even expected your father to bring him to me, Lana. When he didn't, I went looking for them. Your father was doing his best but Jonah was in a bad way. We brought their sleeping tents back to Karonga so I could keep an eye on Jonah.' Again the wicked smile. 'I laced his soup with sherry. That fixed him.'

Moffat smiled. 'He must have been ill. He never drank anything stronger than tea.'

Sarah Fotheringham nodded. 'He was on the

mend. Another day and he'd have been up and around.'

'Did you see much of Dad?' Lana asked.

'We spoke every morning and evening. He told me they were doing a seismic study of the lake.' She leaned forward and bright intelligence shone in her eyes. 'That was rubbish of course.'

Lana nodded. 'He was looking for signs of oil deposits. The survey was supposed to be very hush-hush. The Minister who commissioned it did so without President Banda's knowledge.'

'Ha!' Miss Fotheringham said triumphantly. 'I knew it. Seismic survey indeed. Who did they think they were kidding?' She leaned back again and thought for a moment. 'There were other men up here before them.'

'Yes. They died in somewhat suspicious circum-stances.'

'Never met them.'

Rosalind jumped off Lana's lap suddenly and stalked off into the kitchen. Sarah Fotheringham watched her go fondly. Then, 'When you get to my age, my dears, people sometimes tend to overlook you. That's their mistake of course. You don't sud-denly turn gaga and go blind and deaf.'

What is she getting at?

'I liked both your fathers. The first time I met them the word "honourable" came to mind. I can see it in you two as well. Be careful, children.'

Lana glanced at Moffat before saying, 'Miss Fotheringham, all we're trying to do is find out what –'

'Yes, yes.' She nodded impatiently. 'And in doing so you are both very likely to be in great danger. Think, children, think. Someone killed four men . . . yes, I do believe John Devereaux was killed too, even though he was never found . . . and that person is still out there. I'm talking about Karl Henning.' Sarah Fotheringham looked off in the distance for a long moment, as if trying to reach a decision. 'Listen,' she said finally, 'I will tell you what I know. You can make up your own minds.'

Lana nodded.

'My great uncle, Monteith Fotheringham, lived in Karonga one hundred years ago. He was here at the same time as the slaver, Mlozi.' Sarah Fotheringham smiled. 'He was Mlozi's devoted enemy.'

'I've heard of Mlozi. Karl has a cabinet which he says belonged to him.'

Miss Fotheringham nodded. 'I know. He found it up here. What Karl Henning doesn't know is that I am aware of the contents of the cabinet.'

'A ledger?'

'He told you that did he?'

'He said he donated it to a museum.'

Sarah Fotheringham gave a bark of scornful laughter. 'Bull dust!' she said with gusto. 'The ledger is still in his possession.'

'But why lie about it? Why is the ledger important?'

'Because Mlozi used it to record all his shipments across the lake. Every slave was accounted for, every ivory tusk. He wrote dates, weights and who the captain was in charge of each dhow. Then he recorded payment once it had been received. He was meticulous.' Sarah Fotheringham tapped a gnarled finger on the table. 'Against one shipment, around the middle of November 1887, four dhows carrying slaves and one loaded with ivory left Karonga for Losefa. They never reached their destination. Mlozi had written that all were sunk by a sudden storm – he even estimated where they went down. Interesting, don't you think, that within two months of Karl Henning gaining possession of that cabinet, and coinciding with the first survey team being here, Karl's yacht appeared up here. He was making sure no-one found the ivory, I'll bet my right arm on that.'

'If he had found it I suppose it's reasonable he'd want to keep its location a secret,' Lana protested.

'He was not entitled to kill to keep it hidden,' Miss Fotheringham said sharply.

Moffat shooed Rosalind, who was winding herself through his legs, away. 'You'd have to be fairly certain to make an accusation like that. This country was in political turmoil back in 1983. Government ministers and army personnel were fair game. Perhaps . . .'

'Listen, both of you, listen well. I have been in Karonga forty years. The locals trust me. They see things and they tell me. Karl Henning's yacht was up here at the same time as the first survey team. It was back again just after your fathers arrived. I thought nothing of it at first but when John Devereaux didn't return to Karonga that night I did some snooping on my own.' She stopped, pushed her glasses up, smoothed hair back from her face and continued.

'It's a measure of Karl Henning's arrogance that he didn't bother to cover his tracks. I went up to where your father had been working alone. He'd been impatient, you see, to get back to work and didn't wait for Jonah Kadamanja to recover from his malaria. The equipment was all there. The vehicle he drove was half-loaded with their things. There were bottles of sand on a table. It was as if he had been interrupted in the middle of his work. I could see footprints coming up from behind. I'm sorry, child, but you have to know this. The sand showed that someone had been dragged back down the beach.'

Lana felt the old familiar grief burning a hollow in her stomach. *Dear God, why?*

'I came back to where Jonah and your father had pitched their tents on the beach here. The tents were still there but Jonah was also missing. The local fishermen told me that Karl Henning's yacht had been moored just around the spit for perhaps an hour. It was early morning and too dark to see much but a couple of the men thought they saw Karl Henning carrying something heavy over his shoulder down the beach to a dinghy. They say it *could* have been Jonah. The dinghy then went north and disappeared around the spit. Shortly after that the ketch sailed east.'

Karl! Could it be?

Miss Fotheringham was saying, 'The timing works. John Devereaux went missing one day and

Jonah Kadamanja early the next morning – I know he was there the previous evening because I took him some broth. I remember being surprised that John Devereaux hadn't returned. Karl Henning had plenty of time to sail down the lake and get Jonah before it was light.'

Lana was suddenly aware that tears were running down her cheeks. She brushed at them impatiently. 'Why didn't you report this?'

'I did, child. No-one was interested. Karl Henning could not have planned it better if he tried. The coup attempt was a perfect diversion. Oh certainly,' she added derisively, 'the police looked into it. They dismissed my evidence, said it was all supposition. Karl Henning is an influential man. I wouldn't be at all surprised if a little money changed hands.'

'But why? Why would he kill four men?'

Sarah Fotheringham shook her head. 'I don't know. Perhaps he believed the seismic survey story. He obviously didn't want Mlozi's ivory found but I don't think that in itself would be a reason. I believe he's hiding something else. Something much bigger than a dhow full of ivory.' She smiled sympathetically at them. 'That lie about a seismic survey cost four men their lives. It would seem that they were killed for no reason.'

'How can we prove it?' Moffat asked. 'If nothing was done about it back then, how do we open an investigation?'

'You would need evidence of some kind.' Sarah Fotheringham folded her hands on the table. 'I have lived in Malawi long enough to know that you, Moffat, have other means of retribution.'

'We have been to the Nganga.'

'And?'

'I . . . we're not sure. His advice was –'

'Pretty damned general,' Lana snapped, getting angry. Where was the justice in all of this?

'Tell me the witchdoctor's words,' Sarah Fotheringham said gently, as though she understood Lana's frustration.

Moffat related it in Chichewa and Miss Fotheringham sat for some time, her brow furrowed, thinking. 'You two will stop asking questions, that much is clear.'

'It might be because we stop breathing.' Lana couldn't help it. Moffat's beliefs were one thing, that this woman believed in witchdoctors quite another.

Sarah Fotheringham allowed a small grin of amusement. 'No,' she said finally. 'The clue is that things happen after that. The Nganga is not going to waste his breath telling you things you won't see and hear. *The drums of retribution will stop beating and music of the spirits will be heard.* That's positive, believe me. He's telling you there is danger ahead it's true, but that line is the key to it.' She leaned towards them. 'I don't believe you should join Karl Henning on his yacht, Lana, unless Moffat can somehow accompany you.'

'I don't want to but how can I learn anything if I don't?'

'Why don't you leave it to the Nganga?'

So Lana played the two of them at their own game. 'Because his message indicated that we wouldn't.'

Moffat gave a bark of laughter.

Miss Fotheringham smiled delightedly. Then her expression sobered. 'Be careful then.'

Moffat asked the question that Lana had been tempted to ask. 'You have shown us that nothing happens in Karonga that you don't get to hear about. How is it then, Miss Fotheringham, that until last year I lived here and yet you never saw fit to approach me with this information?'

'Good question.' Sarah Fotheringham did not flinch. 'You were not ready.'

'How do you know?' Lana heard anger in his voice and wondered if he regarded Sarah Fotheringham's words as another example of white arrogance.

Miss Fotheringham's eyes twinkled. She too had heard anger. 'Your father's body was found. He had drowned. You might have had some suspicions though I doubt it. Am I right?'

Moffat nodded. 'It seemed strange at the time that the other man was missing. We didn't know about the first two. I only found out about them a few years ago.'

'And what did you do then?'

'Nothing,' Moffat admitted. 'I thought it was odd but I wondered if perhaps I was being paranoid.'

'Until Lana arrived?' Miss Fotheringham pressed.

'Yes. She'd had one or two strange things happen to her since arriving in Malawi. Put together

405

with my own experiences, things started to add up.' Moffat grinned wryly. 'You're right. I wasn't ready.'

They talked for another two hours, Sarah Fotheringham filling in all the tiny crevices of John Devereaux's and Jonah Kadamanja's last few days in Karonga. They absorbed every word, Lana filing everything away to pass on to her mother and Bernard.

It should have been like a balm over an open wound except that the suspicion of Karl Henning's involvement kept tearing the scar tissue. There was no doubting Sarah's flawless memory and power of deduction and, on the surface, it did appear that Karl had to be guilty of murder. Lana's anger grew as they spoke. And that anger fired determination. But even as her resolution grew, Lana knew one thing for certain. The truth about her father could prove lethal. *Can I do this?* Her father's face floated through her memories – tanned, good-looking, laughing, intelligent, warm and kind. *I must.*

They drove through Old Town Karonga, Moffat showing Lana the sights. Beyond Karonga, towards the south, he pointed to where three hills towered up. 'That's where Mlozi was hanged. He had a stockade there where he held the slaves. When he had captured enough, they were marched to Karonga and loaded into dhows.'

'Man's inhumanity to man,' Lana quoted softly. She shook her head. 'Come on, we have to get down to Chilumba. God knows how I'm going to talk you onto the yacht. Let's pick up our things from Daniel and Dorcas and get moving. We can make a plan on the way.'

They drove back to the Namokos' house. Moffat banged on the door and pushed it open. Lana followed him inside. There was no sign of Daniel or Dorcas. Lana walked to the main bedroom to collect her bag. She glanced around the room, making sure she'd left nothing behind, then went back into the lounge and stopped dead. Moffat stood with his back to her, his hands in the air. Karl Henning was just inside the front door, a revolver held steady and pointing at Moffat's chest.

'Do come in, Lana.'

She stepped up and a little distance away from Moffat.

'Drop the bag and move closer to Kadamanja.' Karl waved the revolver. 'None of your tricks. I'm not as easy as Tony Davenport.'

'Where are my friends?' Moffat asked.

Karl's eyes flicked to him. 'The police will find them. You will be blamed, both of you.' He looked at Lana. 'That car of yours sticks out like a sore thumb.'

'My mistake,' Lana said coldly.

'Not the only one. Your partner here,' Karl sneered at the word partner, 'gave the game away. Stella overheard him talking to the servants.'

'Stella?'

Karl smiled with his mouth alone. 'Stella is loyal to only two things. The gin bottle and me.' He

407

tossed Moffat a length of rope. 'Tie her hands behind her back. Remember I'm watching.' He spoke again to Lana. 'You couldn't leave well enough alone, could you? Now you pay the price.'

With Lana's hands tied, Karl instructed Moffat to turn around and he tied his hands as well. Then he checked that Lana was secure before, walking closely behind them, he ushered them outside and into the back of a newish-looking 4x4 vehicle. Karl got into the driver's seat and started the engine. 'The police will find your car here. They will draw their own conclusions about your friends. Your whereabouts will remain one of Malawi's mysteries.' He put the vehicle into gear and drove quickly away from the house.

Lana glanced at Moffat. He sat staring forward, his face expressionless. She tried to cling to Sarah Fotheringham's interpretation of the witchdoctor's words: that she *would* hear music of the spirits, that the drums of retribution *would* stop beating, but all she could think was that she was in the deepest trouble and that, somehow, Moffat's friends, Daniel and Dorcas, had paid the price for it.

Karl drove fast on the chewed-up road to Chilumba, with no thought for his two passengers. He did not speak to them again. Where the trip had taken three hours the night before, he reached Chilumba in just under two. Lana felt she had bruises on every part of her body. With Karl, once again, walking closely behind them, his body shielding the fact that their hands were tied, they were quickly herded on board *Silver Bird II* and pushed below. Ramón Alzaga's face registered surprise when he saw them but he made no comment. Karl offered no explanation either. The hatch was shut over their heads and, soon after that, the engine started up and the yacht was under way.

Lana sank down onto one of the seats. 'Get up,' Moffat hissed. 'Over here. There'll be knives somewhere.'

With his back to the galley stove, Moffat located a drawer and, with difficulty, opened it. He stepped aside and Lana looked in, shaking her head when she saw the contents. Moffat tried a second drawer. 'Bingo!' Lana breathed. It was impossible to get a knife with their hands. Lana solved the problem by picking it out of the drawer with her teeth.

'Sit,' Moffat said softly. 'Turn your back to me. I'll hold the knife steady and you will have to saw your ropes back and forth, okay?'

It took ten minutes but finally her hands were free. She quickly cut through Moffat's bounds.

'Look for a weapon,' Lana whispered. 'Anything with grunt we can swing.'

She began hunting in the cupboards. Moffat checked the forward and aft cabins. Crouching, Lana reached into the back of a cupboard under the sink. Her hand closed around a metal object and she went icy cold. She knew what she had found, even before seeing it in the light.

Lana stared at the Brunton pocket transit. Not so many years ago, all field geologists had carried such an instrument. It was a compass but, attached to the bottom of the compass box was a circle divided into degrees and half degrees. This attachment, called a clinometer, was used to measure vertical angles. It was also possible, by looking into a mirror on the inside of the cover and sighting on some distant object or landscape feature, to get a horizontal angle reading.

Basically they all looked alike. Her father had one. It had been an essential piece of field kit equipment. She remembered how, when she was just eight years old, and thinking she was doing him a favour, she had scratched her father's initials on the casing using the point of her school compass. Her father had been furious when he discovered what she had done but, as she tearfully explained that now no-one could steal it, he had picked her up and kissed her and said, 'Sorry, poppet, what a clever thing you are, thank you.'

Lana's mouth was dry and her heart hammering. Turning the instrument over, the confirmation she sought gleamed dully back at her. There, scratched into the metal back of the Brunton, the initials J.D.D., and the number 23. Lana had started to put the date on the back as well, realised she would run out of room, and abandoned the idea. It all flooded back as though it were yesterday.

She sensed Moffat crouching beside her. 'I found nothing,' he whispered. 'What's that?' Then he saw the look on her face and his mouth set in a grim line. 'Your father's?'

Lana nodded, words straining through the tight constriction in her throat as she pointed to the initials. 'I did that when I was eight.'

'We have no time for this,' Moffat said urgently.

She knew he was right. She put the Brunton into her pocket and pulled a heavy frying pan from the cupboard. 'Take this,' she hissed. 'And this.' She passed him a carving knife. She grabbed the paring knife they had used to cut themselves free and picked up a two-pronged fork, the kind used for barbecues. 'We have to look as though we are still tied up. Hide those behind your back. You sit that side, I'll sit here. That gives us more room to move.'

An expression her South African grandfather used to use flitted inexplicably through her mind: *'It is better to spend one day as a tiger than 1000 years as a sheep'*. She had always loved the expression. Now she was in a tigress mood she wasn't so sure.

She looked out through one of the windows, it was not a porthole, it was square and slid open. Then she realised that it was big enough to climb through. 'Moffat, look. We can get through here and go over the side.'

'They'll see us.'

'They think we're tied up. They won't be expecting it. Come on.'

Moffat shook his head.

'It's better than sitting here,' she urged.

'Lana, I can't swim. You go.'

Hope died as instantly as it was born. She would not leave him on his own.

The engine was cut suddenly and they heard footsteps overhead, then the rasp of chain as the anchor was lowered. In the silence that followed,

411

they could hear perfectly the conversation between Karl and Ramón.

'I still say we should have gone to the Mozambique side.'

Karl's voice was impatient. 'See that cloud to the north. That means trouble. We'd never make it to the other side.'

'But we've gone nowhere. Just into this harbour.'

'And that's where we'll stay. That storm should hit in about an hour and it's going to be wild.'

'How the hell can you possibly know? It might blow itself out.'

'That fringe of light cloud around the main storm mass is a warning. You do not know this lake as I do. Be patient. It's better to get to Likoma late than not at all.'

'Not this time, my friend.' There was silence for a few moments, then Ramón asked, 'What's the story with those two?'

'You know who they are.'

'Yes, but for God's sake, Karl, I can't get mixed up in anything like this.'

'You won't be. The cave is perfect.'

'I still don't like it.'

'You don't have to like it. Just shut-up, do your job and leave.'

Silence while Ramón digested Karl's words. Then he said, 'Are you planning to leave them in the cabin all the way to Likoma?'

'No. We've got to eat. I'll bring them up later.'

Moffat moved and sat next to Lana. 'Likoma,' he said softly. 'We're safe till then.'

Lana looked through the window. The sun was going down. Capturing its scarlet brilliance on a mirror surface, the lake glowed deep crimson, like a pool of molten rock. A slight breeze touched the silken image sending small ripples of gold towards the shore. Dark cumulus clouds hung low over the Livingstone escarpment to the north-east, the outer edges a shimmering silver. It was a beautiful sight.

Her father's Brunton lay snug in her pocket. Lana turned her head and stared at Moffat. 'If I can, I intend to kill him.'

He nodded. 'Stand in line.'

It was fully dark outside before they heard the hatch open. A torch light shone down into the saloon. 'Up on deck,' Karl ordered. In the glow of the torch, they could see Ramón directly behind Karl.

The darkness of the cabin helped conceal the frying pan behind Moffat's back. He went swiftly up the three steps, past Karl and onto the deck, swinging the heavy based cast iron pan at Ramón's head. Lana, immediately behind him, jabbed at Karl with the barbecue fork, and his gasp of surprise and pain told her she had made contact. Giving him no time to recover, and without stopping to think, Lana launched herself at Karl and the two of them crashed to the deck, Lana's fingers scrambling for the small kitchen knife she had hidden in the back pocket of her slacks. They might have got away with it but, in the cramped cockpit, Ramón had sensed Moffat's movements and shouldered him aside, the frying pan only glancing off his head. Moffat, off balance, staggered back and Lana, who was still grappling with Karl, was knocked forward, giving Karl time to collect his wits. He wrapped her in a bear hug and, with surprising agility, rolled on top of her and stood, using his knees in her midriff as leverage.

The Argentinean's cold voice stilled all movement. 'I have a gun.' He threw a switch and a mast light glowed. 'Over there and sit down.' Moffat moved backwards and sat down. Karl literally threw Lana down beside him and produced his own gun. He was breathing heavily.

'You will be locked in one of the cabins until we reach Likoma.'

'My father was on this yacht,' Lana yelled at him. 'Why did you kill him?'

'Your father was never on this yacht,' Karl denied it. 'I've only had it three years.'

'Then where did you get this?' Ramón snicked off the safety catch of his Walther PPK as Lana, with no regard for her safety, plunged her hand into a pocket and produced the Brunton.

Karl looked at it impassively. 'My staff moved everything from the ketch to this yacht. That must have been with all the other stuff.'

'You murdered my father!'

'Murder?' Ramón sounded amused. 'Really, Karl, you do surprise me. I thought you had more sense.'

414

Karl threw a hate-filled look at Ramón. 'Your mouth is too big, my friend.'

The Argentinean smiled like a crocodile, then turned to Lana and Moffat. 'Your little heroics were impressive but you see, a man like Karl will never let you get between him and his money.' He glanced over at Karl. 'Isn't that so, my friend.'

'Shut-up!' Karl growled.

Ramón shrugged. 'What does it matter?'

Lana realised he spoke the truth. What did it matter? Karl had said something about a cave. Was he planning to murder them and leave them in it? 'What's in this for you?' She was stalling. Up here on deck there might be a chance for escape. Locked into a cabin, there was no hope.

Ramón considered her question. 'On Likoma is proof of Britain's lies and deception. Many have died because of it – but that is of little importance – ultimately we will have what is rightfully ours.'

Lana's eyes met Moffat's. *Great Mother's shame lies hidden, two men seek her secret.* 'Could the other man be Tim?' she wondered. 'Britain and Argentina – the Falklands – it has to be.' Lana realised suddenly just how much danger she and Moffat were in. Karl was evil, no doubt about it, and prepared to kill again to safeguard whatever secret he was hiding. This man, Ramón Alzaga, was possibly more dangerous. Clearly an agent with Argentina's secret service, he would not hesitate to kill. Professional and detached, he would do so in the name of politics, the ethics of his deeds being of no consequence.

Moffat's voice echoed the hopelessness Lana

was feeling. 'We have no interest in your political games. Why don't you let us go?'

Ramón laughed at him. 'I would be prepared to. My friend is not. What happens to you two is of no interest to me. Karl has too much to hide to allow you to live, isn't that right, Karl.'

The antagonism between the two of them was something they might use. Moffat obviously had the same idea. 'You might be implicated. You were seen at his home.'

'It is not in Karl's interest to implicate me. I have too much information about him.'

Karl was dabbing at the fork marks in his arm. He looked up briefly at Ramón and scowled.

'You see,' the Argentinean went on, 'Karl can't afford to come to the attention of Internal Revenue. Nor would he like an international incident if a certain country close to Malawi discovered what he was up to. As I said before, he will protect his back pocket with everything at his disposal.'

'He killed my father . . .' Lana jumped to her feet and flung her hand towards Moffat, '. . . and his, for *that!*' She didn't stop to think. She sprang at Karl, her fingers curled like claws, wanting to rip his eyes out.

Ramón moved quickly, like a cat, his hand whipping up and crashing down again over Lana's wrists. The pain was terrible and she cried out with it. Karl had his pistol trained on Moffat. 'Right, I've had enough of this.' Karl waved the gun from Lana to Moffat. 'Into the cabin. *Now!*'

Lana stumbled down the steps into the dimly lit

saloon, Moffat right behind her. 'Get in there.' Down three more steps was a small aft cabin. The door and hatch slammed shut behind them and a bolt shot home. Like the saloon, the cabin was softly lit. Ramón must have activated all the yacht's lights when he turned on the mast light. Lana hoped they would stay on. She sank onto the bed and put her face in her hands. She felt a slight pressure as Moffat sat beside her and then the warmth and comfort as his arm went around her shoulders and he pulled her close. Lana sobbed onto Moffat's shoulder in helpless frustration and despair as she had done onto Bernard's fifteen years earlier. Moffat said nothing, just held her.

They sat like that for ten minutes before she took a shuddering breath and stirred. 'That African way,' she said shakily. 'I just blew it.'

Moffat grunted, half amused. 'Just a little bit.'

'We're in the deepest possible shit and it's all my fault.'

He squeezed her shoulders. 'If you hadn't done it I would. I've never felt like that before. I wanted to kill him.'

She felt in her pocket for a handkerchief, blew her nose and took another deep breath. 'How the hell do we get out of this?'

Moffat glanced at the small porthole then turned his attention to the floor of the cabin. One panel lifted but it only gave access to the propeller shaft. There was no way out. 'We could open the water valve on the toilet and flood the boat but that could give us even more trouble. Perhaps they'll let us back on deck if we promise not to try anything.'

Lana couldn't think of a better idea so she pushed at the hatch but it was solid and immovable. 'Trust that bastard,' she said grimly. 'Hatches are usually flimsy.' She banged on the door. 'Please let us out,' she yelled. 'We won't try anything again. You have our word.'

Silence.

'You can't keep us cooped up in here.'

Silence.

'Bastards!' she snarled at the door.

'Don't antagonise them.' Moffat patted the bed. 'Sit down.'

'This is hopeless.'

'Let's think rationally.' Moffat calmly responded. 'Ramón doesn't have to kill us but he will if we get in his way. Karl needs to silence us but he's not going to do anything until we reach Likoma. Would you agree?'

'Yes.'

'So there's some hope.'

Lana laughed bitterly.

'You're right, there's no hope.'

'Unless . . .'

'What? Unless what?' Moffat watched her closely.

'Ramón is with the Argentinean secret service, that's obvious. Remember the Nganga's words about great mother's shame and two men? Tim Gilbey is MI6, I'm positive. It's possible he'll be on Likoma too.'

'And then?'

She tossed her head defiantly. 'And then it's three against two.'

He was still watching her.

'What? Why are you staring at me?'

'I've just realised something,' he said slowly. 'The African way won't help us. I called your way arrogance before but I was wrong.' He shook his head. 'It's not arrogance is it? You actually believe we have a chance. You're going to go for it aren't you? You might die in the process but that's not going to stop you. My God!' Moffat gave a short laugh. 'It's blind faith. It's always *been* blind faith. While Africans have been accepting the inevitable because that is our way, the Europeans took control because they believed they had the right.' He banged a fist into a palm. 'Jesus! No wonder we were so easily colonised.'

Lana watched him in amazement. 'Are you quite finished?' she asked with a degree of sarcasm. 'Because I would rather have this profound conversation some other day.'

Moffat rubbed a hand over his eyes. 'You're right. Ignore me. I'm getting hysterical.'

Lana hugged him. 'Many words spring to mind to describe you, Moffat. Hysterical is definitely not one of them. Now, can we hold over the soul-searching for some other time?'

Moffat laughed softly. 'Let us hope, my white sister, that the time is one we've been allotted.'

The hatch sliding back silenced them. Karl stood in the entrance, a look of pure dislike on his

419

face. 'You meddling idiots. You've brought this on yourself.'

Lana stared at him coldly. 'You killed four men. You must have known someone would come looking for you one day.'

'Come looking for me?' His lip curled into a sneer. 'You silly little girl. You have no idea who you're dealing with.'

Lana's voice went soft and flat. 'Oh, I know who I'm dealing with, Karl. A cold-blooded murderer.'

Moffat nudged her. Karl could just as easily shoot them here and now.

'Why?' she demanded. 'What did they do to deserve it?'

He went to step into the cabin, thought better of it and stayed at the doorway. 'I grew up in South Africa. My family were dirt poor farmers and I was one of fourteen children. I got my first pair of shoes when I was eleven.' He smiled slightly. 'They were cast-offs from the farmer next door,' he added.

Lana and Moffat's eyes met and Moffat raised one eyebrow. She could see he was having the same thought as she was. Karl Henning appeared to be seeking sympathy.

Henning went on, 'My father was a brute of a man. He bashed my mother until the poor woman's brains were scrambled. When she wasn't around, one of us kids would do just as well. It was bad enough for the boys but he did more than bash the girls. One of my sisters fell pregnant to him when she was just twelve.' Karl shuddered slightly

420

at the memory. 'I ran away when I was fourteen. Made my way to Johannesburg and worked in the mines for eighteen years. I went to night school and educated myself. One day I read in the newspaper that the British were handing out farms in Nyasaland. I knew about cattle and crops. The thought of having my own place appealed to me, I was sick and tired of the mines, so I came up here. I tried cattle but there was hardly any money in it. Then, just after independence, tobacco took off. Kasungu's climate was perfect. I made the change and, for years, never regretted it.'

Lana and Moffat remained silent.

'Late in 1979 I bought an old chiffonier which had belonged to the slaver, Mlozi. I didn't know this until I found his ledger in a hidden compartment. Remember, I showed you the secret compartment?'

Lana nodded curtly. 'I remember.'

'It was Mlozi's record of trading transactions. Slaves and ivory mainly. Against one of his last entries Mlozi had written that a shipment of four dhows carrying slaves, and one loaded with tusks was lost in a storm. He estimated their position to be between ten to twenty miles north of Likoma Island. I decided to look for it. I needed money. The tobacco boom of the sixties and seventies was over. Prices were dropping fast. A few of my friends went broke.' His mouth set in a hard line. 'There was no way I was prepared to let that happen to me. The ketch was fitted with state-of-the-art echo sounding equipment and I found the dhows on my third attempt. My first dive verified Mlozi's records.'

Moffat stared at him. 'But there was nothing illegal about the ivory, nothing to justify killing four men.'

Karl went on as if Moffat had not spoken. 'I needed somewhere to store the tusks until I could set up links with Asia. Likoma seemed like the ideal solution. No-one goes there. All I had to do was find a place to put it.'

He was speaking as if they were having an after-dinner chat and Lana realised that he was not only evil, he was completely devoid of emotion. 'There was a missionary on the island who was always going on about how little money he had. I talked to him and offered a commission on each tusk sold if he could store the ivory somewhere. He accepted quickly enough.' Karl scowled. 'Then he got greedy.'

Moffat raised his eyes but said nothing. Karl did not seem to see the irony of his last comment.

'The missionary – Frederick Hamilton – told me he had discovered a crypt at the cathedral. No-one knew about it. He said it would be perfect. The entrance was overgrown and, having opened it without authority, he had no intention of telling anyone.'

'So you went into the ivory business?' Moffat commented quietly.

'Only for a while. The dhows had gone down in Mozambique waters. The war there was hotting up and FRELIMO often used the lake to move their forces back and forth. After a while it just wasn't safe. I put the whole thing on hold. The ivory would keep where it was – no-one ever knew of its existence except for Frederick Hamilton and myself.'

Karl lit a cigarette. Lana and Moffat waited in silence. They had been denied the truth for so many years. Now they were about to hear it.

'In 1983 a friend of mine, Dick Matenje, told me that he had commissioned a survey of the lake. He asked if my ketch could be used if needed by the geologists. He said that President Banda did not know about it so I was to keep the information to myself. At first . . .' Karl drew on his cigarette '. . . I was only too happy to help. I met the geologist, Cunningham, and put my boat at his disposal. I didn't expect the bloody man to stray into Mozambique waters and find Mlozi's dhows.'

'So you killed him?' Lana tried to be calm, but the hatred she felt for Karl could not be hidden.

Karl carried on as though she had not spoken. 'He had a drinking problem. Got quite nasty sometimes. I couldn't risk him telling anybody about the dhows. It's funny how things happen. He'd gone on a binge and slipped and hit his head. He was out cold though whether that was the bang on the head or the booze I couldn't say. At first, I just tied him up to keep him under control when he came round. I didn't intend to kill him. Suddenly I saw how easy it would be to drop him overboard. We were miles from shore and in his condition . . . well. I untied his hands. He was still unconscious. He went down like a stone.'

'I suppose his assistant was an *accident* too?'

423

'No. I had to kill him, surely even you can see that. He was the only witness.' Karl took a long pull on his cigarette and spoke around the smoke. 'It was simple enough. He was in shock. Instead of defending himself he just sat staring at the water where Cunningham had disappeared. I tied him up. When we were well away from where I'd dropped Cunningham I knocked him unconscious, untied his hands and tossed him off the boat.'

Lana just shook her head in disbelief.

'But you went on. You killed Lana's father? And mine?' Moffat's voice trembled with suppressed emotion.

'Dick Matenje told me that another geologist was coming to finish Cunningham's work. I kept an eye on him and I wasn't too worried – he was working well to the north but when John Devereaux mentioned the survey was moving to Likoma it was too close, I couldn't risk it. Most of the ivory was still under the lake. Hong Kong was screaming for more. Frederick Hamilton was complaining that he wasn't getting enough money – that it was too slow in coming.' He stopped, as though finished.

'You've told us this much. Please finish,' Lana said coldly.

'I found out where they were working and paid them a visit.' Karl rubbed a hand over his eyes.

'North of Karonga?'

'Yes. But then your father said they were going to Likoma. That settled it as far as I was concerned.'

Lana shuddered and closed her eyes.

Karl went on. 'There's deep water at the mouth of the Kaporo River. It's out of sight from where they were working. I anchored *Silver Bird* early in the morning and went on foot. I expected them to be together so I took my gun. I hid in the trees and watched. Your father was doing something with sand in bottles but there was no sign of Kadamanja. After a few minutes I thought I'd just walk up and start talking but, as I got closer, I could see your father hadn't heard me. He was completely absorbed in his work.' For the first time Karl's voice faltered, although his eyes seemed to gleam with malicious satisfaction. 'So I . . . I walked right up behind John Devereaux and . . . and hit him.'

Oh God!

'I tied him to a tree and went back for the dinghy. He was still unconscious when I got back.' Henning shrugged, unconcerned. 'Must have hit him harder than I thought.'

Blinded by sudden tears, Lana felt Moffat's arm go around her.

'I dragged him down the beach and got him into the dinghy and eventually on board the ketch. It wasn't easy, he was like a sack of potatoes.'

Lana felt a shudder of horror go right through her. Not only because of what she was hearing but at the calm, almost boastful way Karl was telling her.

'When he regained consciousness I asked him about his assistant. He told me that Jonah Kadamanja became sick with malaria and had returned home.' Karl looked angry. 'He was lying, trying to protect the man. Luckily I decided to check it out. Before it was light, I motored down to Karonga.' Karl looked at Moffat. 'Your father was too sick to defend himself.'

The look on Moffat's face was one of pure hatred.

Karl stared back and said spitefully, 'Halfway between Karonga and the Tanzanian side I threw him overboard. Like most of your race, he couldn't swim.'

'You bastard!' Lana gritted.

'What's another black man?' he responded cruelly. 'This country has too many as it is.'

'He was someone's father, someone's husband, someone's son. He was a human being, you stupid, arrogant . . . animal,' Lana burst out, unable to find words to describe her feelings. 'You pig!'

Karl shrugged it off. 'Couldn't leave them in the water together.' He smiled at Lana. 'There is a lot of your father in you, my dear. Misplaced loyalty included. John Devereaux would have tried to save his assistant. Futile really but I decided to take no chances and sailed south, taking your father with me.'

Daddy! My God, how frightened you must have been.

'He knew what had to be done so I kept him tied up. Took it rather well I thought.' Karl frowned at the memory. 'Never noticed him working his hands free.' The frown deepened. 'He came at me like a madman. I had no choice. There was only time for one shot but the bullet took him in the head and he fell back over the side.'

Lana moaned and covered her face.

'He was dead before he hit the water,' Karl went on carelessly. Lana removed her hands and looked at Karl in silence. She was beyond words, even beyond tears now. *There is fear and sorrow for this woman.*

'I looked for him of course. Must have spent half-an-hour searching without any success. For months I expected to hear that the body had been found but it never reappeared. Maybe a croc got him, who knows.'

Her father was dead. She had come to Malawi to find out what had happened to him. Now she knew. The tiny flame of hope that she would find him alive flickered and died.

'You'll both be dead soon, you might as well hear the rest,' Karl said. 'There was trouble in Malawi. Dick Matenje was dead. There'd be no more surveys. The ivory was safe enough. As soon as Mozambique settled down I started diving again. The crypt soon filled with tusks. I couldn't move it out fast enough. You see, everything had to be carried by dugout canoe to the mainland, tusk by tusk. Each trip was at night. That was the bottleneck. I spoke to Hamilton about the storage problem.' Karl lit another cigarette from the stub of the first. 'I don't think he wanted to help but I had the contacts, he didn't. Besides,' the distaste Karl obviously felt for the missionary was clear, 'he's a miserable little man. No guts. Not prepared to run risks.'

'Which of course you are?' His words seemed to stick and Moffat cleared his throat.

'Of course.' Karl seemed surprised. 'Especially when the rewards are so great. Anyone would.'

427

'Anyone but Hamilton?'

'Bah!' Karl discounted the missionary contemptuously. 'Stupid man didn't even know what he'd found.'

'What exactly had he found?'

Karl smiled in pure pleasure. 'I did some research. It's unbelievable but the more I looked into it the more I realised it was possible.' He hesitated dramatically, but, when no-one spoke, went on. 'I believe he's found the missing treasure of Great Zimbabwe.' He looked at Lana.

What does he want? Approval? Admiration? Lana merely stared back at him.

Karl sighed, disappointed. 'There's a cave on Likoma. It's right under the crypt. It might have gone undiscovered forever but for Hamilton's poking around. The crypt is empty, you see, except for one stone coffin.' Karl's lip curled. 'It took Hamilton months to pluck up the courage to open it. When he finally did, the enormity of what he'd found scared the daylights out of him. So, when I came to him asking for more storage space, he took me into the cave.'

Karl leaned toward them. 'You may not believe this but the cave contains an ancient treasure. Gold, copper, bronze, jewels. It's worth far more than the ivory. I'll soon be a very rich man thanks to Hamilton.' He scowled at the mention of the man's name. 'I said I'm a man of my word but nothing lasts forever. Hamilton and I were going to go fifty-fifty on the nest egg of Great Zimbabwe until the little hypocrite got cold feet over the whole deal.

He suddenly decided that the crypt was consecrated ground so his head office should be told of its discovery. I couldn't let that happen.'

'How astonishing that you didn't just kill Hamilton,' Moffat said sarcastically.

'I thought about it,' Karl admitted coolly. 'But I needed him. I couldn't come and go on Likoma without his help. Besides, he said that he'd already told the Bishop about the crypt who'd been in contact with London. There was no point.'

'So where did that leave things?' Moffat asked. 'The crypt was officially opened presumably.'

Karl smiled. 'No. Not yet. I've still got a couple of months. Some church bigwig has to come out and perform a bit of religious mumbo jumbo before that can happen. Not that it matters, I have arranged to move everything well before then. A trawler will ship what's left to Mangochi. From there it goes by road to Nacala and by freighter up the coast to Dar Es Salaam. I didn't want to move it all at once but Hamilton's sudden rush of conscience has made it necessary. He can whistle for his cut.'

'And what's still under the lake?'

'Not much. I've been diving on the wreck quite regularly. I'll have it all up on my next diving trip.' Karl stepped back from the cabin door, smiling at Lana. 'So now you know it all, my dear. A few little hiccoughs – I didn't expect Ramón.'

There was one piece of the puzzle missing. There was nothing to lose by asking, so Lana asked, 'How did Ramón find out?'

'Ramón? He has a lot of contacts. I was selling

some of the ivory to a friend of his in Hong Kong. About six years ago I also offered him some of the gold. Ramón got to hear of it and when he mentioned he was coming to Malawi his friend asked him to check up on me.' Karl looked angry. 'That's the way these damned agents work of course. Get something on you, then blackmail you into helping them if the need arises.'

They had it all. And there was nothing they could do with it. Karl left them sitting in stunned silence. The door and hatch were securely locked from outside.

'*When isi-Kombazana no longer calls over the great water,*' Moffat whispered. '*And the silent ones gather where witches burn.* That's it! That's what the second part means. Silent ones are spirits of the elephants. The cathedral on Likoma was erected at the exact place where they once burned witches.'

'*The drums of retribution will stop beating,*' Lana continued slowly. 'Why? Maybe Miss Fotheringham has got it wrong. Perhaps it's because we'll both be dead?'

Moffat put his hand under her chin and raised it. 'Don't lose your spirit now, my white sister.'

'Spirit,' she said. '. . . *and music of the spirits will be heard.* A band of bloody angels I suppose!'

Moffat grinned. 'You English,' he said, shaking his head. 'How can you be funny at a time like this?'

'I wasn't being funny.'

*

Somehow, they slept. They were not offered food. The storm raged over the lake for perhaps an hour but, tucked into the small harbour as they were, they were spared the worst of its fury. The yacht got under way at first light and Ramón brought them something to eat shortly after that. He offered no comment and they made none to him.

They used the engine for the first three hours and then, with the wind picking up, they set the sails and made good time. Around midafternoon an argument developed on deck between Karl and Ramón. Lana and Moffat could hear them quite clearly. 'That storm's gaining on us. We must ride it out closer to shore.'

'Hold the current course and speed. Enough time has been wasted as it is.'

Karl's voice became urgent. 'For God's sake, Ramón! We're heading towards the deepest part of the lake. If that storm hits we're gone.'

'Please do as you are told, my friend. I'm in charge now.'

'Then we both lose. Just what the hell's so damned important to you?' Karl exploded.

'Honour,' Ramón said succinctly. 'But I doubt very much if that means anything to you.'

'I had no choice,' Karl was still shouting, not enjoying Ramón's censure.

'Oh you had a choice, Karl. You certainly had that.'

'What's it to you anyway? You'd pull that trigger without so much as a twinge of remorse.'

'If I had to. But, Karl, I would be doing it for my country.'

'Shut-up!' Karl nearly screamed at him. 'What do you know? How dare you make such comparisons.'

Down in the cabin Moffat leaned towards Lana and said quietly, 'Hear that? He's losing it.'

She nodded. 'Everything's suddenly falling apart. For fifteen years he's got away with murder. He didn't make that confession to us out of any sense of guilt. He was boasting. He *will* kill us, Moffat, he must. It's the only way he can get his life back in order.' Lana sighed and stretched out on the bed. 'From what we've just heard there's some rough weather coming. Karl will probably be at the helm all night. If he's tired it could give us the advantage we need.'

Moffat sat beside her. *'Fisi feeds on the skill of others but takes the young and weak for himself.'* He turned and stared at Lana. 'Do you think the Nganga was telling us to get aggressive?'

'I couldn't feel more aggressive if I tried.'

'You don't look aggressive. You look half-asleep.'

Lana didn't open her eyes. She felt exhausted and emotionally wrung out. 'I'm thinking.'

Moffat woke her at 4.20 in the afternoon, the pitching of the yacht making him stagger to keep his balance. Looking through the starboard port-hole Lana could not believe her eyes. The calm, serene blue of Lake Malawi had been replaced by plunging grey rollers, white-capped and threatening. As she stared out a waterspout spiralled upwards, as if trying to escape. It rose more than a hundred metres into the air, reaching upwards towards the storm clouds which boiled overhead. Travelling like a tornado, the plume of water headed directly for the yacht until, at the last minute, it veered off, passing directly behind the stern, a hissing, streaming serpent of coiled fury, capable of picking up and destroying anything in its path. Moffat, at the other porthole, exclaimed loudly and, when she looked, Lana could see only a wall of foaming spray and lead grey water. She could only imagine what it must be like on deck.

Torrential rain made pockmarks in the three-metre waves as they raced to catch the yacht. Time and time again, the craft was carried aloft standing on its bow in a suicidal nose dive before arching crazily back with such bone-jarring force that it must break in two. Moffat fell back onto the bed, sprawling helplessly and banging his elbow in the process. In the seething, heaving maelstrom, the yacht was tossed about like a matchstick, rolling, yawing, pitching, suddenly being flung almost broadside to the oncoming waves. Beyond the cabin door a loud crack came from above, followed by the tremendous impact of something heavy falling just overhead. 'There goes the mast,' Moffat cried out, his face white.

The storm boiled around them for over an hour. More than once Lana thought the yacht was sinking. Waves poured over the decks and streamed past their portholes but, gallant as a mountain pony, the boat shuddered, shook free of the water and burst out of one wave, only to be hit by the next. Waterspouts danced across the bucking lake, giant vacuums of water, hell-bent on destruction.

After what seemed like an eternity, Lana could see pockets of blue sky. The storm had passed right over them, leaving the waters of Lake Malawi heaving and panting in its wake. It took more than two hours to soothe its ruffled surface but, by this time, Karl had restarted the engine and they were well under way again.

Up on deck, sounds of frantic cleaning up told them the damage had been considerable.

'When do we reach Likoma?' they heard Ramón ask.

'At this speed, and with no more storms, tomorrow afternoon,' Karl replied.

Tomorrow afternoon. Lana's eyes met Moffat's. Would tonight be their last? She turned to look through the porthole at the final rays of light in the western sky. It was such a beautiful sight. She did not want to die.

SEVENTEEN

Tim Gilbey lowered his compact Pentax binoculars and grunted with impatience. *What is the bloody man doing?* Frederick Hamilton behaved like someone suffering from acute lethargy, rather than someone trying to hold a government to ransom. His actions, since arriving two days ago, were those of a decidedly laid-back tourist.

On Sunday morning, Tim had followed Hamilton from the landing strip, expecting him to go directly to the cathedral. Even though he was no longer a missionary, Tim would have thought he'd at least have paid the Bishop the courtesy of a greeting. Instead, Hamilton checked into the Akuziki Private Rest House and, so far, had not gone anywhere near the priests, the cathedral or the crypt. He spent most of the daylight hours on a beach directly below the rest house. He did not swim or take walks. Despite being well known on the island – which Tim concluded he must be since he'd lived here for twenty years – very few people stopped to speak to him. The only exertion Tim had observed was when he turned the pages of his book. Every now and then Hamilton would raise his eyes and gaze across the water to the Mozambique mainland. Tim had little doubt that the man was waiting for someone.

The fact that Frederick Hamilton had chosen to stay at the rest house was a mixed blessing. While it didn't give Tim an excuse to observe the missionary at close range, at least Hamilton would not become suspicious of, or speculate on, what Tim was doing on Likoma. Passing up what – if the smells coming from the kitchen were anything to go by – promised to be a delicious dinner, Tim went to the rest house to eat on Sunday evening. Gossip that Tim was on Likoma looking at its potential as a tourist destination had circulated and the manager of the Akuziki was delighted to accept Tim's booking for a meal. Ready to enlarge on the tourist development myth if necessary, Tim found Hamilton already seated. 'Do you mind if I join you?' In point of fact, there was little else Tim could do. The 'dining room' was an open-ended verandah, off which four doors led to bedrooms. There was only one table.

Hamilton nodded pleasantly enough. The manager appeared at one end of the verandah and beamed when he saw that his two guests were talking. 'I will serve the soup at your convenience,' he announced formally.

'Any idea what kind it is?' Tim asked Hamilton.
'Chicken, it's always chicken. Not bad though.'
'Stayed here before have you?'
'I've eaten here.'

'Do you know Likoma well?'

'Well enough.'

Tim put out his hand. 'Tim Gilbey.'

Hamilton shook it. 'Frederick Hamilton.' His handshake was limp and damp.

'What brings you to this tropical paradise?' Under the table, Tim rubbed the man's sweat off on his trouser leg.

'Nothing much.'

Talkative little shit aren't you!

The manager, having clearly decided that now was as convenient a time as any, reappeared with two steaming bowls of soup. Hamilton immediately bowed his head and began to eat, spooning the thin and relatively tasteless liquid into his mouth as though he hadn't eaten for days.

So much for Grace!

Hamilton did not raise his eyes until his bowl was empty and wiped clean with a chunk of doughy bread. Up close, he reminded Tim of something straight out of a Charles Dickens novel. He had the kind of face that as a boy Tim would have loved to squash a cream bun into, just for the hell of it. His eyes were permanently moist, like those of a reproachful fish. A long, thin nose dragged down an expression that managed to look perpetually disappointed *and* disdainful at the same time. His sunken cheeks, almost cadaverous in colour, had a number of painful-looking red weals on each, like developing boils. The book at his elbow was a surprise. *It* by Stephen King. Tim would have expected something more ecclesiastical. 'Staying long?' he enquired cheerfully.

'Couple of days.'

Through the trees between the rest house and the harbour, the evening sky was gearing itself for yet another spectacular finale. Tim tried a different tack. 'I've never seen anything like these sunsets. They're beautiful.'

Hamilton dutifully looked but said nothing.

The main course was placed before them. Chambo fillets, boiled potatoes and baked beans. Hamilton virtually inhaled his as though he were starving, reluctantly responding in monosyllables to any attempt at conversation. Tim wondered idly what his reaction would be if asked, 'Found any good secret documents lately?' He stopped trying to make conversation and concentrated on his own meal.

Hamilton finished well before Tim, picked up his book and began to read.

Giving up on food, Tim rose from the table, the fish and baked beans competing unhappily in his stomach.

'Aren't you waiting for dessert?' Hamilton queried, not raising his eyes from the page.

'Why don't you have mine?' Tim said. 'I don't believe I could eat another thing. Good night.'

The double entendre was lost on Hamilton.

Tim walked back to Camp Likoma, confident that Hamilton would be going nowhere tonight. The man was a missionary, not a trained professional. If action, any action, were imminent, the man would have been showing signs of nervous energy. He was obviously waiting for someone, otherwise he would have retrieved the documents and left Likoma. After dark, he wouldn't be going anywhere. Likoma had no electricity so an aeroplane could not land and any vessel arriving by water was unlikely.

As he walked in the gathering dusk, Tim's mind shifted sideways and drifted. Where would Lana be now? Was she all right? Were his misgivings about Karl Henning justified? Why did Hamilton keep that damned book with him? Were the documents lying between its pages? Who was the man waiting for? 'Kill him if necessary,' Martin Flower had implied. 'Christ!' Tim thought, disgusted. 'It would be like stepping on a bug.'

There was a storm brewing to the north-west. He had seen signs of it earlier but now that it was almost dark, the full fury of lightning was awesome. He wondered about the colourful Captain Santos. Where would he go in such a storm? Tim grunted with amusement as he thought about the man. *He'd probably be so full of rum he'd scarcely notice the weather.*

When he reached the camp, Tim sat on the deck outside his tent for some time watching the gathering storm. He tried to keep his mind on the job but it kept returning, time and again, to Lana.

In the morning, Tim had an early breakfast then returned to his tent. From the deck he had a perfect view of the beach but, because the camp was well screened by trees, anyone on the beach would need to get very close before they noticed him. Hamilton was already on the beach, in a deckchair, with his book open. Tim resigned himself to the possibility of a long and boring day.

Around midmorning, Wireless came to see him. 'I beg your pardon, Mr Gilbey. The telephone is working now.' If the man was intrigued to know why Tim, who claimed he was interested in exploring Likoma, had spent all yesterday afternoon and all morning in his room, he was too polite to ask.

Tim followed Wireless to reception where the man cranked an old-fashioned telephone handle and spoke to the operator. He enjoyed several minutes of animated jollity before handing the receiver to Tim. After giving a Lilongwe number and waiting for five minutes, the connection to his secretary was established. Quickly, he explained that he wanted a doctor flown to Likoma and, if it was at all possible, a portable X-ray machine.

His secretary, a seasoned member of the Diplomatic Service and one who, Tim suspected, had an inkling of the true nature of his profession, merely asked, 'When?'

'As soon as possible.'

'I'll get onto it.' She hesitated, then asked, 'Is it for you?'

'No.'

Again she hesitated. 'British?' she asked finally.

'Of course.'

'Life threatening?' she pushed.

It will be if you don't stop asking these damned

questions! 'Head injury – old but nasty. Can't move him but I want it checked. Just get on to it. If there's a fuss I'll take the flak.'

Let off the responsibility hook, she noted the number at the tented camp and assured him that a doctor would be on Likoma as soon as she could arrange it. Since he was supposed to be on an orientation tour she would have been well within her rights to ask him just what, in the name of all things sane, the hell he was doing on Likoma. It was a measure of her professionalism that she did not.

When he hung up, Tim found Wireless studiously polishing the reception desk. 'We have a hospital here.'

'I know, but they have no X-ray equipment.' In fact, they had very little of anything. Tim gathered from Father Smice that if anyone was seriously ill or injured they were immediately flown to the mainland.

'Somebody is sick?' Wireless asked.

'Someone needs attention.' Tim was being cautious. Then he wondered why he'd bothered.

'We have a fish in Malawi,' Wireless said carefully. 'It is called Mpasa.'

'Yes I know,' Tim replied, grinning wryly. 'Lake salmon. A good fighting fish.'

Wireless nodded. 'It will fight very hard to avoid capture.'

'Don't worry,' Tim said, going past the man. 'Mpasa only fights when it is in danger.'

Wireless nodded again, satisfied.

441

Instead of returning to his tent, Tim walked the kilometre or so to the Akuziki, sneaked into Hamilton's unlocked room and gave his belongings and the room a thorough search. As he expected, there was no sign of any documents. Returning to the camp, he resigned himself to the boredom of watching Hamilton who, predictably, had not moved. An hour or so later, a familiar figure in white robes crossed the beach to where Hamilton sat. Tim watched Father Smice carefully. The priest moved briskly, like a man on a mission. He stopped in front of Hamilton and spoke to him. Watching his face carefully through the binoculars, Tim thought Father Smice looked troubled. Hamilton shrugged, then the priest was speaking again. He appeared to be pleading with the missionary.

Frederick Hamilton carefully placed his book on the sand and stood up. From his hands on hips stance and body language, Tim could see he was being defensive. After a few minutes, Father Smice patted Hamilton on the shoulder and left, shaking his head. Hamilton, after a long stare at the lake, sat down and resumed reading.

Tim would dearly have loved to know what transpired between the two men.

And now, at three-fifteen the following afternoon, after yet another long day of watching Hamilton do nothing more exciting than read, Tim was fizzing with impatience. He trained his binoculars on the mainland. Jungle and beaches. Tim scanned the distant shore. More jungle and beaches. 'Christ this is monotonous!' Between the north-easterly tip of Likoma and the mainland of Mozambique, the lake shimmered with reflected brilliance. The glare was almost painful. Something white out there on the glittering blue caught his eye. A boat! 'Could this be it?' Tim focussed on the distant shape. It was well out from the mainland, heading towards Likoma perhaps ten kilometres away.

Fifteen minutes later, Frederick Hamilton saw it too. He jumped to his feet, shading his eyes against the glare. The sudden movement confirmed it. Tim had no doubt that this was what Hamilton had been waiting for.

There was something not quite right about the approaching craft. Suddenly Tim realised that it was a yacht, or, at least, what was left of a yacht. The stump of its aluminium mast, broken off about a metre above deck, jutted defiantly upwards.

Hamilton had abandoned his book and was still staring at the yacht. Tim alternated between watching him and the boat. It was definitely heading straight for Likoma.

The yacht was no more than a kilometre away when Hamilton turned and walked off the beach. Several times he looked back, as though uncertain, before reaching a decision and striding purposefully towards the rest house. 'Here we go,' Tim thought. The familiar rush of adrenalin hit him. Something was happening at last. Was Frederick Hamilton carrying the documents with him – in the book which never left his side? Would he simply board the yacht and leave? That could be a problem if they headed for Mozambique or even Tanzania. Tim was gambling on the documents being hidden on the island. What he couldn't figure out was who Hamilton had been waiting for.

Hamilton, bag over his shoulder, strode down to the beach. As usual, the arrival of a boat attracted a large group of islanders. Tim picked up the binoculars as the yacht drew closer. 'Silver Bird II. Nice boat.' There were two men on deck. The one at the helm was Karl Henning, Tim recognised him from the newspaper cutting in John Devereaux's file. As Tim watched, he rubbed a hand over his eyes, as if weary. 'No sign of Lana Devereaux? Good! She must have decided not to accept Henning's invitation.' Tim turned the glasses to the second man. 'Shit!' he said aloud. Ramón Alzaga's eyes seemed to bore right through the binoculars.

Tim, as part of his training, had committed to memory the names, faces and deeds of literally hundreds of field operatives from all parts of the globe. Ramón Alzaga was one of them. Mentally, Tim flicked through the filing cabinet in his mind.

Ramón Alzaga was an old hand. He had been around for more than twenty years. Cunning and clever he had come up against a number of Tim's colleagues, some of whom were still licking their wounds. Alzaga was a military man, one of only a few to escape after the juntas collapsed when Argentina had been defeated by Britain in the Falkland Islands war. Before that, he had been active in the terror squads which rounded up, tortured and

444

very often murdered, suspected subversives. When the tables turned, Alzaga went underground, re-emerging four years later with the international division of SIDE – Argentina's State Information Service. His presence on Likoma was about as subtle as an atomic explosion. Britain had stalled for too long and, in his impatience, Hamilton had crossed sides. It was Ramón Alzaga he had been waiting for.

Tim scanned the yacht for any sign of Lana Devereaux, relieved when he saw none. Her chances in the company of Henning were bad enough. Alzaga would have made it worse. The man was a cold-blooded killer.

The arrival of Alzaga confirmed that the documents must be on Likoma. If Hamilton had already removed them then Alzaga would simply have met him somewhere outside Malawi.

The boat was close enough now that Tim did not need his binoculars. As he watched, *Silver Bird II* dropped anchor in the small harbour. Karl Henning went to the back of the yacht and, a few minutes later, a dinghy was lowered into the water. Henning jumped deftly into the dinghy and it set off immediately for the beach where Hamilton waited. Ignoring the laughing, waving children in the water, as soon as Hamilton was in the small craft Henning turned it and returned to the yacht. Once on board, Hamilton and Alzaga shook hands. 'What's a nice missionary like you doing with men like that?' Tim muttered under his breath.

He wondered about Lana. Where in God's

name was she? Was she safe? Was she floating face down somewhere between Chilumba and Likoma? 'I don't need this,' Tim was thinking as he checked his Browning automatic pistol. Keeping an eye on Hamilton was child's play. Henning and his games an irritating diversion. But Alzaga was another story altogether. Ramón Alzaga would, more than likely, recognise Tim. As soon as that happened, he would know why the MI6 man was here. 'And from that point in time, he will be trying to kill me,' Tim thought soberly. 'Unless I've eliminated him first.' Tim wasn't unduly bothered by the prospect of killing the Argentinean. From the point of view of agent against agent, it went with the territory. What did bother him was the thought that Lana Devereaux had, quite innocently, been caught up with the job at hand. Tim tried to put her out of his mind. He realised, ruefully, that he wasn't doing a very good job of it.

He waited until just on dark before leaving the camp. Wireless watched him go, a mournful look on his face as he thought of the steamed chicken and dumplings specially made for his only guest. Tim headed for the crypt. Two days ago, when Father Smice showed him around, he had noticed a vantage point from where both the cathedral and the small harbour should be visible.

It was perfect. Several shrubs screened him from being seen but allowed enough of a view in each direction to keep watch. The inhabitants of Likoma went to bed early and rose with the sun. Frederick Hamilton knew this. Tim assumed that Alzaga and

446

Hamilton would waste no time retrieving the documents. Whichever direction they went from the beach he was close enough to follow the two men. His eyes quickly adjusted to the dark. The moon would set around midnight. For now, it threw enough light for him to see quite clearly. Tim settled down to wait, his mind drifting unwillingly to the unknown whereabouts of one Lana Devereaux.

The sound of footsteps refocussed his wandering attention. Then he relaxed. Father Smice's white surplice was clearly visible as the priest made his way to the crypt, bent down and checked the padlock. Satisfied that all was secure, he headed back towards the cathedral. 'Please stay there,' Tim thought.

The luminous dial on his Rolex Oyster read 1.35a.m. when Tim saw the glint of a flashlight on the water. It snapped off seconds later and then reappeared closer, on the beach. Then it bobbed with the rhythm of a man walking. Tim smiled with satisfaction. Somebody was coming up the hill towards the cathedral. As the light drew closer, Tim could make out two figures and hear their hushed conversation. 'After tonight I need never see this island again,' Hamilton's voice laboured with the unaccustomed exercise of walking uphill.

'My friend, you cannot exactly return to England. My country will welcome you as a hero.' Alzaga spoke normally, neither the climb, or any need for silence, bothering him at all.

'I'm not sure about that.' Hamilton sounded worried, as if the enormity of what he was doing had just hit him.

Alzaga's voice went hard. 'It is too late for second thoughts. You should have done your soul-searching before becoming a traitor.'

'Traitor!' Hamilton's voice was little more than a squeak as they passed where Tim crouched. 'I didn't intend —'

'Shut-up,' Alzaga snarled. 'You are becoming a bore. Do as you are told.'

Hamilton fell silent.

'Well,' Tim reflected, 'at least Alzaga got that right. Hamilton is very boring.'

The padlock was a gift to the talents of Alzaga. He had it open within seconds. Both men disappeared into the crypt, pulling the trapdoor shut behind them. Tim waited ten minutes before moving to follow. 'Now or never,' he thought, grasping the iron ring. The heavy, wooden trapdoor began to lift. Tim froze. Soft light flickered through the crack, but no sounds. He widened the gap and looked into the crypt, or what he could see of it down a flight of stone steps. It appeared empty. Stooping inside, Tim moved forward carefully, lowering the door over his head. Although the light was faint, Tim's eyes were used to the dark and he could see quite easily.

He was in a small, bare room, the floor unevenly paved with roughly hewn flagstones. Smaller blocks made up the walls supporting heavy wooden beams which appeared to form the entire ceiling. An arched doorway in the opposite wall was back lit by light beyond. Tim cautiously approached the opening and looked through into another chamber. Like

448

the first, it was empty. A single candle flickered on a stone shelf, lighting the chamber except for several dark alcoves in two of the walls. There was another doorway at the far end.

All his senses alert, Tim heard the faintest sound at the trapdoor. He moved silently forward and into one of the recesses. A few seconds later Father Smice, his face set in uncharacteristic anger, went past the alcove where Tim was hidden. Despite obvious vexation, the priest kept looking around fearfully, as though he expected the hand of God to pluck him from the crypt at any moment. Tim waited, listening. The footsteps slowed, stopped, then carried on again. Father Smice had passed right through the chamber. Following cautiously, Tim stepped through the second archway and into a narrow corridor beyond.

The absence of anything at all in the crypt was eerie. No ornaments, carvings, religious knick-knacks, not even the odd coffin – there was nothing. The passageway ran for perhaps ten metres and appeared to stop at a blank wall illuminated by a second candle. Father Smice reached the end, looked left, then disappeared to the right. Tim had no idea if the priest knew where he was going. He seemed to hesitate, as though uncertain of the way, then his steps became decisive, making no effort to be quiet. Whether that was because the other two were expecting him or because he was too angry to care remained to be seen.

The candle threw a little light along the corridor, its flame showing up a hint of unexpected draft. Tim stopped and watched. Even after any disturbance caused by Father Smice, the candle continued to pick up movement in the air.

The priest had disappeared. Tim followed, his ears on red alert for the slightest sound. Like the priest, he looked left and saw only an alcove. Right led into a small chamber. In the middle of the room was a rectangular sandstone sarcophagus, austere in design, with no inscription or markings. The lid had been turned sideways and, on closer examination, Tim found that it swung, with very little effort, on a heavy vertical rod. The whole stone slab lifted clear of its recessed seating by a foot-operated lever system which terminated outside the coffin as one of many stone squares around its base. Soft light shone upwards through the open stone coffin, bathing the whole room in an eerie yellow glow.

The coffin was empty, but inside several sandstone blocks had been removed. Through the hole, Tim could see a stone stairway. He eased himself into the coffin and onto the first step. It was smooth, slightly basin-shaped, worn down by use over many hundreds of years. Feeling with his foot, Tim located a second slab and stepped down further. Raising both arms in order to fit through the hole, he descended further. His head was now level with the base of the sarcophagus. Uncertain as to how visible he might be from below, Tim lowered himself and sat on the first step.

In the distance, he could hear voices. Light was coming from below. Tim could see that he'd entered a kind of natural funnel in the rock. 'God knows who carved these steps,' he thought. 'Or why.'

Below, some twenty steps away, Father Smice appeared to be having second thoughts. He had reached a corner in the stone steps and was peering around it. Back lit from below, Tim could see him quite clearly. Gathering himself with a deep breath, the priest stepped forward and disappeared from view. Tim drew his pistol, snicking off the safety catch and went softly down the steps. At the turn, he could see why Father Smice had hesitated.

The steps ran down into a cave, lit by paraffin lamps. Tim could see that it was about six metres across, disappearing into blackness at one end. The other sank into a pool of dark water, perhaps two metres wide, before an overhanging rock curved down from above and into the unseen depths. Left of the last step, stalactite joined stalagmite in a giant hourglass of centuries-old calcium carbonate.

Stacked along the far wall were dark brown elephant tusks of every conceivable size and shape. Tim had never seen so many in one place. But in the centre of the cave was a sight he would never forget. Gold and green oxidised copper gleamed dully in the lamplight. An ornately carved wooden chest stood open revealing necklaces and bracelets of gold, set with rubies and sapphires, emeralds and malachite. Pots, stools, crowns, masks and idols of gold were everywhere. In one pile, lying neatly one on top of the other, were wafer-thin beaten sheets of the precious yellow metal.

451

Ramón Alzaga and Frederick Hamilton were frantically pulling tusks off the stack, examining them in turn and discarding them on the floor. 'So that's it,' Tim thought. 'Hamilton hid the documents inside one of the tusks. Clever.'

'It's not here I tell you.' Hamilton sounded desperate. 'The tusk has gone.'

'Keep looking,' Alzaga ordered.

'I'd see it immediately,' Hamilton protested. 'I put it right at the back. It was not big and I sealed the end with mud.'

Their backs were to the steps, both completely absorbed in the search. Alzaga had dropped his guard, the Walther PPK stuffed into the back of his trousers. 'Not very bright, old son,' Tim thought.

Father Smice reached the bottom step. His voice rang out, full of indignation and disapproval. 'I warned you not to do this. How dare you enter the crypt again.'

So unnerved was Hamilton by the unexpected arrival of Father Smice that he dropped the tusk he was examining. It fell to the stone floor with a loud clatter.

'Who the devil are you?' Alzaga barked.

The priest ignored him. 'You must leave immediately, Frederick.' The priest moved towards him. 'Please, my boy, don't make things worse for yourself.'

'Stay where you are.' Alzaga reached behind his back and produced the small automatic, holding it steady and easy, like an old friend, pointing at Father Smice.

The priest stopped, looking around, appearing to notice for the first time what was stored in the cave. 'Is this what made you break the Lord's trust, Frederick? You chose wealth over Grace?' He shook his head sadly. 'If only you had obeyed my letter.'

'You sent it?' Hamilton found his voice. 'You knew all the time?'

Father Smice smiled a little. 'I am from Likoma, Frederick. Yes I knew of the crypt. It is a Holy place.'

'And the cave?' Hamilton demanded.

'I knew only that it existed. It does not surprise me. The storytellers speak of it. They've been relating the story of treasure for centuries. An ancient kingdom was here hundreds of years ago but . . .' He looked pointedly at the ivory. 'Those who tell the tale have never mentioned ivory.'

'But how did you know I'd found the crypt? I'd kept it a secret for so long.'

'It wasn't difficult. You are easy to read, Frederick. You changed – became self-important, charged up with unexplained energy and, yes, it must be said, you lost the love of God. One night I followed you. I saw you enter the crypt. It was a sin, Frederick. I couldn't allow you to repeat it.'

Hamilton's lip curled. 'I've been coming here for years. Way before you sent the letter. I found this place. The treasure is mine.'

'Enough,' snapped Alzaga. 'Go back to your ancestors, meddlesome priest.'

Tim, frozen in the shadows on the steps, was powerless to stop what happened next.

Father Smice advanced towards Hamilton. 'Come, my boy, come away from this place.'

Ramón Alzaga, with no change of expression, no hesitation, fired, the echo of two shots deafening in the confined space. Father Smice stopped in his tracks, a look more of surprise than pain crossed his face as his legs buckled and he fell, a crumpled heap of white gown, the red stain of blood spreading from where he lay.

Hamilton, with a cry of horror, ran to the fallen priest and dropped to his knees beside him, weeping.

Alzaga's professionalism kicked in. Flicking a look of contempt in Hamilton's direction, he said, 'Stay here. I'll check for others.'

Tim had nowhere to go. Alzaga was climbing the steps, automatic ready to use. If Tim fired at him and missed, he was in danger of hitting Hamilton. He did the only thing possible. As Alzaga reached the bend, he launched himself straight at the Argentinean.

Caught unawares, Alzaga fell back, with Tim on top of him, each man grappling for an advantage, each man trying to kill the other, to get off even one shot. Tim felt his left shoulder dislocate as they tumbled head over heels down the stone steps.

The pain was nothing compared to the moment of despair when he lost the grip on his automatic. He and Alzaga hit the cave floor, Tim grabbing frantically for the Argentinean's pistol. But Alzaga had lost his own as well.

Both men scrambled up. The clatter of metal on stone galvanised Tim and he lunged for the weapon, his brain briefly registering that it was his. In a single fluid move, he spun on the ball of one foot, gun coming up ready to fire. Alzaga, anticipating the move, scooped up a burning lamp and swung it viciously at his adversary. Tim flung up his good arm and the hot glass shattered, cutting him to the bone. Alzaga dived sideways, grabbing for his own pistol, rolling, turning and coming to his feet, palming the weapon into firing position. Tim fired first, knowing as he did that he was off balance and the bullet would go wide. He spun left, behind the stalagmite, stopping immediately and propelling himself back the way he'd disappeared, squeezing off a second shot. Perhaps Alzaga expected him to keep going and appear from the other side. That was where his gun was pointing. By the time he realised his mistake, it was too late. He was a fraction too slow. Tim's bullet found the centre of his forehead, snapping his head back, the nine millimetre bullet knocking him clean off his feet, one outflung arm sending the Walther splashing into the water. Ramón Alzaga was dead before he hit the ground.

Panting, one shoulder on fire, blood running freely down his right arm which had begun to throb fiercely, Tim staggered to where Hamilton was crouched in frozen terror over the body of Father Smice. Tim shoved him roughly aside and felt for the priest's pulse. There was none. He checked Ramón Alzaga as well but was just going through the motions.

'They're both dead!' Hamilton's voice strained past the fear in his throat.

Tim nodded grimly. 'Thanks to you.'

Hamilton was reaching the end of his sanity. 'I didn't mean . . . I had no idea . . . I . . . my God, . . . dead.' He drew his knees up under his chin, wrapped both arms around his legs and rocked back and forth, crying.

Tim had no time for this. The man was likely to become catatonic with shock. He grabbed Hamilton with bloody fingers, hauled him to his feet and shook him roughly. 'Where are the fucking documents?'

'Wha . . .'

'The documents you've been hawking to the highest bidder. You hid them inside one of these tusks.'

'I don't know. They must be here.' Hamilton was blubbering like a child. 'But I can't find them.'

Tim looked at the mountain of ivory. There had to be 300 tusks at least. 'Up,' he ordered Hamilton tersely. 'We'll both look.'

'You don't understand,' Hamilton cried. 'It's not there.' He flung his hands helplessly towards the ivory. 'The tusk has gone.'

'If you didn't take it, then who the hell did?'

'That's what I'd like to know as well, Mr Gilbey. I assume that is who you are?' Karl Henning's voice echoed around the cave.

Tim cursed, turning to see an African, hands tied behind his back, standing at the foot of the steps. Lana Devereaux was right behind him. Karl Henning had an arm around her throat. In his right hand, pointing directly at her temple, he held a pistol.

456

'Now, drop the gun please. If you don't, the girl dies.'

Tim's automatic hit the floor. Henning released Lana, pushing her forward into the African. Tim could see her hands were also tied. 'Kick the gun over here. No heroics.'

Tim did as he was told. Beside him, Hamilton moaned with fear. Henning reached down and picked up the discarded pistol. 'You two, over there,' he said.

Lana and Moffat joined Tim and Hamilton. 'What's this about missing tusks?' Henning asked Hamilton.

The missionary found his voice, but only just. 'I hid something inside one. It's not here.'

Karl Henning was staring at the ivory. 'There's more than one missing.' He turned his gun on Hamilton. 'Who else knows about this place?'

Hamilton shook his head. 'No-one, I swear it.'

'You're lying,' Henning said coldly. 'Who have you told?'

The missionary began to tremble. 'I swear to God Almighty, I've told no-one.'

Henning's eyes became slits. He controlled his temper with difficulty. 'Who is this?' He put out a foot and nudged Father Smice. 'What happened to him?' He looked over at Ramón Alzaga. 'Come to that, what happened to my good friend from Argentina?' His eyes came back to Tim. 'Had a busy night I see.'

'Alzaga killed him. He's a priest.' Hamilton was babbling and pointing at Tim. 'Then *he* killed

457

Alzaga. I'm coming with you, Karl, we're partners, you promised.'

Karl smiled. 'Wrong again, you pathetic little man. You're staying here, all of you. I'll be back in about three weeks. By then . . .' he shrugged carelessly. 'Unless of course you're partial to a little human flesh, but you'll have competition. I wouldn't try to get out through the water either. There's a rather large croc who considers this cave his home. I daresay he'll tidy up for you.' He went backwards up two steps. 'Don't try anything, Mr Gilbey. I'll put a bullet in you if I have to. *Ng'ona* will take care of any evidence.'

Tim was helpless and he knew it.

Henning hesitated, then came back down the steps and approached them. He put out a hand to touch Lana on the face but she jerked her head angrily away from him. Something akin to regret shone from Karl Henning's eyes as he went back up the steps. 'Farewell, Lana. A pity. We could have been good together.' He had backed up to the bend. 'I'd save on lighting if I were you. Won't be too pleasant down here once the paraffin runs out. Blacker than hell I'd imagine.' Henning laughed. 'Oh, and forget the crypt. The hatch locks from outside, as Frederick well knows.' He looked directly at Lana. 'I'm sorry about this, my dear, but as I've already explained, you give me no choice.' He turned and disappeared from sight.

Tim followed to the corner, cautiously checked the steps ahead then climbed to the stone coffin, reaching it just as its lid swung back and dropped into place. They were sealed into the cave.

'Tim!' Lana's cry held a note of urgency.

Tim ran down the steps to where he could see the cave. Hamilton was easing himself into the water. 'Hamilton! Wait. Don't be a damned fool.'

'You can't stop me. I won't stay here. Henning's lying. There's no croc here, I'd have seen it.' His lower body was in the water. 'I've got to find Karl – he *must* take me with him – he promised.' The missionary opened his mouth to say more but a scream of pure terror burst from him.

Tim stared in horror as Hamilton rose up in the water. From a flurry of bloodstained foam, the crocodile's head appeared, its massive jaws locked onto the flailing man's waist. The reptile threw back its head and, with almost casual indifference, adjusted its grip. With a swirl, crocodile and man disappeared beneath the surface. 'Christ!' Tim approached the water's edge and stared down. But *Ng'ona*, with the same primitive instincts as his predecessor, had already taken Hamilton to the bottom to drown.

A small sob broke his paralysis. Lana's eyes were wide with shock. 'Here, let me get that rope off.' He untied her hands, the still-running blood making his fingers slippery. 'I take it you're Moffat Kadamanja?' Tim turned to release the African.

'Yes.' Moffat massaged his wrists. 'Is the opening to the crypt shut?'

'Locked solid I'm afraid.' Tim was impressed by the way Moffat wasted no time.

Kadamanja nodded. 'Get your shirt off. That arm needs binding.'

459

Tim needed help. His dislocated shoulder made it impossible to move his left arm.

Moffat ripped Tim's shirt and wound a wide strip around the cut. 'Turn around.'

Tim did.

'This might hurt,' Moffat warned, wrenching Tim's shoulder hard.

It popped back into place at the first try. Moffat hadn't exaggerated. It hurt like hell. 'Thanks.' Tim suspected that ligaments had been torn but at least he could move his arm again. 'Let's get most of these lamps out.' There were four lamps and none had much fuel. They left only one burning.

Lana's temporary paralysis was easing. 'What the hell are you doing here?'

'Seeing the sights.'

She snorted but left it. 'Karl confessed to murdering my father. And Moffat's. There's a wreck, an old Arab dhow, somewhere near here and it had been carrying ivory. He was afraid they might discover it.'

'What made him confess?'

Moffat answered, 'He found out who I was and made the connection that we were on to him.' Then he added, 'That, and the fact that she jumped him. Twice.'

Lana carried on as though Moffat hadn't interjected. 'I guess he decided it wouldn't matter if he told the truth – he seems to have thought of everything. He's quite mad. My God! Will you look at all that gold.'

'You *jumped* him?'

'Not very well. I was too angry to think.'

460

Tim ran a hand through his hair. *'Jumped* him!' He couldn't quite believe it.

'Can we do something with these bodies?' Lana quietly changed the subject. 'Put them somewhere less conspicuous.'

Tim dragged Alzaga back into the shadows. Moffat did the same with Father Smice.

'The grave has three mouths, and one is hungry.' Moffat said, coming back to where Lana stood.

She nodded in understanding. 'So where's the third?'

'What are you talking about?' Tim asked.

'Long story.'

Tim raised his eyebrows. 'Take your time, we've got all night.'

Lana threw a quick glance at Moffat who nodded. She told Tim about their visit to the witchdoctor.

'And you actually believe this stuff?' Tim asked incredulously.

Moffat sighed.

'I know. I didn't believe it either – at first that is.'

'Fact of the matter is,' Moffat cut in heavily, 'whether you believe it or not, this cave will have three entrances. One is blocked. One has a sodding great flat dog in it. All we have to do is find the third.'

Tim's eyebrows went a notch higher. 'I take it,' he ventured, 'that you two have been spending a good deal of time together.'

Moffat pointed at Lana. 'Sodding is hers.'

Lana pointed to Moffat. 'Flat dog is his.'

'And the witchdoctor?' Tim asked, grinning at them.

461

'Ours,' they said in unison.

Tim could only shake his head.

Lana thought it time to convince him. 'You and Ramón were after the same thing, something that Hamilton had hidden inside an elephant's tusk. It's to do with the Falkland Islands *and . . .*' she pressed, seeing Tim was about to interrupt, '. . . *and,* it will cause Mother England a great deal of embarrassment if it gets into the wrong hands.' She glanced at him. 'How am I doing?'

'Ramón told you.'

'The witchdoctor told me first. Not about where it was hidden, I heard that as we came into the cave.'

Moffat coughed pointedly. 'That lamp's about to go out. Would this be a good time to suggest we try and find the third entrance?'

Tim remembered the candle that seemed to be in a draft. Air was reaching it from somewhere, and the air down in the cave was reasonably fresh, not stale and heavy. It couldn't be the entrance to the crypt – Karl had shut the trapdoor behind him – so it had to be close. 'Back of the cave. Good a place as any.'

Moffat nodded. 'Stay here if you like, Lana.'

'I will not.' She looked across at Tim. 'What are you grinning at?' she asked crossly.

'Do you ever take the easy option?'

'Depends on the circumstances.' She moved off towards the back of the cave. 'You two coming?'

'I'm glad I'm black,' Moffat said quietly to Tim. 'Our women are much easier to get on with.'

Lana heard him and rolled her eyes.

The roof of the cave shelved down sharply, almost to the floor. They checked across its full width but there was no way even a small child could get through the horizontal crevice. 'Damn! I'd hoped . . .' Tim held up the lamp which was spluttering and then, quite suddenly, went out. The blackness was total, leaving them disoriented. 'Great!' he said quietly.

'Where's Lana?' Moffat spoke beside him.

'Over here.' Lana's voice was further away. She had been feeling under the crevice about three metres from them.

'Stay calm, I'll come to you.'

'I am calm,' she said calmly. 'You stay where you are. I'll feel my way back along the crevice.'

She reached them a few moments later. 'How much paraffin have we got?'

'Not much.'

'It's so dark.'

Tim put his arm around her, encountering Moffat doing the same.

'Thanks, guys.' Her voice held a tremor. 'I suppose now is not the time to discover that I'm claustrophobic.'

They made their way back to the centre of the cave, feeling their way slowly. There were so many artifacts stacked around that movement was difficult. 'There are matches on the floor near the other lamps,' Tim said. 'I'll try and find them.'

It took nearly five minutes. Cursing people who put dead matches back in the box, Tim finally located a live one and lit another lamp, putting the matchbox in his pocket.

As the reassuring glow strengthened, Lana screamed. 'The croc!' She pointed. The crocodile was half out of the water. Its massive head turned towards them, Hamilton limp in its jaws, the horror of his death a frozen mask.

'Back here, quickly.' Tim jumped the tusks Alzaga and Hamilton had left lying and began to pull frantically at those still stacked against the wall, toppling them haphazardly, trying to create a barricade. Moffat realised what he was doing and pulled more onto the ground. The crocodile raised itself free of the water and dumped Hamilton's body. Turning to face them, it seemed to be deciding what to do next. Five minutes of indecision probably saved their lives. By the time the beast made up its mind, their barricade was waist high, the tusks jumbled in such a way that they virtually interlocked with each other. As protection went, it wasn't ideal but it was better than nothing.

The crocodile was in no hurry. It advanced sluggishly towards them, a calculating look in its slitted yellow eyes. It was huge, at least four metres long and almost a quarter of that in height. Squat, turtle-shaped legs, teeth bared in an evil grin, water dripping from the knobbly hide, dragging its heavily ridged tail, more powerful than any in the animal kingdom.

Tim hurled a tusk at the reptile but it kept coming. 'The lamp. Throw the lamp,' Moffat panted, struggling with a massive tusk and dropping it onto the growing stack around them, urgency lending adrenalin to his already strong arms.

Tim undid the filler cap, took careful aim and hurled the burning lamp. It bounced directly in front of the crocodile, glass shattering, paraffin spilling onto the floor. The flare-up was immediate but lasted only seconds. Before the cave was once again plunged into darkness, Tim saw the reptile back away from the flames. 'Shit!'

'What?' Lana was panting with exertion. The average weight of each tusk was in the region of twenty-five kilograms.

'The other lamps,' Tim said, angry with himself. 'They're over there.'

'Forget them. At least you've got the matches. Let's hope that bloody thing can't see in the dark.' Lana spoke with more confidence than she felt.

They worked frantically and in total darkness, feeling for holes in the barricade and jamming in tusk after tusk. It was impossible work. With no light, they kept bumping into each other, some tusks sliding away and not locking into place. Eventually all the ivory was in a semi-circle around them, the rock wall at their backs. 'I'll try for the lamps,' Tim offered reluctantly.

'No!' Lana insisted. 'The croc's still there. Listen, you can hear its tail.'

The scrape of the reptile moving slowly back and forth seemed to be just on the other side of their barricade. Every now and then it would bump into one of the items stacked in the middle. The resounding crash sounded loud and menacing as it echoed around the pitch-black cave. Lana slipped her hand into Tim's. 'In the morning we may get more light. Sunlight reflecting through that water and into the cave.'

It was possible. It was the only thought they had to cling to.

Ng'ona shuffled ceaselessly up and down, looking for a way through the ivory wall. The sound of its tail scraping and the repetitive plod of one-hundred-year-old feet sinister and terrifying.

Tim checked his Rolex, blessing the inventor of luminous dials. It was only 3.15. So much had happened. Dawn was an hour away. He prayed that some light would reach the cave. If a third entrance did exist, as Lana and Moffat believed, they would have to find it. And soon. Their strength couldn't hold for long.

He became aware of Lana's hand, still in his. Slim and strong. Like her.

'Tim!' she whispered urgently.

He'd heard it too.

The crocodile was closer. *My God! It's through the tusks. It's behind us! Where the hell is it?* The sound was inside the circle of ivory with them. *This is it!* Instinctively, the three of them huddled together. Tim produced the matches but Moffat bumped him and the box fell.

The scrabbling of searching fingers on his backside was the last thing Tim expected.

'Eeeiii! Eeeiii!' The voice was close and very afraid. A barrage of words followed which Tim could not understand.

Moffat shouted something in Chichewa. 'It's all right. It's a person.' The incongruity of his remark didn't matter. It was something all three of them were pleased to know. 'We've given him a hell of a fright.'

More rapid conversation followed. Tim understood none of it but he heard the tension leave Moffat's voice and relief replace it. Moffat translated. 'He says he's taking the ivory. His Chief has been sending him here for years. The third entrance is behind us. We were sitting up against it.'

Moffat asked a question in Chichewa. 'The way out is easy. He wants us to follow.'

The man said something else.

Moffat chuckled. 'He asks if any of us are fat? He wants to feel for himself.'

'Like hell,' Lana muttered.

Tim found he still had her hand in his. 'What the hell,' he thought. He squeezed it. When she squeezed back he found himself grinning into the darkness. 'Tell him the woman is slimmer than us,' he said. Tim felt the man pat his stomach and then feel his upper arms. He appeared satisfied with that.

Outside the wall of tusks, *Ng'ona* made a rush, knocking some of their barricade aside. The man who had appeared so unexpectedly gabbled something in the darkness.

'He says we must go now,' Moffat whispered urgently, awed by the power in the large reptile. 'Him first, me next, Lana after me and then you, Tim. We are to do exactly what he tells us. Down on our bellies. We have to squeeze under this ledge.'

Beside him, Tim felt Lana's start of fear as the

467

crocodile's tail sent one of the lamps flying. The sound of breaking glass, or the smell of paraffin, must have incensed the reptile for it made another charge at them, scattering tusks like fiddlesticks. In the total inky blackness, it was impossible to guess how close the crocodile was to breaking through.

Tim didn't remember seeing any ledge but most of the wall now behind them had been hidden by the tusks. 'Arms forward. Try to keep in touch with the person in front. Use your toes to push,' Moffat instructed, his voice becoming muffled as he slid under the ledge. Then it was Lana's turn. 'See you topside,' she whispered. And was gone.

Behind Tim, *Ng'ona* crashed into the ivory, thrashing in anger. Expecting teeth to close around his legs at any second, Tim tried to wriggle under the ledge but his belt caught on rock. He backed off and tried again. This time he made it, moving forward until his hand made contact with Lana's ankle. The best feeling in the world was when his feet slid under the ledge.

'I can't breathe,' Lana shouted suddenly, panic in her voice.

'You can. Breathe in slowly, big breaths, shut your eyes. It's only in your mind.' Her breath sounded loud in the confined crevice.

The man up front said something and Moffat called back, 'Couple of minutes of this and we're through the worst. Everyone okay?'

Their progress was painfully slow. It quickly became apparent that there was only one route. Any deviation and the crevice narrowed, making movement under it impossible. Ahead of him, Tim could hear Lana's laboured breath as she strained to propel herself along. The couple of minutes stretched into five, and then ten.

'Nearly there,' Moffat shouted back to Lana and Tim. The crevice became wider and it was possible to use elbows as well as toes to make progress. Then, up on hands and knees, they crawled the last few metres. 'Careful,' Moffat warned. 'Move right and keep it very slow. There's apparently one hell of a drop to the left.'

Tim had expected to see light when they emerged. But blackness continued to engulf them. Their guide moved off again. As far as Tim could tell, they were walking along a tunnel less than a metre wide, impossible to know how high, which inclined upwards. A couple of minutes later they stopped again.

'We climb from here,' Moffat translated. 'There are rungs in the rock face.'

'How far now?' Lana asked. 'I still can't see a damned thing.'

Moffat spoke to their guide. 'There are three separate levels, each with a ladder connecting them. He also asks me to remind the impatient young lady that it will be dark outside too. He does speak English you know, just chooses not to.'

'Sorry,' Lana said meekly. 'Can we go? I'm getting a bit desperate to see your ugly face again.'

Moffat chuckled and Tim realised how close these two had drawn in just a few days. He wondered if Moffat Kadamanja was married.

The first steps led them up and into a low tunnel about twenty metres long, terminating with another vertical shaft. At the top Lana exclaimed, 'I can smell fresh air.'

So could Tim. They were going to make it. Progressing through the last section, one which seemed to take them in a complete circle, the air became sharper and fresher. Looking up once they reached the last ladder, they could just make out a lightening in their surroundings and, far away, one beautiful, miraculous, didn't-think-they'd-ever-see-one-again, twinkling star. The guide spoke to Moffat. 'That's the cliff top,' Moffat told them. 'We're out.'

'Thank God,' Lana said with feeling.

Tim felt their still-unseen saviour brush past him. 'Where's he going?'

'To bring out a tusk.'

'Why doesn't he use a torch? He can't be afraid of being seen.'

'He doesn't need one,' Moffat said. 'He's blind.'

'The eyes that cannot see will lead the way,' Lana quoted the witchdoctor.

'Still doubt it?' Moffat asked her.

'No,' she said. 'Not now.'

'Come on,' Tim urged. 'We can discuss this later.' He put his foot on the first rung. 'There's a great deal of unfinished business up top.'

'Henning,' Lana said with grim satisfaction.

Tim was glad she couldn't see his face. 'You don't know the half of it,' he muttered to himself.

EIGHTEEN

The ladder brought them up to a ledge near the cliff top quite close to where Tim had sat with Father Smice only a few days earlier. Five stone steps, hewn out of the rock face, the last crumbling external evidence of King Lundu's ancient kingdom, took them to the top. Overgrown, and partly covered by loose stones, unless you knew where to look, the steps were hardly visible from any angle. Tim wondered how Chief Mbeya knew of them.

Dawn was tinging the eastern sky with a faint blush of pink. Looking down at the dark water of the cove, Lana shivered. Deceptively serene and calm, hiding the horror of what lurked below. So much suffering and deception. The documents which had cost Ramón his life. The treasures – Karl had said they were from the Great Zimbabwe – how much blood had been spilled over them? The ivory. The priest. Frederick Hamilton. How many lives, human and animal, had been snuffed out by man's insatiable greed? She looked at the reddening sky. The God who gave them such stunning displays of nature could never condone such evil. Turning from of the cove, Lana reflected that God must be very angry with His human creation.

She rubbed a hand over her eyes. Tim had killed Ramón. Self-defence perhaps, but Tim had been looking for the same documents, presumably for the same reasons as the Argentinean. They would both have killed further. Why? Government cover-ups? Blind patriotism? Was there a right and a wrong? *Or is the whole damned world corrupt?*

'No! Look at Moffat. He's a man who wanted answers. Now he's got them. He'll go home to his wife and children, go back to his job, go back to his decency. He will not be touched by evil, except maybe to be thankful that he has a small corner of this earth where it has no place. And what about me?' She shook herself mentally, not up to soul-searching. The only thing she knew for certain was that she was glad to be alive.

Tim? Was he a part of it, this terrible hole mankind was digging for itself? Was he motivated by a sense of misguided loyalty? Was it misguided? 'Hell!' she thought. 'What brought this on?' She glanced at Tim and found him watching her. His deep blue eyes were unreadable. Dark hair fell over his forehead. Bare chest and arms, strong, capable, secure. Flat stomach, abdominal hair. With a start, Lana realised she was becoming aroused.

Tim wondered what she was thinking. Fatigue caused faint blue smudges under her eyes. She had a streak of dirt across one cheek. Grit clung to her hair and clothes. She was, he decided, the most beautiful woman he had ever seen. 'And now for my next trick. How much more can she take?' She had to hear about her father and she had to hear it from him. But before she did, Tim had to know about Karl Henning. 'Let's go.'

On the way to the tented camp they told him everything. Tim listened in silence.

'I suppose you're going to say I told you so,' Lana challenged him.

'No.' Tim smiled at her. 'I wouldn't dare.'

'Karl mentioned Tony Davenport. It was obviously Karl who told Davenport to frighten me off.'

So Tim told her about his conversation with Davenport. 'You can report him if you like. He'll do time for trying to run you off the road.'

Lana shook her head. 'He's weak. The man who must do time is Karl Henning. He's evil. All the time he was telling us about our fathers it was as if he was expecting us to congratulate him. I don't believe he has a conscience at all.'

Far out on the lake, they saw Henning's yacht heading north. 'He's in for a shock,' Moffat commented. 'He thinks he's got away with it.'

'He's not the only one in for a shock,' Tim thought unhappily.

By the time they reached Camp Likoma, the local people were up and about, well into a new day. Wireless looked quite overcome when they arrived as well he might; Tim, shirtless, with a bloodied bandage around one arm in the company of two dishevelled strangers. All three were filthy.

473

'Two extra for breakfast,' Tim announced, ignoring the manager's open-mouthed surprise.

Wireless gathered his wits. 'A message for you, sir. It came last night. The doctor will arrive at ten o'clock this morning.'

'Telephone working today?' Tim asked Wireless.

'Open at half-past seven.'

'Thank you.' He led Lana and Moffat to the empty dining room. 'Pick a table, any table. I've got a bottle of scotch.'

'For *breakfast*?' Moffat said faintly.

'For breakfast,' Lana said firmly.

Wearing a clean shirt, Tim came back with a half bottle of whisky. He removed the cap from the bottle, crushed it and handed the twisted red metal to Wireless. 'Three glasses, please, and a jug of ice if you have any.'

Wireless, with an expression of total disapproval, brought glasses and ice. Tim poured three healthy slugs.

Lana let out a satisfied 'Aahhhh,' as the golden liquid set fire to her throat and killed the butterflies still dancing in her stomach.

Tim's dark eyes watched her. He hated what he had to do next.

'I have some news for you,' he began quietly. 'It concerns both of you but mainly Lana.'

Lana looked at him, enquiry in her eyes.

There was no easy way to tell her, no way around it. 'Your father is not dead.'

The shock was total. Her face drained of colour. 'What did you say?' she whispered.

474

Moffat placed his glass gently on the table. 'Would you rather I left you two alone?'

She barely registered his words, simply shook her head.

Wordlessly, Lana stared at Tim as Moffat asked, 'Are you sure of this?'

Tim nodded. 'He's here, on Likoma.' As she went to rise he added quickly, 'No, no, sit down. There are some things you must know first.'

'What? Where is he? Can't we go to him?'

So Tim told her everything. And as he did, he almost believed he could hear her heart break. She heard him out in silence, her face growing paler, lips trembling, eyes never leaving his. Her hands clasped so tight around the whisky glass it was a miracle it didn't break.

'The doctor is arriving this morning,' Tim concluded. 'Then we'll know more.'

'All these years,' Lana whispered to herself. 'All these years,' she repeated. 'We never knew. He was here all the time and we never knew.' She was trying to take it in but her brain refused to function rationally. So many people would have to be told. Her mother. Bernard. 'My God! Mummy! She married Dad's best friend.'

Inwardly, Tim groaned. Could things get any worse for this girl?

Moffat's face reflected the shock and sympathy he felt for Lana. 'Don't worry about that now. He's alive. It's a miracle, Lana, a bloody miracle.' He was trying desperately to cushion the mental blows he knew she was taking. 'Your father remembers nothing. Everything can be worked out later.'

'He must remember,' Lana said fiercely. 'We were too close. There must be *something* there.' She was becoming angry.

'Good,' Tim thought. 'Anger is better than depression.'

Lana snatched up her whisky. Her hand shook but she managed to drain the glass. 'More.' She banged it down onto the table jumping up and turning to the window, looking out, seeing nothing. 'Why did no-one tell us?' She swung to face Tim. 'Who the hell has been playing God?' She leaned on the table, knuckles white. 'Someone will answer for this.'

Tim rose and put an arm around her. 'I'll take you to the village. You can speak with the Chief. It was his decision not to report your father's presence. For months, they expected him to die. When he didn't, they became frightened that they would be punished for not reporting his arrival and condition. Right or wrong, I think you should hear his version of what happened.'

She could only shake her head in despair.

Wireless appeared, proudly bringing breakfast to their table. But when he saw them, two men staring in silence and the woman with tears pouring unchecked down her cheeks, he backed out of the room and softly closed the door. Last night's chicken had been chopped, sauteed gently with mushrooms and onion and then used to fill three huge omelettes. Wireless believed that this was one chicken destined not to be eaten.

476

They used the lodge facilities to clean up. Moffat borrowed some clothes from Tim. Tim examined his arm. It probably should have been stitched but at least the wound was clean. It would leave an interesting scar. Lana had one small problem. All her clothes were still up at Karonga. Wireless came to her rescue, running to the cathedral and returning with a priest's white surplice. 'I will wash your clothes and have this back on the line before they miss it.' Lana wondered if she was guilty of sacrilege or some other religious misdemeanour, but, she reasoned, God would understand. Tim thought she looked rather fetching, the silky material clinging to her slim body.

Tim had realised that there was no choice but to confide, at least to some extent, in the Bishop of Likoma. It would not be easy but he had to be told about the deaths in the cave and the treasures it contained. Leaving Lana and Moffat at the camp, Tim walked to the cathedral. The Bishop, although a man of God, surprised Tim with his understanding of a world far removed from his own. He passed no judgment, asking questions which were both relevant and probing and Tim answered honestly, without embellishment.

Both men knew there was no choice but to inform the authorities. At a little after 7.30a.m., it was the Bishop who rang the local exchange and asked for the British High Commissioner in Lilongwe. He passed the receiver to Tim and sat back, fingertips pressed together, his mind absorbed in unspoken thoughts.

The High Commissioner liked to be at his desk early. By the time Tim had rung off, the man rather wished he'd slept in. He stared down at the pad and mulled over Tim's requests with growing anger.

1. *Charter plane*

   'Gilbey wants a four-seater on Likoma tomorrow morning – three passengers, including Gilbey, coming to Lilongwe. Good! I've got some things to say to that young man.'

2. *Martin Flower – FCO*

   'What the hell does he mean by "Likoma unresolved but situation contained"?'

3. *Karl Henning / Silver Bird II / police / apprehend*

   'I can't mobilise the whole bloody police force.' The High Commissioner stared at the name Henning. 'Murder, attempted murder, accessory to murder, kidnapping, theft – Gilbey's off his trolley.'

4. *Argentine Embassy / body bag??*

   'The Argentinean Ambassador will love this. A dead SIDE agent in a cave on Likoma where a crocodile – a crocodile for God's sake – is likely to eat him.'

5. *Frederick Hamilton / British / body bag!!*

   'He'd have to be British wouldn't he? "Should be there but may have gone if the bloody crocodile was feeling peckish." Anyone for tiffin?' The High Commissioner was feeling hysterical.

6. *Ologists!*

   'No way! The lost treasure of Greater Zimbabwe.

No way! Nothing to do with us anyway. Where am I going to find archaeologists, paleontologists, anthropologists (and any other ologist that springs to mind)? The boy is barking mad.'

7. *Game Department/ivory*

'Hundreds of tusks, old, probably poached. The bloody man doesn't know there's a ban on trade in ivory. Bugger him.'

8. *Hire car/Karonga/Lana Devereaux*

The High Commissioner stared at his cryptic note for a moment before remembering what it meant. Karl Henning, who appeared to be wanted for so many crimes that it was a pity the crocodile hadn't been more selective, had abducted two people in Karonga and, as a result, a hire car had been abandoned there. The car, a Subaru, rented from Avis in the name of Lana Devereaux, a visitor to Malawi, was damaged. "Could I arrange to pick up the car?" Who does he think I am?'

9. *Monkey Bay naval base/car*

'What is it with Gilbey and cars? No doubt this is all on my budget. If he left his car there he can pick it up himself.'

Reflecting that MI6 might do better to concentrate on things other than some totally insignificant, extremely unstrategic and, more than likely, considerably boring little island of no importance whatsoever, the awesomely irritated High Commissioner sighed and reached for the phone. 'Get me Martin Flower at the FCO in London,' he snarled at the receptionist with uncharacteristic ire, forgetting the time in London would be six in the morning. 'Before you put him through, tell him to brace himself.'

When she quietly informed him it would be too early, the High Commissioner, who was normally very composed, honestly felt that the two hour time difference was there specifically to frustrate him.

The Bishop had listened to Tim speaking to the High Commissioner in silence. When Tim came off the phone, all the Bishop said was, 'I will do what is necessary. Go with God young man.'

Tim had returned to camp. Now, as he stood with Lana and Moffat watching the aeroplane circling, preparing to land, he hoped that this doctor could throw a little hope her way. The chances of it happening were very slim indeed.

The Cessna 162 landed expertly and taxied to the large tree where they waited. The doctor, a young man in his thirties, alighted, then turned back to remove a heavy mobile X-ray unit which took up most of the fuselage locker. Tim went to help.

'You Tim Gilbey?' His accent held the lilt of his Swedish first language. 'Lassa Dalberg. We've met before haven't we?'

They shook hands. 'Thanks for coming.'

The doctor stared Tim down. 'I didn't have much choice.'

'Sorry.' Tim grinned ruefully at the doctor's flat

honesty. He quickly explained about John Devereaux. 'So you see, I thought it best if he were
examined on Likoma. Apparently he becomes confused and disturbed if he gets out of routine.'

The doctor eyed Tim with some exasperation.
'There's such a thing as sedatives.'

Tim lost patience. 'The man's been through
hell.'

Dr Dalberg sighed. 'Haven't you heard? House
calls went out with the ark.' He went silent, thinking. 'How long ago did you say?'

'Fifteen years.'

'Wish I'd known this sooner,' Dr Dalberg grimaced at the mobile unit. 'I'd have left this beast at
home.'

Lana had approached the men and heard the
doctor's remark. 'But won't an X-ray –' she began.

He interrupted impatiently. 'No. A CAT scan
will. Not an X-ray, especially a wound that's fifteen
years old.' He looked around. 'Where's the patient?'

'It's a fair walk from here.' Tim shrugged apologetically. 'I thought it best to examine him at
home. Under the circumstances . . .'

'Yes, yes, he gets disturbed.' He looked at Lana.
'This man I come to see is your father?'

'Yes.'

'Does he recognise you?'

'I don't know. I haven't seen him yet.'

Dr Dalberg looked surprised.

'It's a long story,' Tim said. 'I'll tell you on the way.'

'Anywhere I can put this?' The doctor nudged
the X-ray unit with his foot.

'Leave it in the plane,' the pilot offered. 'I'm not going anywhere.'

As they walked, Lana listened to Tim and the doctor discussing her father. The more she heard, the more hopeless she felt. Judging by Dr Dalberg's responses, if her father had any chance at all of recovering his memory, he'd be showing signs of it way before now.

'What does he look like?' she wondered. Fifteen years is a long time to hold the memory of a dearly loved face. She accepted that he would have aged. She felt keyed up, nervous and yet, strangely reluctant as well. *He must remember something.*

The beauty of Likoma went unseen as she walked along, her mind busy with a confusing array of thoughts.

'Holding up?' Moffat asked.

'Just.' She did not look at him. 'It's too weird to talk about.'

He patted her arm. 'I've been trying to put myself in your place.' He hesitated. 'I think,' he said finally, 'that I'm the lucky one.'

She did look at him then. 'I've been having similar thoughts,' she admitted. 'And I've been hating myself for them.'

They had dropped a little behind the other two. 'Moffat,' she said sadly. 'If Dad remembers nothing, if he's just a shell, then perhaps it would have been better if he'd died.' Unshed tears sparkled in her eyes. 'That's what makes this so hard.'

He had no words of comfort but did the next best thing. He gave her a hug.

'Thanks.' Lana sniffed, brushed at her eyes impatiently and gave him a weak smile. 'I needed that.'

Chief Mbeya, in the mysterious way of Africa, had anticipated their arrival and met them outside the village. 'Mpasa's daughter.' It was more a statement than a question.

Tim nodded.

The Chief took him to one side. 'She knows he will not recognise her?'

'She knows.'

Chief Mbeya shook his head. 'Then, Timgilbey, she has the heart of a lioness.'

'She has made a great journey,' Tim replied. 'It is too late to turn back now.'

'Then wait here,' the old man ordered. 'I will take this woman to meet Mpasa.'

As he led her forward, Lana wished she were any-where but where she was. This scene, played out in her mind so many times over the years, should have a happy ending. She knew now that it would not. In her own straight-for-the-jugular way, Lana knew that this would be a scene best not played at all.

'Mpasa's seed is strong in your face,' Chief Mbeya said. 'Your father lives for as long as you do.'

483

Lana nodded dumbly.

'I have seen the talking pictures when they bring them to the island,' the Chief went on. 'I have seen "Gone With The Wind". That man, Clark Gable, he is dead now but he lives in the pictures.'

'What the hell is he talking about?' Lana thought.

'Your father is like Clark Gable. Reach through your sorrow. Not many see their loved ones after they have gone.'

She stopped in her tracks.

The Chief apologised. 'Forgive me. By trying to help you I am perhaps making it worse.'

'No!' Lana said slowly. 'Your words make sense. I just don't know if I can do it.'

Chief Mbeya's wise eyes scanned her face. 'Only a fool believes he cannot fail,' he said quietly. 'You are not a fool. Your doubt is your strength. Come. Mpasa lives this way.'

Lana's heart was thudding wildly. What was the Chief trying to say? That her father was like an old movie – walking, talking but unreachable? *Dear God! What am I doing here?*

It was a rambling, but tidy village. Voices called loudly in conversation. In one of those random flashbacks that occur when the mind is busy elsewhere, Lana recalled her mother telling her that Africans speak loudly so that others will know that nothing bad is being said against them.

The smell of wood smoke was strong in the air. Chickens scratched busily and several domestic pigs rummaged energetically under some bushes.

484

Children were laughing somewhere. The lake glittered in the sunshine. Several women were washing clothes at the water's edge. Lana knew suddenly that her father could not have found a more idyllic refuge. 'Perhaps it's not that he can't remember,' she thought. 'Perhaps he doesn't *want* to remember.'

They were approaching a hut. A woman sat on a stool at the doorway watching them. A man, with his back to Lana, sat on the ground carving what appeared to be a piece of ivory. Around him a display of his wares. Some of them were very good. Lana's heart was in her mouth. Tim had said her father carved things. Her eyes bored into the strong brown back. She found it impossible to equate this half-naked man sitting in the dirt to the elegance which had been her father. The woman rose as they approached. 'Mpasa's daughter,' the Chief told her in English.

At the mention of his name, John Devereaux turned his head.

Lana stared at him. The handsome face was thinner than she remembered with features that had grown chiselled and lean. Lines at the corner of his eyes crinkled upwards. Happy lines but deeply etched. His brow was furrowed. Hair, overlong, had streaks of grey and hung in unkempt waves, covering his ears. He smiled suddenly, his teeth startling white in the heavily tanned face.

A myriad emotions surged through Lana. The smile was the one she remembered. A beautiful smile. Full of humour and intelligence, mischief and concern, a smile which held love and understanding.

Dad! It nearly burst from her in an explosion of happiness. Nearly. Then she saw his eyes. All those things she remembered about his smile should have been mirrored in his eyes. They used to be. Brown, fine eyes, sparkling with life and laughter. Lana looked into her father's eyes and saw . . . nothing.

'*Angello,*' John Devereaux said in wonder, inclining his head to one side.

'What did he say?' Lana whispered to the Chief. *Why am I whispering?*

The Chief looked surprised by the word. 'He called you an angel.'

John Devereaux rose and approached Lana slowly. He was watching her intently, a curious mixture of fear and pleasure on his face. '*Angello,*' he said again.

The walk was awkward, stiff and jerky. Not the one she remembered. He appeared to have difficulty in speaking. Not the voice of her father. A curious thing happened inside her. All her life, since his disappearance, she had remembered him as he was, imagining she would fling herself into his arms if, by some miracle, he ever reappeared. Now she didn't want to. This man was a stranger.

The Chief spoke to the woman. 'Go. Bring the others.' He turned to Lana. 'It is as you have been told. I am sorry.'

John Devereaux stood in front of his daughter, slowly shaking his head. '*Angello, angello, angello,*' he said, again and again.

'Why is he calling me an angel?'

'I do not know,' the Chief said. 'Perhaps it is the

priest's clothing. I have never heard him use the word before.'

Lana did not know this man. She searched his face for her father but could only find someone who looked like him. Did he recognise her? Was there anything, anything at all of his past inside him? 'Lana,' she said slowly.

There was no reaction. John Devereaux simply repeated that one word.

'Can he speak English?' *This is my father! Stop treating him like a stranger. He's my father!* Nothing. There was nothing. Not a damned thing.

'He speaks no English.'

Lana didn't hear the Chief's reply. Now she knew why she and her mother hadn't been told, why her father's presence on Likoma had been kept a secret. The Chief was aware of what she now knew. Fear of reprisal for not reporting his sudden appearance aside, it was very evident that returning this man to his loved ones would have been point-less. There was a roaring sound in her head and a great pain in her chest. All the pent-up grief of fif-teen years, all her determination to find out what happened to him, carrying a picture of him in her head, a love for him in her heart, her father now stood before her and she felt nothing. This was not her father and, as the final realisation hit her, Lana's grief burst from her in heartbroken sobs.

Mpasa stared at the sobbing angel. She was the face under the water, the one who led him away from the terror of his nightmares. He did not know why she was crying. Worried, in case she was angry with him for some reason, he backed away and, picking up an ivory penny whistle, took it to her. He had to prod her twice before she put out a trembling hand and took it from him. Satisfied, he returned to his carving, not looking at her, wishing she would stop crying and go away. Her tears distressed him.

Tim found Lana sitting on the ground, her head on her knees, shaken by sobs which shuddered out of control through her body. In her hand she held her father's gift. She held it as though her very life depended on it. John Devereaux, his back to everyone, was carving another ivory penny whistle. Chief Mbeya stood helpless, a look of deep compassion on his face. Tim helped Lana to stand and, with one arm around her, moved slowly towards the beach. She went with him as though she had no will of her own. 'He's all yours,' Tim said tersely to the doctor. 'Just try and give her some answers.'

An hour later, Lana, composed and pale, listened as Dr Dalberg explained.

'The bullet has severely damaged the fronto parietal and a portion of the frontal lobe. The reason he walks stiffly is that fragments of the bullet also hit the pyramidal tract at the centre of the brain. You see, Lana, when a projectile enters the skull it doesn't go straight through. It begins to yaw and break up and this determines the extent of the damage. In your father's case, you can see from the external evidence that the damage was massive.

There would have been soft tissue injury and major vascular lesions causing haemorrhaging and, ultimately, a huge build up of pressure. Normally this would have killed him – the brain has no way of dealing with that kind of tension.'

'Can the damage be surgically reversed?' She sounded calm, almost detached.

'I'm afraid not.' The doctor's eyes searched her face, looking for signs of hysteria or shock.

'But if the fragments are removed . . .'

She was, he decided, holding up remarkably well. She might as well know it all. 'Lana, the brain learns to live with bullet fragments. Taking them out would achieve nothing. After fifteen years, if they haven't killed him by now they're never going to. The damage to your father can never be reversed.'

'What saved him?'

Dr Dalberg sighed. 'From what I can gather, a witchdoctor's intervention is what saved him. There's a second wound not made by the bullet. When I asked the Chief about it he told me that the witchdoctor had to let out the evil spirits. In other words, using God knows what methods, a hole was drilled into your father's head. It relieved the pressure but it's too late now to say whether your father would have sustained such extensive brain damage if they'd left it alone. On the other hand, if they had left it there is no doubt in my mind that he would have died. I'm sorry, Lana. We could move him to hospital to run X-rays and CAT scans. They would show us exactly what damage was done but that's all it would do. We can't help him.'

Lana remained silent.

'There *is* one more thing I can try.'

'What?'

'It won't help him. I'll do it so that you can see for yourself that your father's memory is completely eradicated.'

'What?' she asked again, a little scared, a little angry.

'Hypnosis. It should tell us how far back his memory goes.'

'You can do that?'

Dr Dalberg nodded. 'If the Chief will translate on my behalf.'

'I don't want to distress him.'

'If he gets upset I'll stop immediately.'

Lana looked at Tim. 'It can't hurt him. It might help you,' he said gently.

John Devereaux was falling, tumbling through water. The little girl was there and he tried to reach her. Falling and spinning, the evil behind him. He was in the greatest of fear. Speaking in Chichewa, he told of the angel who saved him. He kept trying to get to her but she remained out of reach and led him to the island. This was his nightmare. This was his memory. This was it. Lana realised listening to his words being translated that before it, there was nothing.

'Stop,' she said. 'He's getting too scared.'

'Wait,' Dr Dalberg said. 'I think I can take the fear from him.'

Chief Mbeya repeated his words exactly. 'There

490

is no evil, Mpasa, there is nothing to fear any more. When you wake up you will remember nothing. The nightmares have gone, they will never come back. You are going to sleep now. Sleep in peace. You are safe.'

John Devereaux's face relaxed and he slipped from his hypnotic state into a deep sleep.

Dr Dalberg appeared drained of energy. 'He should rest easily from now on. That nightmare was the reason for his fear and the mood swings the Chief mentioned. It should not come back.'

'The little girl, the angel as he calls her, that was me.'

The doctor nodded. 'One tiny piece of memory.'

'And now that's gone too?'

'I'm afraid so.'

'Perhaps,' Lana said, in a small voice, 'it is for the best.'

Moffat glanced at the clock on the dining room wall. 'She's been gone fifteen minutes.'

Tim nodded. Wireless came and cleared the table. 'The young lady has gone for a walk,' he volunteered. 'She went up past the cathedral.'

'I think we should go after her,' Tim said, rising.

Moffat shook his head. 'No. I think it's best if you go.'

Walking up towards the cathedral, Tim could only imagine the turmoil inside Lana. She had been quiet for the rest of the day. When Tim asked if she wanted to stay with her father she had said, 'No.'

As they made their way back to the airstrip with Dr Dalberg, Tim said in an undertone, 'She's too quiet.'

The doctor disagreed. 'There's no evidence of shock. She's had a lot to contend with in the past few hours. She's just digesting it. She's very strong. Let her come through in her own way.'

There was a loose end and Tim wasn't sure how the doctor would take it. 'He's been declared legally dead. Her mother has remarried.'

Dr Dalberg cut straight to the point. 'Nothing can be gained by announcing this to the world. If she wants to keep this to herself she'll get no argument from me.'

'Thank you.'

As they stood watching the small plane banking left to find Malawi air space before turning due south over the lake, all Lana had said was, 'What a nice man.'

She had remained detached and silent for the rest of the day. Wireless apologised that her clothes were not yet dry and all she said was, 'This gown is quite comfortable thank you.' Neither Tim nor Moffat could break through the barrier of politeness she had erected. She had barely touched her dinner. Beside her plate lay the ivory penny whistle. Moffat picked it up and ran his fingers along the smooth whiteness. 'It's good.'

'Yes.' It was all she said.

'May I?' He put the instrument to his lips.

She nodded.

Moffat blew some notes. The tone was pure. *'And music of the spirits will be heard.'* He handed the instrument to Lana.

It put a small crack in her armour. 'The elephant's spirits?'

'That is what the Nganga meant.' Moffat watched her face carefully.

'Yes.' Her face contorted. She was about to cry. With an effort she gained control of herself. *'One will speak yet say not a word.'* She blew the first few notes of 'Amazing Grace', and stopped. 'The head injuries? They speak for themselves. Is that what it means?' She blew a few more notes. 'And he can't communicate in anything but Chichewa and even that's difficult for him.' She lay the penny whistle down and rose from the table. 'Excuse me. Little girls' room.' Lana turned and strode from the dining room.

And now she'd gone for a walk.

Tim took the track past the cathedral. He thought he knew where Lana would be heading. Night was coming in fast. The cliff top, he was positive that was where he'd find her. But there was nobody. Then he saw her. She had taken a winding path down to the small beach at the bottom. Should he wait here? Should he go to her?

'She can only tell me to get lost.' His mind made up, he followed her. By the time he reached the bottom it was almost dark. He could just make her out – sitting back from the water's edge, knees drawn up, staring across the lake. She heard him approach and looked in his direction.

'Want some company?' He sat beside her.

She turned back to face the water, achingly beautiful and so very vulnerable. 'What do I tell my mother?' she asked huskily.

He had no answer for her – she hadn't expected one.

'Do I lie? Is that the best thing?'

Tim put an arm around her shoulders and she leaned into him. She felt tight, like a coiled spring.

'What good would the truth do?' She turned her face to his. 'It's such a *big thing* to lie about.' Her breath was sweet.

Tim didn't mean to. Her lips were so close to his. It was supposed to be a reassuring thing, a trouble shared. He brushed her lips with his, felt the pressure of her response and, before he knew it, she was in his arms and he was kissing her and she wrapped her arms around him and pulled him down with her and she was kissing him back with an urgency that surprised him. But even as he responded, he knew it was comfort she desperately sought and so, clamping down on the desire which suddenly flooded through him, he tightened his arms around her and kissed her deeply on the mouth.

It was not a passionate kiss. He kissed her with an overwhelming desire to help. He wanted her to know he was with her, on her side. The tension rolled away slowly as she relaxed, giving herself up to the gentle caring of his hands and lips. He kissed the line of her perfect jaw and felt her tremble. He ran his lips lightly down her long and graceful neck to where the soft swell of her breasts began, then back again to linger on her lips. The arousal which had flared briefly on the cliff top that morning returned, and she responded eagerly. The tempo shifted and he kissed her with a growing urgency until they were both breathless.

'Lana,' he groaned, his own arousal, so hot inside him that he throbbed with it.

'Make love to me, Tim,' she whispered, and her breath in his ear sent a shudder right through him.

She sat up and he drew the silky white surplice over her head. Under it, she was naked. His hands and lips explored her body and she moaned a low growl of absolute need, her skin on fire where he touched her. 'Take off your clothes,' she pleaded, trembling, committed and eager.

Naked, they knelt facing each other. He kissed the hollows in her shoulders, her belly button, nipples, ears and she responded, feeling the hard muscles on his arms and chest quiver under her lips. At last, when Tim believed he could no longer wait, she drew back. 'Now,' she said shakily.

She cried out when he entered her. Then they were moving together, and all the pain and fear of the past few days departed as the only thing on their minds was the floodgate opening in their bodies and the exquisite pulsating climax, to which they drew inexorably closer, which picked them up and bore them away with such intensity that nothing else on this earth mattered.

Together, they reached an uncontrollable pinnacle of searing passion. Together, their bodies arched and shook with release. Together, they floated down again, holding each other tight, joined, panting with the pure strength of their emotions as the last, sweet, pulsing sensations shook them, leaving them languid and quiet while their breathing returned to normal and they were left with the wonder, safe in the certain knowledge that what had taken place between them had been perfect.

Neither of them wanted to break the spell. 'Lana,' he whispered finally, against her hair.

She moved her head and found his lips with her own. 'Ssshhh,' she sighed.

He held her tightly and, as his head cleared, Tim realised that he would like to hold her like this forever.

Much later, she stirred in his arms and asked softly, 'You're not married, are you?'

'Never come close.' He kissed the end of her nose. 'Bit late to ask isn't it?'

He heard the smile in her voice. 'Just checking.'

He rolled onto his back and she gave a soft cry of protest as he withdrew from her. With an arm under her head they lay in silence, relaxed in the aftermath of their lovemaking, looking up at the stars. Fifteen minutes later he realised that she had fallen asleep. He covered her with the surplice, pulled on his clothes, and curled protectively around her. Together, like children, they slept sound and secure, the fine white sand a mattress under them, the soft Malawi night a gentle balm to ease tired minds and soothe aching bodies, the faintest of breezes a gossamer eiderdown on their skin, and, in the star-studded wide, wide sky a thousand peaceful spirits watching over them.

He woke to the sharp sting of dawn and found her missing. But she hadn't gone far. Still naked, she emerged dripping from the lake, picked up the surplice, raised both arms and let it slide easily over her head. Tim rued the covering of such a perfect body. She came up the beach towards him. The deep pain of yesterday had gone from her eyes. In its place, serenity. The strained smile had become natural. The demons banished. 'It's going to be a beautiful day.' She hitched up the surplice and dropped to her knees in front of where he sat. 'I want to ask you something.' Her blue eyes watched his face carefully. 'In the cold light of day, was last night special for you too?'

He liked her straightforwardness. 'Very.' Tim realised there would never be any half measures with Lana. What she gave she expected to receive. It was a simple enough philosophy and one he respected.

Her reaction was so endearingly childlike he wanted to pick her up and cradle her in his arms. She gave a small delighted laugh and clapped her hands together, holding them under her chin. Then, completely unexpectedly, she hit him with what he would come to call 'a Lanaism'. 'You're MI6, aren't you?'

He was too surprised to fob her off. 'Yes.'

Her eyes regarded him seriously, their questioning depths inviting elaboration.

So he told her of his doubts and of his plans for the future. She heard him out in complete silence.

'And now that time has come. Enough is enough,' he concluded. 'I am leaving the service. The decision is not about you, it's about me.'

She nodded. 'I've done a bit of thinking too.'

He smiled at her understatement. In the soft dawn light Lana's face was relaxed and lovely. As she turned it up towards the sky and stretched her neck, he wanted to kiss the small ticking pulse just under her jaw. 'And what have you decided?'

She took a deep breath. It was hard for her to say it. 'My father is dead. The chapter is closed. That's my decision.'

Her face was calm. He wanted to hold it between his hands. He wanted to look into her soul and tell her he would always protect her. He wanted to hold her beating heart against his and stroke away any doubt. 'I love you.' He had never told another woman that.

She laughed softly. 'Tim.' The way she said his name was a prayer. Her eyes searched his. Then she rose and moved off the beach.

'Where are you going?'

'See those trees back here.' The surplice was coming off again. 'I need to show you how I feel.'

Moffat's relief was obvious but he asked no questions. 'Sorry.' Lana kissed his cheek, smiling. She offered no further explanation.

Wireless brought her clothes, freshly washed and pressed. Lana was still smiling as she went off to shower and change.

'How did you manage that?' Moffat asked Tim. 'She's a different person.'

'Nothing to do with me. She made up her own mind about the future and now she's getting on with life.'

Moffat whistled. 'Amazing.' He did not add that if the change in Lana had nothing to do with Tim then he, Moffat, was a monkey's uncle! There was no rancour in him. On the contrary, Moffat was delighted to think that Lana and Tim were an item. It put her out of reach. And it put Moffat out of danger.

After breakfast the three of them sat in chairs on the lawn at Camp Likoma, soaking up the morning sun while they waited for the aeroplane. Down on the beach people were laughing and shouting. Around the point of the cove, appeared the reason for their excitement. It was Santos, returning his crew to Likoma. The squat Portuguese-African, a bottle of rum in one hand, was bellowing for Father Smice even before the trawler dropped anchor. 'Hey, Father. Quick quick. Same girl. You marry today.' His voice carried easily on the slight breeze.

'Come on,' Tim said, rising. 'Better tell him. I also want him to keep an eye out for Henning.'

'Hey Gilbey,' Santos waved the bottle. He was clearly drunk but in excellent humour. 'Where Father Smice?' The girl next to him giggled.

A small runabout took them to the trawler. Moffat and Lana stayed in the boat but Tim climbed on board, nodding to the girl. He tried to lead Santos to the wheelhouse but the man's attention was, mouth open, focussed on Lana. 'Jesuit priest!' he bellowed in honest-to-God appreciation. 'What tits!'

Lana shook her head and turned away, but not before Tim saw the wide grin of genuine amusement. Moffat, in total embarrassment, stared at something high in the sky.

Trying to hide his own grin, Tim made another attempt. This time Santos stumbled forward. 'Dead?' His voice became a croak. 'The Father? Dead?' He grabbed Tim's shirt. 'You lie, Gilbey, it cannot be.'

Tim prised him off. The smell of cheap rum enough to gag a vulture. 'I'm sorry,' he said, startled to see tears in the old fisherman's eyes.

Sniffling and rubbing his nose with the back of an oil-stained hand, Santos drained the bottle. Staggering a little, he put an arm around the pregnant girl at his side. 'Santos in love.' He glared at Tim. 'Who marry us now?'

'We could ask the Bishop.'

About an hour later, spruced up in a clean overall, as sober as was possible, and with Tim acting as best man, the beaming Captain Santos became a married man. He listened impatiently when Tim asked him to watch out for, but not approach, Karl Henning and the storm-damaged *Silver Bird II*. Santos left for Monkey Bay with his usual lack of finesse. 'You get off boat now. Santos want fuka fuka.'

★

500

The aeroplane arrived just after eleven and took off fifteen minutes later. As they climbed over the northern tip of Likoma, Lana looked down at a small village where the man they called Mpasa carved his ivory. 'I wish you well,' she said softly, fingering the penny whistle he had given her. 'I wish you happiness and peace.'

Tim heard but made no comment. This was her own private farewell.

Within minutes they were out over the lake, the island dropping away behind. 'There's that chap Henning's boat.' Their pilot pointed ahead. The dismasted yacht must have been fifteen kilometres from Likoma. 'Heard about him over the radio – better report on his position. What's he wanted for anyway?'

There was no point in dodging the question. The whole of Malawi would soon know about Karl Henning. 'Murder amongst other things,' Tim responded. 'He killed four good men.'

Lana's hand slipped inside his. 'Thank you,' she whispered.

They flew directly over *Silver Bird II*. There was no sign of life on board, the vessel appeared to be riding at anchor. 'He must be diving on Mlozi's dhows,' Tim said. 'He thinks he's got away with it.'

Moffat, sitting next to the pilot, turned and spoke to Lana. 'There's only one part of the Nganga's words we've still to work out. *The one who fears all eyes and ears will find the jaws of silence.* Obviously it must be Henning but what about the rest? I've tried, but I can't think what it could mean.'

501

Neither could Lana.
Neither could Tim.

Karl Henning, nearly forty metres beneath the surface of Lake Malawi, checked his watch. He'd been down a full five minutes. Only three left if he wanted to avoid decompression stops on the way up. At this depth, and diving alone, he had to be particularly careful. He worked with total concentration. The Arab dhow, or what was left of it, a gloomy ghostly shadow, lay on its side. As it dropped to the bottom one hundred years earlier, its cargo of ivory had moved and broken free on impact. Most of the tusks spilled clear of the wreck and, over time, the shifting sands had covered them. Thanks to an air compressor, only a few remained. The only big ones left were those lying under the wreck. The dhow itself was breaking up, not the heavy hand-hewn timbers but the wooden dowel pins which once held them together. Removing partially trapped tusks was not difficult – just tricky.

During that fateful storm one hundred years ago, two of the dhows had become entangled, the high prow of one smashing into and through the hull of another. Locked together, they sank quickly, Mlozi's ivory carrier hurtling broadside into the sandy bottom. The second dhow, still firmly attached to the first, came to rest at right angles to it, bow down but upright.

When Karl first found the wrecks he examined

them carefully to see if they were stable. Although the second dhow rested on its keel, it was so embedded in the other that he concluded there was no danger.

He shone his torch. The biggest tusk of all, more than sixty kilograms he estimated, lay, thick end towards him, half under the dhow. He checked his watch again. Thirty seconds gone. Swimming down he grabbed the big tusk, braced his feet and started to pull. He expected it to come easily, breaking free as all the others had done.

Under the dhow, out of sight, the curved tip of the tusk moved, then stuck. Irritated, and aware that time was running out, Karl pulled again. It broke free, but a timber beam above it collapsed and the dhow shifted, then settled. Karl drew the tusk towards him. Above, at the point where the two vessels were joined, the movement caused the second dhow to rise at the stern. The extra strain on the heavy cutwater was too much. Weakened by the century-old impact it sheared, and, free at last of the only thing holding it upright, the dhow slowly toppled sideways in a silent but unrelenting path to its final resting place.

Karl had both hands on the tusk. The first he knew that something was wrong was when a skull toppled from those awful decks above and fell past his mask. Looking up, he saw the dhow tipping towards him. Frantically, he tried to kick himself backwards but it was too late. Gathering momentum, the old slaver landed on its side, pinning Karl's legs between its deck and the mighty tusk.

The pain was terrible. Sand flew up and around making the water too murky to see. 'Calm. Stay calm,' his brain screamed as he scrabbled for the torch, found it and shone the light down his legs. One was pinned just above the knee, the other trapped just below. Blood coloured the water. He calculated his air supply. Twenty minutes in total. Nearly fainting with pain, Karl raised himself and reached over to the dhow. It was solid. There was no way he was going to move even one of those heavy timbers and the tusk was too long for him to dig it clear.

He lay back awkwardly against the air bottle. Twenty minutes!

Visibility cleared as the disturbed sand settled. Around him lay a macabre audience of bones and skulls. Hundreds of tormented souls had at last found a reason to smile. One skull slid down the deck slowly, eye sockets empty, jaws grinning in silence. It turned over once and settled gently on his stomach. Karl left it there. It was strangely comforting.

'So many dreams,' he thought. 'For what? For this?' He felt like crying but knew it wouldn't help. He lay there, life performing one last act in his mind. He was going to die. He looked at his watch – fifteen minutes!

Blood from a severed artery in his leg flowed thickly. 'What will it be?' Karl wondered, a calm acceptance now upon him. 'Will I suffocate or bleed to death?' The skull of Ferig, the young Wankonde tribeswoman expected to grace the

504

Sultan's palace in Zanzibar one hundred years earlier, rested on the stomach of this man who would
have profited from her pain and horror and
appeared to mock him.

The irony was lost on Karl. All around him lay
the bones and tusks of those for whom the drums
of retribution would never cease to beat. Above, he
could see the outline of his yacht. And far above
that, if he had but known, Lana Devereaux, Moffat
Kadamanja and Tim Gilbey tried to work out the
last of the Nganga's words.

*The one who fears all eyes and ears will find the jaws
of silence.*

NINETEEN

'Good night, Miss Bagshaw.' Lana waved breezily at PAGET's receptionist, noting that the woman had actually taken to wearing the pink lipstick she'd given her. Miss Bagshaw stared disapprovingly at Lana's departing figure then went back to work. Lana had been, in her opinion, in such astounding good humour since her return from Malawi that Miss Bagshaw considered her behaviour to be unprofessional.

Running lightly down the steps, Lana rued, yet again, the absence of Duncan who had passed away while she was in Malawi. Well past retiring age, the man had died as he would have wished – a heart attack whilst at his post. The office just wasn't the same without him. She missed his snobbish observations and impeccable manners.

The Fat Boy roared into life with all the powerful throatiness of its pedigree. Lana pulled into the street, reached the corner, and sneaked into Marylebone Road between two taxis. She saluted cheekily to the driver who had slammed on his brakes.

Weaving through the heavy rush hour traffic,

she worked her way over to the right hand lane and swung right into Harley Street. She usually took this route home. It pleased her to run the Harley down a street with the same name. A little quirk, she knew, but Lana was perfectly comfortable with her quirks.

The terraced Georgian buildings, which housed some of Britain's finest medical minds, seemed rigid with disapproval as Lana, the skirt of her dove grey business suit hitched high in a most unladylike way, cruised past.

It was a beautiful, late summer evening. London was enjoying one of its best seasons on record. She turned left onto Cavendish, and roared past the Polytechnic. The crash helmet was annoying her. She'd have liked to feel the wind on her face and running through her hair. Briefly, she thought of Likoma Island, of the space and pace of life. 'Exhaust fumes,' she was thinking. 'Who needs them?'

Likoma Island. Mpasa. Tim. Moffat. It was another world. 'I'll be back in London in a few weeks,' Tim had said at Lilongwe Airport.

'Come back often,' Moffat told her when he said goodbye. He had taken Lana to one side to apologise for kissing her. 'I don't know what came over me,' he confessed. 'But I'm over it.'

'The police would like a word with you,' the High Commissioner said, handing Lana a hastily produced temporary passport. 'If you don't want to be tied up with months of red tape I'd get the first plane out if I were you. And you didn't hear that from me,' he added. 'Oh, and by the way, the hire car people are keen for a chat too.' Under her helmet, Lana grinned at the memory. Despite having his patience severely tested by Tim, the man had been helpful and understanding.

There had been an official car waiting at the airport for them.

'Shit!' Tim swore softly, when he saw it. 'This could take hours.'

It had. Tim looked severely savaged when he finally emerged from the High Commissioner's office. 'He's booked you on tonight's flight via South Africa.'

On the twelve hour leg between Johannesburg and London, Lana renewed her resolve to hide the truth from her mother and Bernard. Not even the High Commissioner knew about the discovery of her father. It would remain a secret between Tim, Moffat, the doctor and herself. 'Not an easy choice,' she acknowledged to herself. 'But the other way is worse.' Lana remembered the emptiness when she stood looking at Mpasa – he was not her father. He was a stranger. He always would be. She had loved her father enough to do this for him. Why distress or confuse him any further?

Karen Devereaux-Pickstone had been delighted by the early return of her daughter. She listened in silence while Lana told her that John Devereaux had been murdered by Karl Henning. She wept a little at the thought of her beloved husband falling victim to one man's insatiable greed. 'I knew he was dead,' Karen said. 'I could feel it right from the beginning.'

'You're right,' Lana thought without rancour. 'He *was* dead right from the beginning.'

Waterloo Bridge. She was almost home. Her flat was just off Stamford Street on the other side of the river.

Tim! Where was he? Each time the telephone rang she expected it to be him. 'A couple of weeks,' he'd said. That was six weeks ago! Had he changed his mind? Had something happened to him? She knew that he had to go back to Likoma. 'To tidy up a few messy ends,' were his words. Lana assumed that one of those ends would be a thorough search for the documents which had cost three lives that she knew of.

There had been so little time together. Just before she boarded the flight to Johannesburg he had managed a few quiet words with her. 'I'll contact you the instant I get back.'

She had touched his cheek with her fingertips. 'No more heroics?'

He had grinned. 'You can bloody talk!'

Was that the end of it? Was she fooling herself? Had it meant nothing to him?

Lana turned into her street, noticing with irritation that someone had dumped a skip where she usually left the Harley. 'Bloody hell!' Her neighbour was renovating his flat. The skip would probably be there for weeks. Lana rolled the large motorbike backwards, tail in to the kerb. The Fat Boy's engine shut down with one last classy growl. She swung a leg over the seat and stood, unbuckling her helmet. Removing it, she ran a hand through her short hair.

'I might have known you'd ride a bloody Harley,' the voice behind her said, amused.

'Tim!' She spun around. He was leaning against the skip, a smile on his lips and in his eyes, dark hair falling forward, arms folded. She dropped the helmet as he stepped forward, catching her up in his arms.

'I hate kissing in public,' he complained, lowering his lips to hers.

A wolf whistle from across the street broke them apart. 'Inside,' Lana said, her breathing uneven. 'Before I do something unspeakable in the street.'

There were so many questions to ask and, oh God he looked so good standing there. She wanted to know so many things but he was reaching for her again and they barely got the door shut behind them. 'Bedroom?' he whispered urgently.

'Here,' she moaned. 'Bedroom's too far.'

'Do you think,' he asked much later, 'that we'll ever make love in a bed?' They were lying on the floor just inside the door, clothes spread in abandoned disarray all around them.

She raised herself on one elbow and looked down at him, her fingers playing with the hair on his chest. 'How does ten minutes from now sound?'

He laughed and she noticed that, when he did, he had a dimple on one cheek. So she kissed it.

'Five minutes sounds even better?' he countered, groaning a little. 'I don't think I can wait ten.'

Half an hour later they still hadn't made it to the bedroom but they had progressed to the floor of her lounge. Naked, they were leaning against the settee. 'Have something for you.' His jacket was still in the hall. He came back with it and passed her a plastic bag.

Lana gave a delighted laugh when she saw what was in it. Her father's Brunton pocket transit. 'Thank you,' she said huskily.

He told her then how divers had found Karl Henning's body, pinned under one of Mlozi's dhows and surrounded by skeletons. 'One of the last slave trade shipments of human cargo,' Tim said. 'They'd been down there for around a hundred years.'

'Karl told me that five dhows went down. Four carried slaves and one was loaded with ivory. He said he'd found some kind of record book.'

Tim nodded. 'Mlozi's. The government has expropriated it, along with the cabinet. They say it's a piece of Malawi's history and belongs in a museum. Two more dhows have been located and they're still searching for the last one. Divers are bringing up the bones. They'll all be given a proper burial.'

'God!' She shivered. 'I almost feel sorry for the man. What a horrible way to go.'

'Save your sympathy. He got what he deserved. He traded in death.' Tim picked up her hand. 'I have something else for you. Moffat and I worked out the last of the witchdoctor's words.'

'*The jaws of silence,*' Lana mused. 'Of course. The skulls, the tusks. Jawbones.'

'That witchdoctor,' Tim said carefully. 'Uh, he seems to have been remarkably accurate.'

'You're beginning to sound like a believer.'

He laughed, and there was that beautiful dimple again. Lana didn't think she'd ever get sick of the sight of it.

'Henning's yacht was towed to the naval base at Monkey Bay. I managed to get on board first.'

'Diplomatic privilege and all that?'

He squeezed her hand. 'Are you being seriously sarcastic or do you simply feel morally obliged to challenge everything?'

'Just kidding. Sorry.'

Tim grinned. 'For your information I pulled rank because I was looking for the Brunton.'

'Thank you,' she said again. She looked down at the brass instrument in her hand, then turned it over and stared at her father's initials. 'John Didier Devereaux,' she said softly. ' When I did that . . .' She left it hanging.

Tim could see that while Lana's sense of reason accepted what had become of her father, the sadness of it would always be with her.

'Moffat and I had dinner together. His wife had a baby boy. They're calling him Jonah John Kadamanja. He says to ask if you'll be godmother.'

It broke her sombre mood.

He changed the subject and told her about the

treasure. 'It's early days yet but it looks like it did belong to the Kingdom of Greater Zimbabwe. The ologists are pretty excited.'

'What will happen to it?'

'Robert Mugabe wants it back.'

'That's fair enough as long as it goes into a museum and not some minister's private collection.'

Tim rose one eyebrow. 'Cynicism in one so young and beautiful,' he admonished. 'Anyway, the Zimbabwe newspapers are full of it. National heritage and all that. It's a hell of a find.'

'What about the tusks?'

'Parks and Wildlife have confiscated them. Malawi is likely to follow Zimbabwe, Botswana and Namibia and lift the ban on ivory trading. For how long remains to be seen but, in the short term, it should bring the government some much needed revenue.'

'And the documents?'

'You don't know about them.'

'Did you find them?'

'No. I spent a long time looking for that one tusk but came up with nothing. Chief Mbeya has been providing your f − . . . Mpasa with ivory for years. I'd say he's got a few tusks stashed somewhere but . . .' Tim shrugged, '. . . he sure as hell wasn't going to tell me where.'

'So somebody could still find them?'

'That's a chance we'll just have to take. I'm not even sure they really existed. Hamilton was pretty weird. He may have been making it up.'

'I'm not going to ask you what was supposed to be in them.'

513

'Good.'

She rested her head on his shoulder. 'Because one day, you're going to tell me anyway.'

He turned her head gently and kissed her. 'Am I?'

She rose and pulled him to his feet, winding her arms around his neck and kissing him back. 'Yes.'

'Why would I do that?' They were moving towards the bedroom door.

'Because if you don't,' she said softly, rising on tiptoe and kissing his neck, 'I will go insane with curiosity.'

They fell on the bed together. He ran his hands down the full length of her then gathered her close. 'I'll tell you on our wedding night, will that do?'

'Yes,' she said happily. 'That will do just fine.' She pushed him away. 'Why then?'

He pulled her back into his arms. 'Because,' he said, kissing her, 'you'll be my wife and won't be able to testify against me.'

'Would I do that?'

His eyes smiled into hers. 'The beautiful thing about you, my darling, is that I never know what you're likely to do.'

She ran her hands down his body and found him ready for her again. 'I'm sure,' she murmured, 'that you can guess this time.'

TWENTY

Chief Mbeya made his way slowly along the beach, sedate and proud, his fine Wankonde features burnished copper in the sunshine, his shrewd old eyes watching a fish eagle swoop down and pluck a brightly coloured *mbuna* from the water before powering effortlessly back to the high tree which was his lookout. The Chief chuckled, wishing he too could fly.

It was a beautiful, sparkling August day, the promise of summer already strong in the air. He waited with uncharacteristic impatience for the hot weather. With it would come the planting season and the storms which damaged their houses so that repairs were constantly required. His people needed something new to think about, something to take away the tragic events of a winter which was unlike any he could remember. Around their cooking fires each night, it was all they talked about.

The witchdoctor had foretold of it many years earlier. Not the fool of a young man now, the one before him. The same one who had let the evil spirits out of Mpasa's head. Chief Mbeya recalled the night clearly when, with more than his usual presumptuousness, the Nganga had summoned him to his hut.

'I have had a vision,' he announced. 'You must hear of it.'

The Chief seated himself opposite the witch-doctor. 'It troubles you?'

The Nganga nodded. 'Our lives will never be the same.'

'Are my people in danger?'

'Danger comes in many forms. Some must die but all will be touched in more ways than one.'

'Tell me, powerful one, what is your vision?' Chief Mbeya asked in dread. The Nganga was never wrong.

And, rocking back and forth, the witchdoctor had told him:

'When the riches of the past are revealed, the spirit of Lundu will claim the souls of those who would profit from the evil that men do. A son of Likoma must die to protect the secret of Great Mother,' the witchdoctor had intoned, his features contorted with effort as he heard his inner voice. 'One will come among us who is not of Nyasa and his seed will find great sorrow but also great joy. These happenings will bring many strangers to our land. Others will hear and our way of life will be gone forever.'

And now these events had come to pass. Likoma would never be the same.

It was true. The island had briefly found centre stage as the world's experts gathered to unearth the ancient buildings of Lundu. The tented camps of archaeologists and the rest of them were likely to be a part of the island's life for years to come. Now there were plans to build a tourist complex. The Chief had been shown preliminary drawings. 'We're going to re-create the city of King Lundu,' the enthusiastic young architect from South Africa told the openly astonished Chief. 'Except of course, there'll be swimming pools, tennis courts, a casino, all the trimmings. It'll be an absolute showpiece.'

'Showpiece,' the Chief thought contemptuously, staring at the drawings. 'It looks more like the home of termites.'

The airstrip was already being upgraded and roads constructed. The roar of diesel engines a common sound. Chief Mbeya's lip curled as he remembered the misguided individual who, a few years ago, had decided that the island should have an ambulance. It arrived, gleaming and new, to sit unused at the hospital, unable to go anywhere since the island had no roads. At least now it might get some use. He supposed that was a good thing.

'Nothing stays the same,' Chief Mbeya was thinking as he clambered over some rocks at the end of the cove. Although the village where he lived, on the north end of the island, had remained relatively unscathed, the Chief knew it was only a matter of time before the madness engulfed that too.

Change was inevitable. It could not be stopped. True, the influx of scientists, engineers and the rest brought much needed money to the island. But the

517

innocence of Likoma would be gone. 'And with it,' he reflected sadly, 'the last link to our past.'

Hidden by the rocks, the old man dug with his hands in the soft sand. He looked regretfully at the one remaining tusk. Not large, and strangely twisted, it was all that was left of the hoard he'd saved for Mpasa. Mud had somehow become caked into the nerve end. Hefting it on his shoulder, he made his way back towards the village.

Chief Mbeya knew he was breaking the law – that the Department of Parks and Wildlife, had they known about his secret stash of tusks, would have confiscated the lot. He didn't care. Mpasa loved working with the silky cream of ivory. He preferred it to wood. 'It's not as if he profits from it,' the Chief justified his actions. 'He gives it all away.'

A compassionate and intelligent man, the Chief knew that Mpasa's abilities were limited, that the repetition of carving penny whistles and other artifacts was about the extent of his capabilities. He loved Mpasa like his own son. The man was gentle and kind and completely harmless. Bringing him the tusks, when they so obviously gave him so much pleasure, was a small thing to do. Especially now.

Chief Mbeya shifted the tusk to his other shoulder. Kardiya, the blind man, was sitting on the beach and greeted him respectfully. How was the man able to differentiate between people's footsteps and identify each individual? The Chief suspected that God, in His wisdom, having removed

518

Kardiya's sight more than twenty years ago, had compensated by giving him extra hearing powers, an insatiable curiosity and the courage of five men. He stopped to speak with the man who could not see. 'This is the last one.' Chief Mbeya did not bother to elaborate. Kardiya would know he was carrying a tusk.

'I can get no more.' Kardiya shrugged. 'The way is still blocked by those who crawl over the cliff like ants.'

'You could not get more anyway. The teeth have been taken away.'

The blind man cackled suddenly. 'Lundu carried many spears in his hand.'

The Chief looked at him sharply. 'What are you saying?'

Milky white cataracts covering both eyes glistened in the sun. 'Those who seek Lundu's secrets will find but one small part. Hear me well.'

'You've found more?' The man was incredible. How he'd discovered the cave in the first place was a mystery to the Chief.

'Perhaps Mpasa would like to work the soft yellow metal?'

The Chief wondered aloud how he knew the colour of gold.

Kardiya held up his hands and wriggled his fingers. 'These are my eyes.'

Mpasa ran his hands lovingly over the ivory tusk, appreciating its fine smoothness. He was saddened

519

to think that this was to be his last but the Chief had promised him something better. He picked up a knife and started to dig out the mud caked solid in the hollow end where the nerve had once run. His mind was happy, clear of anything but what he was doing. Somewhere, in the back, was something else, but he hadn't been bothered by it for several months. He accepted this as indifferently as he accepted the food the women brought to him. The only thing Mpasa thought about was the only thing he could do – carve.

Oblivious of his surroundings, Mpasa hardly noticed when, at the Chief's bidding, a stockade was erected around his hut. He never left the immediate vicinity of his dwelling anyway. The explanation, 'Many strangers have come to our island. We do not wish them to disturb you,' had been accepted without question. Mpasa did not care.

The last of the mud broke free and he ran his thumb around the thin rim, clearing it of residue. He touched something inside and, looking, saw three sheets of paper rolled and stuffed into the cavity. They came out easily. Smoothing them open, he took time to admire the fine quality of paper and the red seal at the bottom of each. His eye assessed the documents for their value as material with which he could work. The words were a meaningless jumble.

Losing interest, Mpasa tossed them into his cooking fire. As they flared up, and the wax melted, he was briefly reminded of something else. It was gone in an instant. Frowning with concentration, he picked up his latest carving and went back to work. It was the head of a woman. Her fine features and short black hair were European, not African. Mpasa had no idea where the inspiration came from – nor did he care. All he knew was that this was one carving he would not give away.

MORE BESTSELLING FICTION AVAILABLE IN PAN

Beverley Harper
Edge of the Rain

**Hunger ached in her belly . . . the lioness slid
forward as close as she dared. The little boy
seconds away from death was two, maybe
three years old. He was lost in the heat-soaked
sand that was the Kalahari desert.**

Toddler Alex Theron is miraculously rescued by a
passing clan of Kalahari Bushmen. Over the
ensuing years the desert draws him back, for it
hides a beautiful secret . . . diamonds.

But nothing comes easily from within this turbulent
continent and before Alex can even hope to realise
his dreams he will lose his mind to love and fight a
bitter enemy who will stop at nothing to destroy
him . . .

'Destined to be a worthy successor to Harper's
Storms Over Africa *. . . superbly told story which
will appeal to almost every audience'*
Alan Gold, *Australian Bookseller & Publisher*

TURN THE PAGE FOR CHAPTER ONE OF
EDGE OF THE RAIN . . .

CHAPTER ONE

The blood scent was fresh. Pungent and rich, the acrid smell of it stung her taste buds, bringing saliva. She stopped, turning her head until she caught it again. In the distance, a clump of trees. Years of fending for herself had her instincts honed to perfection. A light breeze floated the scent to her and she savoured it. It came from the trees. But she was wary. Along with the scent of blood, something else, something alien.

Hunger ached in her belly. Cautious, for she could not identify the other smell, she made her way towards the trees, stopping every few seconds to sniff at the breeze. Her eyes flicked over the surrounding land. Nothing there. The blood scent was stronger. Like a wraith she slipped into the shade, moving with exquisite precision, all her senses alert. When she found the source of the scent she slid forward as close as she dared and settled down to watch. She would remain hidden until she was sure—such was her nature.

★

Fifteen minutes later the lioness still lay, motionless as carved stone. Tawny eyes showed she was alert and focused. Invisible from all but the sharpest observer, she was cleverly camouflaged by the dappled shade of a low scrubby bush and the sparse dun coloured grass around her. Muscles tensed along her back and haunches, rippling beige, twenty-three stone of power and speed. Her concentration was total. She was very, very hungry.

The little boy thirty seconds away from death was two, maybe three years old. His fair skin burned crimson from too much sun. Silky blond curls lay damp on his head in the intense heat. A cut on his leg was crusted with dried blood. Face grubby and streaked with recent tears, sobs still surfaced from deep inside him and shook his sturdy little body. He had done the unthinkable, the unbelievable. He was lost in the vast, barren, heat soaked sand that was the Kalahari Desert.

For now, he was absorbed by what he had found on the ground and had no idea the lioness lay, no more than thirty feet away, planning to eat him. Even if he had known, there was nothing he could have done to stop her.

Impending death stilled all sounds. Even the birds were silent, awed by the savage drama unfolding in a land where conscience has no meaning. They watched and waited. The little boy was just another meal but his death would be viciously spectacular.

The lioness tested the child's scent. Her mouth became a silent snarl as she drew her lips back, exposing large yellow teeth, sucking and blowing air over sensitive taste buds. Her stomach rumbled in its hunger, but she hesitated. The small creature before her was edible—she could tell by the blood scent—but it smelled like nothing she had eaten before, looked like nothing she had seen before and sounded like nothing she had heard before.

The object of her interest was squatting beside the remains of a long-dead ostrich. Jackals, vultures and ants had eaten all but a few bones, and the gritty contents of the bird's gizzard. The child was absorbed by a stone which shone with a thousand different lights in the fierce desert sunshine. When he held it up against the sky, and the colours danced and changed as he twisted it in his hand, he chuckled in pure enjoyment, his terror at finding himself alone temporarily forgotten.

The lioness was nearly committed. She knew this was easy prey. One flash of a heavy paw, one slice of razor-sharp claws, one crunch of jaws on that small head, and she could rip out the intestines, then feed to her heart's content. Still she hesitated; caution and stealth had kept her alive till now. As one who lived instinctively, she had a deeply rooted fear of human beings. Her instincts told her to be careful.

On his haunches, the boy hopped sideways around the skeletal remains of the dead bird looking for more shining stones. The movement took him closer to the bush where the lioness lay. She tensed, ready to strike out and bring him down, but he had seen something on the other side of the ostrich, rose and toddled over to it, remaining out of reach. Sobs still shuddered through him but, with the myopic concentration of the very young, he no longer noticed them.

The large and hungry cat inched forward on her belly. Hunger rumbled again. She had not eaten in four days. A front paw throbbed with the poison from a suppurating abscess, caused by a thorn which had broken off and remained embedded. Hundreds of ticks itched as they feasted on her blood but she ignored them. Flies stung as they fed on the sunburned raw edges of her ears. She ignored them as well. Discomfort was as much a part of her life as her instinct to hunt.

Then the little boy began to talk to himself. It was his high-pitched childlike voice which convinced the lioness she was safe. The strange hairless animal was defenceless. Completely committed now, she rose in one fluid motion, disturbing not so much as a leaf. Her tail twitched involuntarily. Tensing front legs she bunched herself, ready to execute her fast, low, deadly rush. The warning growl, something she was powerless to prevent, rose in her throat. It was time to eat.

In that last, intense split second before she acted, her excellent hearing picked up a sound. Self-preservation is strong in those who live by their wits and hunting skills. Hungry as she was, the lioness slid silently from her covering bush and put as much distance between herself and the sound as she possibly could. So great was her ability to move silently, the little boy was unaware she had ever been there.

Beverley Harper
Storms Over Africa

Richard Dunn has made Africa his home. But his
Africa is in crisis.

Ancient rivalries have ignited modern political
ambitions. Desperate poachers stalk the dwindling
populations of the game parks.

For those of the old Africa, the old ways, nothing is
certain.

But for Richard – a man used to getting his own
way – the stakes are even higher. Into his world
has come the compelling and beautiful Steve
Hayes. A woman he swears he will never give up.
A woman struggling to guard her own dreadful
secret.

Richard has no choice. He must face the
consequences of the past and fight for the future.
To lose now is to lose everything . . .

Storms Over Africa is a novel of desperate struggle
and searing passion.

Wilbur Smith
Birds of Prey

It is 1667 and the mighty naval war between the
Dutch and the English still rages. Sir Francis
Courtney and his son Hal, in their fighting caravel,
are on patrol off Southern Africa, lying in wait for a
galleon of the Dutch East India Company returning
from the Orient laden with spices, timber and
gold . . .

'The scope is magnificent and the epic scale
breathtaking . . . Wilbur Smith is one of those
benchmarks against whom others are compared'
THE TIMES

'Meticulous research supports constant excitement
in a fast-moving tale'
WASHINGTON POST

Wilbur Smith
The Seventh Scroll

A fading papyrus, nearly four thousand years old.
Within it lies the clues to a fabulous treasure from
an almost forgotten time . . . a riddle that becomes
a savage battle across the unforgiving terrain of
North Africa.

When her husband is brutally murdered, beautiful
half-English, half-Egyptian Royan Al Simmu is
forced to seek refuge in England. With eminent
archaeologist Nicholas Quenton-Harper, she can
pick up the pieces of her shattered life and find the
courage to return to Ethiopia. For Duraid. For the
long-dead slave Taita. And for the dreams of an
ancient Pharoah . . . Because others will stop at
nothing to claim the prize as their own.

'A desert sandstorm couldn't get pages turning
faster than Smith'
INDEPENDENT ON SUNDAY

'Full blooded, muscle-on-bone-crunching treasure
hunt . . . it is non-stop action'
DAILY EXPRESS